Is America Nuts?

Is America Nuts?

Uncle Sam Takes the Couch

A Trilogy—Part 1—Therapy and Diagnosis

Richard J. Weisman

iUniverse, Inc.
New York Lincoln Shanghai

Is America Nuts?
Uncle Sam Takes the Couch

iUniverse, Inc.

For information address:
iUniverse, Inc.
2021 Pine Lake Road, Suite 100
Lincoln, NE 68512
www.iuniverse.com

ISBN: 0-595-32116-X

Printed in the United States of America

Dedicated to my son Jordan.

A dream is the essence of every story.
Stop dreaming and the story ends.
Continue dreaming and the story never ends.

We hold these truths to be self-evident, that all men are created equal, that they are endowed by their Creator with certain unalienable Rights, that among these are Life, Liberty and the pursuit of Happiness.—That to secure these rights, Governments are instituted among Men, deriving their just powers from the consent of the governed,

That whenever any Form of Government becomes destructive of these ends, it is the Right of the People to alter or to abolish it, and to institute new Government, laying its foundation on such principles and organizing its powers in such form, as to them shall seem most likely to effect their Safety and Happiness.

Prudence, indeed, will dictate that Governments long established should not be changed for light and transient causes; and accordingly all experience hath shewn, that mankind are more disposed to suffer, while evils are sufferable, than to right themselves by abolishing the forms to which they are accustomed.

But when a long train of abuses and usurpations, pursuing invariably the same Object evinces a design to reduce them under absolute Despotism, it is their right, it is their duty, to throw off such Government, and to provide new Guards for their future security. Such has been the patient sufferance of these Colonies; and such is now the necessity which constrains them to alter their former Systems of Government.

Sixty Centre Street in New York City is the location of the Supreme Court. As an attorney, I walked up the courthouse steps a thousand times either to argue a motion, conduct a trial or to file some papers. I was impressed by the buildings architecture. Long steps led up to massive doors. A dome sat upon the building. Standing in the rotunda under the dome made me feel important. I was there to help my client's get justice. I was, I believed, a noble warrior. It didn't take long to realize that anything but justice occurred within this courthouse, or any other courthouse. It was a game. Truth and justice have very little to do with the legal system. Today, this building could be the location of my death, either shot dead under the dome that I loved so much or gunned down on the steps that I had walked up for fifteen years.

I took the elevator to the third floor and went into courtroom 324. For fifteen years, I entered the courthouse as an attorney. Today, I was there as a respondent. My Uncle Sam, the petitioner, sought a temporary injunction to block a book that was ready for publication. I authored the manuscript with his help and permission. A preliminary injunction is a remedy that is not easily obtained. For the court to grant his request, Sam had to show, among other things, a strong likelihood of success and irreparable harm. In addition, Sam was up against the first amendment's protection of freedom of speech and the press. Sam should win but not for legal or even justiciable reasons. Sam should win because I took advantage of his personality disorder that precluded him from telling the Court how he was duped. These kinds of cases are, to a great degree, legal arguments between lawyers. Having practiced law for fifteen years, I knew what the facts and the law were. I wasn't interested in listening to the attorneys go on. I knew, in advance, the result. I was going to defeat Sam. I was recalling my days as an attorney. I had one case before Judge Bruce Wright. He was nicknamed "Cut Em' Loose Bruce." Judge Wright had been transferred from the criminal bench in Manhattan to the civil bench in Brooklyn. He had cut one too many black defendants loose in criminal trials. The administrative judge transferred him to the civil side. A paper merchant in Philadelphia had sued one of my clients for $250,000.00. He owed the money and he simply didn't want to pay. I presented an affirmative defense that Judge Wright couldn't ignore. It wasn't justice but it was the law. Ruling against me, Judge Wright would have been overturned on appeal and I was, as lawyers say, directly on point. Realizing his hands were tied, Judge Wright expressed his anger in an 18-page decision castigating me for being a prick. I guess he thought that his decision might change my life. He called me a sophist. That was all I thought about on this particular day. I never knew what a sophist was until I looked it up in the dictionary: "One who deceives by adroit, subtle and allegedly often specious reasoning." In the paper merchant case I was a sophist. As a young attorney, I was impressed. Actually, I was proud.

Once again, I was a sophist. My shrink once told me that someone like me shouldn't walk down dark alleys. "No good is going to come of it," he would advise me. I was going to win my legal battle with Sam and I'd be dead before I reached the bottom of the courthouse steps. Here I was in courtroom 324. The great Dr. Stanley Warlib, a fucking shrink, sued by his own fucking patient. I leaned back in my chair and dwelled on the course of events that brought me to this Courthouse and possibly to my demise. I knew that I was fucking with the wrong guy.

In real life, as Rick, I take an annual trek to a hidden beach in Baja, California, somewhere between Mulege and Loreto. Here, I feel at home. There are no showers or food. There is a pit toilet. Self-sufficiency is the rule. There is a ban on all news. It is a beautiful place. On Christmas Eve, the dead cactus that "Pam" found in the desert served as our Christmas tree. It was adorned with whatever items we had, old Pez dispensers, candy, an electric light and desert debris. At that point in time, I had been there for three weeks. When night came, the locals showed up from Mulege and the surrounding desert. There were about fifteen children and twenty-five adults. In all, between the locals and the gringos, there were forty people. We lit a wood pit fire. A twelve-volt marine battery juiced the lights on the Christmas tree. On the beach that night were two colorful local Mexicans. A woman accordionist who had just left Church, still attired in her red and white robes and her friend, a guitarist. He had a good voice. They were accompanied by a third local who stood behind them and shouted, "praise the lord," in Spanish. On the gringo side, we had Eric and his girlfriend Emily. Eric played guitar. "Steve" from California played the Dubro guitar. He was nicknamed "Stevie Dubro." Forty people, half Mexican, half international, Christmas

Eve, surrounded by desert darkness gathering to celebrate whatever it was that we were celebrating. The Mexican children lit candles at the foot of the Christmas tree and played with their Pez dispensers. They were delighted. The gringos sang Silent Night. Eric and Steve led us in song. After we finished, the locals sang Silent Night in Spanish. We sang for hours. The locals sang in Spanish. The gringos sang in English. At times, some of us tried to sing in the other person's language. This scene continued throughout the night. Forty people who were alone in the desert celebrating a spontaneous evening in harmony. It was corny but beautiful. Its beauty lied in its sincerity.

When I first arrived at this beach, I inspected each palapa to decide which one I would call home. I passed a guy named Pete who said hello. I told him that I was cruising the beach to find a palapa. A palapa costs $6.00 a night. After looking at all the huts, I decided that the palapa next to Pete's was the one I liked. I told Pete that I would be his neighbor. I settled in. The next day Pam told me that Pete was a "little strange." I sat, read, drank beer and watched Pete for two days. Pete *was* strange. I never observed anyone that would grade the beach sand so that it sloped in a certain direction. Pete did. He also raked the beach every morning and arranged and rearranged seashells to form decorative designs around his palapa. Pete knew that I was an early bird and watched the sun rise, which was a collective beach activity. Every day, before sunrise, while I was having coffee, Pete would peak around his palapa to see if I was in my chair. He brought me Mexican pastry every morning for my coffee. Owing to my propensity to make quick psychological analyses, I decided that Pete was an obsessive-compulsive who couldn't stop himself from arranging and rearranging both his personal belongings and nature. He had to do these kinds of things all day long. It was one of life's random ironies that Pete and I were neighbors. Pete's contentment sprang from always being on the move and my contentment from not moving at all. One day, Pete decided to build a sand castle ten feet in width by twenty feet in length. He started at 9:00 a.m. and didn't finish until 9:00 p.m. I watched Pete for twelve hours build this sand castle. I was fascinated by the activity surrounding the castle's creation. Everyone on the beach participated in molding the sand into an enormous building. Notwithstanding the fact that it was Pete's baby, he never uttered any direction or advice to anyone. He let everyone create his or her own little piece of this sand structure. This was odd since he was an obsessive-compulsive. Normally, letting other people participate in building a sand castle would drive an obsessive-compulsive crazy. Naturally, the children on the beach participated to a great extent. This happy little beach village had a wonderful day. When it started getting dark someone decided that the castle needed candles. About thirty candles were placed on the sand castle and lit. Someone claimed it was our beaches contribution to international peace and it was dubbed the "Castle of Peace." To a former wise guy Jewish attorney from Brooklyn, this Castle of Peace stuff was as corny as you could get. However, as I stated before, its beauty lied within its sincerity and sincerity doesn't suck the lifeblood out of your body. The day ended and I went to my palapa and lied down. I thought about Pete. It was clear to me that in Pete's "odd" obsessive-compulsive behavior he did beautiful things for our beach community. He played a vital role in the beaches well being, more so than anyone else. The next morning when Pete peaked around the corner, I beckoned him to come close. I said, "you know, Pete, you're fucking insane but you do beautiful things." Pete just looked at me. He wasn't angry. I think he felt relieved that someone understood him. Pete and I became friends, at least during those periods of time when he wasn't doing his chores. Pete loved shells and when I went snorkeling, island exploring or hunting for scallops, I picked the finest of shells and gave them to Pete with the understanding that if he didn't like any of them it was all right to throw them away. However, most of the time I knew what Pete liked and brought them back. Few, if any, shells were discarded. Pete to me was special. He was functionally nuts. How often can one be part of someone else's insanity? Pete was just a sweet guy in a very obsessive-compulsive way. Instead of putting him off, I jumped right in and enjoyed his craziness. Pete was a character. Unfortunately, not enough characters exist.

Every morning at sunrise, most people sat in front of their palapa and waited for the sun to rise. It was a daily ritual clothed in silence. One day, I got out my guitar and quietly played the Eagles "Tequila Sunrise." Everyone who heard me play thought that I did a great job. After my initial solo, my neighbors requested that I bring in everyday with Tequila Sunrise. I complied. Another ritual was born.

One day, "Cassidy," a longhaired farmer from California, unintentionally had his Volkswagen bus filled with diesel fuel instead of regular gas. Heading back to our beach the bus died. Cassidy walked back and explained to Paul, another beach rat, and I, what had happened. At that point in time, he didn't know that he had put diesel fuel in the gas tank. The next morning I gave Cassidy a lift to the playa where he had abandoned his VW bus. I told him that I would be back around 2:00 p.m. if he didn't show up on the beach by then. It was 1:30. No Cassidy. I grabbed Paul and drove to the playa where Cassidy was. Cassidy was there with two Mexican mechanics. They were taking out the diesel fuel. All three were half-crocked on Tequila. They were having a great time. No tragedy.

They were having a laughing out loud great time. I joined in on the drinking and caught up to their mental state in half-an-hour. Now, all four of us were just busting loose. Paul stayed straight for driving purposes. He didn't have to. We went to Mulege for a reason that I cannot recall. Perhaps, it was for fresh fish tacos. Back at the beach "Joan" and "David" who had gone clamming, invited the entire beach over to enjoy fresh clams in a great broth.

"Blanco" the dog, mysteriously appeared on the beach that day. He was either abandoned or a stray. Typically, a Baja stray beach dog is thin enough to have his ribs exposed. This dog did not. Blanco created a lot of conversation among the beach denizens as to how he appeared. We concluded that he had been abandoned. Upon his arrival, the other beach dogs tortured him. In order to escape fights, Blanco would drop and assume the most non-aggressive posture he could take. An extended discussion ensued between Cassidy and I about giving him a name. Cassidy suggested "puffster," which, as Cassidy explained to me, meant faggoty. I suggested Blanco because of his color (Blanco is white in Spanish). I won the naming contest and accordingly Blanco became my dog. Blanco was a petite, slim, small boned Yellow Lab type. Blanco had his begging act down to a sweet science and he was well fed. Everyone loved Blanco and took care of him. I'm sure that the story of Blanco would continue with each succeeding wave of visitors and that he would be looked after. If I had a more stable living environment, I would have taken Blanco home. However, I couldn't subject this beautiful little dog to a guy who doesn't care where he may sleep.

There were other equally wonderful souls like "Glen" from Alberta and, at times, Idaho. Glen knew that I was a beach bum. Every day around 10:00 a.m., Glen would saunter over with two beers and toss one of them to me. Glen and I would sit on the beach and concoct wild scenarios about stuff that was happening. For example, we created a story about Blanco. One day during our morning beer buzz, Glen and I wondered what would happen to Blanco in May when the beach became deserted. The weather would be one hundred ten degrees, humid and the mosquitoes would be hell. Out of that scenario, came a short story entitled "Blanco Goes Bad." We envisioned Blanco turning from a subservient beggar to Cujo. Glen and I would go on everyday creating these short fictionalized stories. Glen was a carpenter who had just left Ketchum, Idaho, because it became to "yupped out." Every year, we met on the beach and this year he planned on staying for four months. That was his only plan. When the money goes, he goes. Glen's one principle of life, which I agreed with, was, whatever you did in life "it ain't gonna kill ya." Run out of money? "It ain't gonna kill ya." Car broke down in the desert? "It ain't gonna kill ya."

Eric and Emily were from Quebec. Emily was the fantasy of every guy on the beach. She spoke fluent Spanish, English and French. She was a part time actress and a teacher in Quebec. Emily was adorable. She had a great French accent when she spoke in English. Her boyfriend Eric, whom she wanted to marry, was painfully thin almost to the point of looking like a Nazi concentration camp prisoner. He went swimming everyday even though the cool bay water would freeze him up quick. Eric was about 5'4" and had a shock of black hair and wore thick black glasses just like the Harry Potter character. To a great degree, Emily's attractiveness was because this little cutie loved her man. Eric was a music producer for rock bands in Quebec. He told me that he produced half of Quebec's music acts. He carried a small tape recorder and recorded all the music on the beach that went on at night around campfires. He even recorded my version of Tequila Sunrise. In the spring, Eric was going to Louisiana to musically produce the daughter of a Grammy winner. Every morning, Eric came to my palapa for milk to put in his coffee. Everyday was glorious. Mornings were Tequila Sunrise, pastries from Pete, Eric for milk, Glen with beer and the balance of the day an adventure.

There were many other people on the beach that were equally interesting. Each person was a character in his own right. Beautiful people. Each person contributed to the whole in such wonderful little ways that everyday turned into something special. It was paradise for $6.00 a day. What a gift. On a much deeper level, the beaches real gift to me was that I didn't have to use any brainpower fending off scum sucking Type-A personalities. No shower, no Type-A's.

The previous year, I visited the same beach and met many of the same people. Prior to that trip, I promised some people I knew in Colorado that I would visit them in Cabo San Lucas for New Year's Eve. I left my paradise on December 30 and drove down to Cabo and found an RV park that had tent space. I pitched my tent and went to the restaurant for a beer. There were only two guys in the restaurant. There was an old man who was concerned that none of his buddies were coming down that year. He figured that 9/11 caused many of his friends to stay home. He was from Switzerland. He was a retired bus driver from Zurich who came to America and bought a piece of land in Las Vegas. A hotel bought him out for a lot of money. He moved to California where he bought another piece of land. Again, he was bought out for big bucks. This bus driver was now a multi-millionaire. He passed the days away waiting in the bar for his friends and walking his Doberman around the RV Park. I bought him a beer. The other guy was the bartender. The bartender was a part minority owner, having purchased the restaurant the night before. His name was Juan. His wife, Gabriella, owned the restaurant. The old Swiss man left to walk his dog. Juan and I hung out together. He was an interesting guy. He and Gabriella both came from rich families. I asked him about all the banditos that Americans hear about. He told me that they had to get a job fifteen years ago or they disappeared in the desert. "They work now," he advised me. I told Juan that we should celebrate his purchase of the restaurant. That was all that Juan had to hear. Celebration. He got up on a chair and took out his best tequila from his private stash. He put two shot glasses on the bar and we started to drink. He knew how to drink Tequila. Small shots every thirty minutes. We got buzzed but not high. After three hours of bullshitting with Juan and eating the food that Gabriella made in the kitchen, I explained to Juan that I had to depart and search for my friends. He implored me not to go. We were having a great time. I told him that I made a promise and that I traveled from Mulege just to keep it. Reluctantly, he let me go with the promise that I would return. I asked Juan for directions to the Sheraton Del Mar. The Sheraton was a five star hotel and had five star security guards. With a big smile and "hola" to the local at the security gate, I got in. I was so relaxed and friendly I'm sure the security guard assumed that I was staying at the hotel. I was wearing flip-flops, jeans and a tee shirt. I walked around the entire complex several times looking for my friends. Security finally caught up to me and I was questioned for an hour. Who was I, why was I there and who was I looking for? I decided to go with the flow of the security men and jumped into their game. I gave them just enough to be suspicious and not enough not to cause concern. After all, a security team without security issues is nothing. I supplied their reason to exist at least for that day. Security located my friends at the pool and decided that I posed no security risk. The Sheraton cost $450.00 a day. It had a great beach. No one was in the ocean because of an alleged strong undertow. The rooms were typical hotel. Nothing special. There were people gathered around a good looking woman in her late twenties playing what I later found out was "dirty bingo." She gave me a look. I lingered awhile but she was working the guests. After going down a short path, I came to the pool area. What I saw was fascinating. I always look at the books that people are reading. At this pool, on this day, everyone was reading some kind of financial book. No mysteries, science fiction, historical or biographical books for this crowd. Every person was reading a fucking financial book. "The Millionaire Next Door," "Rich Dad, Poor Dad," "The Money Quadrant." I could not believe it. I circled around the pool area again. Sure enough, every book was about money, who has it, how to get it and how to manage it. The men had an appropriate belly hanging over their bathing suit and a big cigar. The trappings of power and wealth as these people saw it. I made my way over to my friends and pulled the guy away from "The Money Quadrant." "Hey Rick, how are you, when did you get here? Where are you staying?" We exchanged pleasantries and spent some time together. We went to lunch at a small outdoor restaurant run by an American. It was nice. I wanted to get back to Juan and our previous celebration so I made up some good excuses and left. I was relieved to be out of the scene. After all, I was not the millionaire next door nor had any desire to be one. I got to Juan's and the celebration continued with more food and a belly full of laughs. Night came and I retired to my tent and left early the next day. Two beaches, only four hundred miles apart, yet separated by much more than distance.

On January 1, I decided to pack up and head back to the states. I had a full tank of gas and twenty pesos, about two dollars. My plan was to drive all day and sleep out in Yuma, Arizona. Two hundred miles below the border, near San Quintin in northern Baja, I was low on gas and pulled over to a bank to use the ATM. No money at all. The screen showed "00.00." I went to another bank in San Quintin and the screen showed "00.00." I thought for a moment and then backtracked 11 miles to a place named Cielito Lindo located on the beach. I had been there before and felt comfortable sleeping on the beach if it came to that. Over and over, I played out in my mind, the balance I thought I had. Each conclusion was the same. I should have money. I must have screwed up. I thought that if I could cross the border, it would be easier to transfer money to me in Yuma than in Mexico, if that became necessary. I did the only thing that I could do. I sold my camping equipment. I took out a double burner propane camp stove and put a "for sale" on it for $45.00. A Mexican man and his family saw what I was doing and made polite inquiries as to why I was selling the stove. I explained to him what happened. It was time to make a deal. I sold the stove to him for $25.00. I drove back to San Quintin to fill up the tank and drove to the border. As Glen would say, "Broke in the Baja, it ain't gonna kill ya." It was just another Mexican Baja adventure with a minor financial mishap. It was nothing to be upset about. It was nighttime and I took Mex 3 just out of Ensenada northeast to Tecate. The line at the border was long but proceeded expeditiously. I arrived at the crossing in 25 minutes. Not having taken a shower for three weeks I looked suspicious. My hair was matted. I was extremely tan, made even darker by the dirt on me. The American border guards decided that my car and I merited a look-see. I asked them if I could get out and sit on a chair while they proceeded to do their duty. They honored my request. After 10 minutes they decided that I was not a terrorist or a drug dealer. All my papers were in order and I was free to go. The border guard told me that the road to get to the interstate was dark and extremely curvy and that I should drive with caution. I thanked him. I made my way to Yuma and slept in the car in the parking lot of a Wells Fargo bank. In the morning, I walked across the street and spent my last dollar. That was it. No money unless the ATM god was going to smile on me that day. I put the card in, hit the pad to enter my pin number, hit the withdrawal button, then the "other amount" button and pressed in $200.00. I waited. Then the sound of the revolving drum and out came $200.00. The Baja beach story came to an abrupt end. I had the funds that I thought I had. I was going to make it back to Colorado. At that moment, reality set in. Two places: a $6.00 a night beach where it's all about the people and a $450.00 a night beach where it's all about the money. I was depressed. The angst that America exists in today is palpable. I could feel it immediately. Evil-doers, traitors, lefties, libs, pro-abortion, anti-abortion, Democrats, Republicans, poor people, tax cuts for the rich, lies and deception! What the fuck am I doing here? This place is nuts. I would ask myself this question over and over for the next nine hundred miles on the drive back to Colorado. I knew that during the trip home I would question my own sanity. Maybe, I'm the one that's nuts?

At a certain point in my life, I had the opportunity to make a decision that would have landed me at the Sheraton Del Mar. Instead, I choose another path. That choice did not come easy or quickly. In retrospect, I think my choice to follow a simple non-moneyed path was by default. I just stopped putting energy and commitment into a plan that would have put me on the beach at the Sheraton Del Mar.

I was thrown out of Brooklyn College for being, let's say, a character. I screwed "Big Sue" up on the roof of SUBO, the student union building. Later on, I "leered" at a gorgeous teacher in English class who became frightened of me. Of course, her being stoned on LSD had nothing to do with her fear. She barred me from her class. In the sixties, it was more than enough for staid straight Brooklyn College to toss me out. Helping my friend Hilly lock a teacher in a closet didn't help either. My parents were all torn up and disappointed. It was their disappointment that hurt me the most. Prior to college, I was interested in writing songs. I wrote well enough to have an open invitation to Don Kirschner's Rock Entertainment publishing house. On the weekends, I was a "go-go" boy at Trude Hellers, one of the first discothèques in America. It was located on 6th Avenue and 9th street in the heart of the village. A go-go boy in the sixties was a pre-Chippendale dancer. My go-go dance efforts were not supported. My song writing efforts were not supported. I didn't have enough internal strength to continue on the path that I wanted. I caved in to my parent's demand that I do things their way. Reluctantly, I agreed. I was going to be a serious person rather than a creative one. I had to make something of myself. I had an engineering background having gone to Brooklyn Technical High School, one of the elite public schools in New York City. Thereafter, I attended Brooklyn College as an engineering student and lost interest during the second year contemplating the theory of "electron probability." After getting kicked out of college, all hell broke loose. My father immediately took me down to an army recruiting station in Coney Island and when I refused to enlist for the Vietnam War, I was banned from the house. I slept on the streets. I slept in the subways. A nice Jewish boy from a middle class background doesn't do these kinds of things. It was highly unusual. I was obstinate. I was having a good time. It was 1968 and everything was busting loose from their moorings. I worked various odd jobs to make some money and never called my father or mother. One of the jobs I had was at a law firm named French, Fink, Markle and McCallum. They were located on 42nd Street near Park Avenue in New York City. They were labor lawyers. I answered the phone, filed papers and went to the Municipal Building to get copies of pending and passed legislation. One day, Colonel Markle called me in and said, "young man, you appear to have a lot on the ball and perhaps should consider becoming an attorney." I didn't listen nor did I care. Several days prior to Christmas, I handed out envelops to all the attorneys in this small firm. I asked one of the office ladies what was in the envelope and she told me that they were Christmas bonuses. There were five envelopes. One envelope was not licked shut. I looked. It was a Christmas bonus for $42,000.00 (it might have been a partnership distribution). I was amazed and I was hooked. I made contact with my parents and told them that I was going to get serious and go back to college. They were pleased but made it clear that they were done helping me financially. I enrolled in City College of New York, CCNY, during the height of the anti-war demonstrations. I majored in political science. I graduated with honors and was elected to Phi Beta Kappa. I applied to Yale and Harvard with Brooklyn Law School as my last choice. Brooklyn Law School accepted me. I attended Brooklyn Law School for three years and graduated. Everyone was now proud of me. I worked for a two-man office upon graduation and made $200.00 a week. That was enough to support my wife. I took over my parents rent controlled apartment for $33.00 a month. At this point in time, I had been in that apartment, at 632 Ocean Parkway in Brooklyn, for over 30 years. In the first six months of working, I brought in many clients. Billing, attributed to the clients I brought to the firm, exceeded $12,000.00. I was under the impression that I would split some of that money with the firm. It didn't happen. I was pissed. I told my parents and wife that I was leaving and going to start my own firm. To me, it was a no brainer. To everyone else, it was a hasty decision. The firm represented security. Bullshit. As Glen would say "it ain't gonna kill ya." I went out on my own and sat in my office for close to ninety days without a phone call. I sent out all the appropriate announcements and still there were no calls. One day, my father came to visit me and asked what the hell was I going to do. "I don't know dad. I really don't know," I told him. After that visit, I started to think about the question that my father posed and decided that I had to do something. I called everyone on my list that I sent an announcement card to and begged for legal work. My practice grew over the years. I closed my practice in August of 1988.

After practicing law, I started a small business named The Postcard Printer located at 165 Hudson Street in New York City. It printed promotional postcards for many of the art galleries located in the city. The business grew over the years. I loved this business because I made something. I printed little postcards that symbolized the dreams of each artist. Each postcard was my baby. I was dedicated to printing the highest quality card that I could. I met great people. I went to hundreds of gallery openings and people respected me for the product I produced. This experience was totally different than practicing law. During the entire eleven years of law practice I helped three clients. The rest of the time I made money.

In 1992, I had a lung operation. The doctor removed two thirds of my left lung. A major operation leaves scars in your psyche. I questioned my whole life. Why did I marry the women that I did? Why did I practice a profession that I thought was useless and legalized thievery? Why did I do things that I had no interest in doing? Why was I pretending to be a nice guy to my detriment? Answers came.

In 1982, my first wife and I separated. Shortly thereafter, I met my second wife and quickly moved in with her. My second wife was a psychologist. The only thing she did that was of any consequence was to urge me to get into therapy. After meeting different therapists, my wife's therapist directed me to a psychiatrist whose approach was "Sullivanian." That is, during therapy you explore your current relationships with your wife, brothers, sisters, father, mother, and co-workers. In addition to very expensive weekly sessions, there were weekly group therapy sessions. I liked my shrink. I believed that he was smarter than I was. He caught me in all my bullshit. Other therapists would get trapped and bogged down in defense mechanisms that I threw up to block progress. I enjoyed my time with my shrink for many reasons. His office was the only place in my life where the setting was about me. I was an excellent patient. I worked during our sessions and was dedicated to developing an understanding of how my brain worked. This was, and still is, important to me. How does my brain think? After all, that's what the brain is supposed to do. I came to realize that my behavior was generally characterized by long mood swings. On the downside, I did a lot of private destructive damage. I acted in a very sneaky way against my own interests. It was very hard for others to detect my self-destructiveness. It was my private battleground. Writing "Uncle Piggy" on the stub of every check that I sent to the I.R.S. was not a bright idea. My upside mood swing rarely approached mania because I did so much damage on the downside. I arrived at a neutral position. The net result was that I never really advanced.

My shrink and I looked into all relationships that I currently had as well as prior ones. We discussed, my alcoholic father, my mother who went to work when I was five, my sisters that I did not and do not talk to, my participation in a local gang, The Imperial Lords, my fledgling song writing career, my go-go boy days at Trude Heller's, Phi Beta Kappa, law school, marriages, the birth of my son, my feelings about other people in group therapy and how I felt about him. It was a great four years. I believe my shrink enjoyed our sessions as well. I was a character. Most of his other patients, at least the ones I knew from group therapy, were all successful people and medicated. This was of great concern to me because I wasn't medicated. I asked my shrink why I wasn't medicated and he told me they really needed meds because it enabled them to function, whereas my problem was more behavioral in nature. No one ever taught me how to behave. Attorneys don't wear jeans to court. I did. "You wouldn't want a surgeon to operate on you with dirty fingernails would you?" the shrink would ask. Clients don't want their attorneys in jeans. I knew that part of his interest in me was simply that you didn't find many middle class Jewish kids from Brooklyn, New York who acted in the way that I did. It was totally contrary to the norm. I was always the highlight in group therapy since I was always stirring the pot. I demanded and forced the group to act in a real way. It never worked. I tried and that caused conflict. When I got mad, the veins in my neck would pop and my aggression was visible. Others in group therapy, who claimed they were angry, would simply sit there and say, "I'm angry." How the fuck could they be angry and I don't feel it. We were encouraged to go out to dinner after group and interact on our own. One group member always sucked me into her insanity. One evening, she started up with me. On this occasion, I simply sat back and let her go on without a response. She was out there all on her own. She hung herself and I didn't participate. The "old" me would have intentionally taken the bait and subjugated myself to another's nuttiness so I could be self-destructive. The "old" me would have declared that I was working things out with another person and that was a positive thing. However, I knew that I wasn't. There was nothing to work out. It was only my self-destructive side engaging in some non-sense routine to get me nowhere. On the surface, most of the things that I did appeared to be positive, but they weren't. It was all very hard to detect, except to my shrink. I conned just about everyone. I pretended to be a nice guy. What bullshit. Four years of hard work in therapy and I was finally able to dig myself out of my own stupidity. I was very pleased that I was beginning to find out how my brain worked. I took active steps to prevent my brain from working in those kinds of ways. It is a constant, never-ending struggle, but one well worth it. I reached a certain point in therapy that my shrink and I came to a standstill. He had made every attempt to make me see that my behavior should be in synch with who I was in life, father, husband and professional. I went along with that. He was big on "what does it say about how you feel about your clients if you go to court in jeans." When I bought into this belief system, I wanted to know what it said about him that he let his patients sit in a hot fucking humid vestibule outside his office without proper air conditioning. In addition, why would a man who earned over $250,000.00 wear pants that were three inches above his ankle? His suits didn't cost more than $50.00. If I had to dress in $1,500.00 Armani suits and $150.00 ties then my guru shrink had to do the same. I hammered him on it. I hammered the group in session on the same issue. I started a war. Interestingly enough, in a true Sullivanian sense, in exploring my disappointment with him, I caught glimpses of the same disappointment that I had with my father. The Imperial Lords taught me a code of conduct that you do what you preach. Short of that, you're full of shit. I still believe this. The entire issue of short pants, cheap suits and lack of air-conditioning meant that I had gone as far as I could go with my shrink. It was a constructive four years.

It didn't take too long after therapy that it became difficult for me to continue two major items in my life that were self-destructive. Those items were my marriage and the practice of law. I hated both. My second wife was truly evil and I believed that being an attorney was, to a great extent, a rip-off. Being a lawyer is part of the problem and not the solution. I believed in simplicity and the law is not simple. It is intentionally complex and when anything is complex somebody is getting fucked and it's not the lawyer. I slowly closed my litigation practice. I had no new income and lived off the fees of the cases that I closed. I was broke. As far as ending my marriage, I knew that my wife considered herself all knowledgeable and my overseer. On my birthday, while the candles were lit and my son and stepdaughter were seated at the kitchen table waiting to sing me happy birthday, my wife answered the phone and stayed on the line for an hour. The candles burned out and the kids left. When she got off the phone, I told her that she was rude and that I wasn't going to talk to her until she apologized. That's all it took. She wigged out and in thirty days the marriage was over.

My son, at the insistence of his mother, applied for admission to a university in Colorado and he got accepted. There was increasing friction between my son and his mother for several months until I finally asked what the hell was going on. She told me that my son was threatening to go work on a fishing boat in Alaska unless he went to Colorado. The problem was money. Neither his mom nor I had $25,000.00 to pay for out of state college tuition. "Dad, what are we going to do?" he asked. I thought for a moment and told him that when he got his letter of acceptance I would sell everything I owned and move to Colorado. Of course, no one believed me. I saw the letter, held a sale, garnered $600.00 and headed out to Colorado in my Hyundai. My goal was to achieve residence, which I did and my son followed shortly thereafter. This new modern world doesn't like white males over fifty years of age. As a result, any job was hard to get. I sent out hundreds of resumes. No response. Since I had to eat, I worked as a construction laborer, which I still do to this day. No headaches, office politics or sitting in front of a computer all day. Simplicity and a hard days work. From my perspective, the beauty of moving to Colorado was that I had no watchful eyes on me. I could have whatever lifestyle I wanted. In New York I would be considered a bum. In Colorado I was a freedom loving mountain man. Low wages mandated changes in my lifestyle. I love going out and schmoozing with people. I hate paying rent. My answer was to live in a tent until it got cold. Thereafter, I lived in a jeep. I took out the passenger side seat and leveled it out and made a bed out of three quarter inch plywood and covered it with two zero degree sleeping bags and a pillow. I slept like a baby. To this day, I prefer the jeep to an apartment. In the six years that I have been in Colorado, I have had 14 months of "normal" household living. I am a freedom freak. I want my freedom to do whatever I want, when I want. Ownership of material things comes at a price. The more you own, the less freedom you have. It's that simple. This country will burden you down with as much stuff as you can afford and then some. I own very little except my clothes and a guitar. I recently gave my guitar to a friend. I work the bottom of the ladder so I can leave whenever I want. The higher up the ladder you go, the harder it is to back out. Freedom disappears. Most people can multi-task. I can multi-slack. I like the slow food movement. I like sitting for hours having coffee and talking with friends. I like extended families, foreign women and good music. I also like the time to enjoy these things. As the Phi Beta Kappa laborer in my company, me, the lowest of the low, just spent 3 ½ weeks living on the beach in the Baja. I'm preparing for a month trek in Thailand with my son. The Thai trek is only ninety days after the Baja excursion.

After the Baja, I simplified my life again. I decided that I was still too deep into our system. When I came back to Colorado, I cancelled the car insurance and got rid of the car. In addition, I closed my bank account and credit cards. I am off the grid. I did this because I was pissed off at the 68% increase in my car insurance. I was irked at being charged $1.50 for a hard copy of my insurance bill. I was livid at the bank for charging me $31.50 as a "courtesy fee" for honoring a debit charge of $3.25 for a pack of cigarettes.

In light of all the above, I question, once again, whether I am being self-destructive. My answer is clear and unequivocal. Backing out of this system is crystal clear evidence that I am thinking correctly. Becoming more involved is an act of self-destruction. I no longer believe that America is a healthy place to carry on a life. America is predatory and the only way to avoid the predators is to back out or fight. I'm not going to spend hours on the phone, every month with a credit card company to have a charge deleted that they know shouldn't be there.

However, although I continually and actively seek ways to simplify my life, I have, owing to my background in law and political science, kept an active eye on our culture. I read every newspaper and magazine. I watch CNN, MSNBC, C-SPAN and FOX. I cut out articles and catalogue them. I look for little blips in daily events that highlight the unusual. I search for trends. I think, analyze and rethink what's going on in the United States. My background and my current state of being detached, provides me with a more objective analysis of America's current state of affairs than the pundits. The pundits don't have a clue as to what is going on. They have a vested interest in infotainment. I have none. Of course, before you can pose the question, Is America Nuts?, one must conduct an inquiry into whether I am nuts. Hence, the personal background so the reader can draw his or her own conclusions. I know I am a character and I thank God for that. I have some broad general self-destructive traits that I guard against. However, I am happy. The more I follow this path of simplicity and remove myself from this culture, the happier I become. In juxtaposition, the more I watch people who follow the path that our country propagates as the American dream, the more I encounter shallow, empty, unhappy people. Bookstores are a great indication of cultures. In American bookstores there are many books about weight loss, money and how to be happy. I can only assume that America is fat, broke and depressed. So who's crazy, my Uncle Sam or me?

What is it that bugs me so? The short answer is, everything: movies, television, politicians, business leaders, church leaders, the state of men-women relationships, how men are depicted in our society and a million other daily annoyances. America has become immune to the daily horror of its own existence. I know guys who work sixty hours a week. Their wives work fifty hours a week. They have no family life. Their children are cell phone mall brats. The families are electronically interconnected with laptops, desktops and palm pilots. Their schedules are electronically recorded every day. Schedules can extend out for five or six weeks. They complain about time and stress. Everyone within the family has grown apart. They are strangers within their own dwelling. This family is fucking nuts. They don't know it. They have no life. They won't make changes. They do, however, have material possessions. Unfortunately, they do not have enough time to enjoy them.

Politicians seem to have two rules. Never answer a question and always tell a lie. Dr. Howard Dean, the presidential candidate for 2004, recently remarked that a "gaffe" in Washington D.C. is when you tell the truth. I watch, for example, Meet the Press with Tim Russert and Tim is interviewing some congressman. Tim asks a *specific* question. The congressman does not answer Tim's *specific* question. The politico gives a response that (a) has nothing to do with the question and (b) generally appears to be a litany of catch phrases that can be (a) conservative if he is a Republican or (b) liberal if he is a Democrat. It goes something like this: Tim-"Didn't the Republicans *block* that legislation?" Answer: "Well, Tim, we are for a good education program, adequate spending and as you know the President has instituted the leave No Child Behind Act." I sit there and start to moan. This guy, and it doesn't make a difference whether he is liberal or conservative, Democrat or Republican, didn't answer the question. Not even close. I see this pattern of intercourse repeated ad nauseam. Tim might press a little more but never pins the guy to the point of alienation. Never press any interviewee to the point of being uncomfortable. No one will come on your show. Talk shows need bodies to fill chairs. I ask myself about this time honored pattern of asking a question and giving a response that doesn't answer the question. What does it say about us as a culture where this kind of exchange is the norm? Is this a good thing? What concerns me is that this method of exchange has become so deep rooted that it is part of how we interact. This kind of answer is expected. To me, this kind of public exchange is unacceptable. The congressman didn't answer the question. Don't insult me with this babble crap. Am I alone? Americans are working too hard and are too stressed out to pay attention. After all, why should I care if he lies and doesn't answer a question, a friend tells me. "I know this," my friend continues. That's it! He knows that politicians lie. I am naïve. It's all right. My friend is more surprised at me for being surprised. Of course, I extrapolate this cultural norm out to a logical conclusion. Where does outrageous, lying, evasive conduct lead? Nothing good and healthy I can assure you. After all, by tomorrow, it's yesterdays news and everyone's lives are so busy that they don't have time to worry about how our democracy functions. Politicians lie and are evasive, so what is my problem? In the common vernacular, "hello Rick, wake up." I am awake. Are you?

We are not a wise nation. Wisdom is borne within reflection. Reflection is borne within thinking and thinking takes time. When a nation, as a collective whole, does not have time to think it cannot reflect and hence, cannot be wise. Wisdom prevents stupid actions. Invading Iraq was not a wise decision.

Is the average American too busy to care that their politicians lie or is it that they just don't care? Too busy, I can understand. Not caring is really scary. For example, when John Luntz interviews a cross section of people on MSNBC to take our "pulse," they repeat exactly what they heard some pundit say on TV or radio. These people don't have a factual clue but they do have an honest opinion based upon a lie. I don't know how many times I have heard the mantra that Saddam Hussein is an evil monster that uses weapons of mass destruction and killed 1,000,000 of his own people. These are the same folks that couldn't pick out Iraq on a map of the Middle East. These are the same people that believe half of the 9/11 hijackers were Iraqis. They heard it. They repeat it and whether it's true or not doesn't make a difference. I detect a lack of caring. Extrapolate this out and you have a nation that is going to kill thousands of people from a sovereign nation and the sound of that does not prick any sense of morality. After all, Hussein is an evil monster that uses weapons of mass destruction and killed 1,000,000 of his own people. Why don't I ever hear the interviewer challenge this? Names, dates, places, who, what, when, where and how? If I did, I would feel more connected. I don't. I conclude that the American people have been dumbed down, whipped up and freaked out. It's my only explanation of how this occurs. I choose not to believe that they just don't care. Carl Bernstein of Woodward-Bernstein fame recently stated that Americans are an idiot culture.

I have been watching President Bush make his case for war. Usually, it is based upon some single fact and not a totality of circumstances. Nations and people around the world know when to go to war. A legitimate war sells itself. This one is not flying. Witness the millions of people protesting the war. Witness the nations that are struggling to back the United States. Witness the outright hostility of long time allies such as France, Germany, Russia and China. This war isn't selling. Yet, President Bush continues to harp upon some single fact to make his case for war. The exchange between my President and me goes like this: Rick, my citizen, we should bomb Iraq because of "A." Several days later "A" is found out not to be true. I didn't believe "A" anyway. The President moves on and says "Rick we should bomb Iraq because of "B." Several days later "B" is found out to be false. My president then proceeds to "C" and "D" which are also not true. I sit there and ponder reason "A." I assume reason "A" was a true fact based upon credible evidence. But it wasn't. My President lied to me and then proceeded to lie over and over again. Maybe he "misspoke." I ask myself, what does it say about the leader of the most powerful nation in the world who misspeaks? I know he wants my support. But will he lie to get it? I see that his popularity in the polls is high and is getting higher. America buys it. I don't. Once again, the question arises, am I nuts? Am I so far out of the loop that I have become paranoid? No. He lied and lied and lied. I guess I am not supposed to remember the first lie or even keep track of each succeeding lie. But I do. I watch television and see others interviewed repeatedly state that we must invade Iraq because of "A." I am bewildered. I find solace in international opinion that thinks President Bush is a liar *and* crazy. Beyond our shores, I am not alone.

I often wonder what I would do if I were to run against this screwball frat boy President. I would eat him up. Without a script he's lousy. However, I am not a politician so Bush is safe. But where are the Democratic rivals who have more experience in politics than I do? How is it that the loyal opposition doesn't exist? The answer is simply that if you attack a sitting President in time of war you will be branded a traitor and yes, in case you forgot, America, we are told, is in a war. The loyal opposition is stopped dead in their tracks. No balls. Only concerned with getting reelected. Suppose one American dies in Iraq and the congressman who didn't support the war runs for reelection. The opposing candidate would say that the one American soldier might be alive today had you supported our troops. Oops. That's enough. I support, I support, I support. Hussein is an evil man who uses weapons of mass destruction and killed 1,000,000 of his own people. Get with the program. Get with the mantra. Hundreds of intelligent people, our elected leaders, going along with this lunacy, because four words, "you are a traitor," seals their lips. How do they get away with this? America has been dumbed down, whipped up and freaked out. Kill the beast. Kill the beast. Kill the beast. Ah, shades of Lord of the Flies. What is the "soma" that has put everyone to sleep?

The word "lying" is a confrontational word. No one lies anymore. Today, in America, it's spin or misspoke. In Brooklyn schoolyards when you lied, you lied.

On most occasions, someone fucking lied. You didn't "misspeak." You lied. Spin, and then spin upon spin and truth gets so spinned out that no one remembers what the truth is. I always thought that America's greatness was that it could evolve to a higher plane of being. It could lead hundreds of millions of people to a better life. But is this what happened? Instead of seeing shades of gray in any given situation, America has devolved into the simplicity of black and white. Good versus evil. You're with us or against us. You are either a friend or an enemy. The human mind is complex. The mind has been traumatized to accept simplicity. The French don't support us. They are bad. Hundreds of years of an alliance down the tubes and after all, who needs them anyway. Pour out your bottles of French wine and boycott French products. Ban French toast and French fries from the Congressional mess hall. It's freedom toast and freedom fries for my elected leaders. America has been reduced to predictable infantile responses. It's the world's biggest baby. In the international arena of the geopolitical game of Cowboys and Indians, you could not get a better Indian than Osama Bin Laden nor a better Cowboy than George W. Bush. Throughout this movie, we wear the white hats. The Indians are evil savages. Unfortunately, I believe that Osama the Indian is smarter than Bush the Cowboy.

As part of my reality testing, I look for any tidbit that might confirm that I am not alone in my beliefs. Today, I came upon two articles, one in the New York Times and another in my local paper, The Daily Camera. They're my little bits of sunshine that I need to seek out on a daily basis. On Feb. 22, 2003, in the Times under the Women's Basketball Roundup was a small article entitled "Player Jeered for Ignoring The American Flag." It stated: "Toni Smith, who turns away from the American Flag during the national anthem, was jeered by flag-waving students at a road game Thursday night." Further on it states, "Smith, a senior says she is protesting that the governments priorities are not bettering the quality of life for all people, but rather on expanding its own power." What a breath of fresh air. I am not the only one. My local paper reprinted remarks of Senator Robert Byrd that were made on the Senate floor on February 12, 2003. The speech in its entirety was brilliant. I quote only a small part of it: "But to turn one's frustration and anger into the kind of extremely destabilizing and dangerous foreign policy debacle that the world is currently witnessing is inexcusable from any administration charged with the awesome power and responsibility of guiding the destiny of the greatest superpower on the planet. Frankly, many of the pronouncements made by this administration are outrageous. There is no other word." I search for these rays of hope and sanity everyday. I want sunshine right here in America.

Life is not complex. Quantum physics is complex. America has made life complex. It has become a bad business model for people. America's model for living no longer functions. Why people choose a business model for everyday life that totally consumes one with work, electronic gadgets, very short or non-existent vacations, stress and three-hour commutes to work are mind-boggling. Does any man or woman state: "Honey, this is bullshit. I'm quitting my job and we're going to change our lives." The current American life model only produces stress, broken marriages, physical illness, alcohol and drug problems, general anxiety and ultimately death. In quieter moments, some people might reflect on a different lifestyle and yet wake up every morning and embrace the stressful model again and again. I am astounded that very few Americans step back from this insanity and question themselves. Why am I doing this? Our capitalistic democracy has produced exactly what it needs: mindless worker-droids who get the guilt's if they are not producing in everyway, everyday. Give the droids just enough to pay their bills and always keep them stressed. For a long time I viewed American culture as if it was amusing. I analyzed daily events from a political science or legal standpoint. I prided myself on my ability in understanding what "really" was going on. I would say things like "what a great move by the Democrats" or "look how the Republicans boxed those Democrats in." I viewed the entire American process as if it was some clever slick game, which I would wink at if I got the point. I knew it was real and not a game, but I was part of the process at playing the game. After all, I was an attorney. During the mid 1980's, I started to change my point of view. It appeared to me that a big chill started to develop over America. The corporate bean counters took over. Political correctness took root. Being a character was out. Every one needed "space." Everyone was "special." Everyone had "issues." Everyone was dumbed down to act in the least objectionable way. Anger was out. Showing emotions became objectionable and a sign of weakness. No public displays of affection. Don't hold hands and don't kiss. The process of being a good little worker droid was being instilled into the American psyche. The corporate types wanted to have a self-centered citizenry rather than an outer directed citizenry. Outer directed people may care about what's going on. Inner-directed people only care about themselves. No matter how inconsequential, inner-directed people care about their feelings, issues, money, safety, space and time. America can fuck up whatever it wants just don't upset "my being" in any way. Conjure up relativism, so that my truth is my truth and your truth is your truth and therefore I am never wrong and to challenge my perception of truth is upsetting. Therefore, you are a bad person. Who came up with this shit? I didn't learn this crap in the schoolyard of P.S. 134 in Brooklyn,

New York. I actually did a google search on the phrase "personal space," and it's there. The rules of American culture have wrung out every aspect of having an interesting and intriguing personality. So, I am a character in a culture that has been stripped of all its personality. My corporate yuppie friends say, "let's not go there," and "I think that's more than I need to know." Shut off and down all interactions that might lead somewhere. This is not normal. Where have all the characters gone? It goes against human nature. It is an unnatural and unhealthy way of living. Character goes underground. Ever so slowly, our self-centered American culture has turned on itself. We are now our own entertainment. Something is not right. On the one hand, we have nice polite corporate speak, "that's more than I need to know, thank you very much," and in direct juxtaposition are culture plays out through its media, a hostile game of attack. We need to attack something or someone. No advanced dialogue into the shades of gray, but nasty tones of black and white. As I write, I am glancing at the television, watching MSNBC in its coverage of the Feb. 22, 2003, nightclub disaster in Rhode Island. Ninety-Six people burned to death. The bodies have not been identified. The thrust of the coverage is not the pain of it all, but whom to blame. Reality TV shows are popular and cheap. They will become the norm. Many of these reality shows make fun of people. Scare people. Embarrass people. Belittle people. We are not communicating. We are aggressively attacking each other. The Jerry Springer Show comes to mind. The most popular show that caters to the basest parts of our personality. I never saw the Ozzie Osbourne family MTV show. I did see Ozzie on Super Bowl day and thought that the commercial was a put-on. A friend told me that Ozzie is as he is shown. An entire show based upon a dysfunctional family that America loves to watch. Shows that require people to do dangerous and/or disgusting acts. Then, there are shows about people and all their little issues. An MTV show comes to mind. College students sit around and talk about themselves. Heaped on top of all this bullshit, are the cable news networks that just seem to love to get a story with legs. It is usually an event concerning a person that they can beat up on over and over for days or months.

Madelyne Toogood's story comes to mind. This mother was caught on tape in a parking lot spanking her child. This story was raised to the level of national news for ten days. Another story with major legs is The Countdown to War with Iraq. The Gary Condit-Chandra Levy love affair has plenty of media legs. I actually heard a pundit state that he was going to pursue Gary Condit, the murderer, until the end of his career. The current celebrity to beat up on is Michael Jackson. Gloria Allred, a feminist attorney out of Hollywood is suing Jackson under California law because he held his child over a balcony in Germany. Attack.

Attack. Attack. America has recast itself into one big Salem witch trial. We are not evolving as a culture. America is devolving into armed camps of evil, mean spirited people looking for the next witch to burn. It seems the word "alleged" has dropped out of our vocabulary. No one is alleged to have committed anything, anymore. Matters, not proven, are reported as facts not allegations. Innocent until proven guilty is out the window. The government loves this because they can bring baseless claims against anyone they want without factual basis. If the government seeks to destroy someone without a trial, they just claim that the person is "a person of interest." Feed the cable news networks enough information and the networks get the ball rolling. Our media doesn't need facts anymore because they can fill up the airtime with suppositions. For example, they can say, nothing has been proven yet, but suppose this and that. Then go out and get your expert talking heads and debate the supposition as if it were true. Since all of us are so busy with ourselves, the supposition becomes reality and the facts are forgotten. No one ever stops the machine from raging. Fiction becomes fact. We all debate the fiction as if it were reality. Am I nuts? I don't think so. The biggest fiction-fact currently being played out on the international stage is our war with Iraq. America changes the international rules of dealing with other nations and states that it can invade a country and kill its people because America believes that the other country *may* have weapons of mass destruction and that it *may* eventually use those weapons against America. Pure speculation and supposition repeated ad infinitum until people believe that the supposition is fact. If we don't kill Saddam Hussein now, he will attack us with weapons of mass destruction. That's a fact? That's bullshit. As mentioned earlier, Senator Robert Byrd during his masterful speech, further stated: "This nation is about to embark upon the first test of a revolutionary doctrine applied in an extraordinary way at an unfortunate time. The doctrine of preemption-the idea that the United States or any other nation can legitimately attack a nation that is not imminently threatening but may be threatening in the future-is a radical new twist on the traditional concept of self-defense." How is it that you can get away with this kind of thinking? Senator Byrd wondered aloud that very question: he said, "Yet, this Chamber is, for the most part, silent, ominously, dreadfully silent. There is no debate, no discussion, no attempt to lay out for the nation the pros and cons of this particular war. THERE IS NOTHING." Having a change of international policy does not have an immediate impact on anyone's life. Our entire national dialogue consists of attack, reload and attack again. No one has any clue about civilized debate or discussion. It's boring and old. I have always wondered how Nazi Germany got its people to attack other nations and commit horrible acts of atrocities. I am just beginning to get a glimpse of what it must have been like when the National Socialist Party came to power. I hear it every day in my job. "Those fucking French faggots." "Did you see the picture of all those sailors on the deck of the aircraft carrier that spelled out Fuck Iraq?" "Did you hear about Beth, that army chick that was ready to take a French General out of a bar and kick the shit out of him?" "You know, I have to hold a lot of Marines back from assassinating Scott Ritter the traitor." "Those fucking Iraqis should be nuked." "Why the fuck are we playing around with them? Nuke them for Christ sake!" This is America. This is the *real* America. I'm wondering where the hell this hatred came from and the speed at which it arrived. Now, go out and get some kick-ass logical conservative talk show host like Rush Limbaugh and with impeccable logic, he spell's out why we should bomb the crap out of Iraq and 20,000,000 ditto heads nod in agreement. The horror of killing hundreds if not thousands of other human beings does not seem to matter. It is the call of Onward Christian Soldier that seems to propel events. Evil lurks everywhere. Leave no stone unturned. Could the media get a better story with legs than this? Come on Lester Holt, "its countdown to war." When a country's citizens turn on themselves and make themselves their own amusement in a very sick way, they have lost all respect for humanity. Since Americans are not shocked at what it does to its own people, why would they care about foreigners? They don't even care about their neighbors.

Today is Sunday, February 23, 2003. I love Sunday because it is, what I like to call, free floating Sunday. I dwell on whatever comes to my mind. I was just watching Chris Matthews's new Sunday half-hour show right after Meet the Press. Chris wanted to know about reality shows. How is it that 80,000,000 people tuned into Joe Millionaire? David Gregory, NBC's man at the White House, one of the guest pundits stated, "well, you know, we all like to see other people humiliated." Let's watch Ozzie the freak and get another dose of someone we can make fun of. This whole country has turned into a bad life model. It needs to change.

I have been accused of seeing things on a simplistic level. Things are complicated, I am told. No, they are not. I have a theory on complexity. Complexity only exists when one person can't get over on another person. A construct must be created, a matrix, which distorts reality to a sufficient degree that the other person might be convinced of whatever is proposed and freely give his consent. When two modern slick players get together, each creates a construct to get over on the other and the process continues until one achieves victory. If a third party enters into the fray of these dueling constructs, he has no idea of what's really going on. The two parties can then use this spin on an innocent third party. The process becomes exceedingly complex. That's how I view America today. How can I create a sellable construct that has no basis in reality to get the public to buy it? Of course, we have a two party system so we have two spins, each as bad as the other. Each party spins a different set of fictitious constructs. It's all bullshit. Keep it simple stupid. It seems we hate the truth because it may stand in the way of gratifying our own self-centered needs.

Don't wait for the market to go up because it will not over the long haul. Notwithstanding what Wall Street tells you, the market isn't going up. The Street tells you that the market is down because (1) 9/11 and the long shadow cast over the nation and (2) it's the war on Iraq that's holding this economy back and (3) anything to do with Bill Clinton. The truth is another matter and very simple. We have the supply side down. We are efficient to the point of absurdity. What about demand? The war is over. Are you going to go out and buy that new plasma TV? How about a new picture cell phone? With everyone so tapped out there is no longer any extra money to spare for gizmos. One can always refinance. We are in the latter stages of capitalism where we feed on ourselves. Want to buy an automobile or furniture? It's either refinance and suck more money out of your home or the retailers will give it to you with no down payment or interest for twelve months. The big question is: did you make purchases from savings out of your paycheck? If corporations can't get your money at least they can get your promise. They'll sell the paper to the bank for money. We're shuffling paper down the line. How is capitalism feeding on itself? The feeding part comes in when corporations start to earn their money from nasty little irritating fees and penalties. This might be good for the short term but not for the long term. For example, nasty little fee number 1: If I want a hard copy of my insurance bill it will cost me $1.50. Ten million customers at $1.50 a hard copy amounts to fifteen million dollars a month, which is a nice little sum. Insurance companies lost a lot of money on their investments so they raise insurance rates. They are no longer insuring against a risk that I might present, they are guaranteeing themselves a return on their investment. This is not the traditional concept of insurance companies insuring against risk. I thought every state had a Department of Insurance watching over these people. I guess that most heads and staff of these political entities formerly worked for insurance companies. Is the fox guarding the chicken coop? No, that can't happen here. How does the public respond? They cancel insurance and drive without it. Get it for one day when you have to register your car and cancel it the next. Oh, the games that people are *forced* to play. How about ever exploding health insurance rates? Insurance companies want to insure only the very healthiest people who pose the least risk so that all premiums are pure profit. Ask an expert in this field and you'll get such a complex answer your head will spin. Complexity is for screwing you over, plain and simple.

I have always wondered why the path to God is so complex that only those who dedicate themselves to the complete study of God might be able to get close to him. If I were God, I would have devised a message that is clear, simple and easy to understand. According to my theory, God is simple. Man makes it complex and the guy who tells you it is complex, the priest, minister, mullah or rabbi, is satisfying his own human needs to put distance between himself and others. Usually, that distance is vertical not horizontal. That is, he's above and better than you. I'll take a good natured atheist any day over the complex man of God who tells me I must study for years to get close to heaven. It's just another construct designed to confuse and bewilder. Today, I'm also thinking about the continued ever-rising sales of real estate. The number of housing starts and sales is so strong I just can't believe it. These numbers are either contrived or they are real. Let's assume they are real. The only reason housing starts are strong is because of the low historic interest rates. Monthly payments on a home are less than rentals. In addition, there are huge tax benefits and you can suck all the equity out with a home equity loan to continue to buy stuff. This has impacted the rental market. Here's a heads up. Check the second tier rental market. These rents must come down to compete with housing and when they do the strength of the housing market will cease. If interest rates go up, all bets are off.

What a Sunday. I love thinking about all these idle thoughts before I go out and listen to live music. America is an aggressive nation. We have more murders, stabbing, rapes, and child abuse than any other country. We also have the most advanced weaponry in the world. Twenty years more advanced than anyone else. What are these weapons for? An aggressive nation with advanced weaponry for defensive purposes? No. I don't think so. Aggressive nations have weapons for aggressive purposes. There is no nation that would dare act aggressively against our interests. Terrorists might. Nations no. America's defense budget exceeds $450,000,000,000 annually. To justify such an expense to a nation that's broke, you need an exceedingly complex construct that the average person has no hope of understanding. The government opts for a simple construct. America is in a war against terrorism: we don't know who they are or where they are, but they hate us. For the people that do understand that America cannot justify such a large defense budget, the government holds up its trump card up of classified information that they have and cannot share. I know something you don't know and it's this something that justifies spending all this money. So it's Sunday and I have these idle, fleeting thoughts. I offer them as a way of showing the reader how I think. Am I a conspiracy theorist? Is there no good in America? Do I really believe that every time I turn around my country and all its various parts are asking me to bend over? Yes. I do. I also believe that there is no one to protect us. The Republicans? The Democrats? Growing up, I don't recall an America that wanted to screw its own people. I recall a different collective consciousness that was more in tune with the needs of the people. I didn't have such a hard time with my country. I think we "thought" right. As I stated before, sometime in the 1980's I noticed a change. Things somehow got different. There was a steady march towards being inner directed and glorifying each individual rather than the collective whole. Our culture doesn't say get out there and experience all of life. Our culture demands that you turn inward and mind your own business. This comes across in one tiny example. When I tell people that I'm going to the Baja by car they incredulously ask "by car?" as if that is the most dangerous thing anyone could ever do. What about bandits they ask? Aren't I afraid? Americans loved to be scared and will invent stories to keep themselves in check, in place, safe and secure. Anti-bacterial soap plays on the same fears. It will protect you from those nasty little critters. These kinds of beliefs can only exist when you sincerely believe that you are very, very special. Your existence must be protected at all costs. I'm not special. I'm no better than the starving Somali toiling in his field. Since I don't think I'm special, I would never think of bandits on Mex 1 in the Baja because I'm just not that important. Bacteria from all scientific accounts are more healthy than dangerous. We'll buy anything if it protects us. Why? You're special and gosh darn it, you like you. We are so overly concerned with ourselves that the only way to protect our fragile psyches and physical being is to make ever smaller concentric circles thereby preventing anything from the outside getting in. Don't get involved. Don't say hello to your neighbors. Gate your community. Don't . Don't. Don't. Of course this can come back and bite you in the ass. When you develop a country of small-minded gullible hermits and you disturb their perceived well-being, you are going to get in a lot of trouble. Heads have to roll. There are no accidents. There is only culpable conduct and someone must pay a price. Preferably, on national cable news television 24/7 until there is "closure." What an absurd way to live. An entire generation has been brought up within this new inner-directed belief system. What's interesting and scary, is that once you key into this kind of mind set you can affect it in very predictable ways. For example, if Osama told his troops to increase the "chatter" on the internet knowing full well of American intercepts, he could bet his last dinar that America would increase the terror alert code to orange and increase the amount of money that will be spent on that heightened alert. The Federal Government has not included enough money in their budget for the states to support the federal mandates. Impoverished states foot the bill thereby further increasing their poverty. Without actually firing a shot, he can theoretically bring America to financial ruins. I'm sure that what the terrorists didn't expect was the extent to which the United States would show its nuttiness. Tom Ridge issues a duct tape-plastic advisory telling the nation that taping plastic to your windows will help in a biological and/or chemical attack. Every terrorist had to be laughing at this directive. Tom Ridge laughed. When you box yourself in by creating inner-directed self-centered people, a government has to protect its ass. The government tries to cover its butt against events that it cannot control. The only thing America can do is issue a safety directive. Of course, everyone is in trouble if a loner with one stick of dynamite decides to blow himself up in the Mall of America. Just imagine what would happen. In the heartland of America, terror strikes. There would be untold major consequences, the least of which would be plummeting consumer sales. So America has a huge problem on its hands. When you dumb down, whip up and freak out your own citizens, their collective responses are all too predictable in negative ways. There is very little you can do to stop it. To get out of this box, America must start an entire new generation that thinks and acts in a healthy way. You must change the system in its entirety.

Here's a story about my black friend Reggie. In New York, I owned a company called The Postcard Printer located on Hudson Street. I had a corner storefront business at the intersection of Liaght and Hudson Streets. I shared offices with Jonick Trucking, which specialized in trucking services for the printing industry. A guy named John ran it. Jonick is a full service trucking facility that included bike messengers, truck and vans. Reggie owned a van. The Postcard Printer did not have a separate entrance. Clients had to go through Jonick to get to my business. The guys at Jonick hung out at my place when customers weren't present. Reggie and I became good friends over the six years that I was in business. Every Friday was payday at Jonick and Reggie would stick his head in my doorway and shout "I got's mine." This became the Reggie Principle, for as the subsequent years ensued, I noticed that the Reggie Principle became national in scope. As long as "I got's mine," everything is o.k. Right? Once in a while, when Reggie would stick his head in the door and shout "I got's mine," I would say, "hey, Reggie, there are people starving in Africa," to which he replied, "I gots mine." At least Reggie worked hard and earned his money. Unfortunately, the Reggie Principle has expanded to include people who "gots" theirs without earning it. Not even a pretense of earning it. From the mid 1980's to the current time, I noticed that the Reggie Principle was expanding to a greater and greater percentage of the population until it seemed to me that the entire American culture was engulfed in Reggie's formula for happiness. It seemed everyone in America went to greater lengths in their efforts to "gets theirs." The recent period of corporate misdeeds clearly shows that outright theft of monies was indeed a path followed by many to "gets theirs." Corporate chieftains would "gets theirs" even if getting theirs bankrupt their own company and put thousands of people out of work and destitute. Dreams have evaporated overnight because corporate managers decided that earning theirs like Reggie took too long. I worry that with less and less money in this country, a shrinking economic pie will cause all those Reggie's to turn nasty and ugly. When Reggie doesn't "gets his," watch out.

Very little of what I have heard growing up has stuck with me. "I Gots Mine," has. Another little principle of life I learned was from Ronnie Robinson. Ronnie was my best friend growing up in Brooklyn. He died at the age of 18. One day, Ronnie said to me: "Rick, you know what's wrong with you white people?" "What Ronnie?" I asked. Ronnie says: "Two guys are walking down the block and one guy puts his hand in the other guys pocket and takes his wad of bills. A white guy says, 'Hey, you took my money.' A black guy wouldn't say jack shit. He'd punch the motherfucker out, take his money back and keep on walking." The point being, white people debate bullshit. Just look around and listen to how much we debate and argue bullshit. It's not even real crap that we're talking about. A lot of what passes as important is "what ifs" and suppositions. As long as we're arguing something it's o.k. It's our national background noise. Listen to Rush Limbaugh. Yada. Yada. Yada. All day and its all negative all the time.

While I'm on the subject of Brooklyn, another thing I learned was the strongest, toughest guy in the schoolyard didn't pick on the weakest. That was a sign of weakness and the strong boy would be taken down a couple of notches in everyone's opinion. A strong guy picking on the weakest was a big, big, big, no-no. Also, it was the strong-tough boys job to take care of the bully in the schoolyard. When the bully came a knocking, it was the tough guys job to run interference and keep the peace so the ball games could go on. It was against the rules for either the tough guy or bully to pick on the weakest link. It was expected that fights be between equal opponents. You were a punk if you started a fight with someone out of your class. America, at one time was a strong tough guy. It has morphed into the bully and it starts fights with those who cannot fight the "good fight." America starts punk fights. It's like me at 6'1" and 185 pounds with a background in martial arts, carrying a bat, going against a small, petite, fragile grandmother. It has punk written all over it. Now we have America, a world-class bully with the most advanced sophisticated weapons of mass destruction without a tough-strong guy to run interference. The bully is running amuck starting punk fights against weak nations. It is this basic violation of schoolyard fights that has the world so upset. Everyone intuitively knows that this is a punk fight. It's the bully beating up on grandma. It isn't a fight, it's a killing field. That's all we're doing. Killing. Hootin and a hollerin. Lootin and a shootin. In our schoolyard, the strong-tough good guy was Bernie. The bully was Tommy. When Tommy was running nuts in the schoolyard and Bernie wasn't there to challenge him, we had a big fucking problem. On one occasion, we did the only thing we could do. We banded together and challenged him. Twenty to one and we were shitting in our pants. It worked. In the current geopolitical climate, there is no Bernie. So, the world is banding together, just as I did with my friends forty-five years ago. China, Russia, France, Belgium, and Germany are banding together in opposition to a "war" that has punk written all over it. America is going alone to the killing fields of Iraq and there will be hell to pay in the aftermath. I'm concerned about international boycotts of American goods and services. There are ways to punish the bully for beating up on Grandma. Another very important lesson I learned in the schoolyard of P.S. 134 was the saying "don't hide it, divide it." Simply put, if you were the one who had five cents for a candy-bar you didn't go off to the back of the schoolyard and eat it by yourself. Hence, "don't hide it, divide it." Imagine, being in my position, going from the engrained principle of "Don't hide it, Divide It," to "I Got's Mine," in thirty years. I'm convinced the former principle is more worthy.

I am alone on the hill. Ricky Baja, a dedicated multi-slacker, out of the fray, watching what I perceive to be an absolutely unhealthy life model erected in America's name. Ricky Baja living in a nation of inner-directed lunatics whose lives will be shattered. I look out and see disturbing trends developing that will devastate our citizens. An electoral process wholly dominated by large corporations and wealthy individuals. Internationally, nations are increasingly backing away from America the bully nation. Corporations destroying the lives of its workers with rule changes on pension plans. Exorbitant increases in "must pay" premiums for medical, car and house insurance. Forcing seniors who need drugs to switch to a different plan to obtain them. Depriving the educational system of necessary funds to make smart little people. Everywhere I look, I see the average guy under attack on the most fundamental level. On top of all that, a government that pries's into the lives of the average guy in the name of security. The further I back out of the system the happier I become and the more crystal clear it becomes that America is a very strange place. I look for signs that I am not alone. I find temporary solace in the current anti-war demonstrations knowing full well that if America does not proceed, it will be only a respite from its other craziness. The plethora of reality shows will continue this summer. We will continue to denigrate and humiliate our people. We will not promote families, fun, good health, good food, art, dance, music, theatre and friendship. The SUV will still be there. The Palm Pilots will be there. The cell phones will still be there. Rush Limbaugh will continue spewing his invectives at everyone that is not conservative. In America's heart, there is nothing left that is good. When everyday life starts to unravel, all of the self-centered little shits will start screaming and there will be hell to pay. Someone is at fault. Someone must pay. It can't be me. Who can we hang? Michael Jackson? Fed Chairman Alan Greenspan? Violent video games? Someone has to pay. I paint a horrible picture. Therefore, I question myself as to whether I am, in fact, the one that is nuts. Maybe, I am a perpetual doom and gloomer? However, because I do question myself, constantly, I realize that this is a sign of good mental health. There is a mechanism in my psyche that is fluctuating and is attempting to determine whether I am on a path to a better life or a destructive life. What scares me is that I don't see America questioning itself. The internal mental checks and balances all seem to have disappeared. America is on one track, destructive and it is too myopic to see the consequences of its own actions or doesn't care. America is governed by ideologues. They are, by definition, myopic, self centered, idiosyncratic, righteous maniacs. Ideologues view life though a straw. Where is the loyal opposition fighting on behalf of the little guy? As Senator Byrd pointed out in his speech, America is an empty silent chamber. It appears that the powerful and rich are exercising a last ditch attempt in the most blatant example of the Reggie Principle. I wants mine and I'm gonna gets mine. Why? They know that in several years when the baby boomers retire, we're broke. Really broke. They better gets theirs before there ain't nothing left to gets.

Suppose, for example, a major corporation is about to launch a new product and has invested $30,000,000.00 in the process. One day, prior to the launch, the Chairman of the Board discovers that the C.E.O. has lied about everything. The results of the product testing are phony. The results of consumer sentiment are phony. The results of expected sales are phony. Everything is made up. Can you hear the Chairman screaming at the top of his lungs "are you fucking nuts? You need major psychiatric treatment you fucking idiot." Well, that's what I believe. This country needs major psychiatric treatment. I wondered how America would stand up under analysis from a traditional standpoint. I have tried as best as I could, not being a certified psychologist, to formulate an America with a distinctive personality as a whole and put it under the microscope of psychology.

I sent my Uncle Sam to the couch because I think he needs major help. Sam is thinking wrong. He's lying and is acting out his rage. Sam is on dangerous ground and needs immediate help in solving his problems because he can't do it on his own.

The American Psychiatric Association publishes a book entitled "Diagnostic and Statistical Manual of Mental Disorders." It is commonly referred to as the DSM-IV manual. It is used throughout the United States and internationally to classify and diagnose all mental disorders. If you want to get reimbursed by an insurance company in the United States for a mental disorder you have to have a diagnosis recognized by this book. It is a number such as 300.23, which is "Social Phobia" (social anxiety disorder). Each mental disorder listed in the book is followed by a brief explanation under the heading "Diagnostic Features" followed by specifics labeled as follows: "Specified," "Associated Features and Disorders," "Specific Culture, Age, and Gender Features," "Prevalence," "Course," "Familial Pattern," "Differential Diagnosis." Each mental disorder has a rather specific identity in the quest to determine exactly what the problem is and the respective treatment that one might employ to help the therapist "cure" the mental disorder.

DSM-IV defines personality as follows:

> Enduring patterns of perceiving, relating to, and
> thinking about the environment and oneself.
> Personality traits are prominent aspects of personality
> that are exhibited in a wide range of important
> social and personal contexts. Only when personality
> traits are inflexible and maladaptive and cause
> either significant functional impairment or subjective
> distress do they constitute a personality disorder.

Merriam Webster's Deluxe Dictionary (Tenth Collegiate Edition) defines Personality as:

> the complex of characteristics that distinguishes an individual
> *or a nation or group*; especially: the totality of an individual's
> behavior and emotional characteristics.

Does Sam have a personality, which can be diagnosed and analyzed? I think so. Sam has a complex of characteristics that distinguishes us as a nation. Initially, I thought that this would be an easy subject to expand upon. However, my inquiry into Sam is proving to be troubling. Americans love to look at and analyze other nations behavior. It is only recently that some sociologists have looked at America as a culture. We love to study other cultures and their characteristics. That very well might be one of Sam's traits. America is not into self-criticism and self-analysis. There is a lot of foreign interpretation of Sam's traits. Americans are rude people is often a critique that foreigners ascribe to us when we travel. However, I don't want to use what others think of us so I have given some thought as to who my Uncle Sam is. It is based upon what I see everyday in print, television and movies, in short, everything that my eyes and ears consume.

I just came back from Thailand. I was going to go to Japan to visit my son, however, he e-mailed me and wrote that since he already lives there he would rather hook up someplace else. I asked him what other country he had in mind and he told me Mongolia, to which I readily agreed. Several days later, I received another e-mail from my son. He researched Mongolia on the net and based upon the time that he had for vacation, Mongolia was not a good choice. My son suggested Thailand to which I agreed. I read most of the guidebooks in Borders and Barnes and Noble bookstores. I bought a map. Every guidebook pointed out two things about Thailand that were true. It is, indeed, a land of 1,000 smiles and the Thai people like to have fun. It is a cultural trait. If Thais are not having fun, they don't do it. This extends to business as well. A Thai person boxed in a cubicle at a call center is an image that I cannot envision. No fun. Being an early riser, every morning while I was in Chiang Mai, a northern provincial capitol, I had my coffee at 6:00 a.m. The dining area was an open outdoor area bordering the central moat in old Chiang Mai. Every morning I watched the Iraq war on CNN, had coffee and read the Bangkok Post. The editorials were excellent. One particular editorial discussed the difficulties that the multinational corporate managers were having with the local Thai managers. The locals didn't quite get that you couldn't have "fun" at work and that is the true hell of globalization. The pursuit of money reduces everything to the least objectionable common denominator. Only corporate approved politeness dominates. For example, when the bean counters think that the customer would enjoy the ubiquitous phrase "did you find everything all right" at your local supermarket, that's what you hear. I once asked a kid at the Safeway checkout counter if he went to Safeway school and he told me he did. It wasn't exactly school, but rather orientation for check-out people where there advised to ask each customer "if they found everything all right." I always answer no. I have a Safeway card that prints my name. The Safeway checkers are also advised to check out the name and say it out loud. I guess that makes me feel a special bond with the store because they say thank you Mr. Weisman. A stupid little game that some bean counter thinks is good customer relations. I figure I might as well have some fun with it. I always go to the check out lady from Uzbekistan who has a thick Russian accent. She has a booming voice in a halted staccato Rusky accent. "Did you find everything o.k?" "No," I answer. After she rings everything up and the bill is printed out with my name on the bottom, she holds it up and booms "thank you Mr. Richard Weisman." I love it. Might as well be amused. I too, like the Thais, love fun.

There is always a re-entry problem when coming back from an extended vacation. This re-entry from Thailand was more troubling than normal. My expectations are always that many of my friends and relatives are just going to drop everything they're doing and beg me to give them a travelogue about my trip. It never happens. Sara, my son's ex-American girlfriend spent three hours with me listening to a step-by-step travelogue complete with slides. She really wanted to hear about my son. I'll take whatever crumbs I can get. Sara was a blessing. Everyone else I encountered asked, "When was I going to Thailand?" I had been gone for thirty days and came back from Thailand. When I told them that I went they were amazed. "I guess I have been so wrapped up in things," they advise me. What a pity. I am always disappointed. I'm particularly disappointed this time because not only did no one care about asking me about my trip, most people didn't even know that I had left. This is America today.

I'm back to writing and cruising the cable channels for material. The first thing I hear and read about is The Reggie Principle of "I Got's Mine" in full glaring glorious color. In order to prevent a bankruptcy filing, American Airlines demanded extensive pay cuts from all its unions. The cuts ranged from 17-25%. We have to share the pain, the corporate piggies advised. Corporate America has the worker so boxed in, that to preserve your job, you'll take less. After all, where are you going to go to get another job? There are no jobs out there anymore except minimum wage to $8.00 an hour. Want to flip hamburgers? During negotiations, the corporate managers reveal in a document filing that they were awarding themselves seven-figure bonuses (that's millions) and putting $41 million into special pension funds that would withstand a bankruptcy filing. These guys get the "I Got's Mine" 2003 award for a big pair of balls. The same thing happened at United Airlines. Corporate headquarters has decided that there should be less pay for the worker droids and more money for the bosses. As long as I Gets Mine, FUCK YOU.

Previously, I mentioned that a new gimmick is to look you right in the eye and tell you that what is being proposed is good for you. As the saying goes, "let's slap some lipstick on this pig." Lipstick makes it appear that screwing you over is for your own good. For example, since we have fewer workers to do the same amount of work, a corporation will force you to work more. You're more productive. Of course, working more means overtime. Reggie doesn't like paying overtime. How can I Gets Mine if I gotta pay you yours. O.K. the pigs say, let's screw 80,000,000 American workers out of overtime. In the Senate we will propose a bill that, in essence, repeals the right to receive time and one-half for any hour worked over forty. The lipstick the Senate slaps on this pig is calling the bill the Family Time and Workplace Flexibility Act. The House of Representative calls its lipstick the Family Time Flexibility Act. Sounds great. Use the words family and flexibility and you have a winner. Dumb em down and freak em out. In addition to working harder and longer, pay is goings backwards. This is a banana republic and the citizens of this country take it. They should revolt. Is this seditious? Will I be stopped from boarding a plane for writing this? I read yesterday that the ACLU is bringing suit because outspoken liberals have been singled out at airports and harassed. Singled out and detained because of what they believe. Is former Admiral John Poindexter running his super-snooper, Total Information Awareness campaign without our knowledge? Is he infiltrating computers with enemy lists? Is this McCarthyism? Is this sick shit? Has the Homeland Security Act and The Patriot Act eroded our civil liberties? Is the devil under every rock? Are we so frightened and insecure that we allow our liberties to be taken away without a blink of the eye? I'm afraid so.

The mood and beliefs of America have turned ugly. Real ugly. This is not my America. This is not the America I grew up in. America is lurching in fits and starts towards the right. Watch out gays, lesbians, abortionists and everyone else who don't buy the conservative party line. We have injected religion into the debate and cast the debate in terms of good and evil. It is no longer a difference of opinion between two men. It is a war between good and evil. Unfortunately, the so-called good guys are the Christian fundamentalists. These people are true believers. Everyday, in everyway, they're creeping into the individual lives of everyone. The faithful wait for the rapture, which is coming soon. They will disappear. God will bring them to heaven. Life will be peaceful. In heaven, the devil does not exist. Meanwhile, on earth, the fundamentalist mission is to fight the devil at every turn and in every guise. The Bible demands it. Hollywood celebrities are evil. Smash Susan Sarandon, behead Tim Robbins, remove Martin Sheen from commercials and crush the cd's of the Dixie Chicks. Church officials may ex-communicate our elected officials if they don't openly oppose abortion. What a political advantage in an election year. My opponent was ex-communicated by the Church! Church officials must ex-communicate non-believers. They are, after all, good Christian soldiers. Although the faithful are leading the parade, it seems that many in America are riding on their coattails. They may not be religious, but Goddamn, they're buying the message.

A day doesn't go by where my e-mail box doesn't contain at least two French bashing jokes. The Russians are turncoats and Germany will get theirs. It is a daily barrage of negative reinforcement. It is no longer a difference of opinion with other free democratic countries. It is, America is good and if you don't agree with America, you're evil. Simplicity works on simple people. This is not a fun friendly country. America is the Jerry Springer Show. All dialogue is gone. There is no wisdom. It's yell, scream, punch, kick and smear. It's been going on for a long time and appears to be intractable. It is part of our national character. I don't think America hears itself anymore.

We are on a daily witch-hunt to satisfy the most basic horrible instincts that man possesses. Someone must get bashed. Kill the pig. Kill the pig. Kill the pig. The media line, if it bleeds it leads, has been expanded. My theory is that, if it has legs, it leads. That is, if the story can be expanded upon over weeks and months, you run with it. The need to fill up space is paramount in a 24/7/365 environment. Forget the fact that it is not news. It fills up space. Local stories become national stories. I knew we were in trouble when Madelyne Toogood, a mother who was caught on tape spanking her child, made national news for three weeks. The spanking of her child in a parking lot was played over and over. I decided television was no longer a viable means of information. I only watch the cable news networks on a limited basis as an aid for information to write this book. I have asked myself why the death of Laci Peterson is national news. It got legs. Laci was a pretty woman and was eight months pregnant. Laci Peterson is not national news and no one has any balls to stop this madness. The Cable News Networks polls go up. Fox News, the right wing conservative cable news network, number one on cable, has infected every other cable news network. Every news outlet is singing the same song. Laci all day long. Iraq heroes all day long. The war all day long. No news, just a lot of jingoistic bullshit. Everyday I just scratch my head and wonder how this can occur. Reluctantly, I can only conclude this occurs when you have a dumb, mean, illiterate, self-centered citizenry. MSNBC has their hero board. Is everyone who went to Iraq a hero? I guess. Forget the massive bombing preceding our troops arrival. There was complete annihilation of Iraqi forces that didn't have enough brains to run away from superior weaponry. Perhaps, you prefer the sterile pentagon description "degradation." Drive a tank against light rifle fire and you're a hero. This is not a war. It's a walkover. Curious, I opened up Webster's Dictionary and looked up the word hero. Among other things, a hero is one that shows and exhibits *great* courage. At the time of this writing, the weekend of April 26, 2003, a young Mexican teenager in Abilene, Texas was passing an apartment complex that was engulfed in flames. Without regard to his own safety, he ran into the burning building and saved a child. After delivering the child to safety in the street he immediately turned and ran into the building again, over the protestations of the firemen and reemerged with another three children and a woman. Now that's a hero. Am I quibbling? Later on, it was discovered that he set the fire and was arrested for a prior crime. Ain't that America? Everyone who's an American in Iraq is a hero even if he/she got lost and was found wandering down a road. I don't understand why I don't get with the program. Why quibble over the English language in an attempt to use the right word to describe a person or an event when we hang people on national news with only innuendo and assumptions. Was I sleeping when editors of dictionaries dropped the word "alleged"? Gary Conduit, Scott Peterson, Dr. Steven Hatfield, just to name a few, are all people that the media screwed without the niceties of the law. Scott Peterson's distraught mother got it right when she blurted out "what am I living in Nazi Germany." Yes, Mrs. Peterson, you are in pre-Nazi Germany. To get from simmer to boil, we need some fair and balanced reporters. People like Bill O'Reilly, Joe Scarborough, Rush Limbaugh and Michael Savage. Oh, these guys are so fair and balanced. This goes back to my earlier observation, look someone in the eye, make some absurd statement and move on. If a person could find stillness in their life and listened to these guys they would be amazed. Maybe. It might be too late. After all, an entire generation grew up under these lunatics. They're shrill. They bitch, moan, complain, accuse, hang, belittle and steal reputations. They're the furthest from being fair and balanced. They can hang someone was an incredulous lift of the eyebrow as if they were saying "what a smuck." My personal favorite is Dan Abrams of MSNBC, who never met an event or picture that he didn't find "chilling." What a pussy. But why stop there. Why not call all those who disagree libs, lefties, out of touch and traitors. Stifle all dissent. The big problem is simply that with a dumbed down, whipped up and freaked out nation, the O'Reilly voices carry big clout. Every day is hard in America. I can imagine picking on any group as the source of one's problems an attractive solution from picking on the real culprits. A nasty tone permeates our culture. Go one additional step further and air Reality TV shows across every channel. The essence of Reality TV is human humiliation and degradation. As we degrade the Iraqi army, we degrade the human spirit of our own citizenry. Shannon Daugherty states in the trailer for her new reality TV show Scare Tactics, "you could be next," and indeed, you could be. This is a nasty hanging nation and we need hangees. Who's next? The immigrants? The Arab-Americans? The hillbillies? The poor? The liberal traitors?

Growing up Jewish in Brooklyn in the fifties, I heard on more than one occasion the query, "why did millions of Jews go so willingly to the gas chambers?" I recall this question of years ago, because I wonder how this nation of 275,000,000 is going so willingly with nasty, mean spirited, right wing morons. It seems all too easy. I must have been sleeping for other things besides the editors dropping "alleged" from the dictionary. On many occasions, I have wondered how some distinctly American cultural traits came into being. For example, invading one's "personal space." I asked people where this concept came from. No one could give me an answer. But "personal space" is alive and well and something that I encounter everyday. The concept of personal space is very strange for a Brooklyn boy growing up in one of largest cities. It seems everyone younger than me gets it. Go into a bank vestibule in Boulder to visit an ATM machine and at least half the people won't even come in. "Personal Space" at work. If I'm pouring half-and-half in my coffee at my favorite coffee shop and someone comes within three feet of me, they're "sorry" they say. It is an invasion of my personal space. I don't know how many times I hear the words "I'm sorry" as a direct result of someone invading my personal space. Who came up with this shit? Never having got an answer, I decided to do a google search on the web. It seems some guy named Edward T. Hall, an anthropologist, did groundbreaking work on personal space. Americans need major personal space. Maybe that's why we have so many divorces. Not enough personal space after the romance wears off. Maybe we shunt off our parents to old age homes because they invade our personal space. Extended families with uncles and aunts living in close proximity are a violation of personal space. They have to go too. I don't like it. It puts distance between people.

Sam, my former stepdaughter, went to a rich school where she was taught that she was "very special." Every thing about her was "very special." Every child in this school was "very special." Nothing objective. Everything subjective. One problem arose when Sam, who trusted me for an honest answer, wondered if she is "so pretty" how come no one ever asked her out. After all, she was told from an early age that she was beautiful, smart, gifted, etc. She is 13 and no one is asking her out. She is beautiful she was told all her life. I gave Sam a very long-winded detailed explanation of beauty. I pointed out "pretty faces" and told her she wasn't one of those. Sam was very sexy and the boys weren't ready for her kind of beauty. I advised her that within several years she would be number one on every boy's list. She trusted me. Sam, did indeed, become incredibly sexy and grew into a classic beauty. I missed the generation of teaching that plied the youngsters with the concept that they're very special. It flattened out the traditional bell curve. The genius was lumped with the average and the ugly lumped with the beautiful. Everybody was lumped together into this super duper special category. Naturally, when you're super-duper you have to be treated in very special ways. Kid gloves only! Don't ever bruise the psyche of special people. It is not a good thing. Hurt the feelings of very special people and invite a lawsuit. The imbuement of specialty to each individual cannot be shared among all the other super duper people. After all, if I'm special how can you be? The concept of special excludes another person from being within the special person's sphere. In addition, very special people require too much attention to stay happy. Unless they are specially handled, they are forever bewildered why the special treatment never occurs. Indeed, very special people are so concerned with their very special needs, that they don't give a rat fuck about all those other very special people. There is a natural bell curve. Some people are very smart. Some are very good looking. This egalitarian straightening out of the natural bell curve is ludicrous. A very practical example that I often encounter is when I go out with some people and start a conversation. Everyone truly believes that they're bringing a full plate to the table. They believe that they are bright, beautiful, intelligent and gifted. They're very special people. More often than not, they're boring little snots with nothing to say at all. On top of that, they have eggshell personalities that are easily offended. At the minimum, we now have millions of self-centered little shits protected by their very special bubble.

Anger has been wrung from the American citizen. Anger became unacceptable. Hide your anger. Better yet, don't get angry. Today, we have anger management for everything. Basic little husband-wife spat. Anger management. Get caught driving drunk. Anger management. Are you happy? Anger management for you too. I think anger management must have been born in the woman's movement as a way to get men to put their hands down. I don't know. On many occasions in group therapy, the women would take turns respectively being "angry" with me for some bullshit reason. These people were pill poppers who had to be medicated. The doc didn't want me on Prozac or anything else because my problem was behavioral. One night, as I entered into the hollow halls of group therapy, someone starts with me doing the "I'm angry" routine. I had enough of that crap. I asked how the fuck she could look me in the eye and say in the politest way that she's "angry." I yelled back, "that you can't be fucking angry because anger," at this point I get up and kicked the chair across the room, "looks like fucking this, moron." I wasn't really angry; I just had enough of this polite, endless babble. The doc got my point. I saw in their eyes they were really afraid of me. I inquired if any of them ever got angry in that way. No one responded. Anger is a very real visible tangible expression of something that's pissing you off in a major way. The controlled expression of anger, which does not erupt into uncontrollable rage, is a good thing. Anger, and any expression thereof are out. So you can march against the war if you want to. Nicely, mind you and don't get angry. If one gets angry, all of America will look at you as a Neanderthal. Status is lost for blowing your top. Hold on to it until it becomes uncontrollable rage and then pop some students off, Columbine style and have everyone wonder what happened.

If you take this witch's brew of self centered, very special people surrounded by their own little space bubbles all floating around out there and mix in political correctness you really get the pot boiling. Very special people have very special interest and needs. After all, they believe they are further along the evolutionary path than others. They are, a higher species than the rest of us. Well, they see things differently. They have personal space, they are special and they don't get Neanderthal angry. They are in tune with others very specials needs and in partic- ular, feelings. The theory to guides one's life is to strive to be politically correct. Don't offend anyone by speech, gestures and actions. Of course, it is a straight jacket wrapped around the mind, but necessary to distinguish oneself from the Neanderthal. I can imagine, that one spends an awful amount of time rearrang- ing your mind in order to be able to adhere to the strict tenets of being politically correct. Rather than limiting the theory to really offensive words like "nigger," America's propensity to go to extremes, like super size it, has perverted political correctness to absurd minutiae that leaves one dwelling on the tree instead of the forest. Very special people by definition must have their own very special ego. The American Indian only dwells on his concerns, ever vigilant for anything that might offend him. The same for Feminists, Jews and Christians. Everyone is very concerned with hugging his or her own tree. Uncle Sam is left unfettered to con- trol the forest. Recently, I read an article about the governing council of Palo Alto in California. Palo Alto is home to a prestigious university, Nobel Laureates, big money, high tech people and a population that feels pretty good about itself. The article states that the city's web site declares, "Residents are highly educated, politically aware and culturally sophisticated." The Mayor, Dena Mossar, declared, "Palo Alto is the envy of others." This is a perfect example of my self centered, politically correct, very special little bubble people. Now that political correctness has wrapped its tentacles around free speech, the pc people go one step further. The council decided that "unflattering personal *gestures*" be banned.

Everyone smile. The council adopted the rules of conduct but deleted from the rules "body language or other nonverbal methods of expressing disagreement or disgust." Everyone, nationwide, made fun of Palo Alto's non-hostile gesture legislation and it was dropped from consideration. Diane Ravitch in her new book, "The Language Police," makes note that some of the things students shouldn't find in their textbooks are:

(a) Mickey Mouse and Stuart Little (because mice, along with rats, roaches, snakes and lice are considered to be upsetting to children.

(b) stories or pictures showing a mother cooking dinner for her children, or a black family living in city neighborhood.

(c) dinosaurs because they suggest the controversial subject of evolution.

(d) tales set in jungles, forests, mountains or by the sea because such settings are believed to display a "regional bias," and

(e) narratives involving angry, loud mouth characters, quarreling parents or disobedient children because such emotions are not uplifting.

Ms. Ravitch goes on to state the following:

"Owls are out because some cultures associate them with death. Mentions of birthdays are to be avoided because some children do not have birthdays. Images or descriptions showing shock or fear are to be replaced by depictions of both parents "expressing the same facial emotions." Mentions of cakes, candy, doughnuts, French fries and coffee should be dropped in favor of references to more healthful food like cooked beans, yogurt and enriched wholegrain breads. And of course words like brotherhood, fraternity, heroine, snowman, swarthy, crazy, senile and polo are banned because they could be upsetting to woman, to certain ethnic groups, to people with mental disabilities, old people or, it would seem, to people who do not play polo."

Ms. Ravitch further states that:

"The bias and sensitivity reviewers employed by educational publishers work with assumptions that have the inevitable effect of stripping away everything that is potentially thought provoking and colorful from the texts that children encounter and as a result, school curriculums are being reduced to "bland Pabulum.""

The bias and sensitivity reviewers were hatched from the very special bubble people. It is one of the little problems that any government would have to put up with when it permits the concept of "special" to take hold. You create, in effect, a nation of crybabies. However, it is a small price to pay if you want to control the forest. So what, if the little shits want to go off on owls or facial expressions. It is, after all, a dumbing down process, which only further enhances governmental power. I wish I were in the Baja right now. The politically correct exist on the right as well. Although, I equally detest both right and left, if I had to choose one over the other, I would choose the left pc over the right pc. The right pc's are violent nasty people. If you're pc anti abortion, it's morally all right for one to kill abortion doctors. Of course, the pc right is just as stupid. After all, who brought us freedom fries and freedom toast. The left didn't. They are, as Spiro Agnew, once said, "ineffectual negative nabobs." The conservative right is to be feared more than the lefty liberals.

The last and final element to get the pot to a roiling boil is the natural evolutionary process of capitalism. Capitalism, at its final stages is ugly. It's the Reggie Principle of "I Got's Mine" taken to an extreme. Everyone in power lies, cheats and steals. The little guy struggles on a constant daily basis to make ends meet. He works two jobs, long exhausting hours, no vacation and little paychecks are his reward. There is a dichotomy between the top and the bottom. The pc police are well off, "Palo Alto" style, leading the worker drones down a path that they willingly follow because they have too little time and strength to do any thinking on their own. The political right does the same. I sit in the middle watching this great struggle for the hearts, minds and souls of this nation play out in front of me. Right or left are equally absurd. Both the left and the right are dysfunctional. Each side tries to rally support from an exhausted self-centered citizenry. As I watch the struggle, I find that the elements described above, self-centered little exhausted bubble brats are well suited to move a nation in one direction or another. It is my opinion, that the secret ingredient that will motivate all these individual spheres lining up in one direction is anger. Tap into anger and the bubbles will start to line up. Somewhere, down deep, I think everyone must ask himself or herself what the hell is going on in this country. It doesn't feel right. It's not a happy place. There is too much strum and drang. It is a constant grind of bad things. Happiness and fun went on vacation. As Bob Dylan once wrote, "something is happening here and you don't know what it is, do you Mr. Jones." Don't worry, because Bill O'Reilly of Fox Cable News claims that he is looking out for you. It must be true. He wrote a national best seller entitled "Who's Looking Out for You." The "Who" in the title is Bill O'Reilly.

If I was a political science student in pre-nazi Germany and my professor asked me to forge a theory that would permit the regime to execute ten million Jews, Poles and Gypsies without objection from the German citizenry, I don't think I could come up with such a theory. However, if he told me that you could create space between people, make them believe their special, get them bickering over minor issues as if those issues were vital to their health, make them feel that anger is bad and then work them to exhaustion and the people would follow, I wouldn't believe him. I would ask, what then, would motivate people to accept such a horrendous course of action? My professor would tell me, "of course you realize that this would produce angst and worry and when it does, tell your citizens that the cause of their problems are a person, group or an issue. Destroy the person, group or issue and the problem is solved. Self centered bubble turds always like simple answers and the solutions come from a dark place in the heart. Saddam Hussein has weapons of mass destruction and can destroy you in forty-five minutes. America must attack him now. It is for your safety. Support and follow me says Uncle Sam.

As I watch this great struggle between the lefty liberal and the conservative right for the heart and soul of America, it is clear that the left is wholly ineffectual. The conservative right considers the current election year struggle as a bare-knuckled fight. Their hands are wrapped in hemp, soaked in honey and dipped in glass. The lefty liberal is fighting "Palo Alto" style with his hands tied behind his back hiding behind his momma's skirt. Of course, this entire battle is a symptom of some greater dysfunctional malady that is going on in this country. Clearly, the bubble spheres are lining up and leaning towards the right and that is because they have effectively tapped into that forbidden underlying anger. I'm reminded of an experiment that I read about in college in a psychology course. Take a group of people where three-quarters of them take a view that is insane and eventually the remaining one quarter will come around to their way of thinking no matter how preposterous. It is happening in this country today. Everyone knows that something is wrong and the conservative right is scoring points by tapping anger. I saw Peggy Noonan on television stating that President Bush is going to be the next great communicator. She stated that after several days of thinking about Bush and what was going on, she realized that his gift was the "vision thing." She's right. The leader of this country is lining up all these little spheres in the direction of pointing towards a group, the evildoers, whoever they are, that are the cause of their angst. He's wrong, but it doesn't matter, does it? The culprits are terrorism, weapons of mass destruction and everyone who doesn't agree with him. Beginning slowly and currently gaining more momentum, the bubble people line up behind him. He's wrapped in the flag, goodness and God, fighting the good fight against the devil. Any critical commentary against him is vigorously attacked or ignored. The more time goes by the more other bubbles line up behind him. The nation lurches to the right. America commits horrendous acts based upon fiction in violation of international law. It acts alone and believes it's right, notwithstanding an international chorus against it. The world thinks we're crazy and so do I.

Everyday in this bare-knuckle blood sport, I witness broadside salvos being shot with disastrous consequences and without any response whatsoever. The net effect is like the college experiment in-group control. The sane part of the group slowly comes around to thinking insane. The Dixie Chicks stated that they were embarrassed that Bush came from Texas. America organizes groups to stage demonstrations destroying their cd's. Old time book burning. Last week, two Colorado disk jockeys played the Dixie Chicks on the radio in Colorado Springs. They were fired. Senator Rick Santorum equated consensual gay sex in one's own home with incest and that's all right because he is deeply religious. Tim Robbins and Susan Sarandon criticized the war against Iraq and they were unceremoniously yanked out of the Baseball Hall of Fame celebrations. Martin Sheen, another Iraq war critic, was pulled from Visa commercials. Ashleigh Banfield, critical of the media's war coverage is back on the local bullshit beat. Bill Maher, of Politically Incorrect fame, initially critical of America's position had his show cancelled. Daily, and with increased rapidity, high profile people are being destroyed by the right's broadside lethal salvos. If you disagree, you are evil, anti-God and anti goodness. You are an evildoer. Slowly, it becomes apparent that it is better to keep your mouth shut than fight back in a losing battle. Kill the beast. Kill the beast. Kill the beast. The weak bubbles line up willingly because they want to see someone punished. The stronger bubbles change their views to protect their incomes. We lean to the right in a never-ending pursuit of ridding ourselves of evil and all without effective strong opposition. Examine the actions of Senator Joseph Lieberman, a Democratic contender for the nomination of his party and former vice presidential candidate. Is Joe leaning to the right? The week of May 9, 2003, Senator Joe Lieberman took a walk on the conservative side. On Saturday, at a nine-person candidate debate, Senator Joe stated that "we did the right thing in fighting this fight, and the American people will be safer as a result of it." An incidentally, Senator Lieberman advised, no Democrat will be elected president in 2004 who is not strong on defense. On Wednesday, he reveals that he drives a Ford Expedition, a big gas guzzling SUV. On Thursday, during a visit to Florida, he shares his anti-Castro views with Radio Marti. He states: "For years I have believed that the end of the Castro regime would be not only what would give hope and freedom and opportunity to the people of Cuba, but would be consistent with the principles of America's founding. On Friday, Lieberman shares with the Wall Street Journal that he would support Senate legislation providing millions of dollars in federal funding for private school vouchers. Today, you either have God on your side or you're leaning in that direction. Just in case anyone forgot, there is Karl Rove the alleged White House political genius that proclaimed, "it's the terror, stupid."

Where does this lead? Taken as a whole, we have a nation that overturns 50 years of foreign policy, violates International law, conquers a sovereign nation, takes over its oil fields and all actions are based upon fiction. It offers up its fiction as fact and its citizens go along with it together with its commentators, newsmen, priests, rabbis and other persons of interest. A country goes to war against another country based upon outright lies and everyone follows. If this is not crazy than the woman in Texas who killed her two children on May 12, 2003, with stones, because God told her to, actually received an order from God. After all, didn't God tell Abraham to kill his son! It seems God tells a lot of people to kill others. I think it should be recognized as a legitimate legal defense. Well, God told me to kill the liberals, fags, Lesbos, heathens, atheists, Democrats and traitors. The way this country is going, I wouldn't be surprised if the conservative God fearing Christian judges carve out an exception to murder. It is moral relativism. If the majority believes and Judges agree, that God ordered a killing is a legal defense, who am I to say otherwise. I thought about foot-notes referring to various books and articles that I have read to reach some of these conclusions, however, I don't need a footnote as evidence that America has its foot up my ass.

Today, I am disappointed in the media. I'm disappointed in the media because they are traitors. The media are traitors to their country. The freedom of the press is one of Americas most protected and cherished freedoms granted under the Bill of Rights and I'm saddened that most of the media, print and television, don't deserve that constitutionally protected freedom. The press is our fourth estate. They are the guardians of truth and justice. They get paid for ferreting out the truth and digging deep into a story so they can report it to me in an unbiased manner. Unfortunately, I believe that the press has turned news into a game show. News is infotainment. Sometimes, I believe that certain members of the media have side deals with rich conservatives. At every turn, the government's cause is heralded from a conservative standpoint. For example, I listened to Larry Kudlow of CNBC from the show Kudlow and Kramer. First, he shops for clothes at the same store that the pimps shop at. Every time I saw Kudlow during the countdown to war phase, I'm reminded of Arnold Schwarzenegger in Pumping Iron who said that the pump in muscles after working out is better than sex. Watching Larry I thought he was going to come in his pants at the prospect of getting Iraqi oil fields. Larry got visibly excited. Hold on Larry, coming is really better than oil. Maybe not in conservative male circles, but coming is better. Larry got so excited, I could only conclude that he had a side deal for extra money from moneyed conservatives pumping the war and stealing the oil. Larry is not the only one who may have side deals. There are many talking heads on television that just get too excited for my taste. Joe Scarborough is another guy that's just pumping bullshit with exuberance. Michael Savage is another. My gut tells me they have an agenda that is paid for beyond what cable television gives them. Want to make another half a million boys? Keep on pumping. I'm convinced that pumping on the air is inversely proportional to bed pumping. These guys aren't getting any.

I can't watch cable news without recalling the 1987 movie Running Man with Arnold Schwarzennegger. In that movie, people unjustly accused and convicted of a crime were put in a bobsled vehicle and sent down a chute to some abandoned wasteland. Cameras were everywhere in this wasteland. There, they would encounter killers equipped with buzz saws, flamethrowers and other weapons of destruction. Above, a jam-packed studio audience would watch the carnage as an accused man ran for his life. It was a game show hosted by an announcer played by Richard Dawson. Of course, no one survived, except Arnold. The killer's abilities far exceeded the skill of these running men to defend themselves. The audience watched the carnage from above on television monitors. Current cable news is just like the Running Man. Representative Gary Conduit come on down. Your crime? We have suspicions that you killed Chandra Levy because you had sex with her. Do we need more proof? We don't think so. In the bobsled you go. Start running for your life. Next, come all the paid pundits and scumbags offering fact based upon fiction running after this man with slurs, innuendos, assumptions and maybes. Start running Gary. I recall one pundit stating that he wouldn't rest until he got Gary Condit for murdering Levy.

You. Yeah you. Don't turn your back. Come on down Scott Peterson for allegedly murdering your wife. Start running man we're after you. How a local murder turns into 24/7/365 national news is beyond me. But it got legs. Several days ago I was watching MSNBC with the crew discussing the tactics of Scott Peterson's new attorney because he called on national television for an unnamed witness to come forward. The media pundits asked if Scott's attorney was committing illegal acts by coming up with a bullshit story about an unnamed witness?

It felt like the media types were upset that someone was using the same garbage tactics that they use. How dare he! Fictionalizing alleged fact. How dare he! By the way, let's throw Gloria Allred, that feminist lawyer into the fray. Every trial needs a clown.

Here's the kicker. While I'm watching there is a tag line at the bottom of the screen in bold print that states" IS SCOTT PETERSON GUILTY? What fucking arrogance. No trial has started. No jurors have been picked. Not one shred of evidence has been presented. Yet, this cable news network is asking is Peterson guilty. Based upon what evidence for Christ's sake. Upon what we think we know. Assumptions? Innuendo? Upon the crap that you think you know. Day in and day out this goes on and that is the nation we live in. The Bill of Rights and the Constitution have been hijacked by television. You're the running man for the audience's entertainment and your rights are bullshit. You'll run until the media gets the next more interesting or lurid tale, which brings me back to my original point. These people, all of them, in the media business are traitors. They are the vilest, most disgusting traitors that exist today. At least spies put our country in jeopardy for money. These creeps do it for entertainment at the expense of living human beings, the Bill of Rights and the Constitution. Webster defines traitor as one who betrays or is false to an obligation or duty. Incoming! Sean Penn loses movie deal for being in Iraq. Danny Glover loses MCI contract for criticizing President Bush. *Fox News Alert.* MOAB bomb dropped! The trifecta. A journalist made up parts of stories at the New York Times. Oh boy, we get a black, affirmative action and the liberal New York Times all in one.

From my perspective, I am witnessing nothing more than a major sea change back to a period of time prior to the cultural revolution of the 1960's. Almost five decades of cultural history being turned back on its head. At what point do we stop attacking our own people who hold different views. Unfortunately, it is easier for me to envision a continuation of this running man game show than to see its end. We are currently crossing the threshold of attacking those who have been indicted for an actual crime, such as Scott Peterson, to those who hold contrary views like Danny Glover and Tim Robbins. This is, indeed, extremely dangerous ground as the cacophony of attacking voices become louder and louder and those opposing become almost inaudible. To hear any voice of opposition you have to dig deep for alternative sources of information. I do not know of any television station, whether broadcast or cable, attacking the current policies of this administration. Indeed, there is a chilling effect on those ever decreasing remaining voices. They are falling in line. Simply put, if you are visible enough to garner any audience you will be attacked by a sophisticated well-financed conservative right wing that has a large voice. Witness Danny Glover who was attacked by Joe Scarborough. MCI caved in and Mr. Glover lost his contract as a spokesman for MCI. It is incredibly dangerous to the most precious of rights, freedom of speech, when a major cable news network that has a large audience, decides that a private citizen who has only a modicum of exposure, needs to be punished for what he believes. This does not go unnoticed by others who have a small platform to be heard. I, for example, have no platform other than my friends or work associates. When those with small platforms who hold a contrary view are consistently picked off by the jingoistic, traitorous media, such as Sarandon, Penn, NY Times, Glover, Banfield, others of like mind and small platforms will be, to a large degree silenced. Being "outed" for holding a different point of view is frightening. Consider this recent poll: According to a May 1, 2003, Gallup poll for CNN and USA Today, 79 percent of Americans said the war with Iraq was justified even without conclusive evidence of the illegal weapons. It appears that Americans buy their government's current line for invasion or don't care. In the absence of illegal weapons that posed an imminent threat to Iraq's neighbors and the United States, the United States overturned fifty years of foreign policy and invaded a sovereign nation in violation of international law. The United States is the major destabilizing force in the world today. As I write this, al-Qaeda, has set off four bombs in Morocco. Several days prior to this Moroccan incident, Saudi Arabia experienced terrorist explosions aimed at American interests. Iraq was never a threat to the United States or its neighbors. However, since Hussein was such a terrible dictator and tortured his own people, this is enough to legitimize an invasion. In addition, he *might* have used weapons of mass destruction. I cannot believe that we can invade another nation because it *might*, sometime in the future, do something that is contrary to American interests. What is more mind boggling to me is that Americans don't even care about Saddam's dictatorial abuses of his own people. The last time I checked, most Americans don't even know their own neighbors or care to know their neighbors. Americans have this insane perception of who they are as opposed to who they really are. The modern American du jour method of expressing love, caring and kindness is to drive twenty miles and drop off letters and teddy bears at the home of a stranger like Laci Peterson. Of course, it is usually followed by the bus tour to the home of Laci as if it were some tourist attraction to be viewed. This is a typical morbid absurdity of American culture.

Which politicos speak for me? The Republicans don't. The Democrats have morphed into Rupublicrats. The Democrats are so afraid of taking a stand and offending anyone that they stand for nothing and offend everyone. At least these moronic Republicans stand for something. I know what they want. It reminds of the sixties, when I minored in black history at The City College of New York. All my militant black friends echoed the theory that they would rather live in the South because at least they could see the enemy. Up North, in Liberal Ville, you could never figure out who the enemy was. Every day, I see and hear the Republicans. I know what they stand for. I disagree vehemently, but I know what the enemy stands for. The Democrats on the other hand are a bunch of pussies. If you voted for a bill authorizing the President to initiate war on Iraq, when in fact you're against the war, don't cower behind your vote because someone is going to remind you that you voted for President Bush. Stand up you punk. Strap on a pair of balls and admit that you made a mistake. Fight. We need an army of liberal warriors. WarLibs as I like to call them. Stand up and say, I voted for this or that bill based upon lies put forth by the administration. Oh, I see, you can't do that can you because 79% of the American public doesn't give a shit anyway. After all, we were all wringing our hands about Hussein's abuses to his own people. What, no teddy bear bus tours to Iraq at the mass gravesites? In the best interests of American entrepreneurship, I' think I'll organize bus tours via Air France and sell cute little Vermont teddy bears on the plane. It has to be a winner of an idea because we have all cared so much about the Iraqi's lack of freedom. The phrase "weapons of mass destruction" didn't resonate with the American public so the media changed the name to Operation Iraqi freedom. Where is the pussified collective Democratic body? They're out picking on Bush's jet ride to the aircraft carrier Abraham Lincoln. He looked great in his fly-boy flight suit. It was a grand photo-op that not one Democrat could pull off. Let's start an investigation. As a comedian would say, "yeah, that's the ticket." You go boys.

We have these mesmerizing deep throated type Republican men who stand for something, albeit wrong, on one side beating up on these whining stand for nothing shits on the other. It is evidence of the utter, complete slide into a Salem witch-hunt McCarthy America. The voices that are heard are women's voices. This admission is not easy for someone who is concurrently writing a book entitled "Dismemberment by Implied Consent-A Misogynists Musing." I am almost at the point that I think men should stand aside and abdicate their role for running the country to women. After all, they can't fuck it up any more than men have. At least they have balls. I guess it comes from forty years of fighting the hard fight and actually demonstrating out there on the streets. You go girl! Last week, I watched on C-Span Book an interview with Gore Vidal at the 92nd Street Y in New York. My current heroine, Katrina van denheuval, the editor of The Nation, introduced him after a short speech. At one point in her speech she stated that the current Republican reign is "BULLSHIT." She looked right in the camera and said bullshit. Now, this is my kind of woman. She is clear, concise and to the point. Bullshit. How about Sheryl Watkins of Enron. Ms. Watkins is a woman with enough balls to stand up and do the right thing. Saturday morning, having coffee, I decided to read letters to the editor in the New York Times. I never read letters to the editor of any newspaper. Several days prior, the New York Times published an article entitled "Keepers of Bush Image Lift Stagecraft to New Heights," the guts of which had to do with the time and effort that a small group of people in the Bush administration expended to keep the President's image polished. Indeed, they do a very good job.

"Susan" of Brookline, Mass., wrote:

"Describing the administration's elaborate image making, you quote Dan Bartlett, the White House communications director, as saying, 'We pay particular attention not only to what the President says but what the American people see.'

This American sees slick administration maneuvers that are in danger of backfiring.

Dressing the president in a flight suit reminds me that George W. Bush did not fight in a war. Juxtaposing his head against Mount Rushmore shows me the President does not measure up to the presidents commemorated before."

"Barbara" of New York, states: "Dan Bartlett, the White House communicator says: Americans are leading busy lives, and sometimes they don't have the opportunity to read a story or listen to an entire broadcast. But if they can have an instant understanding of what the president is talking about by seeing 60 seconds of television, you accomplish your goals as communicators.

Are these Americans the same "freedom-loving people" President Bush likes to hold up as models to the world? So enslaved by their busy lives that their only opportunity for understanding is to be spoon fed sound bites and visual candy by TV executives turned Presidential image makers." You go girl, in true Katrina style.

Wallace, a man, from Minneapolis states: "Regardless of party affiliation or agenda, the President, as the leader of our country and the embodiment of our heritage and our intentions, should be placed in the best possible light.

As we all know, the broadcast presentation of the president has tactical and strategic importance for sending distinct messages to both the domestic and global audiences.

It is incumbent upon any administration to take full advantage of technique and technology, to do less would be negligent and backward." What a pussy.

Women are today's fighters. The men are strangely absent and accommodative. I guess Wallace thinks that image over truth is more important. Women fight, men accommodate.

I'm getting off my soapbox. My tirade is over and I'll go ponder why America is as great as everyone tells me. I'm sure I'm missing the obvious. What can I say about a nation that beats up on its young, imprisons its minorities, starves it educational system, fiscally implodes its states and cities, neglects its elderly, fosters hatred between the sexes, works long arduous hours and humiliates its citizens for sport and invades sovereign nations. This is not a culture imbued with wisdom. This book is written for one guy. This young man wrote a letter to The New York Times in regard to an article about the plight of recent college graduates. Nicholas wrote the New York Times in response to an article entitled "College Graduates Lower Sights in Today's Stagnant Job Market."

Nicholas wrote: "As an 02 grad, I saw my classmates introduced to the disheartening dose of reality known as the American job market a year ago. This year is no better. Yet a majority of students still seem to harbor the comforting belief, as one put it, that its definitely temporary. Everybody has that feeling-two or three years, and everything will be back to normal."

This is the kind of ignorant optimism that mires our country in economic as well as social and political woes. How bad do things have to get before Americans wake up and take notice?

I implore the fresh faces in today's job (less) market to learn more about the sorry state of our union-particularly the disastrous economic policies of the Bush administration-and then either work to change it, even just through vocal disapproval and diligent voting, *or leave for greener pastures, as I have.*

Nicholas, Shanghai

I imagine that there must be some good old boys sitting around laughing about how easy it was to invade another nation based upon made up non-sense. I can hear them expressing bewilderment at the ease to which the American public bought into this weapons stuff and the prospect of an imminent attack, notwithstanding the Iraqis impossibility of delivering such an attack. How dumb are these American people they must be asking? The more important question is do Americans care? Whatever reasons were stated for the war and regardless of how many times they changed are good enough. The truth. Americans can't handle the truth and don't want to know it. Isn't it good enough for us to have a victory parade and wrap ourselves in the American flag? After all, tomorrow I go back to the boring fucking job that I'm enslaved to.

However, that doesn't work for me. I'm one of those irritating little shits that want to know why we invaded a sovereign nation. How many Iraqi civilians died? How many Iraqi soldiers died, or is that "degraded?" What were those reasons for attacking Iraq? Why did the reasons change? Why was the evidence that was presented refuted after only several days out on the market? To me, these are big issues. I have given my government my consent to be governed. At the minimum, I expect that my consent to be governed be honored in return with truthful information for the acts that my government commits in my name. In this very basic situation, I am the principal and the President is my agent. Agents should never lie to their principals and commit acts in the principal's name based upon bogus information. I am not one of those people who in ten years from now will say: "Oh, I didn't know we conducted a killing field in Iraq to obtain their natural resources." The information is current and is out there. No one wants to examine it, except, the rest of the world. Why not the collective known as America?

In the absence of credible facts supporting the invasion on Iraq, my reality is distorted. I ask myself does this make sense? Am I crazy because 79% of my fellow citizens believe that invading Iraq is all right for any reason as long as we win? Don't they care that our government committed horrific acts in our name based upon lies? I guess not. Since I cannot determine my reality based upon the truth, I am left to my own assumptions, hopefully, somewhat accurate, to make sense of what the real reasons were for invading Iraq, destroying its infrastructure and killing its people. I am forced to connect the dots. My scenario, which makes more sense to me than anything I've heard or read in the media, is as follows: The good old boys are sitting around the barbeque in Crawford, Texas, laughing their asses off about how easy it was to con the American people. Several months prior to this get together, they had a conversation around the same barbeque. One good old boy says that he's fucking tired of them sand niggers controlling the price of oil. After all, he says, he can never know how much money he can make in any given financial quarter, if he doesn't know what the basic cost of his product will be. Another good old boy chimes in that he's right and that they should do something about it. "Well," says one guy, "if we control the second largest known spigot of oil than that sand nigger cartel, OPEC, is busted. OPEC cuts production, I turn the spigot on . OPEC increases production, I turn the spigot off." "Well," says another, "Iraq is the second biggest spigot." "Wait a minute," let's concoct some bullshit about Iraq possessing weapons of mass destruction, after all, we know they have them because we sold them to Iraq. Then we'll whip the public into frenzy about imminent use and create a scenario for an invasion. After all, they're scared little shits post 9/11. I think they will buy it. Most of them think Hussein had something to do with 9/11 anyway." "Think of this," says another. "We invade Iraq, a cakewalk, and then we don't need Saudi Arabia as a base. We'll be right in the middle of this Middle Eastern shit. We'll be next to Syria, Iran, Saudi Arabia, Qatar and not far from Jordan and Israel." "Yeah," another says, "then we don't need those Jew-kikes either." This guy gets a look because the Chief is a reborn and reborns like Jews. "We got the oil and the land right in the middle of those sand niggers home. With our military might, we can go anywhere at anytime. We control the whole damn thing. Yeah, big-time Texas style and we can hand out all sorts of multi-billion contracts to our buddies." The old guy chomping on a big steak chimes in that "if the American economy tanks we'll be sitting pretty to invade Iran or Syria right before the election based upon the same bullshit. Hey, isn't Iran part of the axis of evil? Whatever. Get some of those spin-meisters to come up with a plausible Syria/Iran invasion and the timing before the election." Another inquires whether or not they even need the spin meisters. After all, he says, the bullshit we poured on the American public was so deep you needed boots. They still bought into it. "Hey, George, I'm thinking Iran should be next so we can build a pipeline from them 'Stan' countries through Iran into those water ports." Somewhere in the background, in the shade of a big tree, the man with an ever-present cigar, stated, calmly, "you know George, with Iraq in hand, why don't we get to the real issue. Saudi Arabia. After all, 15 of the 19 terrorists were Saudis. We all know what we have to do. Let them fall. We don't have to fear a depression caused by the Saudis cutting off oil. We got Iraq. It's time we hung those niggers like we hung our own. After all, I think it's better to have all the vipers in one pit than in pits all over the world." There was silence. Everyone knew that the man with the cigar was right. Saudi Arabia must fall.

My reality seems more plausible to me than the non-sense that I read day after day that never pans out. I guess that believing that your own government would have ulterior motives and lie to you is like coming to the realization that your mother, whom you've loved all your life, is a liar and never loved you. Indeed, a reality that no one would easily come to grips with.

If anyone, during this countdown to war, would have commenced an investigation into the evidence supporting the invasion of Iraq, I would have been satisfied that this country is collectively acting in a normal and rational manner. However, everything that I have witnessed indicates that I live in a dysfunctional country. America has psychological issues that must be examined. America sees life through a straw. Its reality is what appears in the small hole at the far end of the straw. Is it any wonder that reality flows from sound bites and mantras. They're the only things that fit neatly within the hole.

Dr. Stanley Warlib, my alter ego, is the psychologist examining Uncle Sam. Before I morph into the good doctor, I leave you with this statement from The Matrix:

> Let me tell why you're here.
> You're here because you know something.
> What you know you can't explain.
> But you feel it.
> Your felt it your entire life.
> There's something wrong with the world.
> You don't know what it is, but it's there.
> Like a splinter in your mind.
> Driving you mad.
> It is this feeling that has brought you to me.
> Do you know what I'm talking about?

> The Matrix?

> Do you want to know what it is?
> The matrix is everywhere. It is all around us.
> Even now in this very room. You can see it when you
> Look out your window, or when you turn on your
> television. You can feel it when you go to work.
> When you go to church. When you pay your taxes.
> It is the world that has been pulled over your eyes
> to blind you from the truth. What truth?

> That you are a slave. Like everyone else you were
> born into bondage. Born into a prison that you cannot
> smell or taste or touch. A prison for your mind.
> This is your last chance. After this, there is no turning back.
> You take the blue pill. The story ends. You wake up in your bed and believe
> whatever you want to believe. You take the red pill, you stay in wonderland
> and I show you how deep the rabbit hole goes.
> Remember, all I'm offering is the truth, nothing more.

Uncle Sam Takes the Couch

My name is Dr. Stanley Warlib. I am fifty-five years old and I am a clinical psychologist. I earned my doctorate at New York University. I live and maintain my practice on the ground floor of an old renovated brownstone located on 88th Street between Fifth and Madison Avenues in Manhattan. On Mondays and Fridays I schedule the patients that I enjoy the most. They are my fun patients that have no major problems. They have an understanding of the nature of the therapeutic relationship with their psychologist. These patients work on their respective problems. Tuesdays and Thursdays, I schedule my most tedious, difficult patients. These patients don't work on their problems. They never will. After I have a good weekend, I don't kill it with Tuesdays den of neurotics. To start off the weekend on a good note, I have the balance of my fun patients on Friday. Unfortunately, every Tuesday and Thursday during lunch, I have to take a little pill to keep me up for the ensuing grueling five hours. If I don't take my little pill, I'll fall asleep. I've always wanted to tell the Tuesday and Thursday crowd two things that I heard in the movies. Number 1-"this is as good as it gets" and number 2, "you have an incurable brain cloud." I take off on Wednesdays to recover from the usual horrible Tuesdays and rest up for the equally horrific Thursdays.

I started my psychology practice with the same temerity that I started my law practice. I opened my door to treat patients the day following graduation. However, I did not want to relive the same difficulty that I had with starting a law practice. In law, I waited for over three months before my phone rang and when it did, it was merely a well wisher. It took five grueling years and caused my first divorce to get my law practice established. In preparation for the opening of my own therapeutic practice, I doubled up on the weekly sessions that I was having with my own shrink. I wanted to pick his brain on everything that I could so that I didn't feel like an idiot as I did when I opened my law practice. I wanted to give the impression that I was an old hand at psychology and was capable of resolving my patient's problems. My shrink wanted to know how I felt. I needed to know the kinds of interventions that I could make. Should I be aggressive or laid back? Should I give homework? I got some help but not much. He asked me how I was I going to get patients. What was my networking game plan? I didn't tell him the truth. I gave him some hogwash that sounded professional and well thought out. The truth was another matter.

While I was going to school for my doctorate I met Gabriella, a graduate student taking courses for her Masters degree. Gabby was the daughter of an extremely wealthy investment banker named Charles Westerfield. I was attracted to Gabby. She was a laid back, dark haired natural beauty, a cross between the American girl next door and a provocative sexy Spaniard. Notwithstanding her father's wealth, Southampton estate, classic Fifth Avenue apartment and her snooty friends, Gabby managed to maintain a rather charming innocence. However, that innocence did not come cheap, as there existed a level of anxiety between that innocence and the exhortations of her friends to join them in high life living. Gabby was grabbed and pulled by everyone for drugs, late night parties, blind dates and constant travel to the latest required "in" places to be seen. Her constant reluctance to refrain from those entreaties caused her to have doubts about which direction her life should take. Gabby and I spent many nights at her apartment talking psych stuff and studying. Occasionally, she would joke that she would be my first patient and I would respond equally light that she probably *would be* my first patient. I never came off to Gabby sexually and that cemented our friendship. However, I always told her that she shouldn't trust me. One night, I told her that given half a chance, I would love to make love with her but thought that it was probably a very bad idea. I thought that it was to my advantage to let Gabby know that I wanted her sexually. This was, of course, my attempt at securing my first patient upon graduation and I worked on Gabby for one and half years. It took all my strength not to come on to her. She was that good. I'm sure her friend's and family bandied about my name since Gabby was always studying with Stan or going to the movies with Stan or having dinner with Stan. I knew she was talking. I was, after all, her "ace" in the hole. It was the natural consequence of our relationship. I was achieving name recognition without ever having met anyone. Gabby and I continued our friendship uninterrupted until graduation and I was pleased with what had developed. For receiving my doctorate, Gabby flew us to Paris for an entire week. Gabby knew that I was going to move from my old apartment to the 88th street converted mansion. While we were in Paris, she had the apartment touched up. She didn't go too far in decorating but far enough to make a dent in the apartment's livability. She gave the apartment a new paint job, several paintings and rugs. In the backyard, she went all out with wonderful outdoor furniture and a great top of the line gas barbeque. She made that backyard special. Needless to say, I was blown away by the Paris trip and greatly surprised by the efforts she made on the apartment. She was truly special.

She spent the weekend with me and we talked about Monday, the official opening of my practice. What exactly I was going to do, I didn't know. Going to the printer to get cards announcing my doctorate and the opening of my practice was the best idea I had. Gabby left Sunday night at my request. She understood that I needed to be alone. On Monday morning I went out to breakfast on Madison Avenue at a diner that should have been closed long ago. After breakfast, I went to the printer and modified a standard announcement card. It was to be engraved on classic off white board. It was 10:30 a.m. That was it. I was done for the day or at least that was what I thought.

At noon, I called my mom and briefly chatted with her. It was the usual standard fare and not because I didn't have anything to say. She is 83 years old and I believe that she doesn't have more than three minutes worth of time left in her for telephone chat. Maybe, when life is finite and you can count the days that you think you have left, I'm worth three minutes. I took lunch on the steps of the Metropolitan Museum of Art. I watched all the comings and goings and chatted on the steps with another man who was taking lunch. My respite lasted until 1:30 p.m. I went back to the office to make believe that I was going to do something important. At 2:00 p.m. the doorbell rang. It was Gabby with a wonderful bouquet of flowers. I was totally surprised.

Overwhelmed by Gabby's kindness, consideration and attentiveness, I was speechless. "Come on in. Welcome to the place where we fix brains," I said. She laughed. In addition to the flowers and kind card wishing all her love and luck, she brought several bottles of wine. "Are you too busy for wine," she inquired. "No, not at all," I said. "My afternoon is free." We drank, laughed, told jokes, remembered Paris and made love. This was not what I wanted. My devious plan was to wait for the natural patient-shrink transference wherein she would fall in love with me and then we would make love. Of course, this plan was legally actionable and my license could be removed upon accusation. However, my plan to build a practice did not include networking. Gabby was bright, beautiful and my ticket to a career. If my mother had finite time frames in which to live, so did I. I needed Gabby to build a practice in a short period of time and was willing to take a risk.

Throughout the afternoon we made love and decided to take a break for dinner. Together in the shower, in an ever so peaceful manner, she whispered, "Doc, how does it feel to make love to your first patient?" "Well, you're not my patient yet, but I will admit that making love with you is the realization of a great fantasy that I have had for all these years and I will confess that the reality far exceeded the fantasy." I just plain liked Gabby.

Over the next several days, Gabby and I made as much love as newlyweds would have on their honeymoon. I saw her as a patient. I committed my first professional transgression within one week of opening my practice. She didn't require much intervention on my part, only 10 sessions. Over those two months,

Gabby radiated. Her family and friends noticed her brilliance. They all thought that I was doing an extra-ordinary job as her psychologist. Of course, what they were witnessing was nothing more than a woman feeling loved and having sex. I radiated as well. Gabby, as expected, chanted my name at every turn. She talked about me at family dinners, parties and in general conversation. The funny thing about the rich elite is that they love having the "best" or at least thinking that they do. They have the best dentists, best pizza places, best Chinese food and as I found out, the best psychologists. I was in and my practice grew. After Gabby's sessions with me were over, we continued our relationship. Not every relationship has to end in disaster or marriage. I loved Gabby and I'm sure she felt the same way. For some unstated reason, neither one of us wanted to go to the next level of marriage. There were other relationships that both of us had but they never intruded upon ours. I didn't ask her about her making love to other men and she didn't ask me about other women.

Gabby's father, Mr. Charles Westerfield, decided to open his estate in Southampton and have a party celebrating the new summer season. Although I didn't attend too many of Gabby's parties, I decided to go to this one. I often heard about her dad's extensive art collection. He had one of the finest art collections in America. Walking back from the beach, I encountered Mr. Westerfield standing on the dunes. "How are you, Stanley?" he asked. "It's not often you come to one of these events." "Once every two years seems to be enough," I answered. "Mr. Westerfield, may I take a look at your art?" "Sure, Stanley. I keep my art collection in the study overlooking this very dune. I can't begin to tell you how lost I get standing on this dune and looking at the night sky. It's my last remaining reality."

I left Mr. Westerfield alone on his dune. I went into the study and slowly examined each picture. Picassos, Modigliani, Van Gogh, Rembrandt and Klee. I was examining one particular picture by Van Gogh. It was a self-portrait done in September 1889, at the asylum of Saint-Paul's hospital in Saint Remy. It is the most distorted, cruel and merciless of all the self-portraits. This one, he sent to his mother. "Freud would have laughed his ass off," I thought. I was deeply lost in the portrait. I was completely startled when I heard, "quite a collection." Someone was sitting in a big armchair facing the window. I assumed, incorrectly, that somehow Mr. Westerfield got back from his dune before me and was sitting in his chair staring at his dune. "Yes, quite a collection," I responded. The chair swung around towards me. I couldn't make out a face. He stood up. He was tall and slim. The only thing I could see because of the light surrounding the figure was an outstretched hand. I shook it. Still holding my hand he said, "I am

Gabby's uncle, Sam." "Glad to meet you Sam, my name is Stanley Warlib," I said. "Oh yes, the great Dr. Stanley Warlib. I've heard your name quite a few times, all spoken in admiring tones. Sit down, Stanley, let's chat before you continue your solo exploration of the great Westerfield collection. "Would you like a scotch?" he asked. "Please, on the rocks," I said. I relaxed into a large armchair. "You wouldn't mind cutting those blinds a little, it's hard talking to a silhouette," I said. "No, not at all, you're just taking away an advantage," Sam stated. "Oh, do you need one?" I responded. "Never, my boy, never," Sam said. "It's only recently that I have been invited around here. Lately, it seems that I've been invited to a lot of places. I receive invitations to parties, clubs, events, everything. I have a full dance card, so to speak. It wasn't always like that, you know. I fell out of disfavor for a long time. It seemed that I made everyone uncomfortable," said Sam. "Well, I feel pretty relaxed around you," I said. "Good, I'm glad," Sam answered. "Now, let me make a point, Stanley. Just who do you think you are having sex with my niece, whether she is in or out of therapy? I saw Gabby two times back in the city while you were 'treating' her. Now, look, son, I've been around the block a lot more than you have and I know when a woman has that glow thing going. While everyone is telling me that you're doing a fine job helping Gabby, I'm biting on my tongue knowing that you're having sex with her. I'm thinking what a low level piece of scum you are. I couldn't prove a thing, so I had to keep my mouth shut. But tell me, are you making love to Gabby's friends too?" Sam barked. I started to squirm in my chair, but didn't respond. Uncle Sam had the floor and it was clear he wasn't finished. "You're a scumbag, Dr. Stanley Warlib. And you know how I know that, because you haven't said one word. Not one word. Back in the old days, any man that had been spoken to, as I just did to you, would have jumped up in my face and told me off. But, you didn't. If you were honorable, you would have said something like, 'that's right sir, and I have been making love to your niece because we love each other. I know it wasn't right, but forgive me.' Or, maybe, 'why don't you just shut your mouth you old piece of shit, what I do or don't do, is none of your business.' Or maybe, say nothing at all. Just lean over the desk and punch my lights out. But look at you, you dumb scumbag, nothing. Maybe, you're going to give me something like, 'that's more than I care to hear,' or, 'we don't need to go down that road.' You're a pussy. One big pussy and you have been one for most of your life. Got anything to say. No I didn't think so," Sam stated convincingly. I was completely glued to my chair. "And you want to know something else Dr. S T A N L E Y. I think what you do is pure bullshit. Therapy! What a convoluted asinine way to make a living. Imposing your view of how things should be on others. It doesn't work. You know what works," and with that he slams a book down on the table. "The Bible, boy. That works. Here is everything you need to know, right here in the Good Book. The only thing I need is the good Lord up above and the Bible down below. You see, Stanley, right here in this book, you have ten little rules for how to conduct yourself. Have you ever heard of the Ten Commandments, Doc? Everything you need to know to have a good life. It's simple. Follow the Lord Jesus and you live well. Follow the devil and you're torn and twisted until you go to hell. It's like I told you. I haven't been around for a lot of years but now I'm starting to get invited everywhere. You know why Doc? It's because your way doesn't work. Instead of telling people some good old simple advice you have been telling this damned mob to express themselves and look at what you got. You have people who claim that another solar system cloned the first human. You have Americanized Buddhists with a touch of Native American spirits practicing paganism. You got people who are nuts. You have fostered an atmosphere that promotes violence, sex, drugs, lying, stealing, homos, lesbians, fags and druggies. All this shit is a reflection of you. What you sow you shall reap. And because this is such a hodgepodge of bull, it's meaningless. Your ways produced a bunch of hollow little whores who don't even know why they're here. What a fucking shit hole. And you want to know something else, D O C T O R. Dr. Jerry Falwell was right when he said that September 11 was retribution for our evil ways but no wanted to hear him then. They'll listen now, Doc. Into this great big vacuum, we stood for the last fifty years silently working the Good Word and bringing it home to those who needed a way. A 'way' Doc, a beautiful way and all you needed to do was open your heart to Jesus, the Son of God. You see, only morons talk to you and the people who wanted the true way spoke to God. Now, how's that for a comparison. Step right up people. You can talk to God for nothing or you can talk to Dr. Stanley Warlib, who will scramble your brains even more, for $200.00 an hour. The bottom line, Stanley, is that you stand for nothing and we stand with God. This mess we're in is the natural consequence of not showing people a Godly path. I don't think you know how badly we have been treated from all you enlightened people. We have been ridiculed, shunned and made fun of. We have been shut out and demonized. We brought love and you brought hate. That's all changing now. You know what happens when good people like us start to get power. We can start to convert people much quicker and easier. You see, Stanley, most people out there just hear the words Republican or Democrat. They think they know what the Democrats or Republicans stand for. What they really don't know is the power of the offices we hold. Well, us God fearing good people conservatives have the power to hire and fire. We start to fire all those devil liberals who caused this horror in the first place. So it's not really Democrats or Republicans, you see, it's the liberal devils. Then we start to hire the people who believe in Jesus and the Good Book. It's easy. The local churches and parishes recommend them. Then we pick God-fearing candidates for office and conservative Bible believers for judges and slowly we start to consolidate our power. And you doctor are standing on the outside and ever so slowly you speak up less and less because you fear that you might offend some of us Good People. And if you speak your mind, you'll get those stares like 'are you stupid?' You can see it all around you. There are prayer meetings at all branches of government. Prayer and Bible readings have sprung up in corporate life. Haven't you noticed all the ballplayers that point to heaven and claim that God hit that home run? How long before the weakest of you succumb and go with the crowd? And it's only a matter of time before they become true believers. And you, Dr. Stanley Warlib, have just been outed. It's the new moral subjectivism and you're out. And why, Stanley? Because, Stanley stands for nothing! Stanley is a hollow little turd with no guts. You have been pussified, my friend. And you know who is leading your little fights that you faggots have been waging. The women. Sheryl Watkins, the Enron whistle-blower. The three nuns, in Colorado, that went to jail for eight years for minor destruction of government property. Everywhere, the women are leading your fights. I gave America's men a real war to fight in Iraq and a moral war to fight at home. You gave them nothing. Onward Christian soldiers. Let me give you a little lesson in political correctness. Take, for example, the National Institute of Health. Well, they give out a lot of money for grants. The word got out that certain words caused consternation to some folks at the N.I.H. Those folks are our folks, the right-thinking folks. We don't like words like lesbian and homosexual. All the grant applications are starting to come in with those words deleted just as we wanted. That's political correctness. It is our political correctness. We are getting stronger everyday in every way and all because you stand for N O T H I N G. And you know what's coming? It's the lesbians and homosexuals that really offend us. They are the next to go. They are forbidden in the Bible and they are evil. And abortion! We stand for something for Christ's sake," Sam concluded. Sam was standing on his soapbox and he was on a roll. I remembered from my legal days that when the opposing attorney is on a roll in the courtroom he is just like a conductor of a philharmonic symphony. He is in total command. The entire courtroom becomes mesmerized. An experienced attorney can recognize this instantly. A new lawyer gets buried. An attorney is taught to break the opposing counsels rhythm. Whatever it takes. Fake a fucking heart attack if you have to, but break the rhythm. I needed to break Sam's rhythm, so I screamed at the top of my lungs, "Shut the fuck up, smuck." Sam was more than startled. He froze in his stance and then just plopped like a sack of potatoes into his armchair. "First, you loud mouthed piece of shit. For the length of time that you have been rambling on, I could have been on my sixth scotch. Now pour yourself and me a double, start drinking and shut up." He poured the doubles, took a long drink and sat quietly. I lowered my voice and completely took him off his rhythm and changed the mood. I continued in a low melodic voice. "Your Good Book, the Bible, has taught you that those who don't follow your path are wrong and evil. The problem, Sam, is that you are so overwhelmingly consumed in your own bullshit you can't see out of it anymore. And that's when you start to make mistakes. You have become myopic. You just keep on moving forward whether you're right or wrong. But you're never wrong, are you Sam? After all, you have God on your side. Unfortunately, Sam, you will move you and your family in a direction that is contrary to your own interests." Sam, blurted out, "America will go in my direction because my direction is right and I'll win." "No, Sam, someone like you already lost. Anyone who thinks like you sows the seeds of his own destruction. Sam, it's simple. Let me give *you* an example." I raised my voice a notch. "You invaded Iraq in what was clearly an easy military victory. The Iraqi people were going to welcome you with open arms. You saw yourself as a great liberator bringing democracy to a new part of the world. You saw yourself as some wonderful prince of goodness. To invade Iraq, you claimed that they had weapons of mass destruction. You changed fifty years of behaving in one way and aggressively turned to another more hostile way. The world watched you exercise your military might. They were shocked and awed. Sam, your personality forces your brain to interpret external events in a way that reinforces your personality traits. However, you have been doing this for so long that these traits have become inflexible and causes you to act in a way that is contrary to your own interests. However, you don't see it and that's when problems arise. You are living in your own fantasy. Yes, you're functional, but you're shooting yourself in the foot. Now, here's the reality." I raised my voice another notch. "You think you showed the world your power. You showed the world the limitations of your power. Just think. All-powerful Sam stuck in the middle of some fucking desert looking for something that doesn't exist. The world watches as Sam spends eighty seven billion dollars for no reason. The world watches as your children die. The great almighty Sam stuck in a desert with no exit in sight and none of your international friends coming to your aid. You started it, cowboy, you finish it. You're trapped in a hall of your own mirrors and you can't get out. Because of what you did, the world is starting to look at you more closely. Your wealth is built on debt. Your behavior is erratic. You are no longer stable. The world is starting to see your limitations and turning elsewhere. No one wants to deal with you. Your dollar is going down and gold is going up. The collective marketplace is betting against you. The power has shifted to Europe and China. The world is a global collective and you're the lone cowboy. You have a major personality disorder. And by the way, it's not a pretty disorder." I lowered my voice. "It's ugly, vindictive, crucifying and bewildering. In your fantasy, you are the strongest richest motherfucker and can make anyone do what you want him or her to do. You are invincible. You see a Sam that is entering his new glory. You see a Sam that is all-powerful, almighty, and all knowing. While your vision might be glorious, it is, in fact, doomed. And Sam, you just don't see any of that. So Sam, all your friends that you have irrevocably alienated are talking, planning, and having meetings about defending themselves against you. Yes, they may be polite to your face, but behind the scenes, they hate your guts. Maybe they're even taking steps to make sure you fall on your face." Here, I pumped out the lines in a loud staccato voice. "That your dollar goes to shit. That your markets go down. That your people go unemployed. Your states implode. Your corporate moguls are stealing billions, your clergy are porking the choirboys, you're in debt up to your fucking ears and you think you're doing well. Are you fucking nuts, Sam?" I put my glass down and quietly walked out of the room. I turned at the door and said, "Nice chatting with you, Sam." I ran into Gabby in the kitchen and she asked me how it was talking to her Uncle Sam. "It was a hoot, Gab. One big hoot." "I'm glad you guys had a good time. I was afraid you two wouldn't hit it off," she said. "Well, Gabby, just let's say we had an interesting time, not necessarily a good time." I finished out the day never encountering Sam again. I said good-bye to Mr. Westerfield and kissed Gabby farewell.

Wednesday morning I went outside to my front steps and picked up The New York Times. I poured some boiling water into a French Press for coffee. The kitchen was right off the backyard patio. I started cooking up some bacon and went out on the porch. I love the smell of bacon. I glanced at the front-page headlines and opened up to the inside last page for the day's editorials just as an advance to see what I was going to read. After a couple of minutes, I got up to turn over the bacon when the doorbell rang. It was Gabby with a couple of bottles of wine. "Busy, Stan?" "No, just cooking up some bacon and eggs and reading The Times. Come on in, I'll make you breakfast." I assumed from the bottles of wine that Gabby was staying the day. I cooked breakfast and we hung out on the patio reading the paper and discussing various articles that each of us was reading. There was nothing of any particular significance. It was an uneventful

day of news. "Gabby, I guess you plan on staying the day," I said. "I thought that
a little afternoon delight would be nice," she responded. If there was anything
annoying Gabby, I didn't pick up on it. We had a salad for lunch and opened up
the first bottle of wine. I put on John Klemmer, a saxophonist with the sexiest sax
music going. It was mood music and I was in the mood. When we finished making love, Gabby whispered in my ear, "What the hell did you do to my Uncle
Sam? I thought that you guys had a good time," she said. "I said, 'interesting'
time, Gabby, not good." "Well, Stan, all hell has broken loose. Dad found Sam
alone in the study crying. He told dad that he was depressed and suicidal. No one
had seen Sam that way before and by the time Sam left, Sam acted as if nothing
happened. He was back to being, well, Sam. After Sam left, there was a gathering
of various men in dad's study and following that a whole series of separate meet-
ings and phone calls. Apparently, a lot of people from all over the world are concerned about Sam's crying episode. Dad didn't tell them about being depressed
and suicidal," Gabby said. "Well, I'm sorry to hear about all this mess, Gabby.
Sam and I had a spirited discussion and based upon what Sam said to me and
what I think, I didn't think Sam would be bothered about anything I said," I
replied. "Stan, it's a lot more complicated than that. It appears that a decision has
been made that Sam should see you for therapy and I don't think that Sam has a
choice." "Yeah, but I do and there's no fucking way that I'm seeing Sam under
any circumstances. Look, Sam hates me. Sam hates therapy and Sam is going to
loathe any relationship with me. It isn't going to work. That is not only my personal opinion but my professional opinion as well. Wait a minute, Gabby. Wait
just one fucking minute. Coming over here on Wednesday with two bottles of
wine for a little afternoon delight and you don't mention any of this until after
we make love. This whole fucking thing was a set-up. You set me up," I said. "I
had to Stan. Dad begged me to do this." "So why the hell didn't you just ask me.
Why go through the ruse. After all these years, did you really think that I thought
with my dick? That getting me high and fucking me would make me any more
amenable to being Sam's therapist. You should fucking know better," I screamed.
"I'm sorry Stan, I'm really, really, sorry. I wasn't thinking clearly at all. All I know
is that after you left the entire household has been in turmoil. Dad has been
working on me for the last three days," she said. "So, I guess this is how your dad
thinks. The way to a man's heart is through his dick," I replied. "Stan, I was
caught between two men I love and since you left the party I haven't been able to
think clearly in this war zone atmosphere," said Gabby. "Gabby, first, what the
hell is going on that everyone, whoever these people are, want Sam in therapy
and second, why me?" I inquired. "The second question is easy. You are the best

and that's what daddy wants. I guess after all these years he feels that you're part of the family. You have kept away from all the parties and the gossip and have kept your mouth shut. In my circles that's worth more than gold. As to what has everybody so upset, I don't know. Sam has been under a lot of stress being so liked these days, I guess it's getting to him," she said. "I think it's more complicated than that. It is way more complicated. I have already made some initial impressions about Sam and I won't treat this guy. No fucking way, Gabby, just no way. You know the way some people have delusions. Well, Sam is totally deluded about himself and he sincerely believes his own shit. He's convinced he's right and there's nothing wrong. They are the hardest patients to treat. They hate their therapists and they hate therapy. I don't have the time, inclination or desire to walk into this clusterfuck situation," I barked. "Stan, they're going to send Sam here whether you like it or not. I'm asking you to do this for me, if that's my last resort. And besides, you'll find your practice a lot lighter in the future and that's not a threat coming from me. I was asked to relay that message to you should I feel it necessary. Stan, I'm scared. And Sam doesn't have any say so in this matter either. They will bring him against his will, if necessary," said Gabby. "Well, that's fucking great. Treating a patient who doesn't want to be treated and is being treated against his will. That ought to take three years to overcome before I can even get to his fucking problems. Go home, Gabby, just go home." Gabby left the apartment soon thereafter. I sat at my desk and stared at the wall. I was numb.

I knew what was coming. My own slow motion train wreck with me attached to the front of the train. It reminded of the last scene in the movie version of Moby Dick with Gregory Peck strapped to the great white whale. I thought about taking some meds or smoking a huge Jamaican spliff. But what would that do. Nothing. I got up and walked the room cursing the day I met Gabby, cursing me and cursing Sam. Fuck this and fuck that. Of course I knew that I was solely responsible for this train wreck. After all, I didn't want to network and develop my practice in a slow way. I wanted instant practice, like instant rice. Take one beautiful woman, one rich daddy, add a little love, throw in some friendship and there you go, instant practice. Nobody's damn fucking fault but my own. I had to curse it up against everyone. So, this is my life. I knew that Sam would appear at my fucking doorsteps exactly one week from today. He would be here next Wednesday and if I had to take a guess I would bet on 2:00 p.m. For the next six days, I was going to be miserable. I would constantly dwell on the matter. I would be less attentive to my patients and tomorrow was Thursday. It was incurable, brain fucking cloud, Thursday. No matter what I did I would not be able to shake the reality that Sam was going to appear in my office in exactly 7 days. Those were my initial reactions. After several hours, sometime around 3:00 a.m. in the morning, five hours from my first patient, I sat back down at my desk. It was my first attempt to calm down. To approach my own impending train wreck in a cool rational manner was impossible. Nevertheless, an attempt was important. Gabby's statement that my practice would be "a lot lighter" meant that her dad would simply get on the phone and request that my patients stop seeing me. A simple request made in those circles would be immediately honored. That amounted to sixty possibly seventy per-cent of my practice. I settled on a sixty-five per-cent loss of revenue as a realistic figure and that loss would be immediate. I expected, that if I did not agree, I would receive phone cancellations by Friday. Sixty five per cent of $300,000.00 was $195,000.00 leaving me with $105,000.00. My life style expenses were $245,000.00. I was in the hole $140,000.00. I was broke, unless I was willing to make immediate substantial sacrifices. And that was the question. I had approximately $100,000.00 in the bank, which would last for one-half year. Thereafter, maintaining my life style would bankrupt me within a very short period of time. The question was at what price do I do the right thing. In this case, refusing to treat Sam was the right thing to do. The consequences were clear. My decision was not. Was I willing to do the right thing and endure the consequences? What price was I willing to put on my values? How honest am I? Can I be bought? I had all these questions. I knew that I would never kill someone except in self-defense. When I worked back from this ultimate moral question, I couldn't put my finger exactly on the scale of one to ten where I would compromise and do something that I knew wasn't right. A time honored line in the movies is that everyone has a price. Here it was, in my life, in real time. What was my price? Yesterday, I saw one of the talking pundits on FOX News television looking me right in the eye and advising me that army inspectors found two alleged mobile units in Iraq with German tags on them. He stated that some things are so vile, like making machinery for weapons of mass destruction, that a nation must stand up to the line and say no. The day prior, I saw a report that American companies through various off shore subsidiaries were selling material to Iran, the biggest evil doer on the axis of evil in spite of a ban on such conduct. It was legal the report said. Selling material to Iran the evildoer. Legal they say, notwithstanding that we may go to war with them in several months. No wonder why I have patients. Things are so screwed up. Dwelling on this stuff was my attempt not to deal with my own more immediate issue. It would not go away. I had a dagger in my back and it would stay there. I dwelled many hours visualizing exactly what my life would be like under severe reduced financial circumstances. My first patient, Rebecca, interrupted me. Rebecca was just some plain down home woman with a great body. Her entire life she got away with everything. She had a false sense of herself because she never got any genuine feed back from anyone. Guys just wanted to screw her so every stupid dumb thing she ever uttered was met with an approving nod or some form of verbalized agreement. After thirty years of this crap she believed she was smart. I tried my best to pay attention but all I wanted to shout was "shut the fuck up bitch." I didn't. For the next several hours, I tried my best to be involved in the therapeutic process with my patients. The more I became involved the less I thought about Sam. I never completely forgot about my problem but there were several hours that I didn't dwell on my own train wreck or whether I would do the right thing and live a reduced life style. While listening to Rebecca, I realized that Rebecca would fade away as she would be one of the patients that would be gone by Friday. So would two of the next three patients be gone. Reality hit home. My Thursday schedule would be with one patient. That was an eye opener. Rebecca blathered on about some flowerpot that an ex stole off her porch. I thought it was an heirloom but it was from Home Depot. Rebecca thought this was meaningful. What was meaningful was that I began to go through each day's list of patients that would leave. Ron, Tim, Sarah, Michael, and Gabby. Putting a face on the very real question of the people that would no longer be with me was frightening. It was very real and very frightening. My life would be sixty-five per-cent empty. I couldn't imagine all those people disappearing within twenty-four hours. No matter how much I ragged on them, they were part of my life. Whether good or bad, they were a part of my life. I didn't need my usual little pill to keep me up. Losing patients was enough to keep me awake. I was going to have a miserable weekend. After the last patient on Thursday, I poured Chivas Regal, put my feet up on my desk and gave out a big sigh of relief. From what, I didn't know, but maybe I already made my decision. I would miss all my patients even the most difficult ones. My place on 88th street would have to be given up. My days with Gabby were gone. This realization hurt the most. There were a lot of little things that would go by the wayside. I wondered whether I would have to give up my daily ritual of mocha latte and the New York Times. I loved this ritual. I sincerely believed that this made me human. It was one of my delights that I would protect at all costs. At this thought, I laughed out loud. "So this is the basis is of all moral decisions," I said to myself. It's the little things that motivate people, not the big ones. I might not have my mocha latte and New York Times. That was rock bottom to me. As long as I could sit somewhere and drink my coffee and read The New York Times, I was all right. Take away my Times and coffee and rock bottom reality would smack me in the face. I thought about all the world's problems and wondered whether the mocha latte syndrome caused them. How about the war in Iraq? Maybe some Middle Eastern beauty offered by an Arabian oil sheik rebuffed some big fat Texas oil guy. He's sitting around with the other fat cats and because of this little rebuff seeks revenge on any Middle Eastern oil state. It might be as simple as that. I'm going to treat Sam as a patient because I might not have my latte. After all, wasn't I the guy who built a practice intentionally screwing some rich kid? Well, I guess Sam was going to be my patient and I awaited Gabby's call. My New York Times and latte were protected.

After an appropriate amount of self-beating, two days worth, I settled down. I hated Sam. All that I had with him was a brief conversation and I hated him. In my opinion, it was court ordered psychiatry. He had no choice although I did. Why should I change my entire life because I thought the guy was a prick? After two days I realized how one could get caught in a crisis situation when a crisis doesn't exist. One of my problems was that I liked to walk down dark alleys and maybe get into problems. I would fight off the ropes and back into the center of the ring. This was my juice. My shrink wanted to know why I just couldn't pass up the dark alleys and walk on by. Why did I always have to fight off the ropes? This was, in fact, the end of the dark alley that I walked down with Gabby. I was forced to treat a patient that I didn't like. Not a hell of a lot of damage after all. To preserve the life style that I built I was going to treat Sam. It was another dark alley that was not my choice. I could hear my shrink screaming at me that it was *my* choice. As expected, Gabby called late Friday, as I was walking out the door. "Hi, Gabby, what's up," I said. Gabby's voice was audibly agitated. "I'm on my way out the door to go for dinner and some drinks, why don't you join me. Meet me at 86th Street and 2nd Avenue. We'll do something German. We'll talk all you want," I told her. "O.K., what time and what corner," she said. "Northwest corner at 8:00 p.m." I met Gabby and we went to a popular German spot. It was Friday night. I acted with Gabby as if nothing ever happened. I was trying to distance myself from her in regard to her Uncle Sam. She brought up her uncle. "The last time we saw each other you told me to get out of your house," she said "Come on, Gabby, all I said was 'go home Gabby, just go home.' I was a little upset." "How come you haven't mentioned Sam?" she inquired. "Because, I have decided to treat him as a patient. I'm not going to talk about him," I said. "Well, do you think you can help him?" asked Gabby. "Are you asking as a concerned niece or as a spy for those who really want to know?" "Oh, come on Stanley, I have to ask." "Well, tell your daddy, that if it is important enough to force Sam into therapy and important enough to threaten my career, then it should be important enough to keep my sessions with Sam private. I will tell you nothing. To aid me in helping your uncle, I need to know exactly why he was forced into therapy and who, exactly forced him," I asked. "Stan, would you believe me if I told you that I do not know the answer to your question?" "Yes, I would Gabby and if that is your answer then we should never again talk about this subject. You can tell your father, or whoever, that the subject is irrevocably closed, I advised her. "O.K., Stan, I understand," she said. "Do you really understand?" "Yes, I do." "Stan, I just have one more question," said Gabby. "O.K., what is it Gabby," I responded. "Why do you hate my Uncle Sam?" she asked. "Gabby, it's like this. I just think he's third rate. He doesn't belong being head of the family. Maybe a mom and pop store in Kansas, just not the head of the family. I think Sam is in over his head and I just don't believe he's running the show. Let's leave it at that," I said. Gabby and I continued eating and drinking for the rest of the evening. She came back to my apartment and we made love. It was better than I expected and it seemed that all issues between us were settled. I told Gabby that she had to leave after we made love. "I have work all week-end and sleeping over is not a good idea," I told her. "You don't work on the week-end," she replied. "This week-end I do, Gab. You know your Uncle is very well known and a lot has been written about him. I have research to do. I want to get to know him and his family at best as I can. I believe that your Uncle Sam will not be as forthcoming as I would like. This weekend I planned to do as much research as necessary to get my arms around this guy. I want to hit the ground running so to speak," I said. "I understand. I hope everything goes well, Stan. Please, please, please, don't let this matter get between us," she said. "Gabby, my crisis in treating your Uncle Sam is over. The only thing that could get between us, is, if you ask me, even once, what's going on with your uncle. Please don't," I told her. "I won't Stan, I promise," Gabby assured me. Gabby left.

I hadn't even met my new patient and I was pissed at him. I was going to do work on the weekend and that always pissed me off. I was attempting to obtain by research, a view of Sam, as I knew that Sam would be uncooperative if not hostile. This was a client intake without the client. However, Sam was popular these days and much had been written about him. In addition, there was sufficient information about him and his family that was easily accessible by the Internet. Saturday and Sunday, I was going to "google" myself to death. Even though I didn't like Sam, he would be my patient. I felt the research would be beneficial in the long run.

Sam's Intake

Sam is the sum total of various personalities such as George Bush, Richard Cheney, Paul Wolfowitz, Donald Rumsfeld, John Poindexter, Dennis Koslowski and Jeff Skilling. They have common characteristics. The list is not meant to be exclusive, but is meant to exemplify that group of movers and shakers that go beyond the mere pursuit of money. They seek grandiosity on an international scale and exhibit a marked hostility towards the average individual. Sam has fifty relatives and each relative has an extended family within defined geographic boundaries. In all, Sam has approximately 285,000,000 people living within his house. Sam's neighbor to the north is Canada and his neighbor to the south is Mexico. Sam does not have neighbors to the east and west of his house. Sam has ample resources to feed his people and what he cannot produce on his own he buys on the world market. Around the world Sam has many acquaintances. Some like him and many don't. Sam is tall, slim and athletic. Many of his family members are overweight. Approximately 127 million people within Sam's family are overweight. Sixty million are obese and nine million are severely obese. Their weight problem is a cause of other related health problems. His family's obesity increases the risk of illness in thirty other serious medical conditions. In addition, Sam's family's obesity is associated with increases from death from all causes. His family's children are showing earlier onset of obesity related diseases, such as type 2 diabetes and they are at a higher risk for impaired mobility. Notwithstanding the health problems associated with their obesity, they experience social stigmatization and discrimination in employment and academic situations. In spite of their continuing problem with weight and its clear associative problems, they prefer to look for an easy fix that doesn't require work, effort or time. A look at what Sam's family reads is informative. There are over 1,805 books written on weight loss most of which promote dubious methods of weight loss with unrealistic claims. His family takes "magic pills" and use "magic belts" that are promoted on television as infomercials. The infomercials make even more unrealistic claims than the books that Sam and his family reads. Lose twenty pounds while you sleep is not an uncommon claim. Nevertheless, Sam and his family look for easy and quick answers to everything. His family is too busy for their own good health. His family has many physical problems besides being grossly overweight. For example, diabetes is a common problem. Seventeen million members of Sam's family have diabetes. In addition, it is estimated that 8.9 million of Sam's family who had a history of cancer were alive in 1999. In this year, it is expected that 1,334,100 new cases of cancer will be detected. Since 1990 over 17,000,000 new cases have been reported. This year 556,500 will die of cancer. His family has heart problems as well. One in five members of Sam's family have some form of heart disease. That is, 57,000,000 members of Sam's family have heart problems. Much of this is related to Sam's obesity problem. Heart disease kills 960,000 people a year in Sam's house. The cost of Sam's family's cardiovascular diseases was estimated to be $392.2 billion in direct costs, such as hospital visits and indirect costs such as lost productivity.

Sam's family is stressed out. Almost seventy-five per cent of Sam's family feels that they have great stress in their lives. It has been estimated that 75-90 percent of all visits to primary care physicians are for stress related problems. Job stress is far and away the leading source of stress of Sam's adult family but stress levels have also risen in Sam's children, teenagers, college students and Sam's elderly relatives. Stress has had a direct impact on the family's physical condition. In addition to other factors, Sam and his family members have turned to various forms of substances and alcohol as a means of escaping the conditions under which Sam has set up his household. Approximately 47% of Sam's family members 12 years of age or older, 104,000,000 indicated that they had used alcohol during a month prior to the taking of a survey. In addition, 46,000,000 family members reported binge drinking and 13,000,000 reported heavy drinking. The highest rates of drinking were for Sam's family members age 21 to 25. In 2000, over 22 million family members aged 12 or older reported drinking and driving during the past year. Cocaine is another substance that his family members use. It has been reported that 24,788,000 of Sam's family have used cocaine in their lifetime. During that report it was reported that 4,186,000 family members used cocaine during the past year and 1,676,000 had used cocaine during the preceding month of the report that I read. Sam and his family members take numerous other drugs but tobacco use is an interesting case in point. An estimated 46.5 million adults in the United States smoke cigarettes even though this single behavior will result in death or disability for half of all regular users. Cigarette smoking is responsible for more than 400,000 deaths each year, or one in every five deaths. Additionally, if current patterns of smoking persist, over 5 million people currently younger than 18 will die prematurely from a tobacco-related disease. Paralleling this enormous health toll is the economic burden of tobacco use: more than $75 billion in medical expenditures and another $80 billion in indirect costs. Sam refuses to outlaw its use. Sam won't stop this unnecessary slaughter.

Mental disorders are common in Sam's family. An estimated 22.1 percent of Sam's family ages 18 and older—about 1 in 5 adults—suffer from a diagnosable mental disorder in any given year. When applied to the 1998 U.S. Census residential population estimate, this figure translates to 44.3 million people. In addition, 4 of the 10 leading causes of disability in Sam's family are mental disorders-major depression, bipolar disorder, schizophrenia, and obsessive-compulsive disorder. Many people suffer from more than one mental disorder at a given time. Mental disorders are diagnosed based on the *Diagnostic and Statistical Manual of Mental Disorders, fourth edition (DSM-IV)*. Further, Sam and his family are an aggressive lot. Recent crime statistics indicate that there were 1,424,289 violent crimes; 10,181,462 property crimes; 15,517 murders; 90,186 forcible rape; 407,842 robberies; 910, 744 aggravated assaults; 2,049,946 burglaries; 6,965,957 larceny thefts and 1,165,559 vehicle thefts. Sam and his family have a love affair with guns. There are approximately 192 million privately owned firearms in Sam's family—65 million of which are handguns. Currently, an estimated 39% of households have a gun, while 24% have a handgun. In 1998 alone, licensed firearms dealers sold an estimated 4.4 million guns, 1.7 million of which were handguns. Additionally, it is estimated that 1 to 3 million guns change hands in the secondary market each year, and many of these sales are not regulated.

Sam's finances are precarious. Although the total amount of goods and services produced are a trillion dollars, Sam's owes over six trillion dollars, which amounts to a tax on each family member and their children of close to $22,000.00. Sam is clearly broke. In addition, Sam's fifty relatives are financially imploding. Sam doesn't have to balance his checkbook. However, many, if not most of his relatives, are required to. In order to do this, Sam's relatives are closing schools and libraries, reducing services and raising the amounts of money that each relative takes from those living within their household. Sam and his relatives cannot manage money. Sam relies heavily on his foreign acquaintances to support his spending habits and indeed, those around the world own 60% of Sam's debt, close to 4 trillion dollars. Sam's foreign creditors didn't have a problem owning Sam's debt because Sam for many years appeared to be a pretty stable guy and relatively predictable. However, recently, Sam has exhibited erratic behavior that has made Sam's acquaintances edgy. Sam has started two wars within the last two years. In addition, Sam has walked out on agreements that he has made with his foreign friends. Sam has quietly seized monies belonging to other people around the world. He claims that this money is being used for terrorist purposes so he is taking it away. Sam is getting increasingly hostile to others and shows an extreme intolerance of others criticisms. Sam is lashing out almost indiscriminately at anyone who disagrees with him. Interestingly enough, Sam is enlisting all his family members in boycotting and slandering his international acquaintances, even though these acquaintances may only have a difference of opinion. Internationally, Sam is being viewed as belligerent, erratic, accusatory and dangerous. Sam is no longer being viewed as a viable friend. Many people are seeking alternatives to dealing with Sam although it is somewhat difficult as Sam's tentacles reach throughout the world. However, Sam's international friends are nevertheless making all attempts to do so.

Sam has become increasingly suspicious of his own relatives and their extended families. He is, with progressive frequency, making all attempts to spy on his family with various tools available to him from hidden cameras and microphones to spying on their most mundane activities. Sam experienced a traumatic event several years ago and is promoting these vast intrusions based upon that traumatic event. He claims that such intrusive techniques will prevent such a catastrophe from happening again. It seems that Sam's attempts on spying on his own family knows no boundaries. Sam enlisted a criminal, although pardoned, to run his vast spy program. It is incredible that Sam's relatives and their families have not shown any anger at Sam's moves. They are strangely silent except for a very small minority. Apparently, whatever Sam wants to do is all right, even if it contrary to their own interests. Sam and his relatives collectively display a certain degree of paranoia that has permitted all this spying. It appears that Sam is frightened that another trauma is imminent and will do anything to prevent it, including encroaching upon his own families rights.

Sam has taken an active path towards taking benefits away from his family members that he had previously given. It has become increasingly difficult to live within Sam's house. Sam wants to change the rules of everything that many of Sam's brothers before him had promoted such as retirement and pensions. It appears that Sam wants to strip himself of all his obligations and only spy on his family members and start fights around the world. Again, it is strange that there is very little anger from Sam's family.

By Sunday night, I got tired of doing research and decided to take a break. However, my interest in treating Sam was piqued, although the realization that Sam would be my patient was frightening. I kept on saying over and over in my mind that there was nothing I could do for him. Based upon my initial impressions, I felt that any attempts to help Sam were going to be a waste of time. I found comfort in the knowledge that in many circumstances therapists have little impact on their patients and present nothing more than a stabilizing effect for them. I had a framework for an initial diagnosis but decided to wait for Sam to fill in the details.

Monday came soon enough. I was, as best as I could be, in the therapy mode. I was relieved that Monday's patients were my favorites and relatively easy to deal with. The last thing that I could handle was a tough caseload. I still had not figured out what therapeutic approach to use with Sam. I was going to make that determination after several sessions with Sam and after my initial diagnosis. Tuesday patients came and went. When the last patient walked out the door a big smile came over my face. I wanted something cool to drink so I fixed a gin and tonic on the rocks and settled in with Ozomatli, a group my son turned me onto. I had another two drinks over the next hour and was developing that kind of slow buzz you get when you're alone. The doorbell rang. I wondered whether I should even answer the door. After an extended period of time, sufficient enough for the person at the door to decide to go away, I got up out of my chair. It was Gabby. "Hi, Gabby, come on in," I said. "Hi, Stan. I haven't heard from you and thought I'd stop by," she said. "Well, Gabby, it's slow buzz time and you're three drinks behind. You missed Ozomatli but you're just in time for the Gypsy Kings or maybe I should put on John Klemmer," I said. Klemmer was a euphemism for making love. "No, I'll take one drink and stay for the Kings," she replied. I knew I wasn't getting any from Gabby that night. Maybe I wasn't going to get any for the rest of our years together. Perhaps this little Sam episode ended our sexual relationship. I was sufficiently buzzed that I didn't dwell on the possibility. Unfortunately, Gabby and I had one of those stilted conversations the kind where one person says something and it just hangs there for a while. Then the other person says something and that hangs there. It is not a conversation. It is more like a series of one-liners strung together by silence. "So, Gabby, why don't we cease this bullshit and tell me what's on your mind." She hesitated, but finally responded, "I was wondering how you were feeling about tomorrow," she said. "Great. Tomorrow is my day off and I have lots of stuff planned," I answered. "But what about Sam?" she said. "I told you Gabby, don't bring up Sam." "But you said you were going to treat him so I don't understand why you planned your day off," she said quizzically. "Wait a minute, what are you talking about?" I asked. "Sam is coming tomorrow," she replied. "What time?" I asked. "I don't know. Don't you know?" she asked. "Gabby, I have no idea what the hell you're talking about. No one has called and this is the first I'm hearing about this. Why am I not surprised? Well, I'm going to plan my day and come back to the office around 1:30 p.m. and then leave at 3:00 p.m. I have a date to go downtown to see some art," I told her. I expected that this information would get back to Mr. Westerfield or Sam directly. This was my first attempt to put boundaries on this upcoming patient. I suspected that Sam would be pissed upon hearing this. "You seem rather poised, Stan," Gabby stated. "Well, Gabby, I'm the guy who gets paid to keep his head when everyone else is losing theirs. Can't have a general out of control on the battlefield in the heat of battle, can you? Besides, I already had my two days of hell over this shit and decided that that was enough. I have decided that although I don't like Sam, I will treat him to the best of my ability and hopefully help him resolve whatever issues he may have." Having said that, Gabby relaxed and a more intimate flowing conversation ensued. "Gabby, how about some John Klemmer?" I asked. "I thought you would never ask," she said. Her lips expanded and came to meet mine. She was inviting me in and I dove. I had a great night. The torture that I was experiencing was turning around to have a good beginning. I felt in control again and that lifted my spirits. Sam is just another patient with problems, I thought. What made me feel well was that the episodes of anger, depression or just being upset were getting shorter and shorter. At certain times in my life, I would have carried on until Sam left therapy, maybe two years hence. I would have got sucked up into his insanity simply because he pissed me off and I would have mixed it up with him to satisfy that anger. Understanding myself reduced what would have been two years of prospective agony to a mere four days. You have to love therapy. I reminded myself that Sam hated therapy and me. He was deeply religious. God and the "Good Book" was his therapy. I would take that into account. Gabby lay next to me while I drifted off into my mind. I stopped and turned around to Gabby and whispered in her ear, "I love you Gab." "I know Stan. I know. I love you too and have for a long time. Maybe one day after all this is over we'll have a chat and talk about why we never go beyond this point in our relationship. How come we never talk about marriage, kids, living together, you know, stuff like that?" Gabby said. "Gabby, I promise that when this is all done, I will sit down with you, in Paris, for a month, and we'll really talk about this. I don't believe that we should talk about this over dinner. We should spend time together," I said. "I agree," Gabby said and finished with "in Paris, huh. Maybe you're a lot closer than you think." Gabby got out of bed, showered, dressed and left the apartment. She looked beautiful, simply beautiful.

On Wednesday I got up, made some coffee and read the Times on the back porch. On that day, Harold Raimes the editor had just resigned over the Jayson Blair affair. Black reporter, phony stories, liberal paper. The conservatives were having a field day. It was insinuated on cable television that Sulzberger, an owner of the New York Times was also going to resign within a short period of time. The scandal was already changing the New York Times. After I consumed as much news as I wanted, I went for a jog around central park and thereafter went to the gym for an upper body workout, chest, shoulders and back. Sweaty, I made my way over to a little café for lunch.

I wasn't thinking about Sam, but I really was. The real reason that I was pissed off was because I didn't want to get into Sam's head. I remembered when the movie Donnie Brasco came out and Brasco realized that he was so deep in as an undercover agent in the Mafia, he almost forgot who he was. I didn't want to get so deep into Sam that he changed my personality. The therapeutic process is like an inverse elevator. The higher you go the deeper you get. To truly understand a patient takes a long time. The commitment eats your soul out and at that end of the process, you don't know who you are. It's not a question of money; it is a question of sanity. These are, indeed, very hard questions. I did not want to go down a road with Sam into his insanity; I wanted to remain on the road with Gabby. My days of fighting were over. It would kill me to take the elevator with Sam. Absolutely, kill me. To help Sam I would almost have to become Sam and stay ahead of him and his games.

These weren't the only questions that raced through my mind as I sat at my desk. My initials impressions of Sam led to a preliminary diagnosis. Patients with Sam's personality disorders are incurable. At best, you might be able to make minor improvements. My reputation as the "best" in Gabby's circles would be destroyed. No one, which included that unseen and unknown jury who forced Sam into therapy, would be pleased. They would not notice any substantial change in Sam or his behavior. Extending Sam's sessions for many years would prolong the inevitable demise of my practice. Mr. Westerfield and his group would slowly abandon me as their therapist and find a new "best" therapist. I was nothing more than the next best pizza place. Easily replaced. If I could extend Sam's therapy I would have time to make arrangements to adjust my practice to withstand the financial blow that was going to happen. I could move out of my current location to a smaller place. I would need to take on more clients with insurance. I decided to take the next available weekend off and come up with a business plan for the next two to three years to deal with the inevitable. Once again, I was voting my own interest as I had voted my own interest when I took up with Gabby. All of this headwork was interrupted when the doorbell rang. It was 2:40 p.m. I expected Sam at 2 p.m., as if it would be a normal fifty-minute session. Sam was at the door. "Come on in Sam, how are you," I said. "Why do you care how I am," Sam said defiantly. I motioned Sam to sit at a chair in front of my desk but he went immediately to the kitchen. His cell phone went off and he answered it. I had the distinct impression that it was all pre-planned and he spoke for almost ten minutes. It was 2:49 p.m. when he ended his conversation and there was only one minute left in our "first" session. "Sam, I expect you here next week promptly at 2:00 p.m. and our session will end at 2:50 p.m. We will discuss what you expect out of therapy and the boundaries that are necessary in any given patient-therapist relationship. In addition, we will discuss how you intend to handle the payment of my fees," I advised Sam. I spoke quickly as it was my intention to finish exactly at 2:50 p.m. "Thank you for coming, Sam." I walked him to the door. Sam was surprised that I ushered him out exactly at 2:50 p.m. "I will not be here next Wednesday if I can help it. You are not my therapist. I do not need help and I will not pay anything for having a chat with you. Good-bye," Sam stated emphatically. My first session with Sam had just ended.

SESSION NOTES

It was clear to me that it was by design that Sam appeared at 2:40 p.m. and went immediately to the kitchen. The cell phone call appeared staged. Sam, by not sitting in my office, made a clear statement that he was not a patient. Although there was not enough time to discuss the issue of payment for my services, I am sure that Sam would unequivocally refuse to discuss the issue of payment. Sam did everything to convey the impression that he was not in therapy and that I was not his therapist. I will not make an initial diagnosis based upon such scant material. I am curious to see if Sam shows next Wednesday on time, as I demanded. I believe that it is important to set the minimum boundaries as to time and payment as anything too demanding would simply antagonize and alienate Sam. I will attempt to avoid creating any appearance that I am his therapist and that he was engaged in therapy. If nothing else, I want Sam to continue to come every Wednesday under whatever labels he needs to classify our relationship. I was going to play his game until I felt that I could proceed to another level of understanding.

When I finished writing my notes, I decided to go out for dinner. If there was an available woman to flirt with I was going for it. I was desperate for a distraction. My brain was on overload and it needed a break. I went to a local eatery that was known to have a rather disproportionate number of women to men. I was not disappointed. I sat at the bar and ordered a Dewar's and soda and the young lady next to me struck up an immediate conversation. "You're Dr. Stan Warlib, aren't you?" she said. "Yes, I am, but how do you know me?" I asked. "I remember you from New York University." Her name was Elicia and she knew her psych stuff. She had obtained a master's in psychology and delayed her doctorate. She told me that it was a decision of obtaining a doctorate and staying within a bad marriage or getting out of the marriage and postponing the doctorate. She decided to postpone the doctorate and end the marriage, which she advised me turned out to be the correct decision. When two psych type people get together they can go on for hours about the mind and I decided that this was not what I needed. "You know, Elicia, it's been a rough day and I came out to eat, drink and more importantly, flirt. I need a brain break and some light banter," I said. I knew that Elicia would understand and much to her credit immediately redirected the conversation to my needs. I was impressed. That kind of conduct exhibited an understanding that at this point in time she was not the center of attention. She attended to my needs. Elicia was getting lots of A's on my scorecard. I glanced down at the floor and told her that she had nice shoes. This was something that I learned from a 21 year old. He told me to comment on a woman's shoes as an opening line. I have used that line for my entire life and it works. Why? I don't have a fucking clue, but it does. Besides the comment on her shoes, I was also checking out Elicia from bottom to top. Not bad at all. "Well, flirt away, Dr. Stan. I'm yours," she said. It was apparent that she had shifted into a total romantic mode with the ease that a racecar driver would shift gears. She did this so well and was so comfortable in this role that I felt a little challenged to rise to the occasion. I wanted to flirt and she was ready. "O.K., E, a little hesitation on my part but I'm getting into the role." I grabbed Elicia around the waist, put my cheek to her cheek and struck a tango pose, universally associated with romance. "I love when you call me E," she whispered. She played the part beautifully. Unfortunately, there was no place to act out this little fantasy. "Elicia, I know a great little Argentina tappas bar with music. Would you care to move this fantasy to another location," I asked her. "Warlib, tonight is your night and I'm yours," Elicia declared. I didn't take her "I'm yours" as anything but her going along with the fun. It was not an invitation for sex. I wondered if I was hitting up on E because I knew that my relationship with Gabby was going to become non-existent, at least until my sessions with Sam were over. Besides, I didn't trust Gabby under these circumstances and would always feel she was a spy for Mr. Westerfield and his unknown jury. I would be too guarded with Gabby to have fun or sex. I would always feel that the next statement that would come from Gabby's mouth would be the one that would force me to tell her that she must leave. Elicia and I got in a cab, went to the tappas bar and faked the tango. We both had too many drinks and too much fun. E gave me exactly what I needed. Elicia created an atmosphere of romance without being overtly sexual. A friend once told me that a good woman is the one that gives credence to her man's fantasies. They're also the most dangerous. "Elicia, tomorrow I have sessions with my most draining clients and I hate to say this, but I think I should go." "I understand, Warlib, then go we must," E said. "E, sometime in near future, I'm going to Montauk Point for a week-end to sort things out. I would love if you would join me," I said to Elicia. Without hesitation, Elicia responded in the affirmative. I took her number, politely kissed her on the lips good night and left.

Thursday was a horror. Thursday I have my most difficult clients with their mind-numbing problems. I took my little magic pill two hours earlier so that I would stay awake. I couldn't keep my mind off of E or Sam. I wanted to see E as soon as possible and I wanted to come up with some kind of game plan for Sam. I was sure that he would show up Wednesday. The day finally ended at 6:00 p.m. when the last patient walked out the door. I went to the kitchen, popped a Stouffer's frozen dinner into the microwave and waited impatiently for four minutes. I love Stouffer's. I took a bottle of wine out to the deck, ate dinner and drank the bottle. The next day I called Elicia on her cell phone and asked her to join me for the weekend in Montauk Point. "What took so long Warlib, I've been expecting your call after our very first kiss. Of course, I'd go. I'd love to go," she said enthusiastically. I told E that I would pick her up at 5:00 p.m. Friday afternoon and that we would crawl out of the city on the Long Island Expressway to Montauk. Friday was a great day. I was really excited about hooking up with E and making a business game plan to soften the blow of my impending change in financial circumstances. It felt good to feel in control even if it was my own financial funeral.

I picked E up at her brownstone. It was not too far from the Queens Midtown Tunnel. She didn't own the brownstone. She rented an apartment. E looked great. She had this boyish thing going on in a Tommy Bahama shirt and guys jeans. "Sexy, real sexy," I thought as she came down the steps of her brownstone. There's something about a woman with great attributes in a laid back earthy kind of way, like a woman in Bergdorf's in a full-length mink coat with jeans and a tee shirt underneath. We stopped for dinner at Conscience Point on the north shore of Long Island. When we arrived at Montauk I requested a room with two beds at the motel check-in desk. Elicia glanced at me approvingly. I knew that getting one bed, even if it was a king size bed would be an act of aggression and an assumption of monumental proportions. It would be a set-up as a sex weekend contrary to my initial request of merely joining me so that I could work out my financial issues. I didn't assume anything. If sex was going to happen, sex was going to happen. I didn't have to force the issue. The best love is always consensual without any hint of forced manipulation. E and I sat on the deck of the motel, had some wine, watched and listened to the ocean. There was some polite chitchat. I was too tired to be witty or charming. Picking up on this E suggested that we retire for the night. It was a welcome suggestion.

The next morning E and I searched for a breakfast place with a view overlooking a harbor. She found a charming spot near the water with fishing boats as a backdrop. I picked up the New York Times prior to entering the restaurant. We both ordered coffee and E grabbed the second section of the Times and left me the first. I discussed a column by Paul Krugman and told her how much I liked his material. "He appears to be one of few with a head on his shoulders," she said. I nodded with approval. "I know why I'm here, Stan, but why are you here?" she asked. "I thought that I needed the week end to work out some kind of financial game plan as my financial circumstances are going to change. I wanted to come up with a plan to minimize the damage. But the more I hang with you the less important it all seems. Maybe I just needed a week-end out of the city," I told her. "Well, why don't you give me a clue about what you think your problem is," E stated. "Simply put, my practice was built upon treating a very rich woman with powerful connections. My practice grew quickly as this rich, powerfully connected circle believed that I was the best. I kept my mouth shut and was constantly recommended by those in her clique. I have relatively easy patients with lots of money. Several weeks ago, it was demanded that I treat her uncle with a veiled threat that if I didn't, my practice would change substantially and quickly," I said. "And is that possible?" Elicia inquired. "More than possible Elicia, probable. These are very powerful people and when they demand something be done, it gets done. I would immediately lose, within seven days, sixty-five per-cent of my income. I would be in the hole immediately. So I thought that if I came here for the weekend I could come up with a game plan. I already know what I have to do. I guess I don't have the fire in the belly any more. There was a time when I relished a challenge. As a matter of fact, a destructive streak that I have since learned to control would create challenges so that I could overcome them. I got tired of fighting. Aging has a peculiar way of dousing whatever fire you have. What once was an inferno is barely flickering. The truth is, I don't have the energy to treat this uncle nor the energy to start the beginnings of financial damage control," I said. "Stan, do you know what to do to control whatever financial damage may occur?" she asked. "Yes, E, I do." "Then that's something we don't have to discuss. That's more of an issue of you just doing what you know you have to do," she said. I loved the fact that Elicia did not demand details of what my financial plan was. Most women would have demanded in excruciatingly minute detail what I was going to do. Laying bare uninteresting details had always bored me. I appreciated her confidence in my statement that I knew what

I had to do. It was sufficient. I did not feel that E lacked any interest in my concerns. It was more a vote of confidence than a lack of interest. "However, I am interested in this uncle that you have to treat. Being forced to treat a patient is certainly a difficult position to be in. Not having the fire in the belly as you stated before, places almost an impossible burden on the therapeutic process. Do you have a plan for this?" Elicia asked. "The short answer is yes. I have a plan. The plan is to treat this guy as long as possible, whether he needs it or not. I want to extend his therapy so that I have time in which to implement my financial plan and replace whatever patients I lose with new patients. This takes time and hence, I can predict without hesitation that this "uncle" will have extended sessions. What's really disturbing is that I hate him and he hates me. He hates therapy. Jesus is his shrink and the Bible is his fucking Diagnostic Service Manual. The realization that I have to treat this guy just pisses me off to no end. When there was a fire in my belly I would have taken up this challenge without hesitation. Now? It all just seems like a big waste of my time, especially since I'm at the stage of my life where time is important. Who the fuck wants to waste time with this prick," I said. My voice was rising and the underlying anger was coming through. "Have you considered going to your shrink to help you during this period," E asked. "Yes, I have, but I'm not there yet. What really gets me is that I will make very little or no progress with this man. That's what my gut tells me. So I'm going to waste the next three years of my life with a patient that I hate and not make any progress," I said. "Stan, I trust your judgment in this matter and strongly recommend that you contact your therapist as quickly as possible, Monday, if you can. You clearly need some guidance in this matter. Anything that will help you get through this period without causing damage to yourself or your patient will be invaluable," Elicia said. Of course, she was right but I wanted Sam to go away. Elicia had a calming effect on me. I stared at the boats across the harbor and Elicia knew enough to realize that I was rolling over in my mind the entire issue that we had been discussing. However, I wasn't thinking about calling my shrink. I was thinking about Elicia. E was this very bright woman trained in psychology only months away from her doctorate. I could use her as my therapist without telling her my intentions. Why? If I called my therapist I would be forced on a weekly basis to do the right thing. I would have to discuss my treatment program and the details of my sessions with Sam so that my therapist could review my ability or lack thereof. Essentially, my therapist would be there to review my conduct so that I wasn't fucking Sam up because all my shit got in the way of effective therapy. Well, I wasn't so sure I wanted that because I did want to fuck Sam up. At least, a part of me did. So why not keep E around as a girlfriend type person? Naturally, her and I would discuss how I was doing, as intimate friends do. After all, psychology type people love to talk shop. Not a bad idea I thought. When I tumbled back from deep thought to Elicia sitting in front of me at the table I said, "Honey, I'm home." She laughed. "You know, you look like Jack Nicholson," she said. I love a woman who understands my sense of humor. "Jack Nicholson has quite a reputation in Hollywood. Did you ever see The Witches of Eastwick? E asked. "Yes, I did Elicia." E was referring to Jack's alleged voracious appetite for sex. She opened the door and I was going to walk right in. I was about to walk down another dark alley. Being with Elicia was all too easy and felt all too good. The remainder of the weekend could only be characterized as a scene out of a great romantic movie. The relationship was cemented. A great woman gives credence to a man's fantasies. E did and I didn't even know what was going on.

Monday was an easy day. Easy patients mean easy days. I looked for any sign in the patients that were recommended by Gabby or Mr. Westerfield or came from that circle that would indicate that they had been spoken to but there weren't any signs. So far so good, I thought. My time frame was three years. I did not know what the time frame was for those that forced Sam into therapy.

SESSION TWO

Sam showed up at 2:20 p.m. on Wednesday. That was better than the previous week. I had made some adjustments in my approach and thought that the changes would make Sam feel more comfortable. "Come on in, the door's open," I yelled. Sam walked in and looked in the office. "I'm in the kitchen, Sam, making coffee," I shouted. Sam walked through the apartment to the kitchen with a swagger. "Would you like some coffee, Sam?" I asked. "Sure," replied Sam. "Sit down, Sam, make yourself comfortable," I beckoned. I had rearranged the bar stools around the granite top so that Sam would sit on a taller chair. I served coffee and sat down. I was at least 6" lower than Sam and he had to look down at me. This pleased him. "Let's have a chat, Sam," I requested. Before he responded, he slid an envelope across the granite countertop. I opened it. It was a gift certificate from Bloomingdale's for $300.00. "Someone gave it to me. I thought I'd give it to you," Sam said. "Thanks, Sam. Thanks a lot," I said. "Stop cow towing to me. I told you someone gave it to me. I didn't go out and get it. You want to get paid for spending an hour with me. So be it. But you should be paying me. By the way, do I look stupid to you? Are these little psycho parlor tricks? You know, the setting in the kitchen? Coffee? My higher chair? Trying to make me feel more comfortable. Are you kidding? Is this the best you have? They say you're the best. What a joke. Even a moron can see through this. I have told you before and I'll tell you again. I don't need therapy and I don't believe in therapy. It's as simple as that. There are a lot of jealous people out there forcing me to do this. So, I don't recognize you as a therapist and accordingly there isn't any need to pay you. The gift certificates you'll receive are given to me by any number of sycophants trying to curry my favor. It is you that should pay me. Really, Stan, what cheap little psycho tricks. You are sophomoric," Sam declared. "O.K., Sam, let's then head into my office and sit in our respective chairs and chat about what it is that we're doing," I told Sam. Sam and I went to the front of my office and sat down. I sat at my desk and Sam sat in the chair for patients. He surprised me by his attack on my strategy. He was absolutely correct. I didn't realize that I was so obvious. I gave Sam more credit than I initially had given him. I thought that I should elevate the level of conversation. "Sam, why don't we get right to the issue and discuss who forced you to come see me," I said. "I wouldn't exactly say I was forced to come to you. Let's just say that it was strongly recommended by some people that I respect. People who travel in circles that you don't know even exist. These people thought that it might be helpful during the next year and a half. They thought that I should have someone to chat with, someone like you. However, after meeting you, it appears to me that you are not an obvious good choice. Perhaps the chief of an acclaimed international institute would have been better. But, others prevailed and I am here. And you, why did you agree to chat with me, Stan?" Sam asked. "Because Gabby strongly urged me to at the request of her father, Mr. Westerfield," I responded. "And did you have a choice, Stan? I don't think you would have voluntarily agreed to see me in view of the antagonism between us," said Sam. "Let's just say Gabby prevailed upon me," I told him. "I see, you were threatened. You were advised that maybe if you didn't chat with me your practice would be, let's say, less profitable. You're a scumbag Stan. I told you once and I'll tell you again, you stand for nothing. You should have refused to see me if you hate me that much. But no, you choose not to lose money. I think you need therapy Stan," Sam declared. "Maybe, you're right," I said. The more I spoke with Sam the angrier I got. He got under my skin. He had my number. There are always some people in this world that ring your bell as soon as you see them. "You're right, Sam. Let's end it right now and call it quits. Our chat is over." I sat in silence. Sam sat in silence. I threw out the challenge and now the ball was in Sam's court. We both stared at each other. I had mixed emotions. One part of me felt that I finally took the first step towards ending the long march down the dark alley and was willing to accept a decidedly reduced lifestyle. The other part of me felt that it was correct therapeutic technique to challenge the patient. I wanted Sam to walk out the door. Fuck him. I was broke before in my life and I didn't fall apart. I could be broke again. I continued to stare at Sam. It was clear that he was weighing the consequences of walking out. He wasn't worried about me. He was worried about his friends. Sam walked out.

SESSION NOTES

Sam was brighter than I anticipated. I should have realized that Sam did not get to be rich and powerful because he was stupid. It was clear that my intense dislike of Sam required me to see him as a person of reduced intellectual capacity. This was my problem, not Sam's. I didn't view Sam as a bright person with emotional problems. I needed to view him as a person of mediocre intellectual capabilities. Sam was consistent in his opinion of the value of therapy and me as a therapist. I challenged Sam to end his relationship with me and he walked out. My challenge was an attempt to see if he would oppose the request of Mr. Westerfield and his unknown group. Sam was willing to end our relationship and stand up to Mr. Westerfield. I still have not formulated an initial diagnosis and it is my considered opinion that I will not get a chance to formulate any diagnosis.

When I heard the sound of the door close behind Sam, I was actually relieved. It wasn't a make believe relief but an actual relief. "Big fucking deal", I thought, "so I'll have to rearrange my financial life." In today's jargon, I felt empowered. I was psyched and ready to get it on. Fighting the good fight instead of hanging out in the shadows trying to manipulate the means to get a desired end. I was elated. It was 2:45 p.m. in the afternoon. Too early to go out so I decided to fix me a gin and tonic and head out to the backyard. Four tonics later, I was feeling good, real good and it was 6:00 p.m. I checked myself out in the bathroom mirror, fixed my hair, sprayed on some cologne and left the apartment. I felt free. I went over to the neighborhood bar. I wanted to call Elicia but I didn't. I didn't need her anymore as my shrink. She was a keeper though. I ordered another gin and tonic and surveyed the bar for new prospects. I wanted to get laid. Among four people down to my left was a lovely young woman who was checking me out. I winked at her in a dramatic way conveying a put on kind of style. She laughed. I knew she had a sense of humor. I was ready to walk over and start the big flirt when someone tapped me on my shoulder. I immediately thought E. It wasn't. "Gabby, what are you doing here?" I asked. I was more than surprised. I was pissed. Just as I was about to celebrate walking out of the dark alley to the light, Gabby pulled me back in. It was a short-lived freedom. "Stan, I have to talk to you," Gabby said. Gabby's eyes were bright red. It was clear that she had been crying. A lot. Out of the corner of my eye I caught E walking through the door. E glanced at Gabby and the new girl who was staring at me. I surveyed in an instant all three women, the new girl, E and Gabby. What a fucking mess. I pulled Gabby to the very front of the bar. Next to the entrance door, on each side, there was a little sitting area that you could look out the window. I motioned to the bartender for another round and asked Gabby why she had been crying. "Stan, I have bad news for you. I have real bad news. Sam announced to daddy that he didn't have to come to see you anymore. That you threw him out," Gabby said. "Yeah, so," I replied. "Unless you agree to see Sam, I must file a report with the authorities that we had sex. Daddy wants me to go so far to say that you coerced me into sex. Not only does he want to strip you of your license but also he wants to put you in jail. I'm sorry, Stan, I'm so very, very, sorry," Gabby whispered. I wasn't going to ask her what she was going to do. E stood five feet away at the front of the bar and didn't take her eyes off us. She watched every move. The new girl in the middle of the bar glanced over periodically and watched every move that Gabby, E and I made. I felt that I was on trial. I thought that I should attempt to re-arrange the scene to my advantage so that Gabby, E and the new girl would look favorably upon me. Unfortunately, anger welled up. I was enraged. "Fuck you, Gabby," I blurted out. I swung around to E and told her to stay away. I glared at the girl in the middle of the bar as if she had something to do with all of this shit. I walked out. When I got home, I fixed myself a gin and tonic. I kept on drinking. I fell asleep in the backyard on the porch.

SESSION THREE

Sam arrived promptly at 2:00 p.m. on Wednesday and took his seat in front of my desk. Sam's presence indicated that extreme pressure had been put on him to continue with his appointments. I did not know whether he knew if the same pressure had been put upon me to accept him into my office. Sam did not say a word. I decided to ask questions and make an attempt to gather information. Playtime was over. My entire existence had been threatened. My license and my freedom were in jeopardy. I was in no mood to play games and decided to take a more direct interventionist approach. "How are you doing with your friends?" I asked. "What friends?" Sam asked. "Your friends. You know, the people that you consider close?" I asked. Sam had a look of bewilderment on his face. "Let me be more specific. Let's take France, for example," I said. Sam thought for a moment. "France is a smuck, plain and simple. I had a problem with Iraq in the Middle

East and I asked France for some help. Go with me and invade Iraq and take care of some business. Iraq had weapons of mass destruction. I thought having those weapons were contrary to my interest and the interest of my relatives and my family. Well, France gets up on its' high horse and decides in its' infinite wisdom to go against me. France goes to my other friends and tells then not to help me. Screw France. France will get punished. I had my spokesman go out and publicly state that France is going to get punished in as many ways as I could think of," Sam stated. "So, because France didn't want to go along with you, you want to punish them?" I asked. "Yes. France said we should let the United Nations go into Iraq and conduct a search for weapons. France said that the United Nations should be given time to find the weapons that I didn't want Iraq to have," Sam said. "So, France only disagreed with you as to the method of how to deal with Iraq? "Yes, that's right," Sam stated. "Well, did you need France's help in your plans against Iraq?" I inquired. "Are you kidding? I kicked the shit out of Iraq ten years ago and they never recovered. Need help? What a joke. You ever hear of that little ditty, 'yea, though I walk through the valley of the shadow of death, I shall feel no evil, because I'm the meanest person in the valley.' Well, that's me. I don't need anyone's help. I am the meanest man in the valley," Sam said. "How long have you been friends with France," I asked. "We've been friends since childhood. He helped me out once when England was kicking America around. I helped him out in World War II." "So you have had a really long friendship?" I asked. "Yes, since childhood," Sam responded. "So, simply because France had a different approach to Iraq, you want to punish them," I asked. Sam responded that it wasn't only that France didn't agree with him. France actively sought to persuade others not to go along with his idea. I asked Sam how he felt about that. "I'm much bigger and richer than France. Nobody goes against me, especially France. France tried to embarrass me in front of other friends that I have. France actively pursued them to disagree with me. That's wrong. When I say Iraq has got to be taken care of, Iraq has got to be taken care of," Sam declared. "Well, did France get your other friends to go along with the French position?" I inquired. "Yes, France did and don't think I'll ever forget that. France is dead in my book. You understand? Dead." "How are you going to punish France?" I inquired. "In as many ways as I possibly can. I am going to undermine France in every way I can. Nobody disagrees with me. Nobody. When France tried to get my other friends on his side, it's like they committed suicide," said Sam. "It seems like a rather severe punishment for a difference of opinion," I said. "Nothing short of killing that French bastard would appease me," Sam declared. It was clear that Sam liked to talk about himself. "Sam, what other friends did France get on their side?" I asked. "Well, let's see, he got Russia, China, Germany and lots of others. France went so far as to threaten some of my friends that if they didn't go along with France, France would not let them into a union France controlled. They call it the European Union. I don't care about those guys. They're little and insignificant. It's the Old Europe. I'm courting the new Europe, Bulgaria, Estonia, Poland and other small countries I can't remember. I have dealings with Germany, China and Russia and I'll get them back too, I swear it. How in the hell can anyone ever think that one can screw with Sam and get away with it," Sam said. "How about your neighbor to the north of you, Canada?" I looked at my watch. "Time's up, Sam." Sam slid a gift certificate in the amount of $300.00 to Paragon Sports and walked out the door. He looked disappointed.

SESSION NOTES

Although this was my first session with Sam wherein we spoke for an extended period of time, it was clear that Sam is experiencing problems with his friends. He boasts of his greatness. He claims that he doesn't need friends who don't go along with his wishes. Sam appears to be vengeful although I didn't fully develop this topic with him. I did not press Sam for details but merely wanted to get a general overview of his current relationships. Sam's problems with Iraq will be fully explored at a later time as well as his plans for "punishing France." Without making any diagnosis whatsoever, I will research DSM-IV section 301.7: Anti-Social Personality Disorder. I believe it best to let Sam talk as much as he wants. I will move from the general to the specific over time. Sam feels at ease in talking about his relationships and has no problem expressing his strong feelings. I am acutely aware, that in most instances, I do not have enough knowledge to even begin to ask the right questions. I'm an easy mark for Sam to bullshit me. Extended research is indicated. As a reminder, I wrote again in my notes, that extended research was indicated.

SESSION FOUR

Sam arrived at 1:55 p.m., five minutes ahead of schedule. The door slammed behind him. It was intentional. I knew he was angry. I thought that this might be a good session. "How are you, Sam?" I asked. "You know how the hell I am," he quickly answered. "I am pissed. I mean really pissed," he said. "About what?" I inquired. Did you see the stock market over the last several days? It's going down, Goddamn down. And the unemployment numbers are going up. Goddamn up.

It's taken a long time for people to like me. Years ago, I couldn't do anything right. Now, I can't do anything wrong. And I don't want that to change. You hear me. I don't want that to change," Sam said. "So, how much money did you lose?" I asked jokingly. "Lose. I don't lose money you moron. You make a living, I make money. I earn thirty per-cent on my money. Guaranteed. I don't worry about losing money. I'm worried about my reputation," he said. "How is it that you earn thirty per-cent?" I asked. "It's where the big boys play. It's an exclusive club. Not for you. All the international big boys." "What's the name?" I asked. "Give it a rest, Stan, you're a little guy making a living," he said. "So, is it this international big boys club that forced you into therapy?" I asked. "Nobody forces me," Sam responded emphasizing "me." "Well, the numbers aren't going to get any better," I declared. "What the hell do you know? If you knew about money you wouldn't be doing this useless crap would you?" Sam declared. "Well, here we are, Sam. It's the summer of 2003. What, if anything is going to pump up those numbers? People are out playing around, taking trips, working in their garden, going to their kid's soccer games. Why would anyone think that all of a sudden, your relatives and their families are going to wake up one day and go on another spending spree? It isn't going to happen anytime soon and the numbers are going to get worse. What's going to happen when your relatives start lying off employees? Look at what's going on. You have had three huge tax cuts over the last three years. Interest rates have been cut thirteen times in that same period and now stand at 1%, the lowest it has been in 40 years and what did you get, maybe 1-2% growth over that same period. My theory is that," Sam interrupted and started screaming at me. "You're a dumb shrink you idiot, not a market analyst. What the hell am I doing here? WHAT THE HELL AM I DOING HERE? If I wanted financial advice I'd go to my club. They're always right and never wrong. This is a bad day. Here I am, the great Sam reduced to sitting in a shrink's office listening to some self proclaimed financial guru shrink who makes a stinking $300,000.00 a year. What a joke," Sam stated. "Well, I'm at a loss about what I'm supposed to be doing. You hate me. You hate therapy. We're both forced into this relationship against our will so I figured we might as well chat about anything that comes up. You walked in here upset about money. So money is a good place to start. Besides what are you going to do, freak out every month watching the numbers go against you when you could be looking at the numbers more clearly and coming up a reasonable plan to improve them," I said. Sam glared at me. He was enraged. "Look you little piss-ant. All my relatives and their families through their representatives agreed with me and passed legislation authorizing the three tax cuts. My friend Alan Greenspan cut interest rates thirteen times and you are telling me that in your infinite wisdom the collective knowledge of the experts are wrong. Stan you need a shrink," Sam said. "And what do you have for all your efforts? A lousy 1-2% growth rate! That rate doesn't insure job growth. Look, Sam you're right. We shouldn't be talking money right now," I said. "Right now," he blurted out. "How about right never," he continued. "Sam, let me tell you what I'm supposed to be doing," I said. "I don't care what you're supposed to be doing," Sam responded. Right then, the anger started rising from my feet and marched inexorably up to the very top of my head. I knew the veins in my neck were protruding because I could feel them. I lost my temper. I was enraged. I stood up and presented all of myself to Sam. Sam stood up. I was large and fit. Sam was large and fit. "Look you fat fuck. I'm going tell you what I'm supposed to be doing whether you like it or not." Right then, I circled around my desk and moved quickly towards the door blocking his exit. It was going to be a confrontation. "What I'm supposed to be doing is helping you and I think you need a lot of help. Major fucking help. Number 1-Personality traits are enduring patterns of perceiving, relating to and thinking about the environment and oneself that are exhibited in a wide range of social and personal contexts. Number 2- when personality traits are inflexible and maladaptive and cause significant functional impairment or subjective distress they constitute Personality Disorders. You Sam, have a lot of fucking disorders and you don't even know it." Sam made a motion towards the door. I was so fucking pissed off that I blocked the doorway. I was ready for a fight. Fuck this fucking moron I thought. "Number 3-The essential feature of a Personality Disorder is an enduring pattern of inner experience and behavior that deviates markedly from the expectations of the individual's culture and is manifested in at least two of the following areas, cognition, affectivity interpersonal functioning, or impulse control. This enduring pattern is inflexible and pervasive across a broad range of personal and social situations and leads to clinically significant distress or impairment in social, occupational or other important fucking areas of functioning. This pattern is stable and of long duration and the pattern is not fucking better accounted for by another mental disorder and is not due to drugs or a medical fucking condition. Now, I want to know, do you take huge fucking quantities of drugs and fall on your head, because if you didn't, then you have a fucking personality disorder, Jack," I shouted. Sam moved back, regained his composure and stared at me. I could tell he was contemplating his next move. The possibility of physical violence hung over both of us. I thought I was done shouting but I wasn't. The anger swelled up again from my feet and raced to my head. I wasn't done. It was uncontrollable and renewed and I felt justified. As Sam would say, I was standing up for something. Myself. "And another thing, you fat piece of shit. I can see by the way you're looking at me you don't have a fucking clue what I'm talking about. Well, let me put it in plain English so even a joke like you can understand. Your boys are being picked off, shot and killed in the fucking desert and you go on national television for the entire world to see and say, "bring em on." Guess what. You increased the number of attacks threefold. You break off agreements with your international friends. You start fights with your friends Gerhard, Jacque and Vladimir and now you're stuck in the middle of the fucking desert and the whole world is watching and hoping you fail. You got that, fuck face. And nothing is ever your problem. It's always something or someone else. You're great. You're right. And I hear it on good authority that God himself told you to do these things. You got a huge, severe Personality Disorder." With that, Sam stepped back another foot, sucked up some air and plunged his body right through mine. On the way in, he looked me right in the eye and spit in my face. I went flying from his weight and the force of his blow, which knocked me into the center vestibule between my office and the kitchen. That was the first physical confrontation I had had since I was six. He stormed out of my office and I thought that I finally got rid of Sam. I lied on the floor propped up against the closet door. I felt good. Confrontation was good. Actually, I enjoyed myself. I had no thoughts of Gabby forcing the issue to the point that I would be poor, in jail and destitute. None of that entered my mine. Fuck it. It was one on one in the face of justified physical violence. I must have sat there for an hour. I was lost in my mind although I cannot recall exactly what I was thinking about. Finally, I stood up, somewhat wobbly and made it to the kitchen table. I opened up the refrigerator, took out a bottle of chardonnay and poured a glass. All I could think of was the physical feeling that my body was experiencing. I felt elated and exhausted at the same time. It was a new experience for me. It was a feeling that I hadn't felt for a long time. I imagined that the extreme athletes felt this way as often as they could. Scared to death, exhausted and exhilarated. Just like going down a huge mountain on skis for a world speed record. Either you crash and burn or make it to the bottom. That's when I realized that Sam was doing the same thing. He was either going to crash and burn or make it to the bottom victorious, nothing in between. The big issue was that Sam honestly believed that he would be victorious. He could never contemplate a crash and burn situation. The only difference between Sam and I was that if I crashed and burned I took no innocent people with me. If Sam went down to defeat a lot of people would suffer. I tried not to think. I dwelled on the recession of anger as it went back down to my feet and disappeared. I held my hands out across the kitchen table and watched the trembling stop from the rage that previously engulfed me. What a trip.

SESSION NOTES

There are no notes of any therapeutic value as it regards Sam. As I wrote the first line of my session notes "that there are no notes of any therapeutic value" I knew that I was employing a defense mechanism. I didn't want to deal with my anger. I lost my temper and became enraged, something that should not have happened. I told Sam that he had personality disorders and didn't even know it. He stormed out of my office. He spit in my face. I felt good about the whole episode and as the saying goes, it was "empowering." The possibility of physical confrontation existed on all levels. I do not know if Sam will ever be back. I think it might be an appropriate time to call Elicia. I reminded myself, once again, that I was a sitting duck for Sam's bullshit unless I did research, research, research. I wrote the word research several times, so that the word would be branded in my mind.

Of course, there are times when you don't want to write down everything in your notes as they may be used as evidence against you in a court of law. I called Gabby who was surprised and concerned to hear from me. After an exchange of pleasantries, I asked her to go out and meet me for a drink. There was distance between us with all the associated caution that ensues when a breach in a relationship has occurred. Both of us had our radar screens up watching for incoming hostilities. After all, we were two lovers who had been reduced to adversaries. I was confident that both of us could go back to the way we were. It just wasn't going to happen quickly. It seemed so long ago that Gabby and I were lovers. Only weeks had passed. She asked if everything was all right with me and wanted to know why I wanted to take her out for a drink. It was obvious that Mr. Westerfield had instructed her not to see me under any circumstances. From his perspective, he was keeping Gabby isolated and well protected in the event that he needed to blow me out of the water. He didn't want me to work on her. I wasn't going to encourage our friendship to soften any testimony that she might be forced to give against me. I explained to her that I needed to talk with her for our mutual benefit and that I had no intention of compromising whatever position she had to take. I might note, that at this point in time, I had lost two patients who had poor excuses for leaving. It was clearly a message from the Westerfield group of what I could expect if I did not play along with them. Gabby reluctantly agreed to meet me on Madison Avenue. I was going to use Gabby as a conduit to pass along what I wanted from Sam. I knew it would get back to her father. I told

Gabby to meet me at 6:00 p.m. I also told her that I had an appointment at 7:00 p.m. and that I would have to leave her at 6:45 p.m. I assured Gabby that what I had to say wouldn't take long and would be to our mutual advantage. I was still feeling empowered from my fight with Sam. I called E and told her to meet me at the same bar at 7:00 p.m. E was pissed at me for not having called her after our weekend at Montauk Point. I didn't blame her at all. My conduct warranted more than a slap in the face, it warranted a knee to the balls. I apologized to E and the sincerity in my voice convinced her that I was truly remorseful for not having called. I wanted to tell E the truth but it all sounded like a huge mess. I could hear the words coming out of my mouth and it sounded like I was a wacko. Fucking patients, forced therapy, international big boys club, secrecy, etc. It just sounded bizarre. I had to fudge the truth. Then again, I could tell the truth in a very benign way and spin my way into normalcy. I decided that that was the course of action to take. After trying to weasel my way into E's life again, she abruptly said "no." "Sorry Sam," she said, "I won't meet you. After making love with you all weekend and not following up with a phone call is unacceptable behavior, plain and simple. I'm sorry, Sam, I'm truly sorry." After that, the conversation was stilted and ended shortly thereafter.

I walked over to the Madison Avenue Bar at 5:45 p.m. and ordered a scotch on the rocks. The girl in the middle of the bar was now at the end and waved to me. I nodded back. I didn't know whether to walk over to her or not. I didn't want Gabby to see me talking to her. I didn't know why, it just felt as if I shouldn't be talking to some girl I didn't know when Gabby arrived. Then again, what I had to tell Gabby it didn't make a difference whether I was talking to some woman or not. I walked over and introduced myself. The woman's name was Haven. She told me that her parents thought naming her Heaven was a little off so they named her Haven. "And as close to heaven as you can get," they always told her. I bought her a drink. "It was quite a night for you several weeks ago," she said. "I sat there wondering whether it would be me, the woman who had tears in her eyes or the one that you were having a drink with. I lost. Heaven lost out. It looked like hell conquered you." If she was talking in riddles, she was pretty smart I thought. I told her that hell was going to walk in that door at 6:00 o' clock and that I had to talk to her and asked Haven if she would excuse me for a short period of time. Haven said she would excuse me on the condition that I would immediately return to her when my conversation was over. I agreed. At one minute to 6:00, I excused myself and walked up front. Halfway up to the door, Gabby entered. I turned around and noticed that Haven was watching every move. I politely kissed Gabby on the cheek and held her hand as I began to speak. Gabby pulled her hand away. "Gabby, I'll make this brief. It is simply to assert my position in regard to your Uncle Sam. I'm telling you this, as I am confident that you will relay what I am about to say to your father. I will only treat Sam under the following conditions. This is not a threat. It is simply a way to make the next few years' tolerable. I am no longer concerned nor will I be held hostage to whatever allegations your father forces you to make against me. I am prepared to lose my license. I am prepared to be poor and I am ready for jail. Because I am prepared for all of this, your father's threats no longer have any grave danger to me. I will accept whatever comes. I have no anger against you either." Gabby gave me a half smile and I could see she was visibly relieved. I continued, "unfortunately, should your father take the route of forcing you to bring me up on charges it will be nasty and public for all of us. Hopefully, it won't come to this, however, if it does, I fully understand that it contrary to your wishes and forgive you in advance." Gabby interrupted, "Stan, I am not at all comfortable with you talking to me this way. What happened to us? This sounds so businesslike. This is all so sad. I hoped that one day we would, you know, kind of get together. Maybe not marriage, maybe live together. Here we are in the middle of a bar and you're talking to me like I am some kind of stranger. Whatever happened to us?" she asked. "Gabby, I'm real sorry for this state of affairs. Maybe when this is all over, we can start again. Hopefully. Here is what I want to tell you. I will only treat Sam under the following conditions. Number 1-Sam must abide by the time rules. From 2:00 p.m. to 2:50 p.m. Number 2-Sam must pay me money for my services and not give me gift certificates. That's it. Other than that, Sam can be whoever he is. I don't mind the fights, anger, and the belittlement of my profession or me. After all, that's who Sam is. I am giving Sam only two basic rules to follow. I don't care how difficult Sam makes it to have a therapeutic relationship. It will only help in making a diagnosis. I guess all that I'm trying to tell you is that I'm ready to go to the mat. I won't back out if Sam follows those two simple rules, time and money. Remember, I'm willing to fight. So if Sam decides not to show up anymore and therapy is over, whatever your father decides to do; so be it. I am no longer afraid of the consequences and I don't blame you," I said. "Thank you, Stan. I was so worried you would hate me forever," Gabby said. I turned around and clearly indicated that our conversation was over. Gabby stood still and watched me walked back to the end of the bar. When I reached Haven and touched her on the shoulder, Gabby turned towards the door and left. I watched as Gabby walked out. "Well, that didn't look so bad from the back end of the bar. It was short, sweet, no tears and no yelling. Do you mind telling me what that was all about?" asked Haven. "Yeah, I do. I don't mean to be nasty but I was just wrapping up some loose ends so I could close an open wound." "I don't think it's over," said Haven. I motioned to the bartender for another round. "Hell comes in two's," said Haven. "What?" I asked. "Hell, comes in two's," Haven repeated. "Turn around, Stan," she said. I turned around and Elicia was just about in my face. E quickly glanced at Haven and looked her over. "Are you busy?" E asked. "Perhaps you need another Montauk vacation with a new partner. Someone you need to discuss your *business* plan with. Is that your line, Stan?" E asked. Before I could answer, E said, "I'm sorry Stan. I didn't come here to hassle you. I came here because I thought you needed someone to talk to. I guess I'm still a little angry about this whole thing. However, I just thought I should get over my anger and offer whatever help I could. Of course, I won't go to Montauk anymore, but that's your loss," E said. Haven tapped me on the shoulder and said she had to leave. She motioned to Elicia to take her seat. "It appears that both of you have something to talk about. Perhaps another time, Stan, when you're not so busy," Haven said and walked out the door. "What's up, Stan. How's your business plan?" E asked. "It's not the business plan I'm having trouble with, E, it's my current patient, Sam. Elicia, before we sit and down talk shop, why don't we just chat like we're friends. This is too businesslike for me. How the hell are you?" I asked. E said she was all right but that she was really pissed that I didn't call. Unfortunately, in these circumstances we weren't going to be friendly. We had to discuss why I didn't call and E was entitled to that. Being friendly was somewhere on the other side of the room. Why I didn't call was right in front of me in the form of Elicia. I figured it was either why I didn't call or nothing. "I'm thinking I didn't call because my life is so screwed up. There are things going on, that if I told you would sound like a huge mess. But now that I'm thinking about it, nothing really prevented me from calling you. Nothing. I realize that no matter how screwed up things were and are, I still could have picked up the phone and called. I apologize. I know that it doesn't answer your question. I could have called and asked for your help. I could have called and simply said hello. I could have called and asked how you were. I could have called just to touch base. Since I'm the one under analysis, I guess I should really think about why I didn't call you." "I guess you should," E said. Sometimes it's the analysis of the little things that produce the most profound insights. The question was, why I didn't call? Simple enough. The answer was elusive. I spent the entire weekend making love with this woman and I didn't call. Everything that happened to me subsequent to that weekend with E did not prevent me from calling. So why didn't I call? Elicia could see that I was really pondering this question and seeking an answer for her benefit and mine. "I didn't call because you're too fucking young. I had a great time with a great woman and you're too fucking young. It's as simple as that," I said. "I don't think you're too old. I really liked you. I had a great time. I loved making love to you. I loved your sense of humor. I loved Sunday on the porch reading the New York Times discussing articles. I loved everything about that weekend and you screwed it up because you didn't call. You know, I thought it was something I did. All this time, I have been pondering what I did wrong and the only thing I did wrong was something that I didn't do at all. It was because I was too young. Well, the way I see it, this is your issue, so let's talk about it. What hang-up do you have about age? You're in good shape, a good lover, fun and smart. You have lots of things you bring to the table. And your age is not an issue with me," E said. She repeated, "so what is your problem with being with a younger woman? Come on, Stan. You're in therapy and this is your free fifty minutes. Make the best of it. Dig deep. You've been in therapy. I'm sure this subject came up. Rehash it out." I thought about what E had just said. This subject had not come up in my therapy. "I don't think this subject came up in my therapy because I was dealing with marriage issues when I was in therapy," I told her. "So, it's a new issue," said Elicia. "That's even more interesting," E said. "Well, I'll just talk about it. I know I'm in shape and I know what I bring to the table. When I look in the mirror I see the same image that I saw when I was young. But I'm fifty-five. I know that I'm not young. But when I walk down the street or drive the car I see young woman checking me out. I say to myself, "don't they know I'm fifty-five. What's a young chick checking me out for. For some reason, it distorts my reality. The ladies should know better I say to myself." "Wait a minute, Stan. You realize that this is all in your head, like some great debate. First, you're an attractive guy to any woman at any age and yes I'm sure the young ones know you're older than them. But what if they want to meet you. Why is that such a big deal? Young or old, I think you have an issue with woman. You don't talk to or have any dealing with women your age, do you? Elicia asked. "No, I don't. I don't like them. They seem old to me. The spark that I want just doesn't seem to be there with women my age. So that leaves younger women that I find attractive," I said. "But, Stan," E interrupted, "look at how you set up the equation. You don't like the older women and the younger ones are verboten. That leaves you with no women and that's a pity because you're a pretty cool guy. So, why don't you like women," E asked. "I hate to admit this, but the bottom line is that I simply don't trust them. I think they're sneaky. Not a deep mysterious reason is it," I said. "No," E said, "but the answer lies with the early relationship with your mother and sisters if you have any," E stated. Elicia was a Freudian. "You should think about that because it is preventing you from having a full life. Bringing it all back to me, you didn't call me because you don't trust me. You think I'm sneaky. Was there anything that happened between us during that week-end, that wonderful week-end, that indicated that I was untrustworthy or sneaky?" Elicia asked. "No," I said, "nothing at all." "So," E continued, "you have this great internal discussion going on in your head, without me, the very person you had a good time with, debating with yourself whether I'm sneaky or not. I suppose you thought that I was going to hurt you somehow. Stan, I like you. I like you a lot. Right now, I have nothing going on in my brain that would make me untrustworthy or sneaky. I just want to have a good time. If you promise me that you'll think about these issues and continue talking with me about this subject, I promise you there will be other Montauk's. I like you and I want to continue building a relationship with you," said Elicia. All I could feel was that hate that I feel when another person is so disgustingly direct and correct. She was right and I was wrong. It was my issue. "E, I promise you, I'll work on it." Of course, I had no choice. I believe in therapy and talking about one's issues can only help. I thought about Sam. What could I do with a person who doesn't believe in therapy and doesn't like therapists? Elicia interrupted my mind meanderings. "How can I help you Stan?" E asked. "I got this patient, Sam, that I almost came to physical blows with. I was enraged. Sam doesn't like me. Sam doesn't like therapists. Sam believes in God and that all answers to life are contained in the Bible. I can't find a way to help him or even to get through an hour. I don't know how to approach this patient," I said. E asked if I made an initial diagnosis. I told her that I did not but that I believed that he might be bi-polar along axis 1 and had some personality disorders along axis 2. Elicia said it was clear that a therapeutic bond had not been formed and that I felt it was all right to attack my own patient, notwithstanding how obnoxious he might be. She suggested that I ask Sam, very simply, what kind of relationship would make him comfortable coming to my office every week. Seemed simple enough. "Thank you, E, thanks a lot. I will think about my issue with women and the equation that I have set up to prevent me from moving forward. I do not want to be alone for the rest of my life because I set up an equation that was contrary to my own interests." I kissed E on the cheek. She moved towards me and whispered in my ear. "That's not enough," she said. "Give me your tongue." I did. I almost felt human again. I spent the rest of the evening being charming and funny. Elicia laughed throughout the evening. "We got a shot to make this last for however long it lasts. This is too wonderful, Stan, not to work on the stuff we talked about," she said. I promised Elicia that I would work on my issues. I further promised that I would talk about them with her. She wouldn't be left out no matter how embarrassed I felt. Elicia smiled. We didn't go home together. "How about Montauk this week-end?" I asked. "Don't push it Stan. Maybe the following week-end and maybe New Hope, Pennsylvania instead." "That sounds all right with me," I responded. We'll see," Elicia said.

I was glad that Elicia and I were resolving our differences. I realized how important it is to have someone in your life that you can talk to. It's so easy to get caught up in your own bullshit and make delusions, reality. I had a patient that didn't like me and didn't like or need therapy. I planned, as suggested by E, to let Sam dictate what he would be comfortable with. I realized that there might not be a next time, that the next time could be a cop with handcuffs locking me up in the tombs of the Bronx with all sorts of nasty criminals. Or it could be a lawsuit seeking fifty million dollars in damages that would bankrupt me. Or it could be both. The horror of all those alternatives shot through my body and I felt electrified. I quickly dispensed with the bad feelings and thought about everything good that had happened with Elicia. Thursday, usually a bad day, worked out well. I still needed my little pill at 11:00 a.m. to keep me up. Actually, I listened more attentively to my patients. My patients noticed. They all said "thank you" on their way out, something I hadn't heard in a long time. I wanted to call Elicia for the weekend but decided to be patient and not to push it. Instead, I went to the Madison Avenue Bar in the hope that I would meet up with Haven. It was going to be my therapy. Take my age and her age and remove it from the equation. Whatever happened I would let happen. Of course, everything in theory is easy. Getting rid of the equation in practice would be extremely difficult. After all, how do you get rid of fears that you formulated in childhood and still held on to fifty years hence? I was determined to try. I surveyed the bar upon entry and there was Haven at the front. "You move around a lot don't you," I said. "Got to keep all the boys happy at all ends of the bar, Stan. How are you? I see you've been stirring the pot. Got all the little girlies in the world upset, do you?" Haven stated. "All the little girlies, huh. I guess you've heard the rendition of Just my Imagination by Gwenneth Paltrow and Huey Lewis in the movie Duets." "Excellent, Stan," Haven said. She was impressed. "How is it that you know this stuff?" she asked. "I rather whisper in you ear Barry White tunes," and with that I leaned over and in a calm sexy voice said "can't get enough of your love baby." "I thought romance was off the radar screen, Stan. I didn't think a guy your age would ever do something like that," she said. "Too bad, Haven. Romance is the spice of life. It's what makes a great day even greater, if you know what I mean," I told her. "Yeah, well, why don't you older guys teach the younger guys that flowers still go a long way with us little girlies," said Haven. "I guess the feminists got in the way," I said. "Well, don't let them stop you. I still like flowers, Stan. Have you worked out your problems with your women?" "I think so, Haven. I really think I have. Well, let's just say I think that I understand what the problems are. Maybe over time, I can work them out." The rest of the evening I flirted with Haven with a view towards making love at my house. I asked her to go home with me and she agreed. We sat on the back porch and drank gin. We made love. Several times I had to dismiss the thoughts that she was too young. Leave age out, I repeated several times to myself. I did. For the first time in a long time, I had a good time and didn't let my brain get in the way. Haven had a great time and that was that. I made Haven a knockout breakfast in the morning and catered to her. Actually, she was quite a young lady. I didn't even know what she did for a living and didn't care. Unfortunately, Haven had to leave as my first patient was going to arrive in an hour. "What are you doing this weekend?" I asked. "I have plans but I can cancel them if you like," she said. "Yeah, I think I would like if you cancelled them. I'd like to go Cape May in Southern Jersey." "A weekend with Stan the man. Yeah, I'd like that. Call me," said Haven. "I will, Haven, I promise." Friday was a breeze. I loved all my patients. I loved my practice. I loved my life. I didn't know what I was so happy about but I was happy. I called Haven and we went to Cape May. It was a great weekend. I was at my best, notwithstanding the fact that Haven was 25 years my junior. So be it. I let it rest. Sunday night I realized I was in a lose-neutral situation with Sam. I could lose everything or I could be in a neutral situation listening to Sam for the next two years. I didn't know what was going to happen. Wednesday loomed large on Sunday. Monday and Tuesday went by quickly. I called Elicia and touched base with her. She reminded me of our conversation as to her suggested approach with Sam and my own personal issues. I told her that if Sam showed up I would attempt to employ her plan and reassured her that I was indeed thinking about my issues with women. She told me that she had a vested interest in me. I told her that I felt the same way about her. It was clear that New Hope was going to happen. "I'll call you Thursday," I told Elicia. "Don't forget Stan and don't let the mind gremlins get hold of you," E advised. I was somewhat anxious about whether Sam would appear. I was hoping that he would, as this was the first time I felt as ease dealing with Sam. It was clear that I had to disassociate myself from Gabby, at least temporarily. She was too close to the situation and her presence in my life enveloped me in a dark inescapable "Sam" world. I read my session notes and realized that I did not do any research. How was I going to understand Sam if I didn't know what his game was?

SESSION FIVE

At 1:59 p.m. Sam knocked on the door. I didn't know how to interpret the fact that he knocked. On all occasions he just came straight in. I decided that Sam was at least respecting the ground rules that I demanded. He arrived on time, a condition for continuance. I was hoping that he would pay at the end of the session, the second condition. "Hello, Sam, come on in." Sam followed me back to the office and sat down. "Sam, I've given a lot of thought as to how we can both make this a better relationship, at least for the fifty minutes that we are together. I think that you should tell me how you want to structure the time that we spend together," I said. Sam paused. "I have no interest in what you think. I do not care for your opinion, suggestions or beliefs. I have nothing to learn from you. You on the other hand, if you keep your mouth shut, might learn from me. After all, I am Sam. I lead this great family. I'll do all the talking. Ask one question in one area that you're interested in. I have nothing to hide and plenty to share. Most people listen to what I have to say. I strongly suggest that you do the same," Sam said. "O.K., Sam, I can live with that. I may need to ask you questions concerning matters upon which you are speaking so that I have a better understanding of what you mean," I said. Sam responded, "if you need to ask a question for clarification, that's all right, but I do not want you to interject into our conversation anything that might suggest that I'm wrong or that what I'm saying doesn't make sense. Everything I say makes sense. I have more knowledge than you. I know certain things, which you and my family are not privy to. You should sit there and learn. I want this to be more of an interview with a great figure in history than a therapeutic session. If we conduct ourselves in this way, it will be a great moment in your life. I wouldn't be surprised if that at the end of our relationship, you refund me all the money that I will have paid you," he said. The mention of money was a clear indication that Gabby had spoken to her father and the message of payment had been received, the second necessary condition to continue therapy. I was sure that Mr. Westerfield was going to make the payments. Sam would never pay me out of his own funds, as this would be a visible sign that Sam was in a therapeutic relationship. "Sam, I can live with the structure that you have suggested," I said. "The first question that I have for you is the problem that you are having with your long time friend, France." Sam sat back in the chair and made himself comfortable. It appeared that I was in for a 50-minute monologue. Hopefully, I would be able to ask several questions. However, I was presenting no opposition. Sam was a regular patient and this is how he wanted to play it. "First, let me say that France is no longer my friend and second, it is France that has the problem, not me. There is a saying among my friends, something in Latin, which I can't remember, but it means that I don't care if my friends like me as long as they fear me. France fears me. France made a huge mistake several months ago by opposing me in my quest to punish my enemy Saddam. Nobody opposes me. I put hundreds of thousands of my troops in countries surrounding Saddam in the heat and France decided to oppose me and actively went out and gathered others to oppose me. France said Saddam, an evil person, should be given more time to come up with the weapons that I wouldn't let him have. It's true, that we had some ineffective inspectors looking around for forbidden weapons, but those guys were monkeys. They couldn't find a hat on their head. France said give those inspectors more time. I said no. After all, I had all my boys sitting out there. What the hell was France thinking? I was going to let my soldiers sit there forever? I sent them there to invade Saddam's house and kill him. I don't like Saddam. He's been screwing with me for too long. He screwed with my father and he screwed with me. But I'll tell you the biggest mistake France made. He tried to screw with me in public. Can you imagine that? France wanted to take on Sam in public. Nobody screws with me in public. He got up in my face. Who the hell does France think they are? In my face! Then France goes out and tries to round up my two buddies Russia and Germany. Guess what, Russia and Germany decide to stand with France in their opposition to me. Well, screw them too. Those two little piss-ants will get theirs, but I have the biggest hard on for that weasel France. Cut off the head and the body dies. When I get rid of France, you'll see Russia and Germany sucking up to me for forgiveness. Life is simple in the big city. Now, you probably want to know what the hullabaloo was about all those weapons of mass destruction. Well, that's exactly what it was. Hullabaloo. Listen, we supplied a lot of the materials for those weapons back in the eighties. We backed Saddam in his fight against that idiot ayatollah living next to him in Iran and I knew he was using chemical weapons. But that was all right. Then Saddam straps on his jock and decides to take a stroll into his neighbor's house, Kuwait. During a meeting with one of my ambassadors, Saddam asked if it was all right to invade Kuwait and she winked at his proposal. So Saddam takes a stroll and I get a call from my friends in Saudi Arabia who are freaking out about Saddam's little walk into Kuwait and they demand action. Well, unbeknownst to you, the King of Saudi Arabia and I go back a long way, so I agree to kick the crap out of Saddam and prevent his walk into Kuwait. Now, listen, Saddam, being the little shit that he is, starts crying and begging for his life and promises to be a good boy. So, I demand that he allow my agents in and that he get rid of all that nasty stuff that we supplied him. Everything is fluid, you see. Sometimes you're my friend and then stuff happens and sometimes you're not. That's the way the international game is played. There is no consistency like you little guys want. I can love a ruthless dictator one year and kill him the next. I need to protect the future of my family. So, I divide up Saddam's house into no fly zones, north and south and monitor Saddam from the sky. I got people on the ground to watch what he's doing. I know what weapons he has and we destroyed a lot of them during the years after we kicked the crap out of him. I place an international embargo on Saddam so nothing can go in and out. I got Saddam pretty much boxed in. I don't know if we got all those weapons but then again it doesn't matter. Got any questions, Stan?" asked Sam. "No," I said, "please go on." "Good. I hope you're learning something. This is how the big boys play. Saddam has very few weapons and he doesn't have the means to deploy them, so I am not really afraid of him, but then again I'm not really afraid of anybody. Who out there can challenge me? I have the most advanced weaponry known to man. I can deploy and destroy anyone in a matter of days. Screw respect when you got fear. So you're probably wondering why I wanted to kill Saddam in the first place. Because I can! For too long, I have been the biggest, strongest, richest man in the world and I'm screwing around playing nice like I give a crap. Well, I don't give a crap and I can do what I like. It is time for Sam and his world vision to stand up and be recognized by everyone. I have it on the highest authority, from God himself that I have been called upon to take up this mission. It is the new millennium of Sam and no one is going to stop me. You got that, no one and no one can. My very select group of real friends and I decide that it's time we flex a little muscle and so we pick on Saddam. First, we kicked the crap out of him back in 1991 so we know how weak he is. Second, we know that we can kick the crap out of him even quicker than we did the last time with few, if any, casualties. That's a condition that I have to respect for my families sake. In other words, Saddam is the easiest target. Third, Saddam is sitting on the second largest reserve of oil. It's a win-win situation. Saddam was the easiest and richest target to launch the new millennium of Sam. We all agreed that we needed an excuse to get the world to sit up and take notice. I wanted to get everyone's attention that Sam is here, so Saddam was the first. It is easy, fast and lucrative. But you know as well as I do, that I can't get on the airwaves and say I'm going to screw over Saddam. So, what do I do? Well, we take this germ of truth called weapons of mass destruction and spin it into some global and immediate threat. It's all marketing. That's what my friends and I decided. Weapons of mass destruction were the best way to market an invasion and the killing of Saddam. Fear is a great motivating factor. Any questions?" Sam asked. It appeared to me that Sam enjoyed explaining to someone, even me, his grand plans. I think he wanted me to ask questions. I decided not to. "No, Sam, no questions, yet." "So, we market the crap out of this weapons stuff and everybody buys it. Much to my surprise, I am not getting any opposition, except from France. I'll get back to France later. So I market this invasion stuff and stir up my family who is already nervous from the attack on the World Trade Center. I think they're suffering from some kind of posttraumatic stress syndrome. So I equate Saddam with 9/11 as a constant reminder to my family of the danger and stir them up. Every time I mention Saddam I know they're thinking 9/11. But what's strange to me is that no one is calling me on this except for some liberal lefty little worms crying out there in the wilderness because no one is listening to their bullshit. Guess what? Most of my family believes that Saddam's people commandeered the planes of 9/11. I was stunned. I couldn't believe how easy it was. My family was buying into everything. Can you imagine that anyone would believe this would be a real war? This was going to be a cakewalk. So I gave them the trappings of "war." We marketed this cakewalk with embedded media, tanks, good graphics, heroes and all. Did you ever see a war without dead bodies? We have video games that are more violent. Rule number 1 of modern warfare is no blood and no bodies. It's got to be as antiseptic as possible. My family doesn't like blood. Give them good graphics. That's what they want. My buddies and I decide that Saddam is the easiest way to set off the new millennium of Sam with a bang. The world is now on notice. Don't screw with Sam. I have demonstrated my power. Besides, look at all the benefits. I use all sorts of weapons to destroy his country. Then I get a chance to rebuild it and buy new weapons." I interrupted Sam. He was surprised. "You have a question, Stan?" he said. "Yes, I do. Does this have anything to do with your guaranteed 30% return on your money?" I asked. "Now, now, Stan. Are you suggesting that my buddies and me are profiting from the misery of others. What a horrible suggestion." Sam's last statement was said with a little sarcasm. "So, the world's on notice. Sam has arrived. Guess what happens? That weasel France gets up in my face and tries to prevent me from launching my new era. Nobody screws with Sam, nobody. Now, I'm after France with a vengeance," Sam said. "Sam, I have a question. Your problem with France is that they simply saw things different than you. They thought that giving the inspectors on the ground more time to find those weapons would prevent the need for an invasion?" I asked. "Yeah, Stan. But France is playing it straight as if those weapons were a serious issue. The weapons weren't a serious issue. Saddam presented no problem. Every time I presented proof of Saddam's threat, people started poking their noses into the evidence presented and came up with issues about its veracity. Well, I took the best of the evidence that I had, spiced it up and spun it around to my advantage. Think about it. Aluminum tubes for uranium enrichment. Really. Buying nuclear material from Niger from someone that doesn't even exist. What a crock. It's almost laughable. Talking about laughable. I saw my friend Tom Ridge on television who cracked a smile when he advised the public not to run out and buy duct tape and plastic, which they did en masse. We were hysterical. It was then that it became clear that we could do just about anything we want. France knows what I'm doing as well as Germany, Russia and China. It isn't about weapons. It about dominance! Screw France for trying to stand in my way and to get Russia and Germany on their side," Sam said. "Sam, you can understand France making an attempt, can't you?" I asked. "Yeah, I guess. But France! What an arrogant country. I bailed them out fifty years ago and they owe me one. I didn't think France would give me any problems. I thought that my buddy over in China would give me problems. At the United Nations, France led a campaign against me and they lined up Russia, Germany and China. Now I got to go out and get a coalition of the willing. What a stupid idea. Something left over from the old days. But I have to play by some rules. To get my coalition of the willing, I have to pay these stupid little countries and make all sorts of promises. I mean, the great Sam hanging with the likes of Bulgaria and Romania. If anybody bothered to look they would see that Romania is another country that makes weapons of mass destruction. What a joke. Well, that's one idea that's going by the wayside. No more 'coalition of the willing.' From now on, it's the Sam doctrine. I can and will act unilaterally against anyone even if they present no present threat. If I perceive anyone to present a danger to my authority or my people whether now or in the future, I'll act alone. Screw the United Nations and screw some bullshit coalition of the willing. I had to promise those little brats that they'd have a hand in rebuilding Saddam's house. They aren't getting any contracts worth jack. Maybe some crumbs. Sam and his buddies gets jack," Sam stated. "Well, aren't you going to alienate a lot of people?" I asked. "I don't care! What are they going to do about it. I have the most advanced weaponry known to man. I have all the weapons. I spend more on weapons than anyone. I spend four hundred billion dollars a year on my defense. I spend sixty-four billion dollars a year on research for weaponry alone. In a short period of time we won't need troops anymore. Wars will be fought by advanced drones capable of flying at supersonic speeds carrying 12,000 pound bombs and it will all be done from some hole deep beneath a mountain. Ever hear of Falcon? Research it. You might find it interesting." I interrupted Sam. "Sam, if you fight future wars with robotic drones, aerial and ground, doesn't that leave people as the only target to go after?" I asked. "Stan, we have too many people as it is. The only thing that matters is the opinion of my family and right now I'd say I'm looking pretty good. They're buying what I'm selling," he said. "Sam, I have a question?" "Yes, what is it, Stan," Sam said professorially as if he was conducting a class. "What about those weapons of mass destruction that you used as a basis for beating up on Saddam in the first place?" I asked. "Well, France knows that I'll find very little, if any. Certainly nothing that presented a threat. If that were true, I would have killed him a long time ago. Besides, and listen very carefully, I don't care. The new Sam doctrine says that I'll do what I want when I want. The only thing that I care about is my family and what they think. Now here is crux of this whole little puzzle that we have been trying to figure out. I have been sitting down with my buddies for years trying to figure out how we can get the family to go along with what we want to do. We were coming up with all sorts of very complicated intellectual theories. One day, my buddies and I are sitting around playing black jack at the ranch. The television is on and one news story on CNN catches someone's eye. It's a story about how much my family knows about its own history. I mean real simple stuff. The dumbest idiot in France's family would know the answers. Some guy pounds on the table and screams for everyone to shut up and watch. The game stops and we watch this story on CNN. The interviewer asks random people what their unalienable rights are. Half the idiots don't know what the word 'unalienable' even means and the other half doesn't have a clue of what the hell the answer is. I mean, the unalienable right to life, liberty and the pursuit of happiness in our Declaration of Independence. Our very own constitution, the model the whole world strives for and my family is laughing like it's some joke. 'You got it, guys. You see this is the answer that we've been looking for,' he says. We all looked at him like o.k. what are you getting at? He says the answer to the puzzle is right in front of our face. 'It's not some complicated theory of how to control collective behavior. We don't have to figure out how to get the family to agree to what we want to do. Just to it. These people are stupid. Get it! They're fucking stupid. If you can't convince stupid people you don't deserve to be at this ranch. For us to pull off all this crap is proof that they're stupid. For example, the headline the war against weapons of mass destruction doesn't ring true, let's try Operation Iraqi Freedom. A complete change in midstream to a different issue and our family thinks the Iraqis are their best friends and that we should start a war to free these poor suffering people. Yeah, they're screaming, free those poor Iraqis from evil Saddam. Freedom. I mean we couldn't get away with that before. The media would have ripped our asses open. Now they're lying in bed with us. Let's face it guys, our family is stupid. Don't pay them any mind. Let's just do what we want.' It starts to sink in.

My family is dumb. I mean really dumb. You can sell dumb people anything. So I give it a try. We find two mobile units sitting outside some refinery, which could have been used to make weapons of mass destruction. Under close examination by experts, they would probably tell you that they weren't mobile labs. I go on the airwaves and say we found the weapons of mass destruction outside a refinery. The media says, 'Sam declares weapons of mass destruction found' and that is what my family hears. Weapons of mass destruction have been found. I commission a group to poll my family. We ask, 'have we found weapons of mass destruction in Saddam's house?' Three out of four people in my family say oh, yes, we found weapons of mass destruction. It's unbelievable. We go from two stinking broken down vehicles in full view of everyone and my family thinks that they are mobile weapon labs for chemical weapons and that we found them. It's truly unbelievable. I couldn't believe it, so I try it again. We find about six little parts and some plans that one of Saddam's scientists planted under a bush in his backyard twelve years ago. You got that. Twelve stinking years ago! Six little parts that you could hold in both hands that had been buried for twelve years. I go on television and tell my family that we found evidence of Saddam's nuclear program and guess what, my family thinks that those six little parts are evidence of some nuclear program. Show my family an image. Tell them whatever you want to tell them the image is. Tell them you saved their lives by finding these broken down vehicles and hopefully, we always get a laugh out of this, hopefully, you'll get a world renown Dan Abrams 'chilling.' If we get a Dan Abrams 'chilling' we know we did a good job of marketing. Can you picture that! Abrams showing a graphic of two rusty old vehicles and saying, 'chilling.' Or how about showing the rose bush where the scientist hid his nuclear reactor parts, 'chilling.'" Sam went into gales of laughter. He was laughing so hard his body started to hurt. "Sam, Sam, hold on. Times up. It's 2:50. Times up," I said. When Sam's laughter lessoned he realized what I had said. He looked disappointed. He put his hand into the inside coat pocket of his jacket and took out an envelope. I walked him to the door. "Stan, I had a good time. Maybe you do know something about psychology. Good shrinks listen and don't talk. This format I like. I talk and you listen," he said. Sam continued out the door and at the bottom of the steps turned around and said, "Stan, remember Stan, chilling." He walked down the block with renewed laughter. I closed the door and took a look in the envelope. It was cash. I could live with that. Sam fulfilled the two conditions, he arrived on time and he paid. I normally follow each session with notes. However, I felt like I was just blown away and had not yet come to my senses. I didn't know what to make out of my session with Sam. I walked into the kitchen and fixed myself a gin and tonic. I nonchalantly picked up the phone and called Elicia. "Elicia, Sam just left. I was blown away. I took your advice and didn't fight him. I just let him talk. You gotta come over. I'll start the bar-b-que and we'll have some drinks," I said. Elicia said she'd be there in thirty minutes. When I hung up the phone I realized that my first instinct was to reach out to Elicia, as if she were my best buddy. For some reason, I felt real close to her. I wanted her to come over. I wanted to share my feelings with her. It made me feel good to hear her voice. I thought about what E had told me. I should examine my feelings about women. Well, here were good feelings. Feelings I hadn't felt in a long time. That was certainly a place to start. I was lost somewhere in my mind thinking about Elicia when she came in. I immediately gave her a huge hug and kissed her. "Well, at least there is one person in this world who is happy to see me," she said. I fixed E a drink and ushered her out to the porch. "E, I'm blown away. I offered no opposition and Sam just went on and on. He enjoyed it. I certainly picked up enough information to begin to understand him. And by the way, don't think I didn't think about why I called *you* right off the bat. I wanted to be with you. For a moment, you felt like home base. Go figure. So, I am thinking about my issues with women. I haven't forgot. I will tell you one thing. It felt good reaching out to you," I told her. "So, what is he, Stan?" E asked. "What?" "You know, is Sam bi-polar or a paranoid schizophrenic. What kind of personality disorder does he have?" she inquired. "Hold on, E. I have got to settle down and recover. It was quite a session. I'm not back to normal yet." I needed time to get out of my shrink head. I told Elicia I needed more time and she fixed another drink. By the fourth gin and tonic I was more settled. At least, it felt that way. "Well, Elicia, if I had to tell you what went on it would be difficult. Sam is quite a character. Number one he is a fighter. He's big, strong, has lots of money and doesn't mind using all his assets aggressively. He doesn't like his family. He thinks they're dumb. He is extremely manipulative and deceitful and he has a grand plan for the world. Sort of like 'The World According to Sam.' He doesn't suffer any opposition well. Having a different opinion incurs his wrath. He speaks to God and God gives him answers. E interrupted me. "You mean he's delusional?" she asked. "I don't know what it means, I'm just telling you bits and pieces of our session." "So what do you make of it?" E asked. "You mean an initial diagnosis," I said. "Yes, that's exactly what I mean." "I'm not ready to make a diagnosis. I just want to talk about this. When I'm thinking clearly, I'll make a diagnosis. I have to think about this for awhile," I told her. "Stan, where am I sleeping tonight? With you?" she asked. "I wouldn't have it any other way, E."

SESSION NOTES

As I told E, Sam is big, powerful, rich and aggressive. Sam exhibits a rage against those who disagree with him. He is hostile and vindictive. He aggressively pursues others with whom he feels have slighted him in any way. It is clear that Sam distrusts anyone who is not within one of his select groups. Sam demands loyalty. He clearly believes that he and his friends are special and unique. He is deceitful and deceptive. Sam doesn't like his family and belittles them. I believe that Sam barely tolerates his family. This is an area to explore. I wanted to explore who the others were in Sam's special group but I didn't think Sam was ready to reveal such information. Sam has a plan to mold the world to what he wants. He believes in God and speaks to him. I will respect Sam's belief in his God, as it is clear that this belief is not yet delusional. At present, I think Sam has several personality disorders. I find that Sam's personality can comfortably fit within the following disorders (a) paranoid (b) antisocial and (c) narcissistic. Although there are some elements that could be ascribed to other areas as well, these disorders clearly fit best. This analysis is along Axis 2 and I make no assessment of the severity of any disorder. I will not bring up certain subjects like the stock market and in particular unemployment numbers. This is a sore subject with Sam and it completely knocks him off his stride. I will narrow the limits of my inquiry to develop more information about Sam plans, his friends, relationships and family. I will pay particular note to the severity of the personality disorders. Some elements might not be as strong as others.

New Hope, Pennsylvania, turned out to be one of the most pleasant weekends that I had had in a long time. I wondered if Elicia picked New Hope as a sign of symbolism. I won't describe in detail the events of the weekend. When I kissed E good-bye on Sunday night she said, "find any reason to distrust me, Stan, or did you find some reason to love me?" Immediately, I thought that E was fucking with my brain. I didn't hear this woman simply say "find some reason to love me." I heard something much more sinister. I heard bad entanglements. All she said was "find some reason to love me." I decided that just being aware was a good sign. Even though my mind screamed mistrust, I forced myself to let it go and believe that E was simply giving me reasons to love her. After the weekend, E gave me plenty of reasons to love her. Dwelling on the nice side of life is a lot more pleasant than living on the wrong side. When it came to women, I was always on the wrong side of the street. I forced myself to believe that Elicia was a good woman and not some sneaky little bastard with a destruct mentality. For my money, I could skip Monday and Tuesday and go with Sam on Wednesday.

Two weeks ago, I hated this guy and now I wanted to treat him. Life is just one big fucking series of ups and downs and ins and out. I even started to trust E a little. I kept on repeating up, down, in and out. Up, down, in and out. I had an insight. That was one of Sam's problems. Sam wanted his life to be linear. No ups, downs, ins or outs. Entirely straight and predictable according to the way Sam wants it. I knew instinctively that Sam would suffer major disappointments in his life if the rest of the world did not act in the manner that would make Sam comfortable. Worse, I didn't think Sam cared at all. I didn't think Sam had any problem with being hated. Nothing bothered Sam. Sam is right. Everyone else is wrong. I recalled Sam advising me to do research on something called the Falcon and I recalled my own notes that I should do research. Another week went by with no research whatsoever having been commenced.

SESSION SIX

Sam arrived at 1:55 p.m. He didn't just come in. He bounded in. He flew to his seat before I could even sit down. "I got to follow up on our last session," Sam blurted out. I knew Sam didn't realize what he had just said. He used the word "session." A milestone even though it was unknown to Sam. "I'm excited because I want you to completely understand what's going on here. I don't know where to start. After I stopped laughing about the Dan Abrams Chill Index so many thoughts rushed into my mind I almost called you on the weekend. I couldn't wait to be here. Let me get back to where I left off. I believe I was telling you about the function of the media. You remember, show the people a graphic and tell them what it is. Have an expert describe the object to give an air of credibility and move on. It works. In and out with a mantra or graphic and tomorrow nobody even remembers what we said, let alone understand it. They heard "we found weapons of mass destruction," and that's their reality. My entire family knows the truth as yesterday's tag line. Now take my friend Rupert. This man is a genius. He sees that the media is a pain in the ass to people like me. So he comes and tells me that he is building a major news network, with my help of course, and he'll sell my family on what a great man I am. He'll use all the fancy techniques that the media can employ today, you know, motherhood, apple pie, freedom, Sam is great with patriotic songs, boards of hero's, the whole nine yards. Guess what, Rupert turns out to be number one in the ratings. Everybody stands up and takes notice. He sells me and I help Rup if he needs a favor. Got it. Now, you may think that all my buddies and me are just sitting around at the ranch in some vast right wing conspiracy. We aren't. It's just the natural consequence and the final resting place of democratic capitalism. All the elements just come together. News is business. Politics is business. Government is business. Defense is business. Everything in my country is business. And the business of business is money. Now all my buddies are on the same page. This is a final synthesis of our mutual collective interest. It's the money stupid. We can all help each other because our only interest is money. How can I make you money? Well, you can help me make money by doing this. O.K. I can do that but I have to bring in so and so to get it done. Is there anything you can do for him to get money? Yeah, I can fit him in. It's all one big circle of money. I'll tell you, if I didn't believe in God, I'd swear that Darwin was right. Survival of the fittest! The fittest are the wealthiest and we have one common interest, money. You want to get ahead in the media, don't screw with Sam. I'll give you an example. My poor friend Tony goes on record that Saddam can launch a biological attack in forty-five minutes. The poor dumb guy sticks his neck out with a statement like that. With what for Christ's sake? With the rose bush trinkets? "Jesus," I said to myself, "Tony, how could you be so stupid." Just how the hell is Saddam going to launch a biological attack in 45 minutes. Tony is overboard. My friend Tony is a novice. There's a part of him that still wants to do the right thing. Anyway, Tony's media, the BBC gets all over his case. I have to bail him out. I call Tony and tell him to get on the airwaves and start calling the BBC traitors and screaming that they're helping the enemy, that their conduct is leading to more deaths of Tony's soldiers. I tell him to keep on hammering it home so that the totality of the repetition raises the allegation to truth. The people will do their part. They'll start to believe the allegation as truth. After all, if you say it enough times it must be true. Tony starts a campaign and bingo. Tony's people start to turn against the BBC. Tony's Queen gets in on the act and starts to question the validity of the BBC. Problem solved. So you see, don't screw with Sam. I'll make your life miserable. Now, since the media is owned by big business they know how to play the game. People who use to work for companies that my agencies regulated, now staff the regulatory agencies. When the regulators quit their positions they go to work for the very companies they regulated. We just didn't realize how fucking dumb my family is. We can do all this shit right out in the open," Sam said. "Sam, I have a question for you. You got a lot of smart people in your family and I'm sure a lot of stupid ones as well. Do you think that maybe they don't care?" I asked. "Now, that's a great question, Stan. My buddies and I have thought about that too. We think that we have a combination of both. We call them stupey dopes. Well, what can I say? The smart ones are too busy trying to get into my little club. They're the hardest working self-centered sons of bithces you ever saw. It's this group that we think doesn't care. If it ain't about them, they don't give a shit. Either way, it's working. I'm doing what I want. My buddies and me are building the future and no one is standing in our way. It just all came together. Get a bunch of people chasing the same carrot and after a while they'll start to realize it's to their mutual advantage to get together and work out ways where they mutually benefit. All of us understand this. Do you realize what's been going on with my family? Their houses are imploding. They're working themselves to death. They take no vacation and when they do they feel guilty about it. They're working longer and harder. They're maxed out on debt and they still think they're living in the best place in the world. Don't ask me? I don't have an answer. I'll tell you something even funnier. Because they're such a miserable lot of little shits give them someone to hate and they go at it. And I mean at it with a vengeance. Take that jerk France, for example. God, if my family ever heard me say France the jerk they would be repeating it like crazy. They would eat that up in a New York minute. Maybe I'll tell my media guys to use it. France the jerk, chilling." Sam burst out laughing. "Any questions, Stan?" Sam inquired. "No, Sam. You're on a roll, please continue," I responded. "Well, my family takes on France with a vengeance. We don't have French fries. We now have freedom fries. No more French Toast, we have freedom toast. No French kissing. Besides these stupid little things, my family decides to boycott French wine and French restaurants. They won't even go to France and to go one step further the student exchange program between France and America isn't working because no one in my family wants to house France's little kiddies. Remember the movie Twins with Arnold and Danny. In that movie there's a line that Danny says, 'you fuck with me, you fuck with my family.' Life is good. They love me, Stan. They just love me." This seemed like a perfect place to ask a question. I didn't want to ask Sam a fluff ball question where he goes on again for another twenty minutes. I didn't want to shut him up either. I remembered the last time I brought up numbers. I knew the subjects that I should, at least for the present, stay away from. I decided to ask Sam a question about his family. He seemed to both admire them and dislike them. "Sam, I would like to know something. Do you like your family? I'm having trouble figuring out whether you like them or not?" I asked. "Actually, I don't. I like my very special small circle of buddies. It's an elite club, an elite club of very special people. People like me. There aren't a lot of people in my family that are like me. I'm far and away the best, except for my buddies. My family, well, they're whiny little shits. All they care about are themselves. Give me this. Give me that. My issues, my health, my wealth. Me, me, me. All they think about are themselves. My brothers before me created this mess. They gave those little brats everything. I always carry around two things, Stan. The Bible and the Constitution of this country. Now, if I gave you the Constitution, you would be hard pressed to find things like Medicare, Social Security or the right to privacy. We handed them everything and they became spoiled little brats. Now, I've got to start to take things away. They got a right to their life. I won't kill them. They got a right to their liberty. Well, I won't jail them. Maybe. If you agree with me, I won't jail you. If you disagree with me, well, let's just say I can call you a lot of things and get you locked up indefinitely without charges or any other little nice-ties. Oh yeah, my family got a right to their happiness, whatever the hell they think that is. But where does it say they got a right to freebies. It doesn't and they don't have a right to all this crap. This little document says the following: The Congress shall have power to lay and collect taxes, duties, imposts and excises, to pay the debts and provide for the common defense and general welfare of the United States; but all duties, imposts and excises shall be uniform throughout the United States. It doesn't say and give goodies to Sam's family. It doesn't say to give food stamps and free bus rides and subsidized rents. My family has grown fat. These little babies think they're entitled and I'm going to change that with the help of my friends. We need money for the defense of Sam not the common good or general welfare. Times are a changing, Stan, yes, times are a changing. How does that song go, 'you better start swimming or you'll sink like a stone, because the times are a changing.' My family better start taking swimming les-sons. They're already sinking. Personal bankruptcies are at a record high. Just who the hell do they think they are escaping their debts to my business buddies. We are going to change that at the end of the year. If anyone in my family can pay anything they are going to pay. I don't care if they're miserable. Screw them. I like them when they are messing with France and I hate them when they're whining. Just look at them. They want to sue my business buddies for making them fat. Did McDonald's grab them off the streets and force a fat burger down their throats. No. My family marches in voluntarily and eats that crap. They don't even get off the couch. They eat more than they need to. They don't exer-cise and then they want money because they became one big fat family. Their insane, I swear to it. What's the nature of the lawsuit? I'm too stupid to under-stand that this crap and my sedentary life are going to make me fat. There you go again. They're a bunch of dumb mothers. Well, things are going to change. From my perspective, what my family has is a right to a job ifG they can find one. They can work their little asses off and give all their money to my business associates," said Sam. "Sam," I interrupted, "what makes a person a buddy or a friend or an associate?" I asked. "Not a bad question. Suffice to say that an associate is someone who I can make money off of but don't like him. A friend is someone that I like because he wants to curry my favor and I can make money off of. A bud, well, a bud is a bud. You Stan are less than an associate. Sorry. I mean my family has been cuddled for way to long and it's become way to expensive. Things have got to change and I'm going to change them. There is no better time than now. My family is worried to death over terrorism and it's clear that they're not paying attention. For example, the unemployment rate went up. I send out my associate Elaine and she says 'wow, unemployment went up, that's a great sign. Good times are just around the corner.' The dumbest shit I ever heard but that's what it comes down to. I can say what I want, no matter how stupid, move on and declare victory even though I'm screwing them up the ass. I'm not worried about any of this. I'll raise hundreds of millions of dollars to get reelected as head of the family and spend another four years beating up on my allies and family. I know this sounds terrible to you and you probably can't believe I'm telling you this, but that's how I feel. This is who I am. It's my personality Stan, take it or leave it. But, I'll get my way. There isn't anyone who can stop me. There are certain times in history when a person rules an era. It's my time and my era," Sam stated. I thought it was a perfect time for a question. "Sam, have you been acting on orders from God. I read in the paper that you have?" "Yes, I am. Sam. I believe you read that in an Israeli newspaper after my meeting with the new Palestinian Prime Minister Mahmoud Abbas. I told him that God told me to strike at al-Qaeda and I struck them. God told me to strike at Saddam and I did that too. Yes, I said that. What you don't understand as well as my detractors is the breath and depth of my convictions. I have nothing to hide. I'm right out front as to who I am. I have accepted the Lord Jesus as my savior and I have been saved. The rest of the world is sitting around scratching their heads trying to figure out who and what I'm all about. It's easy. I'm Sam, I speak to God and I believe in the New Testament and the Lord Jesus Christ is my savior. Knowing this, would anyone be surprised that I would be against anything forbidden by God. Gay marriage is wrong and evil. It is an act against God's will. Abortion is an act against God's will. I will not go against God's will. In my era, God will not take a back seat. God will be everywhere in my country because God is everywhere. For too long we have hidden God in the closet and now I have opened the door and I am introducing God to my family. I am proud and honored to have been chosen to lead the way. God is here and I am doing God's will. There is no mystery. There is only bewilderment among the unbelievers. Who in the right mind is going to go against me? Going against me is going against God. Only evildoers go against God. I will do whatever is necessary to protect my family and myself and whatever I choose to do is right because God is steering me. Just today I pronounced to the world that without my active involvement in the world, the ambitions of tyrants would go unopposed and millions would live at the mercy of terrorists. Tyrants have learned to fear and evildoers are on the run. This is all because of me. It is my mission given to me by God. Why should I talk to you when I can talk to God? Certainly you don't claim that your answers are better than God's. Your roadmap to salvation is that book on your desk. What's it called, DSM-IV? My roadmap to salvation is the Good Lord Jesus Christ and the Bible," he said. I decided to ask another question. I thought that a second question might be pushing it but I asked anyway. "Sam, that book on my desk, the DSM-IV, is not my roadmap to salvation. It is merely a guide to help me understand people so that I may help them understand themselves. That's all. Suppose, for example, one of my patients is having problems with his friends. I look for guidance in the book. How about your friends? France, Germany and Russia are mad at you. Their families and most of the world's families don't like you. I just read that your friend of forty years, Turkey is very upset for capturing several of their soldiers. Your best friend Britain, is very angry with you for subjecting two of their citizens that you are holding in Cuba for military trials that might lead to their death. I look in my book for guidance for those who seem to be having issues with their friends. I'm afraid you'll be left all alone in the desert heat while members of your family get killed," I said. "So, what's your question, Stan?" Sam asked. "I guess my question is how you think you're doing with your friends?" I asked. "The short answer is, I don't care. It's just not sinking in, is it? Let me use words that frighten people. I am on a messianic mission from God. People don't like to hear that, but that's the truth. France, Germany, Russia and what the rest of the world thinks about me is irrelevant. I know that those guys and the rest of the world are secretly hoping that my mission concerning Saddam fails. I know that they will not help me in my quest to rid Saddam's house of evil. In every crusade there are casualties. Members of my family will die and they will die for the glory of God. They are God's soldiers. Right now, France has incurred my wrath and France is suffering. If I choose to go after Germany and Russia, they too will suffer. I have not yet instructed my family to declare war on them. For the moment, I am confident that if I chop off France's head the body will follow. Germany and Russia will fall in line. France is suffering significant financial losses," Sam stated. "Are there other reasons for your anger at France other than the fact that he disagreed with you?" I looked at my watch. "I'm sorry, time's up, Sam. We will have to pick it up, next week," I said. "Fine," Sam responded. Sam handed me his envelope and left. I wanted to call Elicia but felt compelled to review the session immediately.

SESSION NOTES

I am deeply concerned about Sam's deep rooted and utter contempt for his family and international friends. His opinion of his family is that they are "stupey dopes" and self centered little brats. His lack of concern in regard to his relationship with his international friends is nothing short of astounding. I fear that Sam will be isolated and will continue to act out in a manner that is inconsistent with his own interest. It is apparent that Sam sincerely believes that maintaining good relations with both his family and friends is not necessary for a healthy life. I'm struck that Sam does not realize that the very fear and hostilities that he is actively creating by a crusade of his own making will not improve the "numbers" (stock market and unemployment) that he seeks. Sam is enveloped in his own world and misinterprets or reinterprets all events to reinforce his own belief structure. Sam has locked up his Turkey friends. He has even threatened to try two of Britain's soldiers in a military court. Britain is Sam's best friend on the international scene. Such a trial could result in death by military tribunal, which is wholly against Britain's beliefs. Sam doesn't seem to care. Sam is wholly focused on money. In addition, while I respect Sam's beliefs in God, I believe that Sam's getting his instructions from God is disturbing. Sam's only friends on the international scene are those friends that he has given money to. Sam is disturbed by this fact and promises to do whatever he needs to do without buying more friends so that the rest of the world sees that Sam has a "coalition of the willing." I am afraid that Sam will act out again and start fights with others in the international community and his family. Sam is becoming increasingly more aggressive. What is equally disturbing is that Sam's family seems to be in full support of Sam. That Sam would laugh at his family's own stupidity is revealing. Sam's analysis that they are stupid and self-centered might have some weight. I am further concerned that Sam's family will have an active and aggressive backlash against Sam when they realize that he's been "screwing them." Self-centered brats have a tendency to strike out when they don't get their way. It appears from all circumstances that Sam's conduct is going to produce an international and domestic disorder of significant proportions. I am leaning at the present time to an initial diagnosis that Sam has all the trappings of an anti-social personality disorder. On the Global Assessment of Functioning Scale (GAF) I am giving Sam a 35, major impairment in several areas, such as work, family relations, judgment, thinking, or mood.

However, in the area of international relations I am giving Sam a 10; persistent danger of hurting himself or others.

The DSM-IV manual states that the criteria for having an anti social personality disorder are as follows:

A. There is a pervasive pattern of disregard for and violation of the rights of others occurring since age 15 years, as indicated by three (or more) of the following:

    1. failure to conform to social norms with respect to lawful behaviors as indicated by repeatedly performing acts that are grounds for arrest.

    2. deceitfulness, as indicated by repeated lying, use of aliases, or conning others for personal profit or pleasure.

    3. impulsivity or failure to plan ahead.

    4. irritability and aggressiveness, as indicated by repeated physical fights or assaults.

    5. reckless disregard for safety of self or others.

    6. consistent irresponsibility, as indicated by repeated failure to sustain consistent work behavior or honor financial obligations.

    7. lack of remorse, as indicated by being indifferent to or rationalizing having hurt, mistreated, or stolen from another.

B. The individual is at least age 18 years.

C. There is evidence of conduct disorder with onset before age 15 years.

D. The occurrence of antisocial behavior is not exclusively during the course of Schizophrenia or a Manic Episode.

Notwithstanding Sam's protestations to the contrary, it is clear that Sam has violated the law and rules governing international conflict. Saddam did not pose an immediate threat to Sam and therefore Sam did not act in self-defense. From a technical standpoint, Sam could be indicted as a war criminal. Indeed, there are indications that several of Sam's family members have had suits brought against them for international war crimes. Although Sam, prior to beating up Saddam, invaded Afghanistan and beat up the Taliban, no one in the international community harbors any bad feeling about that crusade. Apparently, post 9/11, their was worldwide sympathy for Sam and he got a pass on the Taliban. I am only bringing up this issue as an indication that this might be considered a "repeated act" necessary according to criterion (1). As for criterion 2, deceitfulness, as indicated by repeated lying, use of aliases, or conning others for personal profit or pleasure, I believe Sam had made many repeated lies and was intentionally deceitful in regards to his actions invading Saddam's country. I do not know if this was done for personal profit. I am somewhat confident that I can rule out that that Sam beat up Saddam for pleasure. I was disturbed that Sam knew that beating up Saddam was going to a "cakewalk." Clearly, Sam knew that Saddam could not defend himself or his family and Sam's media buddies presented the horrors of war as sterile as they possibly could. I'm not sure if this exhibits "pleasure" but I do have questions in regard to area. It might be my own reluctance to believe that Sam could possibly murder for pleasure. This would be hard for me to believe. I might bring this matter up with Elicia the next time I see her. As to criteria three, impulsivity or failure to plan ahead, Sam exhibited some impulse control by restraining himself in not beating up Saddam as soon as he wanted to. I believe that Sam made an attempt to get the world community to go along with his plans. However, no one bought it except those that Sam bribed. I think Sam exhibited impulse restraint although the impulse was always there and colored many of Sam's desires. As a result, I believe that Sam became deceitful and conned others into believing that Saddam posed a threat. Accordingly, it is clear that Sam will lie in order to get his way. I do not believe based upon what Sam has said to me, that he will any longer seek approval from anyone. I think Sam will act upon his impulse as needed without resorting to or consulting with any of his friends, even though his relationships with his friends are severely strained. In regard to failing to plan ahead, the two most recent examples of Sam's assaults are telling. Although Sam successfully routed the Taliban out of Afghanistan, Sam never completed the job of rebuilding the country, which everyone deemed necessary to prevent Afghanistan from falling back into the very hands that Sam went to war with. It has been reported that no reconstruction projects have been commenced and that there are increasing attacks on Sam's troops. The Afghan warlords appear to be back in control of the provinces and Sam's friend Hamid Karzai, who was once the darling of Sam's buddies, is now begging for help. Clearly, Sam's expertise lies solely in destruction and not in cleaning up the mess that he makes. It seems that once Sam's impulse for acting out aggressively has been satisfied, Sam no longer exhibits any interest. It has been widely reported in the media that although Sam had a successful war plan in invading Saddam's house and beating him up, Sam had no effective plans for running Saddam's house once Sam got rid of him. As a result, Sam's troops have been left in extremely hostile territory and many are dying. I have read reports that Sam actively sought out and engaged with many of Saddam's former family seeking advice. Many reports indicated that Sam believed that he would be welcome with open arms. I am under the impression that Sam sincerely believed that all he had to do was kill Saddam and that Saddam's house would run on its own under the leadership of Sam's direction. It is also possible that Sam only listened to those former family members of Saddam that offered up information that reinforced what Sam wanted to believe. I don't think Sam understood that the source of the information about running Saddam's house might be tainted since everyone would want a chance to sit on the second largest oil reserves in the region. Whatever the truth might be, clearly both situations present evidence that Sam fails to plan ahead. Although Sam has demonstrated and said enough that I could conclude that three criteria have been met to state that Sam has an anti-social personality disorder, I believe that Sam has exhibited elements of the other criteria mentioned in the diagnostic criteria for anti social personality disorder.

I could not proceed to an analysis of criteria four. The fleeting thought that Sam might get pleasure from killing people stopped me in my tracks. I kept on going back to that line that my Sam., my Uncle Sam might get pleasure from killing people. Now, that's chilling. That's number 10 on the Dan Abrams chilling index. I couldn't recall ever having met another person that got pleasure in killing. I could understand Sam getting pleasure from his weapons but I couldn't believe that Sam might be some red-neck that believes that killing another human is fun. I could hear Elicia telling me that you can't separate the pleasure of Sam's technological killing weapons from the fact that those weapons kill people. E would say that getting pleasure from advanced weapons that kill is the same as taking pleasure in the death of the humans that were killed. I knew that I had to talk to E.

I went out to the Madison Avenue Bar for a couple of drinks. I sat at the windows looking out into the street and just stared at the traffic going up Madison Avenue. I was lost in my mind. I just couldn't believe what I was thinking about. Could the guy sitting right in front of me during our sessions take pleasure in killing? My mind was just a garbage can full of stuff. I thought about every image that I had watched on CNN, MSNBC and FOX cable news network. I couldn't recall a single image of a blown up body. The images I recalled were that of the bombs and their pin-point accuracy. The plumes of smoke going up. The fireballs lighting up the sky. Nothing about the people under those bombs with body parts strewn all over the ground. Some guy's head over in a corner and his torso twelve feet away. An arm hanging on a nail on a fence. How about the commentary by the media concerning the destruction. "Watch this," one commentator would say. "Look at that, right through the window. Unbelievable." Then the retired generals would wax poetic about the advanced state of Sam's weaponry. How Sam is the most powerful man in the world and that no one could match Sam's strength. However, I believed that Sam was fascinated and took pleasure with his weapons; I just couldn't believe Sam took pleasure with killing people, but how could you separate the two. I thought that maybe Sam didn't care. Maybe Sam was only interested in testing his weapons to see if they matched his expectations about performance. "Kill people, who cares!" I could hear Sam say. "Just look at how those weapons performed," he would add. I thought about that bomb reported in the press that got to Saddam's house to late to be dropped. I think it was called MOAB. It was a 20,000-pound bomb that was capable of killing and leveling everything in its immediate area. One of Sam's generals stated that it was great for building airfields in a hurry because the bomb leveled everything. I recall at the time that I thought it was Sam's answer as a non-nuclear alternative. I didn't think Sam would ever use nuclear bombs. Then I remembered that Sam said that if he didn't like the way his assault was going against Saddam, nuclear bombs were on the table. The more rumblings that went on in my mind the more I believed that Sam was ruthless. Nothing went off in his brain that was outside the boundaries of a "fair fight." After all, he just kicked the shit out of Saddam, at best, the equivalent of me starting a fight with an infant. The first section of the New York Times lay next to my glass. I picked it up and turned to the editorial page. There was an op-ed piece by William Safire. It was a make believe conversation between Nixon and Safire by cell phone wherein Safire was picking Nixon's brain for analysis of the political strategy of Sam. Safire wanted to know from Nixon how Sam would keep the center of his family in tow behind him. Safire wrote that taking charge of the world would dominate the center, intimidate all but the looniest on the left and keep him high within his family. I was beginning to think that this job was beyond my capabilities. I wondered about Sam's family. Were they really stupey-dopes? Were they self-centered little brats concerned only about their welfare? Maybe they liked the fact that Sam wanted to dominate the world. Maybe they loved the power of destruction of Sam's bombs as long as there were no blood or body parts, the ultimate in reality television. Real live death and destruction in your living room, rated for a general audience. No foul language, no blood, no sex and nudity. A fireworks display courtesy of Sam. To me it was surreal. I was sitting in the middle of a cyclone with the very man who was producing the cyclone. Once again, I felt that this whole matter was over my head. I thought that I could deal with Sam if he didn't act out aggressively. But it was the aggression and open hostility that frightened me. Sam exhibited a total disregard for the consequences of his actions. Dwelling on this, I concluded that Sam did not take pleasure in killing. It was just that Sam didn't care. Although, this was a much more frightening conclusion, it was easier on my mind than thinking that Sam enjoyed killing. I had a vision that Sam was just like a bull in a china shop walking around bumping into everything in sight and causing massive amounts of destruction. He was an animal who had no comprehension of what he was doing. He didn't plan ahead. Had he, Sam's family members would not be getting killed in Saddam's house. Sam is a psychopath.

"Hi, Stan." It took awhile to tumble back out of mind. It was Haven. "Hi, Haven, how are you?" I asked. "I have been watching you from the street for two minutes and you didn't even notice me," she said. "Yeah, well, I have been lost upstairs in the brain department." "Want to be alone?" she asked. "Yes and no. Yes, but later on and no, not right now. Sit down and have a drink," I said. Haven and I engaged in some polite conversation for about an hour and then I left. I promised Haven that I would call her the following week to go out Salsa dancing. She loved to dance. So did I. A salsa break sounded like what I needed.

I went back to my office. I grabbed my notes, made a gin and tonic and went back to porch to complete my session notes. The fourth criteria for antisocial personality are irritability and aggressiveness, as indicated by repeated physical fights or assaults. Just then, I was overwhelmed by tiredness. My brain was fried. I decided to pick up on the notes over the weekend. Thursday morning when I woke up I had one thought and one image in my mind. The image was that Sam and his family were like Dr. Evil and Mini Me and that Sam's "buddies" were the ones who forced Sam into therapy. My gut told me that Sam's buddies were getting worried about Sam getting his orders from God instead of them. I was not having a good time. It was one of those times in life that you experience a lull after a major start. I was excited for the last two sessions that I had with Sam but I felt exhausted. Even my forays with Elicia and Haven were wearing me down. It was just too much too soon. I decided to spend the weekend by myself and do a little more research into anti-social personality disorders. Thursday felt like the longest day of my life. I could hardly keep my eyes open during sessions. I popped my little magic pill that helped with my 1:00 p.m. patient but I crashed with my 2:00, 3:00 and 4:00 o' clock patients. Friday was better. I realized that not one of my patients had the same intensity that Sam did. With Sam, I always was blown away after the session. Friday finally ended. I did not go out. I did not answer the phone. Elicia had called and left a message. I decided that I would return her call on Saturday.

When I awoke Saturday, I returned E's call and told her that I was wiped out from my last session with Sam and stayed in on Friday night. She asked if I wanted company and I told her that I reserved Saturday for r& r. Elicia understood but was disappointed. She wanted to get together. I did not suggest Sunday during our conversation and after I hung up I thought that was strange. I always felt better after having spent time with E. I liked Elicia. I went out front and grabbed the New York Times, started the coffee and settled down to read. I went back to thinking about why I hadn't followed up with E and suggest that we get together on Sunday. I had no answer. Somehow I felt that I just didn't have the energy. I assumed that I had to entertain E. I had to be funny, bright, witty, charming and make love that would leave her exhausted and happy. Why all these assumptions existed I didn't know. Clearly, I was setting up an equation all based upon my own internal assumptions to reach a conclusion that I wanted to achieve. I wanted to spend my time alone. Saturday and Sunday. I was sure that I could tell Elicia that I wanted to be alone and I was sure that would be all right with her. I also knew that I wanted to be alone on Sunday because I was tired right now. Another good night sleep and it would be quite possible that I would wake up with a clear head and a body full of energy. I choose to cut off my contact with E based upon how I felt right then. I could have taken a different course of action. I could have told E that I was so tired I couldn't think of having company over on the week-end but that a good night's sleep and I could have a different feeling about the whole thing. I realized that the worst thing I did was not say something. Here was a woman that I knew wanted to be with me and I left her hanging. It would not have made a difference what I said to E so long as I said something. I realized that Elicia was sitting there hurt and disappointed trying to figure out what my problem was or maybe whether she did something. If I liked her why would it be all right for me to permit that kind of thing to exist? I probably had done that a lot in my life, left women hanging and wondering. I could smell that the coffee was ready. I went inside to pour a cup. I called Elicia. "E, it's Stan." "Hi, honey," she said. That caught me off guard. A simple, "hi honey" and I immediately was taken to a different place. A gentler place. A place that I felt was home where a little loving could heal all my wounds. "I need a shave. I thought that maybe you could come over tomorrow in the afternoon and give me a shave." "Well, o.k. No man has ever asked me to do that. I have never given a guy a shave. But why not," she said. "We'll eat, have a little wine, listen to music and if you're feeling particularly kind to me, I'll take that shave. If you're hostile we'll skip the shave," I told her. "Very funny, Stan. It's the most unusual request I've had in a long time. Sounds like a relaxing day. I'll be over at 1:30 p.m." E said. I felt a lot better. I went back to reading my paper and spent the entire morning watching the action in the garden. The cat walking on the fence. The birds perched in the tree. The squirrel that ran along the telephone wire. The bees. It was quite an active backyard. I hadn't stared at nature and listened to its peaceful quietness in a long time. I didn't think at all about my work or Sam. I just wasn't ready. Around noon I lit the bar-b-que and cooked some burgers. I went back to sitting on the deck and continued staring at nature's little play that was acting itself out in my yard. I put on some classical music and achieved a state of contentment that had not existed since Gabby first threatened me with exposure to the authorities. I was so mellow that the thought of doing some research was so distant that I didn't even bother to think about it. I fell asleep. I cannot recall what time that was. I woke up around 2:00 a.m. and was surprised to find myself in the chair. I made my way to the bedroom and fell asleep as quickly as I awoke. In the morning, I felt like going fishing or playing catch with someone. After a bagel and the Sunday Times I went to my closet and found my old base-ball glove. I took a walk to Central Park and found a teenager having a catch with his friend. I asked the kid closest to me if I could join in. He yelled over to his friend and asked if I could join in. The other kid shrugged his shoulders and nod-ded that it was o.k. The ball was tossed to me and I slowly walked away throwing the ball back and forth until I arrived at a distance that was equi-distant between the two kids. They were kind of surprised that I could throw the ball. I always believed that the best way to communicate with your child or friend was to have a catch. Conversation just flows naturally. The mind's natural guardedness is somewhat lessoned when a ball is coming at you. What comes out of your mouth is truer and cleaner. I don't think you can have a catch without having a little chat among the catchees. It all feels so natural. There should be a law that all moms and dads must play catch at least four times a week for at least an hour each time with their children. You can get more honest information in an hour than you ever get could in an 8-hour interrogation. I operated on three levels dur-ing my catch with my two teenage buddies. On one level, I asked the kids simple questions. I found out their names, school, brothers or sisters. Introductory stuff. On another level, I was remembering the times I played catch with my son and on the third level I was thinking about Sam. Not heavy thinking. Light thoughts. I thought that it would better if I didn't write session notes after Sam left. Sam was so intense and I was so blown away that I could not reflect on what I had wit-nessed to accurately describe what had transpired. I was too sucked into Sam to be objective. Waiting a day or two to write session notes would be better. I thought I should review my session notes, as they might not be accurate as to my initial diagnosis. Maybe Sam had a personality disorder other than anti-social that would be more accurate. Maybe? I missed the ball thrown to me. It was over my head. I had to go chase it. I tried to throw the ball to one of the kids from the point where I had picked it up. I got close. The kid picked it up on one bounce and screamed "nice throw." Unfortunately, I hurt my arm. I waved to the kids to get their attention, as I did not want them to throw the ball to me. I pointed to my shoulder and they smiled. One kid yelled "anytime" and I smiled acknowledging their invitation. Playing catch felt good. I walked back to my office and realized that treating Sam was having more of an impact on me than on Sam. In the five weeks of dealing with Sam, I ran the gamut of emotions. Treating Sam evoked some of the strongest feelings that I had had in a long time. At times, I wanted to both kill him and help him. At other times, I was just too blown away to feel anything. The bottom line was exhaustion and that's exactly how I felt this weekend. I decided that I needed more of a life than just therapy and working on my own personal issues with Elicia. I needed fishing, hiking, camping and more time outside. Life's answers are more abundant when you're doing nothing than when you're busy. I got back to my apartment as Elicia was walking up the stairs. "Where have you been, Stan? You're one big sweat ball. Well, I am going to make a little change in plans," said E. "Yeah, what do you have in mind?" I asked. "Just get inside and do what I tell you," she said. "I love when you talk dirty, E." She smiled. "O.K., what do you want me to do?" I asked. "First, you're going to take a shower. So get your little butt inside the bathroom," she said. "Do I stink that much?" "Stan, in the shower, now," E barked. "Yes, ma'am," I said. I stripped and got in the shower. I started to lather up the soap when Elicia said, "wait a minute, Sparky, that's my job." E was standing next to me naked in the shower pressing her body against mine. "The soap is my job. Now turn around with your hands up against the wall." I complied. E lathered up the washcloth and gently scrubbed me down from my head to my toes. "Now, turn around and I'll do the other side." Once again, I complied. E took any opportunity she had to press her body against mine as inconspicuously as she could. It was as natural as could be. It was the sexiest turn on I had in a long time. She knew what she was doing. I was sure that if I asked Elicia about pressing her body up against mine she would give me a blank look and say in a most innocent way "what are you talking about?" "O.K. cowboy on your knees," she said. Here's the sex part I thought. "Now, lie your head where it fits because it's time to wash your hair." I was melting. Fun time was over and I was out of the tub. E toweled me down and dried me off. "Buddy boy, get your butt on the toilet and relax. Stan, I want to put on some music. Do you have any favorites?" she asked. "Put on John Klemmer," I told her. E returned shortly and the sweet sounds of Klemmer's sax could be heard in the background. I rolled my shoulders and let out a big sigh. I was totally relaxed. Elicia reached into the tub, grabbed the hand towel and rinsed it out in the sink. Then she turned on the hot water, soaked the towel until steam came from it. "O.K., Stan. Sit back and relax," she told me. "E, if I get any more relaxed I'll go into cardiac arrest," I said. E laughed. "Come on Stan, I'm trying to do my job. Now this might hurt just a little but it softens up that little stubble you got there." With that, Elicia gently placed the hand towel on my face and made sure that I could breathe. I started to speak but E shushed me to be silent. When she removed the towel, I asked her what she was doing. She told me that she stopped into an Italian barbershop in Little Italy and told some guy named Salvatore that she wanted to give her boyfriend a shave and asked if he would teach her. She told me that Sal told her to stick around, watch and ask questions. She hung around for an hour, about four shaves worth and by the time she left she had all the guys cracking up. Elicia became knowledgeable at understanding the mechanics of a good shave. The guys insisted that she had to have two grappas before she left. Sal made it himself. It was homegrown white lightning in a plain bottle. Actually, E told me it looked like an old bottle of after-shave lilac. Elicia obliged. Sal told her that the grappa would steady her hand. I sat back and enjoyed. E pulled out a straight razor and a length of leather and started swiping away sharpening the razor to perfection. "A little gift from Sal, I assume." "No. It's a little gift from me to you." E proceeded to give me a shave with the perfection of a seasoned barber. I was in heaven. The shave was a compliment from a beautiful woman inside and out. I was pampered into butter. E said it was all over and we went outside to the deck. She poured us a glass of chilled white wine that she brought over. She fixed finger food to munch on. She let me settle in and then asked, "what are you thinking?" "I'm thinking that I could fall in love with you," I said. "Come on Stan, you know what I'm talking about." "Yeah, I know, but I have been doing my best to avoid thinking for the last forty-eight hours," I told her. "Well, we don't have to talk shop," E stated. "No, no, it's o.k. I don't mind. Being this relaxed will probably give me more insight than I have had since Sam came to my office." I put my feet up on the table, took a sip of wine and munched on some celery. "I'm thinking that Sam has such a powerful personality he blows me away after each session. Normally, I write session notes right after a patient leaves but it's not a good idea with Sam. He stirs me up so fucking much that I don't think clearly. I'm also thinking that talking to you is a great idea and

I'm thinking I need another shave," I said. "Well, you'll just have to wait. Any thoughts about what you're dealing with?" Elicia asked. "I'm leaning towards a diagnosis that Sam has an anti-social personality disorder. Sam's a psychopath," I told her. The psychology profession changed psychopath to anti-social personality. However, I made this diagnosis right after a session with Sam. I'm thinking that because he stirs me up so much that maybe I'm not seeing him clearly. I know he definitely meets certain criteria for that diagnosis. I had to take a break from finishing my notes and when I restarted my notes several of the other criteria that I felt confident Sam would meet didn't feel so right anymore. I should review my notes," I told Elicia. E had a question. "You know, other personality disorders may be confused with Antisocial Personality Disorder. Many disorders have certain features in common. You may have elements of Antisocial Personality Disorder but you should examine the criteria for Narcissistic and Histrionic Personality Disorders as well. However, I'm sure you were planning to examine all personality disorders before you made a complete evaluation," she said. "No, E, I wasn't going to do that. If I wasn't this relaxed I would never admit that," I said. "So, you weren't going to do your job and I imagine you don't want to do your job. You know, Stan, these kind of patients are some of the hardest to deal with and the experts suggest that therapists go into therapy while they are handling these guys," Elicia stated. "And ladies," I added. "The truth is that I wasn't going to do my job. Antisocial is close enough. I figured I could leave it at that," I said. "I don't understand what you're saying. That's malpractice," E stated. "I guess you could look at it that way," I replied. "Stan, you're to nonchalant about all this. We're talking about a complete failure of your responsibilities. If Sam is your patient, you owe him one hundred per-cent of your ability to help him. You just can't say oh, well, antisocial is close enough. You need to do a lot of work here, Stan, a lot of work," E reminded me. I knew I should have kept my mouth shut. I was truthful with E and I got slammed. But E was right. I was doing only half my job. Actually, I wasn't doing my job at all. I was faking it and I admitted it. I was sure Elicia made judgments about me. I thought E was terribly disappointed. "How pissed off are you at me, Elicia?" I asked. "If I say I'm not that angry with you, you'll continue to neglect your responsibilities and if I say I'm real angry with you, you'll do your job. That's not the issue. The issue is why weren't you going to do your job. Why was it o.k for you to fake a diagnosis? This is exactly the reason that you should be in therapy. You should be examining with your shrink why you don't want to tackle this patient with a one hundred per-cent commitment and dedication to making him well," she said. I was honest with E and now I felt like some little kid being admonished for doing the wrong thing. Even though I knew she was right, she was pissing me off. I wanted to ask about the skeletons in her closet as a way to deflect her criticism of me. But attacking E was not the issue. I was on the hot seat. "Well, Elicia, Sam gives me a lot of trouble." Elicia interrupted. "No, No, No, Stan. I'm not your shrink. Don't start talking to me about your problems with Sam. Talk to your shrink. I'm here to be with you on an entirely different basis. Not as your shrink, hopefully, as your woman. The shower, the shave, the munchies were not done so I could listen to your problems. I did those things as a women who is interested in you," she said. I wanted E to piss me off so I could start a fight and avoid being on the hot seat. Instead, I sat and listened. I had a vested interest in Elicia. I really liked her. I decided to go one step further down the path of truth as an experiment and tell E exactly why I wanted her in my life. "When I first met you Elicia, I formulated a plan that during my sessions with Sam, I would see you once a week and pick your brains. I was going to use you as my shrink. The reason is that I would have more wiggle room with you than my own my shrink. My shrink would keep me on a short leash. Why? I wanted to keep my options open with Sam. I hate him. He pisses me off. He brings up a lot of issues. Simply put, I was going to use you. It's not an admission that I am proud of, but it is the truth. One of my problems is that I like to walk down dark alleys and see if I come out unscratched on the other side. I do it a lot less these days than I did when I was growing up. It's where I get my juice. My heart pumps a little faster. The blood moves a little quicker through my veins. There is a part of me that wants to fuck around with Sam and screw up his brains a little bit. I knew I needed some therapy while I was treating Sam, so I figured I use you as a sounding board and still have a little wiggle room. So that's it. I never claimed that I was a sweetheart." E asked me if Montauk was a sham. "No, Elicia, Montauk was not a sham, but part of it was designed to start the process of getting you involved. Instead I got involved with you and not in the way I expected. I like you. You're screwing with my brains with every thing that you do. Part of me wants to just ease up and settle in with you and the other part of me wants to start a fight and back you off because I don't want to fall in love with you. I mean, slugging grappa with Sal and bringing over a straight razor after shaving lessons. I just eat that kind of stuff up. I'm just not use to these kinds of feelings. I have been single too long. I want you with me." I shut up and looked at Elicia. I couldn't see any visible sign of aversion to what I had just said. After a long pause, E said, "well, Stan, it takes a lot of nerve to admit the kind of things that you just admitted. It's not easy to sit here and listen to a man that you like admitting that he wanted to use you. You're very cunning. You have certainly given me enough justification to get up and leave. You like me and I like that. I could get upset but it would only be because my brain tells me to. Deep down, I respect your honesty. I'm not upset. I'm a little concerned for you. I don't like you walking down dark alleys. You could get hurt and hurt me in the process. Just keep on talking to me, Stan. We all have some baggage and that includes me. I'm not going to walk out. There are lots of things that I love about you. The dark side of your personality does not overwhelm all the wonderful things about you. What do you plan to do?" she said. I felt relieved. I thought that E would box me into a corner like some little kid and then I would strike back and say things that I couldn't retract. I would have been so nasty that E would have no other choice but to leave. Instead, I held my tongue and things didn't get out of hand. "Well, Elicia, I'm going to finish the night the way you started it, with a lot of love." E smiled. "Then tomorrow I'm going to get up, call my shrink, Dr. P., schedule an appointment and hit the books after I'm done with my patients. After that, I'm going to think about you," I told her. "I like that part the best," E said. I looked at Elicia and wondered to myself where Elicia came from. Either she's for real or she's just playing me like a fiddle. I couldn't believe that Elicia was for real. The rest of the night we sat there like two little kids laughing out loud and chatting away. Nothing stood between us. Elicia and I reminded me of newlyweds. Two people wholly wrapped up in themselves oblivious to the rest of the world.

"Dr. P., how are you? This is Stan Warlib." "My Stan Warlib?" Dr. P. responded. "Well, Stan, what dark alley have you walked down this time? I hope you're not in too much trouble?" Dr. P. asked. "No, I'm treating a patient with a personality disorder that brings out the worst in me. The kinds of things that mandate that I see you." "Well, Stan, knowing you, I'm sure there is a little more damage that you have done to yourself before you made this phone call," Dr. P. said. "What is a good time for you?" I asked. I'd like to see you sooner rather than later," Dr. P. said. "Tomorrow morning would be fine with me Dr. P, if you have the time open." "Tomorrow morning at 9:00 is open." "That would be perfect," I said. "Then tomorrow morning it is. I'm looking forward to seeing you again." I wanted to call Elicia immediately like some little kid saying look ma, look I did the right thing. I didn't. Somehow I felt confident that E knew that I would call Dr. P. and take care of business. After all, doing the right thing didn't need her approval. Anyway, that's how I felt. Monday's patients were a pleasure and once again, everyone one of them noticed that I was somehow different. My 2:00 p.m. patient asked if I was in love. I asked him what made him say that and he told me I seemed more alive. "You know, Doc, you got the look," he said. I just smiled. I decided that I was going to do some research at 6:00 p.m., one hour after my last patient. I also decided that I was having too much alcohol. It felt like I was open-ing up a bottle of wine or fixing me a drink at every turn. I was having drinks at the bar, in the house and on the porch. It was too much. I thought that dealing with Sam was taking a larger toll on me than I even knew.

I was tempted to go to the Madison Avenue Bar, but I didn't. I reached for a bottle of wine in the refrigerator and aborted that as well. I sat down at my desk and reviewed my notes of the last session with Sam and made an attempt to recall the meat of that session. I wasn't entirely comfortable with my initial analysis of Sam. When I wrote the notes, I was confident that Sam met at least three criteria of Anti-Social Personality Disorder but it seemed to me that I was stretching the facts to meet other criteria. I was confident that Sam fit into criteria (1) failure to conform to social norms with respect to lawful behaviors as indicated by repeat-edly performing acts that are grounds for arrest (2) deceitfulness, as indicated by repeated lying, use of aliases, or conning others for personal profit or pleasure and (3) impulsivity or failure to plan ahead. Much of what Sam said and did (invad-ing Iraq, lying about weapons of mass destruction and having no exit plans) could fit into these categories. I wasn't going to abandon Anti-social Personality Disorder. I reread the DMS-IV sections on personality disorders. I felt like a nov-ice and as novices do I acted in a scatter-brained approach. I decided to start at the beginning. There are 11 different personality disorders. I wrote them down with a brief description, hoping that the most relevant ones would reveal them-selves to me.

(1) Paranoid Personality Disorder is a pattern of distrust and suspiciousness such that others motives are interpreted as malevolent.

(2) Schizoid Personality Disorder is a pattern of detachment from social rela-tionships and a restricted range of emotional expression.

(3) Schizotypal Personality Disorder is a pattern of acute discomfort in close relationships, cognitive or perceptual distortions, and eccentricities of behav-ior.

(4) Antisocial Personality Disorder is a pattern of disregard for, and violation of, the rights of others, central features are deceit and manipulation.

(5) Borderline Personality Disorder is a pattern of instability in interpersonal relationships, self-image, and effects and marked impulsivity.

(6) Histrionic Personality Disorder is a pattern of excessive emotionality and attention seeking.

(7) Narcissistic Personality Disorder is a pattern of grandiosity, need for admiration and lack of empathy.

(8) Avoidant Personality Disorder is a pattern of social inhibition, feelings of inadequacy and hypersentivity to negative evaluation.

(9) Dependent Personality Disorder is a pattern of submissive and clinging behavior related to an excessive need to be taken care of.

(10) Obsessive-Compulsive Personality Disorder is a pattern of preoccupation with orderliness, perfectionism and control and

(11) Personality Disorder not otherwise specified.

After reading the list of personality disorders and a detailed description of each contained in the manual, I discounted eight disorders and focused on Paranoid, Antisocial and Narcissistic Personality Disorders. I realized that I had become too comfortable in my practice. I built it on fluff. No hard cases and no challenges. My Tuesday and Thursday patients were difficult but not challenges. They were merely crybabies who understood what their problems were but didn't want to work on them. I had winged it for a very long period of time. Being an excellent psychologist is like being a detective. To find the truth of someone's being you have to wade through years of defenses that an adult patient had been developing from childhood. Patients put up roadblocks, roads to nowhere, a multiplicity of roads designed to confuse and rarely reveal the core of who they are. You have to dig to get at it. Digging takes time and you always have to be one step ahead of your patient's bullshit. Dr. P., for example, was always one step ahead of my crap. They'll try to suck you in to their issues, spin you around a couple of times and spit you out in the wrong direction. Sounds crazy, but you have to wade into a morass of a mixed up brain and maintain a steady course. I had gotten lazy. Now I had to work. I felt that at least I had the makings of a team. There was Elicia, and now Dr. P. I felt like I was back in school. I was pouring over the material in the manual. I couldn't recall the last time I picked up the manual and actually read it. At its core, it was nothing more than a roadmap for the mind detective to arrive at a conclusion as to what he was dealing with. I was intrigued. The manual was a reminder of how difficult analyzing another human being could be. It felt like the manual was always screaming at me it might be this, but it could be that, or it could be that, but then again, it might be this. The manual was going to be my bridge to Sam. I reviewed the eleven disorders and skipped past the general diagnostic criteria for a Personality Disorder. Once again, I did not start at the beginning. That was my first bridge to cross. Was I even dealing with a personality disorder? For some reason I just kept on passing over it. I stopped and read it several times. On the top of page 633 the first line read, "personality disorders must be distinguished from personality traits that do not reach the threshold for a personality disorder." It then went on to state "personality traits are diagnosed as a Personality Disorder only when they are inflexible, maladaptive, and persisting and cause significant functional impairment or subjective distress." Even before I answered that question, the manual wanted me to first cross a different bridge. Wait a minute, the manual tugged on my sleeve, many of the specific criteria for personality disorders describe features, such as suspiciousness, dependency or insensitivity, that are also characteristic of episodes of Axis I mental disorders. The manual follows a multiaxial system that involves an assessment on several axes, each of which refers to a different domain of information that may help the clinician plan treatment and predict outcome. Personality Disorders are found on Axis II. Once again, I decided to start at the beginning and that was Axis I. There are five axes:

> Axis I Clinical Disorders
>
> Axis II Personality Disorders
>
> Axis III General Medical Conditions
>
> Axis IV Psychosocial and Environmental Problems
>
> Axis V Global Assessment Functioning

The personality you think you're seeing may not be the real one because the patient has a substance related disorder. He may be high on drugs or withdrawing and the personality you see is not the personality you'll get when the patient is off drugs or when he withdraws. Don't forget this little bridge the manual points out; the clinician must be cautious in diagnosing personality disorders during an episode of a mood disorder or an anxiety disorder because these conditions may have cross sectional symptom features that mimic personality traits. In addition, the manual reminds you that personality traits may emerge when a patient has been exposed to extreme stress and hence a diagnosis of posttraumatic stress disorder. The bottom line; the personality you are dealing with may only be real to the extent of the stress and that once the patient deals with the trauma a new personality will emerge, the real one. There are bridges to cross and a need to understand what bridge to cross first. I looked at my watch. It was 1:15 a.m. in the morning. I turned out the lights and went to bed.

I arrived at Dr. P.'s promptly at 9:00 a.m. Dr. P. was at the door and waiting to greet me. He looked genuinely happy to see me. "The last time I saw you was under very unfortunate circumstances. It is extremely difficult when an attorney loses a client to suicide. However, we made it through that and I'm confident that we'll make it through this. Come on in and sit down," said Dr. P. Dr. P. was referring to a client of mine that had committed suicide. I wondered if Dr. P. made that statement as a reminder that basic everyday issues were something that did not require his attention. Nevertheless, bringing me back to my client who died by his own hands while I was conducting his trial was riveting. I didn't see the stress that the trial had on my client. He shot his brains out in the courtroom. It was the reason that I filled my practice with fluff patients. I didn't want any more suicides. If Dr. P. was telling me that he didn't want any bullshit from me the message was loud and clear. I sat down. Dr. P. started to talk and got right to the question. He wanted to know why I was there. "I'm here because," I paused, feeling compelled to come up with something that required his attention, "because I want to kill my fucking patient Sam. I have never met another human that I find as detestable as this smuck. When he walks in the door, I get pissed off. I want to kick him in the balls and then when he is hunched over at the waist bring my knee up under his chin and snap his neck backwards. I conned myself that I was interested for two sessions, but I just hate him." I expected the first question from Dr. P. "You don't literally mean murder, do you?" he asked. "No, I don't literally mean murder." "So what's your fantasy, Stan? How do you in your fantasy murder this patient." I didn't expect that question. Well, maybe I did expect that question. The problem was that I actually did have a fantasy and I didn't want to reveal it. It would show a side of my personality that I didn't like to deal with. "Stan, what is your fantasy?" Dr. P. asked again with a little agitation in his voice. It was almost as if he was annoyed with me. Two shrinks knew how to play the game and he didn't want any bullshit from me. Dr. P. asked a simple question. "My fantasy, Dr. P. is simple. I want to beat this patient's mind to a pulp. I want to slowly shatter his image until he goes into a deep depression. Hammer home, week after week after endless weeks that he is nothing but a piece of shit. Pound on him until he exists in a catatonic state curled up in the corner of my office or does the world a favor and blows his brains out," I said. My reference to "brains being blown out," caused Dr. P. to sit straight up in his chair. He put his hands on his desk, looked over his bi-focals and quietly stated, "I'm glad you called. It seems that this patient really summons up strong angry feelings in you. Is there any possibility that you might, let's say, pound this patient into a vegetable until he winds up in some catatonic state in the corner of your office."

Dr. P. used my language in framing his question to me. It had an impact. "Or that you'll cause this patient to take his own life?" he added. "I don't think so, Dr. P." Dr. P. strongly recommended that I schedule an appointment with him every Thursday morning after seeing Sam. I could tell that Dr. P. had concerns, as he immediately wanted me to visit him. My anger caused deep concern with Dr. P. I figured it was the choice of words and tone in my voice that got Dr. P.'s attention. After all, no one would ever know what I did to Sam. When someone goes to a shrink, everyone automatically makes assumptions none of which are true. People who go to shrinks are troubled. If Sam lied catatonic in my office, I couldn't be blamed for it. I'd pick up the phone, call an ambulance and have him thrown into some hospital. Who would believe him if he accused me of trying to fuck him over. My answer? He's paranoid! Life goes on. "Stan, are there any women in your life?" Dr. P. asked. "Yes, I met a great women. Her name is Elicia," I told him. "Are you here because Elicia told you to come or are you here because you know that you should be?" "Both reasons," I responded. "Stan, this is not a game to curry favor with some woman in your life. I know, you know, that I know you. I know your tricks and deceptions. Don't make me wade through bullshit," said Dr. P. "I'm not giving you bullshit. I gave you an answer. I'm here for both reasons. Elicia and I discussed the subject and prior to our discussion I was thinking about it for a while." "What is your patient's name?" Dr. P. asked. "Sam," I answered. "Now, how long ago did you start treating Sam?" "About five weeks ago," I answered. "And how long have you had these feelings?" "About five weeks," I answered. "So you have wanted to 'fuck' Sam up from the moment you laid eyes on him?" Dr. P. inquired. "Yes," I said. "And you waited all this time to call me. I suppose you have been debating this issue over and over for the last five weeks. Stan, I'm concerned. You know that you should have called me immediately. Not only do I want you here Thursday mornings, but I also want you to call me immediately after your session with Sam if the need arises. Stan, you're a professional. I don't want any of your bullshit. Straight talk, straight answers and straight living," Dr. P. admonished. Dr. P. and I continued until the end of the session. Dr. P. shook my hand and stared me down, "No nonsense, Stan." I walked out. On the walk back to my office, I knew that I had done some good things. I didn't drink as much. I had Elicia on my side and I was in therapy with Dr. P. Doing the right thing never made me feel good. I had to stretch to do it. It comes naturally to most people but not to me. I had always walked down dark alleys and got knocked around a little. Most times I escaped harm, but I always had to fight my way out. I could have used all this energy living a good life. For many reasons, I expended all this energy staying away from a good life. However, until Sam, I had been rather calm and maintained a fairly steady course down the center of the street. I looked down the dark alleys but didn't feel compelled to take a stroll. I felt a heavy burden had been placed on me. I had work to do. No more coasting. I resented Sam. I wondered what life would have been like had I not screwed Gabriella Westerfield to get a practice going. I was going to hit the books and prep for Sam. I realized that an effective evaluation required more information from Sam. I decided to ask more questions regardless of Sam's reactions.

The best place to start was at the beginning along Axis 1: Clinical Disorders, such as Schizophrenia, Psychosis, Mood and Anxiety Disorders. As stated before, there are five axes for an effective evaluation. Axis 1 is a list of clinical disorders and other conditions that maybe a focus of clinical attention. Axis 1 lists the following:

> Delirium, Dementia, and Amnesic and Other Cognitive Disorders
>
> Mental Disorders Due to a General Medical Condition
>
> Substance-Related Disorders
>
> Schizophrenia and other Psychotic Disorders
>
> Mood Disorders
>
> Anxiety Disorders
>
> Somatoform Disorders
>
> Factitious Disorders
>
> Dissociative Disorders
>
> Sexual and Gender Identity Disorders
>
> Eating Disorders
>
> Sleep Disorders
>
> Impulse control disorders not elsewhere classified
>
> Adjustment Disorders
>
> Other conditions that may be a focus of clinical attention.

Sam was in good physical condition. He had been a heavy drinker up to the age of forty. Sam maintained a vigorous physical conditioning program. As far as I knew, Sam did not have any issues with sleep, eating or sexual/gender disorders.

However, there was a marked discrepancy between Sam's physical program and that of his family. Neither did Sam appear to have any mental disorders due to a general medical condition. My sessions with Sam did not lead me to believe that Sam exhibited any symptoms of delirium, dementia amnesic or other cognitive disorders. My focus centered on Schizophrenia and other psychotic disorders and mood and anxiety disorders. After a brief look at the information on Schizophrenia and ruling that out, I moved on and stopped at 297.1-Delusional disorder and its various sub-types. I was particularly interested in the Grandiose subtype and Persecutory subtype. Delusional disorders differed from schizophrenia in that delusional disorders are of the non-bizarre type. They involve situations that occur in real life, such as being followed, poisoned, infected, loved at a distance or deceived by spouse or lover. Non-bizarre delusions are the kinds of things that can actually happen. Schizophrenic delusions might involve more of the bizarre types such as a person having had his entire organs replaced by aliens but he had no scar marks on his body because the aliens had a special method of doing this kind of operation, which was scar less. The two subtypes of a delusional disorder, grandiose and persecutory, presented themselves as areas that might require some attention. The onset of a delusional disorder occurs in middle or late adult life. The persecutory type is the most common subtype. It was going to be difficult to differentiate Mood Disorders with Psychotic Features from delusional disorder, because the psychotic features associated with Mood disorders usually involved no bizarre delusions without prominent hallucinations and delusional disorders frequently have associated mood symptoms. I was shaking my head and saying to myself all these bridges to cross in the right order just so that I can help some prick that I didn't like. The Grandiose subtype interested me because it applies when the central theme of the delusion is the conviction of having some great, but unrecognized talent or insight or having made some important discovery. Less commonly, the individual may have the delusion of having some relationship with a prominent person or being a prominent person. Grandiose delusions may have a religious content, for example, the person believes that he has a special message from a deity. This was of particular interest as it had been reported in an Israeli newspaper that Sam claimed God instructed him to bomb and invade both Afghanistan and Iraq. When I asked Sam if that was true, he freely admitted it. One area of questioning will be the extent to which Sam has a special relationship to God.

The persecutory subtype is more prevalent. Although Sam directly confirmed his special relationship with his deity there were overtones throughout Sam's sessions that felt like Sam might belong in this subtype as well. This subtype applies when the central theme of the delusion involves the person's belief that he or she is being conspired against, cheated, spied on, followed, poisoned or drugged, maliciously maligned, harassed or obstructed in the pursuit of his long term goals. Small slights may be exaggerated and become the focus of a delusional system. The focus of the delusion is often some injustice that must be remedied by legal action. The manual stated that individuals of persecutory sub-type are often resentful and angry and may resort to violence against those they believe are hurting them. My thoughts on this were that Sam seemed to feel that his enemy Saddam was going to destroy him, if not immediately, then sometime in the future. Sam also had feelings that others were after him such as a group of terrorists called al-Qaeda. I didn't feel entirely comfortable with the persecutory subtype, but decided that I would keep my ears open and hear if there were any threads running through my sessions with Sam that might indicate I should explore this subtype further. Exactly what struck me was the sentence that included the language "long term goals." Sam had long-term goals. Sam was in a never-ending war on terror. I decided that tomorrow's session would center on Sam and God. Did he have a delusional disorder of the Grandiose Subtype? Was Sam God's right hand man? Was Sam's family delusional of the persecutory subtype? Something terribly wrong was going on. I feared for Sam and his family. I went to bed.

SESSION SEVEN

Sam arrived promptly at 2:00 p.m. and appeared eager to go. "Sam, I have been reviewing my notes for the last six sessions and thought that I should take a step back and get some more detail about one particular area. I'd like to know more about your relationship with God?" I asked. "Ah," Sam sighed, "my favorite subject." I knew that this week the unemployment claims rose unexpectedly and the stock market went down. I expected Sam to be in a lousy mood. Perhaps I cut him short with the question on God. After all, it is his favorite subject. "Well, I don't know where to start. My relationship with God goes back such a long way." "Well, tell me about how you talk to God," I asked Sam. "No, no, no," Sam barked back, "that's putting the cart before the horse." "Well, then, why don't you start wherever you want," I said. "From the beginning would put everything in perspective for you," Sam said. "O.K., then from the beginning," I answered. I knew that I was in for a non-stop Sam type speech, but that was exactly what I wanted. I figured that somewhere at the end of the session, I would be able to ask a question or two. "Well, Stan, I'm not going to go way back to 1946 when I was born on the East Coast. In 1948, two years after I was born, mom and dad moved to a western state, oil country, and they joined a local church. I was a cut-up growing up. I went to three named prestigious schools and got married. Prior to marriage I had a pretty good time with the ladies. Five years into my marriage, my children were born. But here was the problem, Stan. I was a big drinker. I had an alcohol problem, a big alcohol problem and my wife was fed up with me. When I turned forty I knew I had to fix my problem. Well, about that time, my friend Evans, who was in a crisis of his own, took me by the hand and together we marched to a Bible study group, which was a boot camp for God. It was an intensive yearlong study of a single book of the New Testament. Each week we read a new chapter and had detailed discussions of what we had read. I did this for two years. There were two themes, one political and one spiritual. I liked the conversion story. I liked knowing Jesus as a friend. I stopped drinking. Cold turkey. I knew that Jesus was my savior. I knew that Jesus was my hero. I read the Bible word-by-word and line-by-line. I was enraptured, so much so that I stopped drinking. It was good-bye Jack Daniels and hello Jesus Christ. Do you have that, Stan? Do you really know what I'm talking about? I don't think you do. You see, we are the true believers. The Lord Jesus is my savior and the Bible is my path to holiness. But you're just not dealing with me, you're dealing with millions of people like me. One out of three Christian's are evangelical. We are fervent. We are fighters and we will not hang out in the closet any longer so as to spare your feelings. I can lay on the hands. I can walk the walk and talk the talk. While guys like you were smoking dope and fornicating, my buddies and I were slowly spreading the good word and building larger and larger bases of support. We got teenagers involved. They like music and we gave them music. We gave them music with the message. They are our new Christian warriors," he said. "Sam, hold on," I said. Sam was somewhat taken aback as he was on a roll, talking the talk. "You said, 'my buddies and me were slowing spreading the word,' is this the same group of buds that you previously talked about?" I asked. "No, this is a different group. These are God's buds. Those other guys are my financial buds. Anyway, just listen to this. Did you know that almost sixty per-cent of my family believe that what is written in the Bible's Book of Revelations will come to pass? Glory-be to God! Give me an amen, Stan, come on, Stan, give me an amen." I reluctantly gave Sam "an amen," as I thought that this would be the only way he would proceed. "Now didn't that feel good? Come on, Stan, tell me the truth. Didn't that feel good? Didn't that feel good? Praise the Lord. Jesus is my Lord and Savior and the Bible is my book. Witness what the Lord Jesus did for me. I accepted him as my savior and bam; he got alcohol out of my life. What power, what glory! Seeing what the Lord's wonders did for me, I realized what the Lord's wonders could do for everyone. Talking about my teenage Christian warriors, do you know what the largest group on college campus's are today? The conservative groups! Not those left wing liberal leftie traitor pieces of garbage. Those evildoers. My children. Gods' children! And you know why? You Stan, as I told you before, stand for nothing. I stand with God. Imagine, nothing versus God. Who do you think is going to win Stan? God, Stan, God." Sam raised his hands to the ceiling and shouted "glory be to God." I thought that Sam was going to ask me to give him another amen but he didn't. He continued apace with the rhythm and rhyme of an old time preacher. I realized that Sam was indeed a true believer. I also realized that it wasn't only Sam. Sam had millions of true believers right under the radar screen of our society that no one paid attention to. When he spoke in the manner that he was speaking, it was odd language and very unfamiliar to my ear. I recalled that moment when Sam's friend, Jerry Falwell, went on television and said that 9/11 was God's retribution for all of America's evil ways. Even though he retracted the statement and claimed that he "misspoke," it was clear to me that Sam and tens of millions of people really believed that 9/11 was God's retribution for America's evil ways. "So you see, Stan, millions praise the glory of God. But it wasn't enough to go around converting one lost soul at a time. We needed to gain political power and retake this heathen nation and rid it of evil people. You see, you either walk with God or you don't. You either accept the Lord Jesus as your savior or you don't. If you don't, you are either misguided or evil. If you are misguided Stan, I will show you the path and if you're a true non-believer I will smite you with the fury of God's wrath. Then, God called upon me and said, 'Sam, you must run for political office. That is my calling for you.' Praise the Lord. So I ran for office and was elected. During all this time, I connected with pastors, religious leaders and every one of the faithful that I could reach. The sheer number of people that are out there with me, hands raised to the heavens, flowing back and forth praising the Lord. Can I get an amen," he said. "Amen," I said. Sam moved quickly on. "And then the good Lord spoke to me again. He said, 'Sam, I want you to lead my family and show them the way of the Lord and my son Jesus Christ.' It was my calling. It was my mission. God had called me and I heeded his mission. I gathered many ministers and leading pastors for a lying on of the hands and told them that God had called me. 'Glory be,' all of them shouted. 'Glory be. Signs and wonders.' God works in strange ways. My good friend Karl told me when to chill on the good Lord because people like you weren't ready for it. I conducted my campaign below the radar screen, through the Internet and letters. I spoke to my troops and they listened. They knew that I was chosen to lead the flock to the

Promised Land. Praise the Lord. Praise the Lord. And then God rewarded me for my unflagging obedience to him. He made me, Sam, his chosen leader. Give me an amen. And then God spoke to me again and again. Evildoers, that's right, evildoers, bombed my beloved land and God instructed me to get those evildoers and I heeded his call. God told me to bomb Afghanistan and I bombed Afghanistan. God told me to get Saddam, a man of unspeakable evil. I heeded God's calling and went after Saddam. It was enough for me to heed God's call. But it wasn't enough for my financial buds and some of God's less brave buds. They told me they had to make up a story that Saddam had weapons of mass destruction and to pound it into my family's head. Over and over and over again we pounded home the message that Saddam had weapons of mass destruction. I pounded home the message too, although I didn't need to do that. Saddam was an evildoer. Iran is an evildoer. North Korea is an evildoer. Do I need more than that? I ask you. If God says to kill the evildoers do I need any more? Right now, they're not finding weapons of mass destruction over at Saddam's house. So what. Praise the Lord! The evildoer is vanquished to do no more evil. Isn't that enough! My friend Karl says point to two abandoned trucks and called them weapons of mass destruction, so I do. My friend Karl told me to point to some trinkets hidden under a rose bush in some scientist's back yard and call them evidence of nuclear weapons, so I do. He tells me that my family will believe me. So I tell them and they believe me. You will not find weapons that evil Saddam could have used against me. They were gone in sufficient numbers long ago. But Karl tells me to send David to Iraq and he'll make sure that weapons are found in the name of the glory of God. But I don't need any of that. God spoke and commanded me to kill Saddam and I heeded the call. That is sufficient but I sent David over there anyway. I'm sure he's doing what he has been commanded to do. He will show you evil Saddam's weapons. You'll see, he'll show you. But my faith in God is not complex, Stan. It is destiny. I do my best and everything else is in God's hand. God will work things out. Can anyone out there second-guess me? Doubting me is the same as doubting God. I will not tolerate doubters. In my house Stan, there is an aura of prayerfulness in seeking God's help during these difficult times. When I awake, I engage in prayer to God, praise the Lord, before anything else, even before I kiss my wife good morning. God tells me that my body is a temple and I treat it as such. I have no sweets, run and exercise everyday. Are you with me Stan? My brothers want me to bring the fight in the name of God to my family. God through the Bible clearly indicates that abortion is wrong. Homosexuals are wrong. Lesbians are wrong. I cannot now, or ever, abandon the fight against these evils. I will always fight against the evildoers that believe that this kind of conduct should be permitted. While I have been called upon to fight the evildoers from all over the world, I have placed many of my friends in positions of power to fight domestic evildoers. They are engaged in a day to day fight to get conservative pro-life judges appointed; new HUD regulations that allow federal grants for construction of "social service" facilities at religious institutions; a ban on human cloning and partial birth abortion; a sweeping program to allow churches to use federal funds to administer social-welfare programs; strengthened limits on stem cell research; increased funding for teaching sexual abstinence in schools rather than safe sex; foreign aid policies that stress right to life themes and money for federal prisons that use Christian tough love in an effort to lower recidivism rates among convicts. God is here and I am God's man because I have a calling and I have a mission. So to answer your question, do I speak to God; the answer is yes. I speak to God everyday and God speaks to me. Praise to the glory of God and Amen. Come on Stan, can't I get an Amen out of you." I looked at my watch. It was 2:50. "Sorry, Sam, time's up. There's always next week." Sam handed over an envelope.

SESSION NOTES

As I started typing my session notes, the phone rang. "Oh, Dr. P., why I not surprised." "Just a friendly reminder, Stan, just a friendly reminder." "I know, tomorrow at 9:00 a.m. I'll be there." "Thank you," Dr. P. said and hung up the phone. That was an irritating, but I guess, warranted phone call. I opened up the DSM-IV manual and turned to Schizophrenia and Other Psychotic Disorders along Axis 1.

I was sure that Sam was not schizophrenic. He did not have, as the manual stated, for the last six months, including 1 month of active phase systems, at least two of the following: delusions, hallucinations, disorganized speech, grossly disorganized or catatonic behavior. However, I was confident that Sam had a delusional disorder, number 297.1 in the manual. The diagnostic features stated that the essential feature of a delusional disorder is the presence of one or more non-bizarre delusions that persist for at least 1 month. I could not give Sam a delusional disorder diagnosis if I could also give Sam a diagnosis for Schizophrenia. They are mutually exclusive. Apart from the direct impact of the delusions, Sam's psychosocial functioning was not markedly impaired and his behavior was not odd or bizarre. However, I was concerned about Sam's moods. The manual reminded me that if mood episodes occurred concurrently with the delusions, the total duration of the mood episodes must be relatively brief when compared to the total duration of the delusional episodes. I leaned back in my chair and thought about the entire contact that I had had with Sam. It appeared that his moods were fairly consistent and outside of bursts of anger, Sam had relatively stable moods. Had it been otherwise, I would have to seek another diagnosis along the lines of mood disorders and psychotic episodes. Sam, being a religious man treated his body as his temple. Sam did not take drugs and was in perfect health. As a result, Sam's delusions, if in fact, speaking to God was a delusion, could be ruled out because of substance abuse or a general medical condition. Delusional disorder must by definition be non-bizarre delusions. Bizarre delusions would throw Sam into the Schizo category and at times bizarreness may be difficult to judge. Delusions are deemed bizarre if they are clearly implausible, for example, as stated before, an individual's belief that a stranger removed his internal organs without leaving any scars. In contrast, non-bizarre delusions involve situations that can conceivably occur in real life (i.e., being followed, poisoned, infected, loved at a distance, or deceived.) There were seven subtypes of delusional disorder but only Grandiose and Persecutory were relevant. Although, I had toyed with this before, I was more confident than ever that Sam's grandiose delusion that he had a special relationship with God, "his right hand man," as he put it, clearly indicated that Sam had a delusional disorder of the grandiose sub-type. What had given me pause and concern regarding the persecutory subtype was not present after this last session with Sam. It was clear to me that while Sam was fighting evildoers coupled with his insistence with people were with him or against him, Sam would not easily believe that he was "being conspired against, cheated, spied on, followed, poisoned or drugged, maliciously maligned, harassed or obstructed in his long term goals." It was Sam that conspired against, cheated, spied on, poisoned, drugged, maliciously maligned, harassed and obstructed his enemies. The term "long term goals" had given me a problem before, however, I saw that Sam's fight against an unknown enemy that you couldn't see and that existed everywhere was Sam's long-term goal. Sam had been given a calling and a mission from God. Sam had a delusional disorder of the grandiose subtype. I thought about Sam's plans for regime change in various parts of the world. In addition, I thought about Sam's Middle East Initiative Proposal. Sam was not only nation building, he wanted to change cultures. It went hand in hand. The manual stated that the persecutory subtypes could exhibit marked anger and violent behavior. I was concerned that the manual stated delusional disorders could be associated with Obsessive-Compulsive Disorder, Body Dysmorphic Disorder and Paranoid, Schizoid or Avoidant Personality Disorders, a group of personality disorders along Axis II. I was thinking different personality disorders and this concerned me. I reminded myself that I was a mind detective and that I shouldn't be discouraged because the manual suggested different personality disorders than I was thinking about. The manual raised a flag. Under the topic Specific Culture and Gender Features the manual advised me that Sam's cultural and religious background should be taken into account. It stated that some cultures had widely held and culturally sanctioned beliefs that that might be considered delusional in other cultures. Sam speaks to God. God speaks to Sam. Millions of people, indeed, tens of millions of people believe the same way that Sam does. Within Sam's culture, speaking to God is not delusional. I asked myself, if this is the case, who am I to diagnosis that Sam has a delusional disorder? I had two questions to discuss with Dr. P. Is Sam delusional within his culture and couldn't Sam have other personality disorders even though delusions disorders go more with the ones that I *wasn't* thinking about? I hadn't had alcohol in a long time and went to the refrigerator to get some chilled white wine. I thought of Sam's alcohol problem. I raised my glass to the ceiling and with all sincerity said "chilling." I laughed out loud. I needed a good laugh. I wasn't finished with my notes. I went out to the back porch and watched the silent parade of insects and animals on their daily spectacle. I didn't sit down because I knew that I would get too comfortable and I had more session notes to do. I had some thoughts about Sam's family that I needed to get down on paper and see if they made any sense. I limited myself to only one glass of wine although I wanted to finish the entire bottle. I felt like I needed a clear head for the next part of my session notes.

I read the following passage: "it can be difficult to differentiate Mood Disorders with Psychotic Features from Delusional disorder, because the psychotic features associated with mood disorders usually involve non-bizarre delusions without prominent hallucinations, and delusional disorder frequently has associated mood disorders." The manual further stated "the distinction depends on the temporal relationship between the mood disturbance and the delusions and on the severity of the mood systems. If delusions occur exclusively during mood episodes, the diagnosis is Mood Disorder with psychotic features." I thought about Sam's family. Most of them were not holy rollers speaking in tongues or evangelical Christians. Sam might not be delusional in his subculture; however, Sam was indeed delusional in regard to the greater whole of his family and the international community of families. Throughout my session with Sam, I wondered if Sam's family was delusional as well. After all, I did not believe that which Sam's family so easily believed. For example, I did not believe that Saddam posed a threat under any circumstances. I knew that Saddam had been defeated and ripped apart in 1991. He presented no threat whatsoever in 2003. However, while I watched Sam try to convince his family over and over again that Saddam presented an imminent and grave threat, Sam's family easily succumbed to the delusional belief that Saddam presented a threat. I put Sam's family in the persecutory delusional subtype disorder in that they believed Saddam was going to poison them with biological and chemical weapons and even worse, bomb them with dirty bombs. Notwithstanding Sam's attempts to convince his family, I was unmoved. I didn't believe Saddam was a threat and neither did the rest of the world. Sam's family did, notwithstanding the basic reality to the contrary. What Sam was telling his family just wasn't true and yet, they almost gleefully consumed all the lies that Sam put forth. I thought they were delusional as well. When I read the passage that advised me that it was difficult to differentiate between delusional disorder and Mood Disorders with Psychotic Features, I realized that Sam's family wasn't delusional at all. They had mood disorders with psychotic features. Sam was intentionally trying to hype up his family to create non-bizarre delusions. Saddam is going to climb into your bedroom window with VX gas and sit at the edge of the bed and watch your skin melt off your body. I remembered the movie Gaslight with Ingrid Berman and Charles Boyer. Boyer did the same kind of things to Ingrid and tried to make her believe things that weren't true. He tried to create delusions. Sam was intentionally destabilizing his own family. He was gas lighting them. Sam's mood was always consistent. He was unflappable in his convictions. Sam speaks to God and follows his orders and let's God take care of the rest. God is, after all, never wrong. I felt that if Sam had any moods they were contrived. I felt more confident than ever, that Sam, along Axis I had a delusional disorder and that his family, along Axis I had some kind of mood disorder with psychotic features. As far as Sam was concerned, he let his minions make the case for beating up Saddam, although Sam just wanted to beat up Saddam because he was evil. Sam's buddies, both financial and religious knew that Sam couldn't beat up Saddam just because Sam thought he was evil, they needed something else. So Sam's minions went out and came up with weapons of mass destruction and gas lighted his own family. I wondered how Sam could do that. How did Sam really feel about his family? More importantly, why would so many others jump on the bandwagon in the face of such an obvious fraud? It was clear to me that Sam's family had been gas lighted. Religious, financial, government and media giants were ripping apart Sam's family to their own advantage. What rang out was that Sam had a direct influence on his family's mood. They were co-dependent. Sam gained a significant position of dominance in his family's life. At one point, Sam wasn't liked, as he had told me and now he was using his newfound popularity to burrow into his family's life and take a controlling position. Indeed, the mood of Sam's family was largely controlled by the personality of Sam and was at times directly and severely affected by Sam's delusions. Sam and his family were hopelessly locked up in a very unhealthy dance. Sam and his family forgot that life was supposed to be fun. Sam's family was suffering. There was no true enjoyment of life.

I sought to make an analysis of the family's Axis I mood disorders. It would be helpful to have another session with Sam about his family before I delved into my own initial diagnosis that his family had a mood disorder with psychotic features. However, I just couldn't take my mind off the subject. I felt like I was on to something, like a real detective when he uncovers one little item after another that reinforces his analysis of the previous piece of evidence that he just discovered that leads him to believe that each succeeding item will lead him to the truth. It's juice. The blood starts flowing and the adrenaline rushes through your body. Somehow, it seemed to me that I would lose the trail if I didn't proceed following up the leads. I needed more evidence about Sam's family but the thought process seemed crystal clear at the moment. I hadn't visited the mood disorder section along Axis I of the Manual in quite a while. Unfortunately, most of psychotherapy is pharmacological in nature. Give them Prozac! Prozac nation. Chilling. Therapy takes a long time. It takes a long time to get to know a person. Snap judgments don't work with people who appear functional but by their own admissions are upset about something. You have to wade through defense mechanisms that have been built up over the years just to get to one item of truth or a real feeling. Most patients will evade and lead the therapist in as many false directions as possible. To read these kinds of maneuvers takes a lot of time. Insurance companies don't give you a lot of time. Give your patients a pill and fix them up. Insurance companies want therapists to get their patients in and then out. The insurance companies don't pay for a therapist to get to know their patients. Over time, a therapists detective skills decrease. I forgot what a wonderful, valuable aid the manual was. It was *my* bible. I noticed that I wasn't so hostile to Sam and part of me was actually enjoying getting into Sam's head. Sam was my patient and I wanted to help him. I thought about Elicia and the shave that she had given me. I had to work on my women issues I reminded myself. I was prepared to go back to my desk and tackle the mood disorders. I sat down with authority as if I were Sigmund Freud with an air of confidence that stated, "Siggy is here to crack the case." I was in the company of Sherlock Holmes, Poirot and all the other great detectives of our time. I was actually having fun. I realized that Sam was having a profound effect upon my moods. First I hated him and now I was having fun with him. I was up and down. Bipolar? That was the first thing I thought as I walked into my office. I wondered if I was talking about Sam or me, or both.

It was time to hit the books. I read the manual several times until the information sunk in. First, the predominant feature of a mood disorder was simply a disturbance in mood. There are four mood episodes; a major depressive episode, a manic episode, a mixed episode and a hypomanic episode. These episodes do not have their own diagnostic codes and cannot be diagnosed as separate entities. They are the building blocks for the mood disorder diagnoses. The mood disorders were as follows:

Major Depressive Disorder

Dysthymic Disorder

Depressive Disorder Not otherwise Specified

Bipolar I Disorder

Bipolar II Disorder

Cyclothymic Disorder

Bipolar order not otherwise specified

Mood disorder due to a General Medical Condition

Substance Induced Mood Disorder

Mood Disorder not otherwise specified.

I remembered my school days at New York University. I had this great professor who took all these words on paper which our young minds had various degrees of trouble grasping and he turned the words in the manual into a great visual. "Look," he says, "without getting into a detailed analysis of what a mood *episode* is, we all know, through daily usage of the words what we're talking about. A major depressive episode is the guy who sits in his room, all alone, refuses to come out and doesn't come out to eat, shave or take a shower. I would say, 'man, that guy is depressed.' Now, take the same guy. He runs out of his room, laughing out loud, cleans the house, doesn't sleep, is doing everything he likes and this goes on and on. I would say 'man, this guy is manic.' Now this same guy, stays in his room for one full week and then bounds out and runs around the apartment like a nut, I would say this guy is up and down, now that's a mixed episode. Now this one's a little harder, the hypomanic episode." The professor states to "think manic but not that manic." "Half manic," he says.

"Leave it that. Now visualize these four different mood *episodes* as four little wooden blocks. There is glue on the ceiling of this room and we're going to throw these four little wooden blocks up to the ceiling and see which ones stick and which ones come down." "O.K.," he says, "now take these four little blocks in your hands, like the game of Boggle, shake them up and throw them up to the ceiling. The whole class does this and he says "look, only one block came down." He holds up this imaginary block and reads the label. "Hmm," he says, "I got in my hand the block that says major depressive episode. You know what class? This guy has a Major Depressive Disorder. Now let's take the same blocks and change one of them to Manic episode, so that we have two blocks labeled Manic. O.K., shake them up real good and throw them up to the ceiling and let see what comes down. Look, one block stuck and three blocks came down." He makes believe he is picking up one block at a time. "O.K. let's see, we have one block Manic, the second block is manic and the third block is depressed. Now, class what do we have, anyone?" Someone shouts out Bipolar I Disorder. That is, two manic and one depressed episode. "O.K., class, two major depressive episode blocks come down together with one hypomanic block? What do we have?" Another student shouts out Bipolar II Disorder. "Now, you all know that it is somewhat more complicated than that, but the details are in your homework. However, sometime in the future when a patient is sitting in your office take these four episodic wooden blocks, throw them up to the ceiling and see what comes down on your desk. That is what you got." I never forgot that lecture. It was one of those simple illustrations that spoke more than the words themselves. I leaned back in my chair, put my feet up on the desk and thought about Sam for a long time. Then I took these little imaginary wooden blocks put them in my hands and threw them up to the ceiling. Nothing came down. I stared at the desk and repeated the process. I thought about Sam. I took my four wooden blocks and threw them up to the ceiling. I looked at my desk. Nothing came down. I stared at the ceiling and there they were, hanging ten feet above my head. Sam had no Mood Disorders. I didn't think so. Afterwards, I thought hard about Sam's family. Everything that Sam had told me and everything that I had watched, read, heard and seen. I recalled, for example, the interview on television by a reporter asking Sam's family what their unalienable rights were. Most people didn't know and many of them laughed at themselves for not knowing the answer. I took these four little wooden episodic blocks, shook them up in my cupped hands and threw them to the ceiling. Amazingly, the blocks stuck a little bit to the ceiling and then started to fall one by one. What was amazing was that none of them landed on my desk. They just kind of hung there suspended right above my head. I grabbed the blocks and started the process over again. I threw the blocks up to the ceiling and once again, each one broke away and was suspended in mid air. "I must have missed the follow up class on what to do when the blocks hang suspended," I mused. It was time to hit the books. I looked at my watch. It was 4:00 in the morning. I knew that I had an appointment with Dr. P. I set my alarm clock for 8:00 a.m. and went to sleep. I wished the index of DSM-IV manual had "suspended blocks" listed right after substance abuse disorder. It didn't.

I arrived at Dr. P.'s right on time although I had to hurry. The door to his office was open so I went in and sat down. "How are you, Stan," asked Dr. P. "I'm fine. I have been busy doing research. Hitting the books so to speak. I haven't really checked out the manual in a long time," I told Dr. P. "And how are you doing with your patient Sam?" inquired Dr. P.

"I'm doing fine. Just fine." "So, let me get this straight. Last week you were very upset with this patient and now you're just fine," said Dr. P. "Right, I'm fine. I started doing research and got into diagnosing Sam," I said. Dr. P. leaned over his desk, put on his bi-focals and stared down at his notes. I hated this part. This is where you're boxed in with your back up against the wall. It's psychology's answer to the Tim Russert "got ya" moment. In other words, you're fucked. Dr. P. read out loud. "I'm here because I want to kill my fucking patient Sam. I have never met another human that I find as detestable as this smuck. I want to kick him in the balls, bring my knee up under his chin and snap his head backwards.' Now I'll ask you again. How are you doing with your patient?" Dr. P. said somewhat louder. I hesitated and sat there for several minutes without a response. "So you want to know where all that anger went?" I said. "So, now you're answering a question with a question," Dr. P responded. "Come on, Stan, you're not new to psychology. What happened to your anger?" Dr. P. demanded. "I guess we're talking about my defense mechanisms." "That's a good place to start," said Dr. P. A defense mechanism is a coping style. It is an automatic psychological process that protects the individual against anxiety and from the awareness of internal or external dangers or stressors. Usually, patients are often unaware of these mechanisms as they operate. "Well, Dr. P., I guess, right off the top of my head, I'd say that I have a reaction formation together with sublimation." A reaction formation is where I would deal with emotional conflict or internal or external stressors by substituting behavior, thoughts, or feelings that are diametrically opposed to his or her own unacceptable thoughts or feelings. Sublimation is where I would deal with emotional conflict or internal or external stressors by channeling potentially maladaptive feelings or impulses into socially acceptable behavior, for example, turning into a "mind detective" and studying the manual until late at night. "That sounds very nice Stan, but I think that those feelings that you expressed last week were so powerful that you tucked them away real quick, a little too quick. So, I'm thinking something a little more basic, like repression or suppression and if I had to take a guess, I'd put my money on suppression." What Dr. P. was saying was that if I repressed my feelings I expelled my disturbing wishes, thoughts, or experiences from conscious awareness and if I suppressed my feelings I was intentionally avoiding thinking about disturbing problems, wishes, feelings or experiences. "For arguments sake, Stan, let's say you have been intentionally avoiding thinking about Sam so you could avoid your anger. As you know, the anger is still there. My question to you, Stan, is what makes you so angry with Sam?" "I get angry because he's so God damn arrogant. It's like listening to Rush, Hannity, Savage, and all these little right wing smucks on radio or television. They're such self centered, egomaniacal little twerps that repeat the same party line. They don't care about nothing but themselves. I have always had a problem with people who care only about themselves. I just don't know what to do with these people. You just can't reason with them. Even if they're wrong they're right. It's just so frustrating for me. They will never admit wrongdoing or change they're mind even if you prove it to them. The bottom line to me is that they just don't care. Sam does not care. Even if I showed him how he was wrong about certain things, or that he was seeing reality in a way that was contrary to his own interests, I'd be wrong. I can't deal with these guys and women, I said. "Well," said Dr. P., "you only have seven sessions under your belt. Perhaps it's not too late to suggest another therapist to Sam, one that might be better equipped to deal with him," said Dr. P. "I don't feel angry right now. However, I would love to get Sam out of my life. I don't want him as a patient," I said. "Do you think you can bring this matter up with Sam at your next session?" Dr. P. asked. "Yes, I think I could. I'll feel like a loser, but, yes, I think I can bring this matter up." "In the interim, Stan, until you successfully conclude your relationship with Sam, if that is what you decide to do, do you think you can stay out of dark alleyways. I mean, I don't want to see you lose your license because you kicked this guy in the balls and then kneed him under his chin." Dr. P. added that remark as a reminder. The session ended.

I walked slowly back to my office. I felt rotten. I was a bad apple. I didn't tell Dr. P. the truth. I didn't tell Dr. P. that I had walked down a dark alley when I made love to Gabby and built my practice literally off her backside. I didn't tell Dr. P. that Gabby threatened me with exposure and the possible loss of my license and could put me behind bars. I didn't tell Dr. P. that I was forced to treat Sam. I didn't tell Dr. P. anything of any consequence. I didn't tell Dr. P.

jack-shit. I was still angry. Maybe furious would be a better word. I was furious at Sam and myself. It was near the end of July and my vacation was coming up. I was taking August off as most psychologists do during the summer. I planned on going to the coast of Maine. I use the word "planned" in the past tense, because my real plan was to double or triple up sessions with Sam. I had just told Dr. P. that I would consider getting rid of Sam as my patient when it was my real intention to expand my sessions. "What a fucking liar I am," I thought.

I expected Friday to be my usual good day. Easy patients, light headwork and the weekend at hand. Something unusual happened on this Friday. Patricia, my four o' clock patient advised me that she could no longer afford treatment and that today was her last day. At 5:00 o'clock just as I was going out the door, Daniel called and told me that he would not be back in September to continue his treatment. Both patients were "Gabby" patients. Apparently, Sam's financial buds didn't like the progress of Sam's treatment. I couldn't figure out why Sam just didn't keep his mouth shut. I was sure that Dr. Westerfield was working on Sam. In a matter of sixty days I lost four patients. It was a monetary loss of $42,000.00 per year. I was pissed. I bit my tongue on the way out the door. I met Elicia at the Madison Avenue Bar. I was restraining myself. The dark alley was really starting to punch me around with some serious consequences. I didn't want to ruin my meeting with E, but I was livid. It took every once of strength just to walk straight. It was clear to me that Sam's financial buddies were reminding me what they could do. They were poking me in the eye as a reminder. I didn't know what the fuck they expected or wanted. I made a mental note to tell Sam to keep his mouth shut. I hadn't seen Gabby in a long time so I knew she couldn't be a mole and she never asked me any information about treatment with Sam. She only came to bring bad news.

I met Elicia at the bar. She gave me the biggest hug that she ever had given me. "What's up E," I said. "Oh nothing, just thought I take your mind out of whatever it's into. You're wearing it on your face. Besides, I am happy to see you." E certainly turned my head around, at least for a while. Unfortunately, despair set in and finally I had to tell Elicia was going on. I filled her in on the details. "How about a shave. A hot shower, shave, some wine, music and me," Elicia said. "E, I really appreciate the offer and absolutely fucking yes. Let's go." Elicia and I went back to my apartment. E took my mind off of Sam, losing clients and money. She was a great diversion. I confided in E a little more than I thought I should have but once I got talking I couldn't stop. I needed an ear. I needed to hear my own words and look for justification that I had to do what I did and that I was right. I told Elicia that it was my opinion that Sam's financial buddies forced him into therapy and that I was losing clients because Sam was telling them what was going on and that whatever they expected from me as Sam's therapist they weren't getting. I had no clue what they expected or wanted. Elicia listened intently and asked pointed questions. She wasn't intrusive. She just asked questions that added detail to my story. Naturally, I didn't disclose anything to Elicia that would cast me in a bad light or force her to conclude that I wasn't playing with a full deck. E didn't have any real suggestions or answers, however, she did provide needed comfort. I felt like a cornered rat that had its' own personal nurse.

I knew the following week was going to be easy. Generally, the week before a therapist's month long vacation is exploring the client's feelings about his or her therapist leaving. For example, would my upcoming absence cause angst? I was looking forward to seeing Sam on Wednesday and dreaded seeing Dr. P. the next morning. I had thoughts of canceling my appointment with Dr. P. with some bullshit excuse knowing full well that Dr. P. was going on vacation in August and that if I missed Thursday's appointment I wouldn't see Dr. P. until the month of September. I decided to leave the issue open and see what happened with Sam on Wednesday.

SESSION EIGHT

Sam arrived five minutes late and apologized. He explained that there was a lot of traffic and that he thought all the shrinks in the neighborhood were getting an early start on their August vacation. I laughed. Sam was visibly tired and so was I. The week prior to vacation is easy in one sense but very tiring in another. I asked Sam how he felt about me leaving for vacation but he told me that we would discuss that at the end of the session. "You look upset, Sam, what's troubling you?" I inquired. Sam responded with a question. "You look upset as well, what's bothering you,?" Sam asked. "Why do you want to know Sam," I said. "Let's skip the shrink crap." Sam's tone was not hostile. The tone was annoyance rather than hostility. "Nothing," I said, "but what's troubling you?" "I'm upset, very upset about two different matters. The first is that my friend Tony came over from England and gave a great speech to Congress, my family and the world. I can't compete with him. He's a barrister and very gifted in the art of rhetoric. I just can't compete. His speech reminded the world and my family of the larger issues involved in the war with Saddam. He tried to give me a lift in an attempt to get some in my family off the nit-picking stampede that has ensued because we can't find weapons in Iraq. He makes me feel like a know nothing. But it's more than that. He could have accepted his gold medal from Congress, given a short speech and walked off the stage. My gut tells me that my financial buddies got a hold of him and persuaded him to go further and help me out. That means that my buds are losing faith in me. They're getting worried that my family will remove me in a couple of years. That's one matter. The second matter, in my opinion, is worse. I'm really upset about this. The same week that Tony's giving a speech, my friend Pat is on television, holding his wife's hand, in a national prayer among the faithful, asking God to send a message to three Supreme Court justices telling them to retire. That prayer session was picked up by the networks and broadcast internationally. I know people like you see national prayer as stupid and lots of people are making fun of it." I interrupted Sam and asked him, "what is so troubling to you about this." "Let me continue," Sam said. "What troubles me is that if Pat had confidence in me he wouldn't be on television. If Pat believed that I would be the head of the family in two years he wouldn't be on television praying to God for the justices to retire. He would let me take care of that. I am very upset at what I perceive to be a loss of faith in me. I feel like my financial and religious buddies are losing faith in my abilities to run the family. So that's what I am upset about. How about you, Stan, what are you upset about?" "As you know, Sam, therapists don't answer questions like that, but I'm going to make an exception. I lost another two clients this week. I have lost four clients since we started 'chatting.' That's a total of $42,000.00 a year and that's going to make a dent in my lifestyle. I think that Dr. Westerfield is behind all this. I believe that he doesn't think I'm going in a direction that he wants me to go with you. I don't know what's he's looking for and I don't know what he is basing his actions on which leads me to this question. Are you talking to Westerfield about what's going on in here?" "The short answer is no," Sam replied. "I saw Westy on one occasion at a party in New York City and we exchanged pleasantries, that's all," Sam stated. "Well, I haven't seen Gabby since I started with you, so if you're not talking and Gabby doesn't know what's going on, I'm at a loss to explain why I'm losing clients." "Stan, I think you're getting paranoid on me. You do know that there's a recession going on out there. Maybe those clients you lost just can't afford it anymore. Maybe you're not that great a therapist. Maybe those clients you lost have some sense of morals and got wind of your affair with Gabby and decided that they didn't want a therapist with a low moral threshold," said Sam. "Maybe you're right. I wanted to know whether you were the one leaking information to Westerfield and if you were, I was going to tell you to not to talk with anyone about our chats. Now, I have been doing some research into that speech you gave and I have got some questions," I said. "Oh no, not those infamous sixteen words," Sam blurted out. "No, as a matter of fact, not those words at all. What caught my interest was the line wherein you said, "there is wonder-working power in the goodness and idealism of my family." It was the phrase 'wonder working power,' that caught my interest. I was listening to a report on cable news network and the report referred to your ranch as Prairie Chapel. After that I went on the Internet and did a google search for the word 'wonder' and there were 22 references to signs and wonders. I got lost in my research and found reference after reference about Sam and Pat Robertson, Sam and Ralph Reed, Sam and Billy Graham and Sam and Jerry Falwell," I said. Sam interrupted, "you mean you're just getting into this. I told you straight up and out that I was the real deal. I am one with God and walk with him everyday. I don't know why people like you have such a hard time getting it into your head that I'm a real deal reborn Evangelical Christian. I am a true believer along with tens of millions of other people. The tide is turning Stan and you should come on board. Besides, a Jewish shrink walking next to me is a big feather in my cap. It's like a liberal having a best friend who is black. A conservative Christian evangelical walking with a Jew is a blessing. Can I get an Amen, Stan? You'll get use to it. I will admit that you must have something going if you picked up on that 'wonder' word in my speech. It's like a lot of people in my family are in denial. They just don't get it and even if they do, they just don't talk about it. Oh, Sam is appealing to his base, the commentators say. They don't get it either. I'm the real deal. Bringing up religion is like the third rail in politics. No good is going to come of it. Debunking me is like debunking God and who out there is going to debunk God?" Sam asked. "You know what's interesting Sam. While everyone was focusing on those sixteen words in your speech that you gave to your family, I was focusing on something else. Everybody was talking about uranium and I was stuck on this coalition matter. I wanted to know exactly what other countries had ground troops in Iraq in your war against Saddam. I researched the Internet for one month and couldn't find an answer. Everyday, I researched the Internet for an hour looking for the names of 19 foreign countries that had ground troops in Iraq. I couldn't come close to an answer. The first article I encountered was on the MSNBC website. In that article, Sam, a reporter for Slate, Fred Kaplan, had this discussion with General Tommy Franks:

"Gen. Franks said at yesterday's hearing that 19 countries have forces in Iraq, with another 19 preparing to send some and 11 discussing the possibility. But nobody is telling just which 19—much less 38, or 49—countries Franks is talking about. Consider this Hellerian conversation I had yesterday with a Pentagon public-affairs spokesman:

ME: How many countries have, or soon will have, forces on the ground in Iraq?

PENTAGON: There's a dozen nations now, a dozen more very shortly, and a dozen more considering it.

ME: How many people does this add up to?

PENTAGON: You'll have to talk with the individual countries about that.

ME: Which countries are they?

PENTAGON: We can't go into that.

ME: How can I talk with the countries if you won't tell me who they are?

PENTAGON: Well, Britain, of course. Poland has publicized its involvement. But, as I'm sure you understand, this is a very discreet subject for many of the others."

"Sam, on Tuesday, July 21, 2003, @ 4:45 p.m. E.S.T., Mr. Paul Bremmer, the U.S. Administrator to Iraq stated on Buchanan and Press, stated that 'we now have troops of 19 countries on the ground in Iraq already which makes it international and pledges from 37.' The very next day, on July 22, 2003 at a press conference with Donald Rumsfeld at 12:37 p.m. E.S.T. said 'there is already a coalition. There are nineteen countries with troops on the ground in Iraq.' Then on Sunday, July 28, 2003 in a CNN exclusive interview between Wolf Blizter and Lt. Gen. Ricardo Sanchez at 10:11 a.m. E.S.T., the general stated that there are '18 countries presently on the ground in Iraq.' Sam, I am just trying to figure out what countries are in Iraq. Forget the sixteen words. Who are the nineteen countries?" Sam started giggling which soon turned into outright laughter that ended with Sam holding his sides in laughing pain. "What's so funny, Sam?" I asked. I must have asked that question sixteen times. Sam couldn't answer me he was laughing so hard. Every time he started to calm down and look at me, he started laughing all over again, louder and harder than the last time. Sam laughed for twenty minutes. The more he laughed the angrier I got. Sam regained control and struggled to talk. He laughingly blurted out, "Stan, you have got to get a life. I hate to cuss, but you are God damned anal. You remind me of that guy on the Odd Couple. What's his name? Felix. I mean the dates, the times, wow, get a life Stan. You're losing it. What would you shrinks call anal?" he asked. "Obsessive-Compulsive," I said. "Yes, that's it. Give me that book, the manual you have on your desk, what is it, the DSM-IV manual." Sam started to chuckle again. "Really, Stan, I hope you didn't stay up all night on this stuff. Didn't lose any sleep did you?" With that, Sam opened the book and turned to the index and looked up Obsessive-Compulsive. He thumbed to the correct page and started to read. "The essential feature of Obsessive-Compulsive Personality Disorder is a pre-occupation with orderliness, perfectionism, and mental and interpersonal control, at the expense of flexibility, openness and efficiency," Sam read out loud. Sam continued to read silently. He was looking for something that rang true. "O.K., Stan here we go. Individuals with Obsessive-Compulsive Personality Disorder may be excessively conscientious, scrupulous, and inflexible about matters of morality, ethics, or values. They may force themselves and others to follow rigid moral principles and very strict standards of performance. They may also be mercilessly self critical about their own mistakes. Individuals with this disorder are rigidly deferential to authority and rules and insist on quite literal compliance, with no rule bending for extenuating circumstances. For example, the individual will not lend a quarter to a friend who needs one to make a telephone call, because 'neither a borrower or lender be,' or because it would be bad for the person's character." Sam stopped reading and then picked up where he left off except this time louder and he enunciated each word. "These qualities should not be accounted for by the individual's cultural or religious identification. Well, Stan, or should I call you Felix, that leaves me off the hook and you on. What is your point of trying to prove every little mistake I make?" asked Sam. "Well, they are not mistakes. They are lies and half-truths," I said. "Stan, it is spin, my boy, just plain spin. However, since you have an Obsessive-Compulsive Personality Disorder, I can see you have a need for the literal truth. What happened to you when you were younger? Did your father preach to you the sanctity of marriage and you walked in on him with someone who wasn't your mother and as a result you developed this Obsessive-Disorder for the truth?" asked Sam. "No, Sam, I am part of your family and I have to go to great lengths to find out what God damn 19 countries have ground troops in Iraq. I know that you're creating an illusion that we don't need to ask NATO, France or Germany for troops because you're waiting for things to settle down so you can be the big enchilada in Iraq. So you can control the scene and all the rewards. But from my perspective, such conduct is deceitful and manipulative. You know, it took me one full month to find out some semblance of truth. I finally found an article on Slate.com that asked the same question. Who are these nineteen troops someone posed to Slate.com? I assume that Slate put someone on the issue and found only 14 foreign countries with ground troops in Iraq. I handed Sam a copy of the article that I had printed out. He sat silently and read the following:

WHICH ALLIES HAVE TROOPS IN IRAQ?
A postwar roster of men on the ground.
By Brendan I. Koerner
Posted Friday, July 25, 2003, at 2:30 PM PT

The Pentagon is <u>planning</u> to rotate American troops in Iraq, who currently number about 145,000. There are also approximately 13,000 non-American soldiers patrolling the embattled nation. Where do these other "allied forces" come from?

Obviously, the bulk of these troops are British—about 11,000 of the non-American total. Another 1,000 or so are Australians, down from a peak of 2,000 during the height of combat. After that, it's a mishmash of small units, primarily from European countries. Getting exact figures on troops sent by other participants is tricky, in large part because Centcom and the Department of Defense are pretty cagey about keeping such data hush-hush. (Click <u>here</u> for a *Slate* "War Stories" account of the Pentagon's vagueness on these matters.)

What is known, though, is that 380 Danish troops are keeping the peace in the southern Iraqi town of Qurna, purported to be the site of the Biblical Garden of Eden. The Danes also have command over 45 Lithuanians belonging to the <u>Grand Duke Algirdas</u> Motorized Infantry Battalion. The Lithuanians are preparing to commit another 50 troops shortly, and these newcomers will be joined by a tiny unit from Latvia, too. Romania sent its first contingent of 77 troops on July 16 and aims to have 400 of its finest in place by month's end. And Albanian Defense Minister Pandeli Majko has announced that 70 of his nation's soldiers are assisting the 101st Airborne in Mosul, the city where Odai and Qusai Hussein were recently killed.

The Poles currently have between 200 and 300 men in Iraq; several Polish news sources report that at least 50 of those soldiers are members of <u>Grupa Reagowania Operacyjno Mobilnego</u>, the country's elite special forces unit. The Poles are scheduled to beef up their presence to 2,300 troops by Sept. 1, however, when they'll take over command of a large swath of southern Iraq. Joining them will be 1,300 Spaniards and a smattering of Bulgarians, Romanians, Hungarians, and Slovakians. And just yesterday, the Dominican Republic announced that it will be contributing 300 troops to this Polish-led effort, too.

The other contributions are a bit more piecemeal. Last month, a unit of about 100 Italian troops arrived at Nasiriyah to help with humanitarian duties rather than peacekeeping. Their ranks are slated to eventually rise to 1,700, though it's unclear when this buildup will be completed. New Zealand will be sending 60 armed engineers to aid in the reconstruction effort. There have also been reports that Czech troops are assisting with the peacekeeping efforts, but these may merely be remnants of the chemical-weapons teams that Prague dispatched near the beginning of the war.

Last week, British Foreign Secretary Jack Straw <u>announced</u> that, aside from the United States and Great Britain, nine nations had troops on the ground in Iraq. However, Explainer had no luck trying to locate data on precisely how many Norwegian, Dutch, and Ukrainian soldiers are helping out right now. (Curiously, Straw failed to credit the Aussies or Albanians in his speech.). Got any intelligence on these or other nationalities currently within Iraq's borders? Let us know.

After Sam finished reading the article, he looked up and said, "yeah, so, now what. I still think you are a moral obsessive and you are not exempt by religion," Sam stated. "What do you mean yeah, so, now what?" I asked. "I mean exactly that, yeah, so, now what. I don't think I ever said there are 19 foreign countries with ground troops in Iraq. I know I have said there is a coalition of the willing. So, let's see, Tony and I. I would say that fits the definition," said Sam. "And you don't think that that is deceitful and manipulative? I mean, aren't you creating the impression among those members of your family who have a life, that aren't obsessive, like me, that there are a lot of foreign countries with troops in Iraq. That they're all helping you and that for this reason alone you don't have to go to the United Nations, France, Germany, Russia or China. I mean you bought those little countries. You are paying for their troops to come over. You're paying for their food and shelter and salaries. There is no real coalition helping you. So I ask you again, don't you think that this impression, whether spin or outright lies, is deceitful and manipulative?" I asked. "No," Sam simply answered. "Stan, why don't you let it go? We were having such a good time," Sam said. "Sam, I can't let it go and it's not because I have an Obsessive-Compulsive Personality Disorder. How about telling the world that Saddam was actively seeking uranium from Niger, which was based on forged documents? How about claiming that several parts buried under a rose bush twelve years ago are evidence that Saddam was reconstituting his nuclear program? How about pointing to two rusted old trucks and claiming that it is evidence of Saddam's chemical and biological weapons? How about having invaded Saddam's country and occupying it for three months and you haven't discovered one shred of evidence of weapons of mass destruction. Last week, someone went into Iran and took a tiny soil sample and discovered tiny traces of elements that could only have been produced if Iran was pursuing nuclear weapons. I assume that you have the same testing equipment in Iraq. Yet, you have discovered nothing. Now, don't you think you were creating an impression that Saddam was an imminent threat that justified you invading Iraq. Isn't this deceitful and manipulative?" Sam just looked at me. I thought that he was about to get mad and storm out of the office, but he didn't. "I'm not going to get mad at you, Stan. You have promise. After all, you picked up on the 'wonders' in my speech. I believe I can save you. I will save you. It may take time but I will do this for you. Now, let me tell you this. You know what a believer I am. After 9/11, I received a calling from God. Not many people receive callings, but I did. God's mission to me was to rid the world of evil. God will return to earth and reign for 1000 years after Armageddon and the place of the war is ancient Babylon, now Iraq. I accepted his mission and call upon me for service. I am leading the forces of goodness in overcoming evil and the fight starts in Iraq. At the conclusion of Armageddon, God will reappear and peace will reign supreme. I called for regime change because Saddam was evil. I have always maintained that Saddam was evil. However, many of the closest members of my family told me that you can't attack and invade Iraq simply because Saddam and his sons were murderers, rapists, torturers and evil people. My handlers told me that my family had to be convinced that their safety was in imminent danger and so they made up this story supported by the flimsiest of facts and spun out a tale of mushroom clouds and death. However, I was right. The polls indicate that most of my family doesn't care if we find weapons of mass destruction. Seventy per cent believe that I did the right thing because Saddam was evil. I wasn't forceful enough. Had I stuck to my guns there wouldn't be any of this non-sense. So now it all starts to fall apart and we have little Felix's like you standing on the sidelines picking us apart because of all these inconsistencies. There would be no inconsistencies had my close associates followed my lead. Good versus evil," Sam said. "But wouldn't that violate international law," I asked. "I don't care about international law. Yes, it violates international man made law. I follow God's law and mission. It is, after all, a calling higher than any other. It supersedes man-made law. It is the battle necessary for God's kingdom to reign on earth. One thousand years of peace," stated Sam. "So the end justifies the means?" "Yes," Sam answered, "the end justifies the means. The next time I see my friends I'm going to tell them of that Obsessive-Compulsive Personality Disorder and issue talking points to all my subordinates to get it on the airwaves. That will stop them dead in their tracks. The next time people see those liberal leftie Democrats they'll see Felix. Little Felix is whining about catching his dad in bed with someone other than their mother," Sam laughed. "Don't get angry Sam, there is no need," I advised him. "I'm not angry. I'm just getting a little annoyed being picked on all the time. You can understand that. I don't have the gift of gab like my friend

Tony. If I did I would be on the airwaves all the time. I see the larger picture and let me tell you the probable outcome. My troops just killed Oday and Qusay, Saddam's sons. Very shortly, we will capture Saddam. I have told my general's to capture him alive rather than dead. We will put him on trial and then execute him. We will support the Iraqi people and rebuild their infrastructure. The schools, public institutions and all vital services will return over time. Iraqi oil is flowing at 100,000 barrels right now and it is only 90 days since we won the war. One year from now, do you really think anyone out there is really going to care whether or not Saddam presented a threat? Of course not! My family's attention is only as long as the last news cycle. What? Maybe 12 hours. Why not spin for-eign troops on the ground to keep the United Nations and France and Germany out? Why should they benefit at all in the spoils of war. I am six months away from all this nonsense fading into memory. No one will remember. I will be hailed as God's liberator," Sam stated. "What about next time?" I asked. "I don't know what you mean, Stan." "Well, what about the next time you invade another country that presents a larger and more sophisticated military solution. Won't you need real allies? After all, all your military men thought that Saddam was going to a cakewalk," I said. "The answer is that there is no other foreign country that can present any threat to my family or me and no other country that I cannot deal with on my own. I do not need help from anyone. After all, I have God on my side," said Sam. "Sam, this unilateral view of omnipotence can get you in trouble. I don't mean trouble with your family. I mean trouble with the international community. You know what amazes me Sam? Nobody in our coun-try challenges you. The fourth estate, the revered fourth estate has dropped the ball. The press in this country has a special position. It is protected by the consti-tution. It is a privilege to be a member of the press and also poses a grave respon-sibility on them. Why hasn't the press raised the issue of your religion as a matter of discussion? Why didn't one reporter on cable news raise his hand and ask which foreign countries have troops in Iraq. I just can't figure it out," I said. "Well, Stan, I really don't have an answer for you but it definitely works to my advantage. The press in my family would rather discuss the Laci Peterson death trial or the Kobe Bryant rape case. What's interesting Stan, is that if you question them about this, they'll all tell you that the public, my family, has a right to know and more importantly wants to know. I don't get it myself, but my family just never speaks up about anything anymore. They're so complacent. That's why is will be so easy for a mere twenty per cent of my true believers to take this family in an entirely another direction. There are some people out there that we keep an eye on. To give you an example, take that moment you had about twenty minutes ago, when you were reading to me all that stuff about the 19 troops. That is what my friends and I call a Tim Russert moment. Russert likes to be the master of the "got ya" moment. You know, ask someone a question and then show something they said a year ago diametrically opposed to their current position and there you have it, a Tim Russert 'got ya' moment. To which I say: yeah, so and now what. That is where that expression comes from. All those reporters have their little fiefdoms and that is what they care about. The pursuit of the truth is something that's a vague memory. The pursuit of their own goals is what they care about. However, take Chris Matthews. Now, there's a guy who is having a Woodward-Bernstein moment. He smells the truth and he is obsessed with finding it out. Now, he is the one that I'm concerned about. We don't like people who have Woodward-Bernstein moments. You can have all the Russert 'got ya' moments you want, but not Matthews's kind. Thank god there are very few of those guys left. You can bet we keep our eyes on him," Sam stated. "So, I shouldn't expect anything from our press, should I?" I said. "Not unless you like extended trial coverage," Sam replied and added, "and guess who's sitting in the cat bird seat on that one, your friend and mine, "Dan, that's chilling Abrams," said Sam. "I am somewhat compulsive and obsessive especially when it comes to reading news articles and magazines. I read as many as I can find. I have a pretty good memory. I can remember, for example, when the tag line was the 'hunt for weapons of mass destruction' and that was changed to the 'war for Iraqi freedom,' or when the Defense Department changed their program from Total Information Awareness to Terrorist Information Awareness or when we went from Saddam has weapons of mass destruction to Saddam had weapons of mass destruction programs. It seems you move the goal post at every chance," I said. "Let's just say my friends and I are creative," Sam responded. "And you don't think this is deceitful and manipulative?" I asked again. "Well, I guess you can make an argument if my family was paying attention, but they are not. I guess you can't be deceitful if the one who is deceived is not aware of it. You know, it's the old argument, if a tree falls in the forest and no one hears it, did it fall?" stated Sam. "Aren't you debasing the standards by which you and your family are conducting themselves?" I asked. "If this were peaceful times, perhaps, but this is the apocalyptic war between good and evil and so I believe rules can be bent. It is, after all, God's war," Sam replied. "I'm almost at the point of not reading or watching anything that your family produces as news. I have turned to Britain to read more informative articles that have some meat on them. For example, today I read in the Guardian, a British newspaper an article entitled "America is a Religion." I deleted many parts and only left those in that I thought you might find interesting. I wanted to show it to you and ask your opinion." I handed Sam the article and he read it:

AMERICA IS A RELIGION

Sam's leaders now see themselves as priests of a divine mission to rid the world of its demons

George Monbiot
Tuesday July 29, 2003
<u>**The Guardian**</u>

To understand why this failure persists, we must first grasp a reality which has seldom been discussed in print. The United States is no longer just a nation. It is now a religion. Its soldiers have entered Iraq to liberate its people not only from their dictator, their oil and their sovereignty, but also from their darkness. As Sam told his troops on the day he announced victory: "Wherever you go, you carry a message of hope—a message that is ancient and ever new. In the words of the prophet Isaiah, 'To the captives, "come out," and to those in darkness, "be free".'"

So Sam's soldiers are no longer merely terrestrial combatants; they have become missionaries. They are no longer simply killing enemies; they are casting out demons. The people who reconstructed the faces of Uday and Qusay Hussein carelessly forgot to restore the pair of little horns on each brow, but the understanding that these were opponents from a different realm was transmitted nonetheless. Like all those who send missionaries abroad, the high priests of America cannot conceive that the infidels might resist through their own free will; if they refuse to convert, it is the work of the devil, in his current guise as the former dictator of Iraq.

As Clifford Longley shows in his fascinating book Chosen People, published last year, the founding fathers of the USA, though they sometimes professed otherwise, sensed that they were guided by a divine purpose. Thomas Jefferson argued that the Great Seal of the United States should depict the Israelites, "led by a cloud by day and a pillar of fire by night". George Washington claimed, in his inaugural address, that every step towards independence was "distinguished by some token of providential agency". Longley argues that the formation of the American identity was part of a process of "supersession". The Roman Catholic church claimed that it had supplanted the Jews as the elect, as the Jews had been repudiated by God. The English Protestants accused the Catholics of breaking faith, and claimed that they had become the beloved of God. The American revolutionaries believed that the English, in turn, had broken their covenant: the Americans had now become the chosen people, with a divine duty to deliver the world to God's dominion. Six weeks ago, as if to show that this belief persists, George Bush recalled a remark of Woodrow Wilson's. "America," he quoted, "has a spiritual energy in her which no other nation can contribute to the liberation of mankind."

Gradually this notion of election has been conflated with another, still more dangerous idea. It is not just that the Americans are God's chosen people; America itself is now perceived as a divine project. In his farewell presidential address, Ronald Reagan spoke of his country as a "shining city on a hill", a reference to the Sermon on the Mount. But what Jesus was describing was not a temporal Jerusalem, but the kingdom of heaven. Not only, in Reagan's account, was God's kingdom to be found in the United States of America, but the kingdom of hell could also now be located on earth: the "evil empire" of the Soviet Union, against which His holy warriors were pitched.

Since the attacks on New York, this notion of America the divine has been extended and refined. In December 2001, Rudy Giuliani, the mayor of that city, delivered his last mayoral speech in St Paul's Chapel, close to the site of the shattered twin towers. "All that matters," he claimed, "is that you embrace America and understand its ideals and what it's all about. Abraham Lincoln used to say that the test of your Americanism was...how much you believed in America. Because we're like a religion really. A secular religion." The chapel in which he spoke had been consecrated not just by God, but by the fact that George Washington had once prayed there. It was, he said, now "sacred ground to people who feel what America is all about". The United States of America no longer needs to call upon God; it is God, and those who go abroad to spread the light do so in the name of a celestial domain. The flag has become as sacred as the Bible; the name of the nation as holy as the name of God. The presidency is turning into a priesthood.

So those who question Sam's foreign policy are no longer merely critics; they are blasphemers, or "anti-Americans". Those foreign states which seek to change this policy are wasting their time: you can negotiate with politicians; you cannot negotiate with priests. The US has a divine mission, as Sam suggested in January: "to defend...the hopes of all mankind", and woe betide those who hope for something other than the American way of life.

The dangers of national divinity scarcely require explanation. Japan went to war in the 1930s convinced, like Sam, that it possessed a heaven-sent mission to "liberate" Asia and extend the realm of its divine imperium. It would, the fascist theoretician Kita Ikki predicted: "light the darkness of the entire world". Those who seek to drag heaven down to earth are destined only to engineer a hell.

Sam looked up after reading and said that it was great article. "So why doesn't your press have the same insight that the world media seem to have. I just don't understand why I find more sanity across our oceans than right here in my own country," I said to Sam. I pulled out another article and slid it across the desk when Sam stood up and said time's up. I looked at my watch and almost two hours had gone by. I couldn't believe it. It was the first time in my practice that I forgot time with one of my patients. I was embarrassed. I started to discuss my vacation with Sam. Sam leaned towards my desk extended his arm and grabbed a notepad and a pencil. While I was talking, Sam jotted down some sentences and pushed the pad across the desk so that I could read it. He kept it covered with one hand until I looked at him and with the other hand put his index finger over his lips and gently whispered "shhh." He did it again and again until he saw that I understood to keep quiet. I read the note. Sam wrote; "look under your desk on your left. That little black box is a transmitter." I continued to talk about my vacation and leaned over my chair and peered at the bottom of my desk. There was a little black box. I felt light headed on the way up and broke out into a sweat. This was way over my head. I found out how Westerfield was checking up on Sam's progress. I wondered how long Sam had known. Sam could tell I was shaken at the discovery of the transmitter. "You probably missed dinner. Why don't I take you out for dinner, my treat and we'll belt down a couple of scotches," Sam said. I knew that it wasn't a good idea, but Sam continued, "I know that it not correct therapeutic behavior for a shrink and a patient to have dinner but we have broken every rule so far why not one more," he said. It did not go unnoticed that Sam said "shrink and a patient." Sam and I got in a cab in front of my office and Sam instructed the driver to go to a little Italian restaurant on West Broadway in the village. Sam and I got out of the cab and Sam stopped at the entrance to the restaurant. "No, No, I don't think so," Sam said. I'm sure my friend John, the statistical and numerical genius probably figured out we would come here. This place is not secure. Take a walk with me. We're going for Chinese food. Poindexter knows I hate Chinese food. The probability that I would go for Chinese food would be statistically insignificant. Come with me, we're going to Hung Fat's on Mott Street," Sam said. "Sam, what the hell are you talking about?" I asked. "Security Stan, security. You don't think I could walk out the door of your office with you without some attempt by those concerned to monitor our conversation," Sam stated. "Sam, all of this stuff is way over my head. I am beginning to believe that I'm in the wrong ballpark. The game that's being played here doesn't look or feel like anything I know," I told Sam. "Calm down, Warlib, you're with me. All we're doing is trying to protect whatever conversation we have. The powers that be want to know what we're talking about. They want to know what I'm thinking. Knowledge is power, Stan." We entered Hung Fat's and Sam walked to the back of the room. He told me to sit with my back to the entrance and that he would sit facing me so that it would be difficult for anyone to read our lips. "Is this the kind of world you live in? Mystery and intrigue at every turn. It's a real James Bond movie," I said to Sam. "No, it's not that complex, Stan, it's about power. Who's got it and who doesn't? How to get power and how to take power away? It's not that complex. Don't get carried away," Sam said. Sam gave the waiter $50.00 and told him to get us the best sake he had in the back. The waiter returned and Sam pushed away the little sake cups, poured both water glasses into another empty glass and filled up the glasses halfway. I knew it was going to be some kind of night. I had been down this road before where two people who don't like each other start drinking together and end up the evening drunk professing love. It's like that beer commercial "I love you Man." But it's all bullshit. It's really two enemies looking for an opening, a weakness in the other guy's armour when inhibitions and defenses are gone. Both parties declare friendship and respect for the other person. It's a game. Sam and I exchanged polite banter as we drank the sake. Sam poured us another half glass and we drank that too. About ten minutes later, I could feel the alcohol take over. The waiter came over for our order but Sam waived him off. The waiters were pretty cool about heavyweights drinking in the back of their restaurant as they were used to meetings among Mafia people. They knew it was talking time not eating time. Sam poured another half glass except this time both of us began the sipping process instead of slugging it down to get the quick buzz. Sam and I weren't quite in the freedom zone. We continued the polite banter and continued sipping. Eventually we slowly slipped into the alcohol defense free zone. Inhibitions lessened and Sam took the opportunity to fire off the first question. "So, Stan, what kind of name is Warlib anyway?" "It's short for Warlibowsky," I said. "Is that Polish?" Sam asked. "No, Polish is Ski not Sky. I'm Jewish, you know. Tom Delay is my best friend. You know Tom Delay, don't you? The head of the Christian Zionist movement in Congress." Sam laughed. "That's a good one Stan. You know, don't you, that you would probably be the first one on Delay's hit list?" "Yeah, well, screw him too," I said. "Look, Stan, do me a favor and cut out the cussing. I won't deal with it," Sam said. I thought for a minute and realized whom I was dealing with and reluctantly agreed. "Brooklyn boys have a hard time talking without their hands and using foul language," I told Sam. "I'll try," I said, "but I don't know if I can be 100% cuss free." "Give it a try," said Sam. "By the way, Sammy boy, how come you guys say cussing and not fucking cursing. It's right up there with pop instead of 'Coke' or 'Pepsi.' Hey, Stan, would you like a pop? I'm sorry Sam, I know I said the word fucking. I'm aware, I promise, I'll do better." Sam poured another half glass of sake. We were there in the zone. Buzz time, big time. "So, Stan how are you doing. How are you really doing?" Sam inquired. "How am I doing? How am I really doing? Well, how much time have got Sammy boy." "All night," Sam responded. "Well, I'll tell you how I'm doing. My practice is slowly going to pot. Gabby is sitting on my face with a criminal prosecution and my license could be lifted. I've broken every rule of therapeutic relationships with patients. I'm in a ballpark where I don't get the game that's being played. There's a transmitter under my desk and I'm sitting with a guy who can't go into an Italian restaurant because his friend John Poindexter would have statistically proven in advance that you would be there with me and listen into our conversation. Other than that, I'm doing just fine. That's the long answer. The short answer is that I'm out of control. I'm way in over my head and the life that I had sixty days ago seems like a pleasant fantasy. I went from a musical comedy to a horror movie in two months and I'm drinking with a guy who found God because he was a drinker. I'm in fantasyland, Sam. One big amusement park and I'm the main attraction. So, how are you and why are you drinking?" I asked. "Well, God will forgive me for breaking the rule on drinking and to answer the question about how I'm doing, I would say I'm doing fairly well with some minor problems." Sam seemed in control. Either he wasn't that buzzed from the sake, was telling the truth or was giving me a lot of shit. I really couldn't tell. For someone who had not had a drink in years he had to be buzzed. I realized that his stability was his belief in God. All he had to do was the best he could and God would see to the rest. "Well, this is great Sam. I'm the shrink out of control and you're the delusional nut in control. The classic case of the screwballs running the asylum." "Is that what you think, Stan. I'm delusional?" he asked. "Yes, and not only that Sammy boy, I would diagnose you as having a narcissistic personality disorder with features of and/or a full blown diagnosis of having the additional disorder of anti-social personality disorder. Formerly a psychopath." "Well, well, well. All this after eight chats! Am I suppose to fall down on this news, Dr. Sigmund Freud or is it Dr. Carl Jung?" Sam asked. "No. You can sit right here and listen to all this crap. But the bottom line is, I'm out of control and you're not. Right, Sam?" "Yes, that's the bottom line, Warlib. You're out of control and making mistakes. Big time." Sam kept on pouring sake like it was his one big treat and he was going to make the most of it. "So, Dr. Sam, how do I get out of this mess that I'm in?" I asked. "Why, Stan, you're asking me questions. You're looking for my help. Who's the shrink here, Sam or

Stan?" "I'm getting drunk and I really don't care," I said. "Well, you know my
answer, Stan. Follow me. Follow God and follow the Bible. The truth shall set
you free. You are engulfed in grayness because you are trying to get out of all your
mistakes without punishment. Admit your mistakes. Declare the truth and God
will forgive you. The grayness will disappear and blue skies will arrive immediately. You'll feel renewed," Sam stated. "So, it's that simple for you guys?" I
asked. "Yes, it's that simple." "I don't believe it," I said to Sam. "Try it," Sam
calmly replied. "Stan, in the game of power you never tip your hand under any
circumstances, drunk or sober. I have had a lot more experience in this than you.
We never lose sight of power politics. You really are a babe in the woods," said
Sam. "Yes, I am a babe in the woods Sam. Look, I'm just a little guy making a living. I try to do the right thing most of the time, have a little fun and don't try to
hurt anyone intentionally. I am a member of your extended family. You and your
financial and religious buddies are the head of the family and I don't like what
you guys are doing and where you guys are taking us. I am truly bewildered. I'm
going to do you a favor and tell you what's going on down in the pits among your
family members. There are cracks showing up Sam. And you don't see the cracks.
Not everybody loves you. Since you're a narcissistic piece of shit, your own personality stands in the way of noticing what you're doing to your family. Not only
that, you don't care. You have this huge grandiose scheme that you're leading
your family down the road to salvation and everything you do you interpret in a
way that's to your advantage even when it's not. For example, your brain won't
filter in any information that says occupying Iraq will be a problem. Your brain
filters out all negative information and you only allow in information that you
interpret that the Iraq people will embrace you and sing and dance in the streets
to you as the great liberator. Your brain needs to seek out those people who will
reinforce that belief. It seeks constant reinforcement that supports your position
no matter how dubious the source or quality of the information or people that
provide it. So, up pops a guy named Ahmed Chalabi, a former Iraqi citizen, a
convicted bank embezzler, who hasn't been there in twenty years and he tells you
what you want to hear. 'Yes, my people will dance and sing in the streets for Sam
the great liberator. They will welcome you with open arms,' Chalubi says and you
buy into it. You're Sam, you're great. It's like the emperor's cloths. No one
around is going to tell you that you're standing there naked except you're family.
The only problem is that even you're family thinks you have clothes on and that
is why I'm bewildered. This terrorism stuff! I don't believe it at all. Yes, I do
believe that there are terrorists in this world but nowhere near the extent that you
guys actively seek to promote. I think you're gas lighting your own people. I

really believe that your family has features of a Paranoid Personality Disorder and you feed into that. You're making them nuts. It's terror, terror and more terror. You say it over and over, again and again. Why would you do that to your family? I'll tell you why. You don't like them. You despise them. They're a bunch of heathens who took the wrong road. Do you think your family knows the direction that you're taking them? Do you really think that they fully comprehend that you will criminalize homosexual behavior, ban abortions, ban books and movies that you think are offensive? I don't think they understand that Sam. Not really. So you feed into their paranoid personality over and over taking their eyes off the road you're really going down. Fear, fear and more fear. You're going to be attacked, I'll protect you. I'll protect you. You see guys, there have been no attacks since 9/11. Look what a good job I'm doing. I have been protecting you well. Love me and I'll protect you more. I don't believe any of this bullshit. I think 95% of this terror crap is crap," I said. "Are you finished, Stan?" Sam interjected. "No, I'm not. I'm drunk, rambling and I'm not finished. You know, I have tried to follow proper therapeutic guidelines in treating you. I have done an incredible amount of research into you and your family as an aid to help me understand who and what you're all about. So, I'll give you just one example, which is representative of hundreds of examples of the same type. The question is how is Sam doing on the war on terror? The answer is, great. I have arrested hundreds of terrorists and made my family safe. So, here's the example. Your boy, John Ashcroft, needs a high body count of arrested terrorists to add to the absurd delusion that we are under attack by terrorists. Sixty-two Middle Eastern students are arrested. Wait a minute, I have the article. I cut these things out and put them in a file or carry them around and read them over and over thinking that maybe I'll gain some insight." I reached into my wallet and pulled out a folded piece of paper. I opened it and gave it to Sam. The article stated in pertinent part the following:

At first blush, New Jersey's District Attorney's office seems like a model of federal law enforcement in the war against terrorism. In the year after 9/11, after all, they nabbed 62 individuals for acts of "international terrorism"—individuals who, arguably, would no longer be threatening American lives. But on closer inspection, there's less to this success story than meets the eye. Sixty of the 62 international terrorists, according to a March story in *The Philadelphia Inquirer*, turned out to be Middle Eastern students who had cheated on a test; specifically, they had paid others to take an English proficiency exam required for college or graduate school. Only one of the other two cases involved charges that might normally be understood as relating to an act of terrorism: Ahmad Omar Saeed

Sheikh, who was indicted for his role in the kidnapping and murder of *Wall Street Journal* reporter Daniel Pearl in Pakistan.

After Sam finished reading the article, he said, "yeah, so, now what. You're having another one of those Tim Russert "got ya" moments. "Don't give me that crap Sam. That is one example among hundreds of the crap that you pull all day long. Now, my theory is that no one is paying too much attention so you take this phony information and spin it out of control to come up with an overall impression that your family is under attack and that you're doing a great job to save them. I think its bullshit. Here's what I think. I'm not looking for what's missing in the crime scene. I'm looking for what should be there. If we were under attack by terrorists, a real coordinated attack by terrorists, it would be like Israel. Terror attacks should be there and they're not. Imagine three lone wolfs each with a stick of dynamite. One is in the mall of America and one each on the west coast and east coast. They all walk into major malls and blow themselves up. Reality dictates that scenario if terrorism is as real to the extent that you make it out to be. Retail sales would plunge and your family already teetering on the brink of financial ruin would topple. Your answer is that terrorists have a signature. They look for big targets, like the The Statute of Liberty. I say bullshit. Ninety-five per cent of this terror stuff is bullshit and I'm convinced that it's the intentional gas lighting of your family. Now, that Sam is sick shit. That's what I believe. Sounds like I'm crazy, doesn't it? But here's the kicker. I see all sorts of reports of you and your buddies not funding homeland security. Everybody makes hay that you don't care and I sit there and I think that it makes perfect sense. Why should you spend a ton of money for a threat that is at best, inconsequential? Makes sense to me." I paused and grabbed the waiter by the sleeve and ordered roast pork chow fun. Good greasy food. "Stan, are you done? You are way, way, out there. You are starting to sound like a guy from the planet of conspiracies. Do you really believe this kind of stuff?" Sam asked. "Yes, Sam, I do and I'll tell you why. I'm not going to let up. I'm having a Woodward-Bernstein moment. If I accept your reality that we are under attack and that you have arrested 1,000 terrorists in our homeland and therefore the threat is real and I do some research, your reality starts to fall apart." I was drunk but I think I was making sense. "So, let's take another example." I pulled out a second article and handed it to Sam. It read in pertinent part:

And thanks to an expansive, non-standardized, and often subjective definition of the term "terrorism," it's easy to make mundane criminal cases look like terrorist threats. When two *Philadelphia Inquirer* reporters studied Department of Justice cases between 1996 and 2001, they found numerous misclassifications.

Among those counted as terrorist cases were a tenant impersonating an FBI agent to try and escape eviction by his landlord, a commercial pilot who falsely implicated his copilot in a hijack plot out of personal jealousy, and seven Chinese sailors who stole a Taiwanese fishing boat to seek political asylum in Guam. (Not to mention the Arizona man who got drunk on a United Airlines flight, kept ringing the call button, and "put his hands on a flight attendant," according to the article—and was classified in Justice's records as a case of "domestic terrorism.") As Jonathan Turley, a professor of constitutional criminal procedure at George Washington University Law School, told the *Inquirer*, Justice, like all agencies, needs to "justify past appropriations and secure future increases." Bagging more terrorists, even if they probably just need a few A.A. sessions, is a good way to do it.

So now you have the entire fourth estate, our grand illustrious media, bringing on the pundits discussing terrorists and the possible terror scenarios. The terror plot de jour is, can ferries be used as weapons of terror? What bullshit. These guys should be pouring over the articles that I just showed you. They should be determining the nature and extent of the terror threat and the exact extent of this issue. Is it real or imagined? But they don't because reality doesn't sell, does it? Freaking people out with grand headlines is what sells. All you have to do is make one simple statement and the media does the rest. They even go so far as to make up their own scenarios and I have to look at the expert pundits giving me this shit. And the loyal opposition who wants to unseat you and become the head of my family doesn't run away from this bullshit, they want to show me that they'll spend more money and protect me better. They could do a better job against this threat called terror. Well, let's just get the duct tape and plastic and seal me off in a little bubble, lock me up in the closet and surround the house with the national guard. Whoop de freaking do, I feel safe now." I realized that many in Sam's family exhibited features of Paranoid Personality Disorder and Dependent Personality Disorder. For some reason, whether it was the alcohol or the free floating rant that I was on, many questions that I had before started to become clearer. Sam knocked on the table with his fist. "Stan, are you with me?" "Yeah, Sam, sorry about that. I got lost somewhere in my mind," I said. "I can see that you have. You have been lost in your mind for the past thirty minutes. Do you know what you said to me?" Sam inquired. "You have been telling me that you think to a large degree, I believe you said 95%, that this terrorist threat doesn't exist. Are you crazy?" Sam asked. "Sometimes I think I am, Sam. However, a psychologist can be a functional loony and still be a good therapist and yes, I sincerely believe that this alleged terrorist threat is largely a delusion emanating out of your family's Paranoid Personality Disorder largely instigated by your insane dislike of your family due largely to your Anti-Social Personality Disorder. You know, we used to call you guys psychopaths and sociopaths. I mean, just look at what you and your buddies do. You point to two broken down trucks and claim they are evidence of manufacturing weapons of mass destruction. You hold up some trinkets found under a rose bush and claim evidence of nuclear intentions. You stand in front of a big sign that says Jobs Growth and Opportunity and claim that your tax cut to the wealthy will create jobs. I could go on and on. It's all misleading and deceptive. I think you are a psychopath. But why would you do that? What do you gain?" I asked. The greasy chow fun came and I dug in. Sam didn't touch his food. Several minutes went by and not a word was said. Finally, I asked Sam again, "so what do you gain by gas lighting your family?" "Oh, you're really looking for an answer?" Sam said. "Yes, I'm really looking for an answer," I replied. "Are we back in session?" asked Sam. "Yes, Sam, it looks like we're back in session." "Well, I'm out for dinner and drinks," said Sam. "Can't be Sam. You brought me here for Chinese food and you don't like Chinese food. So you didn't come here for dinner. You also don't drink, although you're doing it tonight. After you answer the question and I'll repeat it, 'what do you gain by being deceitful and manipulative with your family?' you can answer this question, why did you bring me here tonight? What exactly do you want and what exactly do your financial buddies expect. Come on, Sam, let's get down to the nitty gritty," I said. "Feeling pretty good, aren't you Stan?" said Sam. "Yes, as a matter of fact I am and that's because you're right, Sam, the truth will set me free. From this day forward, I'm going to tell the truth and put it all on the line. The truth will set me free. I'm not going to live up in my head anymore. Tomorrow, I'm going to my shrink and confess all and take the heat. Right after that, I'm calling my attorney and find out exactly what the downside risk is for nailing Gabby under therapeutic circumstances. So, you're right, the truth will and has as of right now, set me free. I'm starting to gain back a little respect. So, answer my question, Sam, what do you gain and what do you want?" I asked again. "I don't gain anything. I'm not gas lighting my family," he responded. "Well, you know the hardest question for patients to answer is exactly what they gain for continuing bad behavior. This question would be particularly hard for you because you're a narcissist. You think you're great. Well, guess what, you're not. Seen the polls, lately, Sammy. You're slipping. We'll leave these questions for our sessions. The next question is exactly why did you want to go out. It was all very mysterious at first and I was scared. The transmitter under my desk shook me to the bone, I'll admit that. However, I am setting myself free so let's give me an answer as to why you wanted to go out to dinner." Sam sat silent for several minutes. I continued eating my chow fun. I forgot how much I loved greasy chow fun. What a treat. By now the effects of the alcohol were starting to wear off. "Come on Sam, it's getting late and I have a shrink appointment first thing tomorrow morning," I told Sam. "I invited you to dinner because I had a plan that I thought you might find interesting. What is going on, Stan, I mean, the reason that you're being tweaked by Westerfield and losing patients is that he's not hearing what he wants to hear," Sam said. "Well, what does he want to hear?" I asked. "Hold on, Stan, I'll get to that. Listen, you have been talking for nearly two hours, non-stop and now it's my turn. Westerfield is merely a liaison between my financial buddies and me. I don't have that much access to them and I hardly know any of them. There are five hundred "financial buddies" and I have only met a handful. There is a huge separation between us," Sam stated. I jumped in with a question, "so why do you call them your buddies?" "Don't get hung up Stan, it was a figure of speech. They are not really my buddies. I hardly know them and for political and other reasons everyone is better off if we maintain distance between us. However, they're very rich and very powerful. They are from all over the world. Well, Stan, my religious buddies are exactly that. They are good friends and all of us are on the same page. It seems, from the limited information I get from Westerfield that these financial buddies are somewhat upset by my affiliation with my religious buddies. They're worried that I'll neglect their interests and walk down the road with my religious buddies to their neglect. They're all about the money. Period. So they're protecting their interest by forcing me to see you," Sam said. "How is that protecting their interest?" I asked Sam. "Well, just like you think I may be delusional, these money men are just as leery about my walking with God and so they figured that you might be able to persuade me to walk down their road rather than walk down God's path. They were protecting their interest," said Sam. "How was I supposed to figure that out?" I asked. "I guess they heard that you were good and would figure it out on your own. I don't know. I'm sure they would have whittled your practice down to nothing in the hope that you would finally figure it out. Let me give you an example. You know that I have stated many times that North Korea was part of the axis of evil. Well, I really believe that. Right after I was elected head of the family, I changed the previous administrations position on North Korea and that was contrary to the interest of my financial buddies. Well, guess what? It didn't take more than two hours before they got my father, my father, to call me on the carpet and change my position. I mean, they made it plain that I wasn't going to be around too long. The next day I had to publicly change my stance and suffer humiliation. Apparently, I didn't know they owned a large South Korean bank that had some possible dealings going on with the North. It didn't take but two stinking hours before I was hauled on the carpet. The bottom line seems to be that I can lead my family in whatever direction I want as long as it doesn't have any effect on their financial holdings. You know the Bible says that it is easier to get a camel through the eye of the needle than to get a rich man in heaven. I will see them at the gates of heaven," Sam said. "Here's the problem I have with what you're saying. You're gas lighting your family and freaking them out. For example, just when the airlines are trying to obtain some financial footing and gain traffic, you guys come out with an alert and warning that al-Qaeda is going to attempt, sometime in August, a possible 9/11 type plane high jacking. That is contrary to your financial buddies own interest. They should be trying to make people feel safe, not freak them out. Your family is going to close their pocket books and retreat from the airlines. They're broke as it is. Do they want to put the nail in the airline coffin? It just doesn't make economic sense," I said. "Well, that assumes that these financial buddies have interests in airlines. Maybe they don't. Let me say this. The recent GDP figures showed a surprising 2.4% increase. In large part that was based upon a 44% increase is defense spending. Are you starting to get the picture, Stan? Terror sells a lot of offensive and defensive weapons systems and that is all that I'm going to say on this matter. To get back to the point of why we're here, I was going to suggest to you that you should slant your questions towards convincing me that my religious buddies have too much influence over me and then I would kind of go along and see the light and slant my beliefs a little more towards my financial buddies," Sam said. "So, we are going to stage therapy lessons and read from some kind of script. Is that what you have in mind?" "Yes," Sam answered. "The theory being, that you discovered with my help, a more correct path that was similar to theirs and then you wouldn't have to come to therapy?" I asked. "Somewhat correct, Stan. It would be more like I had an awareness that their interests had to be protected and that I wasn't going to be a loose cannon. Not many people feel comfortable with evangelical conservative Christians. Can you imagine me requesting Congress to give me 'ah amen' after my speeches. All hell would break loose. They started to feel uncomfortable with my religion and wanted to remind me that financial support would not be forthcoming. The bottom line was very simple. Don't make God your only buddy," Sam said. "Sam, I think I'm starting to get the picture but I have to give this a lot of thought. You want out of therapy and I want out of therapy with you and the answer to our mutual problem is to stage therapy sessions until we reach that point in time that your financial buddies feel comfortable. I suppose you even have a script in mind?" I asked. "Not yet, but I can have some of our shrinks prepare one," Sam answered. "I have to think about all this Sam." "You can't. This is a one shot deal. It won't happen again. These people are information freaks. If you remove that transmitter from under your desk the game is over. If we go out again without supervision the game is over. I'll have no support to become the head of the family again and you'll have no practice, no license and you'll be spending time with Martha Stewart for a very, very long time. This game is real and for keeps. We need to stay here until we arrive at some conclusion one way or another," Sam said. "Let me ask you some questions, while I think about this for a minute. Since your financial buddies aren't really your buddies, let's give them a name," I said. "Just call them the Carlisle boys, O.K.," said Sam. "How do they financially support you. Wouldn't that be a violation of the law?" "I'm sure you are aware that I have no opponent running against me from within the ranks of my own support group. What I'm sure you don't know is that any unused campaign funds belong to me and I can assure you that without any opponent from within my own group I will have lots of unused funds which the law says I get to keep. Got it. Unused campaign funds are probably the easiest way to make $100,000,000 that I ever heard of. Nod bad, Stan. I have a lot of money riding on your decision. You know, Stan, it just occurred to me that they'd just get me another therapist. Maybe you aren't that important after all. Maybe I'm getting myself all whipped up in this nonsense just like you. Maybe the truth will set me free as well. I'm just being greedy. I don't need their support and I probably don't need their money. I can get money from my religious buddies to run my own campaign," Sam stated. "So, is that it, Sam? Have we arrived at our mutual solution? Are we going to let the dice roll for both of us. You go your way and I'll go mine so to speak?" I asked. "Yes, Stan, that's what we're going to do. We're going to let the truth set us free. Amen," Sam said. "Yes, Sam and I agree, amen." "Good luck, Stan." "Good luck to you Sam."

Sam got up, left the restaurant and left me sitting there alone. All the patrons had left. The waiters were busy finishing up their respective jobs. Two of them just sat in their seats glaring at me waiting for me to leave so they could go home to their wives. Sam didn't believe in slow decelerations. He practiced mind blowing sudden stops and they always left me in a surreal world. This mind blowing sudden stop left me alone with two Chinese waiters in Hung Fat's on Mott Street in New York City.

I grabbed a paper for the cab ride home. The battle had begun. Sam and his religious buddies were coming down hard against gay marriages. The gays were appearing on the Bravo channel in a new reality show. The battle lines were drawn and each side's cavalry was lining up. The cable news networks were working overtime with Saddam, weapons of mass destruction, the Vatican, gays and terror. My family was in turmoil and they didn't even know it. It was business as usual except the degree of the turmoil was on high. Rodney Kings "why can't we all just get along" was good advice at this point in time. It seemed that after years of equal splits in Sam's family one side or the other wanted to break out and win the war. The heat was on. Sam and I were about to roll the truth dice each in our respective ways. The world did indeed seem extra turbulent tonight as I rode up Madison Avenue. It was two o' clock in the morning. The battles were beginning. The war had commenced.

As the cab drove up to my stoop I noticed a figure standing outside the door. It was much too dark for me to make out who it was. I expected someone to be waiting. C.I.A.? F.B.I.? D.I.A.? N.S.A.? Condi Rice? As I walked up the steps it became clear that the "figure" was Gabby. "I expected someone from the Westy camp to be here, but I didn't expect you," I told Gabby. I opened the door and asked Gabby to come in. "I don't think it's a good idea, Stan," she said. "O.K. Gabby then stay right here and I'll take my leave and go to sleep." "But I have to talk to you, Stan. It's real important," said Gabby. "Then I suggest that you come on in otherwise there will be no talking," I answered. Gabby reluctantly came into my apartment. I motioned towards the deck in the garden and she followed me. I thought that I should check the area for "little black boxes" and sure enough, under the windowsill was a thin 6" cylinder glued to the brick wall. In all respects unnoticeable, whether in daylight or darkness. I must have passed that transmitter a thousand times and never noticed it. I ripped it off the brick and broke it in two. I handed it to Gabby. "Here, tell your father he doesn't need it anymore," I said. I sat down with my back away from the brownstones on the other side of the garden and pulled my chair as close to Gabby as I could. I talked quietly. I was trying to prevent anyone from eavesdropping on our conversation. I learned quickly the lessons the night had taught me. I told Gabby that I was tired and that she should speak quietly. "Now, Gabby, how are you?" I asked. "I have something important to talk to you about," she said. "No, Gabby. First we talk like normal adults without the drama. I haven't seen you in a long time and you are very special to me. I missed you. Do you know that? I had thought for a long time that someday you and I were going to wind up living together and that thought was a mere 90 days ago. It seems like a lifetime." The more I spoke along these lines the more Gabby relaxed. I could see the frigidness in her body start to dissipate. Her shoulders were slowly coming down from next to her ears and came to a normal position. I was determined to keep on talking until I noticed that her entire body was relaxed. Talking to Gabby while she was upset would be useless. She was only there to deliver a message and I already knew what it was. She had been so whipped up in this mess that she wasn't the Gabby that I knew. Gabby had undergone a complete transformation or so I thought. I had undergone a complete transformation. Gabby put her arms around my neck, drew my closer and kissed me. I responded. Within that embrace and kiss it was as if we had never been separated and that the entire mess that had gone on between us was a dream. Gabby slid her mouth away from my lips to my ear and whispered, "I love you Stan." I wasn't aware how tense my body was until that very moment. I felt my shoulders leave the vicinity of my ears and slowly droop to a more normal position. My eyes were closed and I lifted my head and let out a big sigh of relief. All the turbulence in my life had left with those simple words "I love you." It felt like I was home again. No pretenses, no defenses and no more expending an extraordinary amount of energy protecting myself. I realized at that very moment, how difficult and draining it was treating personality disorders. Your guard is up all the time protecting yourself from your own patient. I opened my eyes to a figure in the doorway. I couldn't make out who it was as the kitchen light was on. I backed off Gabby and got off my chair and moved forward. "Sorry, Stan. I didn't mean to frighten you. It's me, Dr. Westerfield. It has been a trying three months for both Gabby and I and we can here to apologize. I no longer have any association with, let's say, some groups that I have been associated with and Gabby, well, I guess she can speak for herself. Needless to say, we all acted very poorly and therefore, I apologize," Mr. Westerfield said. "I'm sure you and Gabby have much to discuss. I have no idea what your August vacations plans are but you're welcome to my house in the Hamptons. We will be there for the entire month. It might be a good opportunity for you and Gabby to get reacquainted. Once again, I apologize. Gabby I'll be in the car waiting." Dr. Westerfield stepped back, turned and went back into the kitchen. He grabbed my arm and motioned for me to follow. In the kitchen, out of earshot of Gabby, Dr. Westerfield whispered, "I might inform you that Elicia is the human version of that little black box that you found under your desk. She is human intel. I hope to see this weekend. Good-night." Dr. Westerfield left the kitchen and I turned towards the deck. I stared at Gabby. I forgot how beautiful she was. I forgot what a great time I had had with her. The concept of Gabby and I seemed years ago but only a short period of time had passed. Time had been distorted. "Gabby, it's late and I have a lot of work left to do. I have an appointment with Dr. P. in the morning. Will you be at the house this week-end?" I asked. "Yes, Stan I will and I'm not going to ask you if you will be there because I know you will." "Gabby, I think it's going to be sunset and sunrise walks on the beach." I grabbed Gabby by the waist with one hand and pulled her close while I placed my other hand on the back of her head at the same time. Our lips came together. Gabby turned and left. I sat down and placed my feet on the deck table and waved to whoever might be on the other side. "The truth shall set you free" was probably the greatest quote of all time I said to myself. If there was a mystery man across the garden in the brownstone south of mine I ignored him. I leaned back and stared at the stars. I thought to myself that Sam, Elicia and the rest of this unknown group were a sick bunch of people. Sneaky, clandestine, egomaniacal loonies hopelessly trapped in some power and money game that no one wanted to escape. I mused what life would have been had the essential motto of the hippies; love, peace and happiness, still permeated my families psyche. I thought that that was better than the words money, buy, sell, me, 24/7/365, at the end of the day, weapons of mass destruction, terrorists and chilling. How far into insanity had we gone?

The next several hours I spent making copies of my session tapes and notes that I had had with Sam. I packaged the tapes and notes for mailing to my mother, an editor friend, Dr. P. and a politician. I wrote on the package "Do not open-Hold for Security." I was sure that I would receive phone calls from these people when they received the packages. I arrived at Dr. P's office on time. After he said hello, I told Dr. P. to sit back and relax because I was going to tell him my latest venture down the dark alley. He was not surprised. I told Dr. P. the whole story from the very beginning right up to the reason for the package that I slid across the desk. The hour was up and Dr. P. said welcome back from the alley and wished me a pleasant vacation. I knew that Dr. P. would have had more to say if it were not for the August vacation. We shook hands and I left his office. I recalled that I did not discuss with Sam the fact that I was leaving for my August vacation and wondered if Sam would show up next Wednesday to a closed office. I felt that we terminated our relationship, but I wasn't sure if Sam really understood that therapy was over. I called Sam's cell phone. I left a message and wished him a good productive August. I looked forward to Friday with great anticipation. I packed my clothes, some summer novels, tennis racket and fishing rod. While I was closing my apartment door someone tapped me on my back. I turned to discover Elicia. "If I wasn't so happy right now I would punch your teeth in you stupid mother fucker spy." Elicia stood there shocked at my anger but didn't say a word. I pushed E out of the way and walked towards my garage and made my way to the L.I.E. I was sure that Elicia would contact me again thinking that if I was stupid the first time I would be stupid a second time. I believed Dr. Westerfield. He might be a powerful moneyman of great influence but he was old school. He epitomized honor, dignity and grace. If Westy said Elicia was a human black box, she was. Dr. Charles Westerfield was too old to play games. I couldn't remember Dr. Westerfield and I having a longer conversation than the one we had late Wednesday night. It was clear he loved Gabby with all his heart. I arrived at the Westerfield estate late. It was almost midnight. Gabby answered the door with a glass of white wine and led me to the study. Dr. Westerfield was sitting in his chair admiring his books and art. "Gabby assured me that you would come. I wasn't so convinced. However, Stan, I am more than pleased that you have arrived. Life's pleasures are somewhat limited to the cerebral when you reach my age. Gabby and I were just discussing that Van Gough painting over there. Not the paining itself but how I acquired it. This, Stan, is one of life's little treasures. To be here at my age with the daughter that I love so much and tell her stories of her father's youth. It is the creation of another memorable moment. Sit down, please." I did and Dr. Westerfield continued with his story. I was ashamed. This man acquired one of the greatest works of art walking down well-lit paths, endured all of life's suffering and enjoyed all of life's passages. I acquired little insignificant trophies walking down dark alleys. Westerfield was a man of great wisdom that only living life to its fullest in the most open, honest and sincere way could bring. He celebrated his ups and analyzed his downs. When the greats of his generation die, the world would be left with tortured souls. Dr. Westerfield asked me to pick another piece of art and began to tell Gabby and I another wonderful story of how he acquired the painting and why he wanted it. I was mesmerized. Had my vacation-ended right then, I would have been satisfied. "Stan, I have scheduled only one party within the next two weeks. I have invited only those from the arts. Soho painters, sculptors, playwrights and theatre type people. I'm sure you'll enjoy the gathering. Gabby, Stan, I must take my leave. Good night." Dr. Westerfield retired to his bedroom. "I kissed Gabby good-night and went to bed. I felt that everything was going to be o.k. It was the start of what would turn out to be one of the greatest two weeks of my life.

Gabby woke me one-half hour before sunrise. I got dressed. We walked out the long wooden slat walkway from the back of her house over the sand dunes to the beach. The sand felt great beneath my feet. I ran to the edge of the water and Gabby ran after me grabbing my hand as she approached. I grabbed Gabby and pretended that I was going to throw her in the water and she howled with laughter. As I swung her around I noticed that Dr. Westerfield was standing in his study with a smile. I could tell he was pleased. I continued swinging Gabby and then placed her gently on the sand and we walked east towards Montauk. Two of

Gabby's neighbors were out early walking towards us. Their dog, Murph, ran towards us. He was a blue point, a working dog. As the people walked by I asked them if this was the famous Murph the Surf and they nodded yes. The couple told me that the original Murph had passed away. This was the son of Murph the Surf. Gabby and I talked with them for ten minutes and right before we left they invited us to a clambake on the beach at 7:00 p.m. Both gabby and I accepted willingly. We continued our walk, holding hands and laughing as if nothing had happened a mere 60 days ago. It was a blip. An episode best left forgotten because it was not real. It was an outburst of irrational behavior because of the horrible consequences that we both envisioned. I was confident that one day we would talk it over but not during these two weeks. I didn't make any sexual overtures towards Gabby nor did she towards me. "Daddy has a little surprise for you today," Gabby said. "Really, what is it?" I inquired. "Come on Stan, be patient. We have to be back at 10:00 a.m."

We arrived at the house at 9:50 a.m. Gabby grabbed my fishing rod and we went out to the front of the mansion. Dr. Westerfield was waiting in his limousine. I noticed the license plate. It wasn't a vanity plate, something like Westy. It was just a plain old plate. "Where are we going Dr. Westerfield?" I asked. "Stan, please call me Charles," he said. "That may be a little difficult, for me. For whatever reason, I have always paid respect to those older and wiser than me by using Sir or Ma'am or their full name. However, I'll try, Charles. Do you have a middle name?" I asked. "Yes, I do. It is Garfield. Charles Garfield Westerfield." "That is a great full name, Charles." The limousine made its way on to Montauk Highway for a short distance and then headed north towards the North Shore. I knew we were going to Sag Harbor. The car pulled up to a marina and the chauffeur opened the doors. The Captain of Charles fishing boat was waiting. The family, so to speak, was going fishing. It was a great honor to go fishing with Charles. I didn't know why it was a great honor but it was. "I haven't been fishing for quite a while and if we catch some fish it would be as exciting to me as telling you the story of the acquisition of the Van Gogh," Charles said. "Charles, I haven't got skunked in fishing in twenty years. We'll catch fish, I promise you." "Captain, I guess we're going for striped bass," I yelled out. "You guessed right," the Captain said. We got on the boat, the mate untied us from the moorings and out we went. Gabby, Charles and I sat at the back end of the boat and the first mate walked over with three chilled cans of Bud Light. "Charles, you can't get any better than this. Bud and a boat," I said. "You didn't expect some fancy microbrew from Colorado or Boston, did you?" said Charles. "I grew up with Pabst Blue Ribbon and Schlitz, Stan. I can't imagine anything but a boat, a bud and a bass,"

Charles stated. The boat left the harbor and headed out towards Montauk Point. The Captain watched the fish/depth finder carefully. The mate rigged the poles and all three of us swiveled around in our chairs facing rear. The lines were let out and we slowly trolled the south part of Long Island Sound. I just couldn't believe what was happening. It was a glorious time with Gabby and her father. I hadn't done this kind of stuff since my son left 10 years ago for Japan. We drank our Buds and cracked jokes. For all the power, money and influence, Gabby and Charles were the most laid back non-pretentious family I ever met. Charles had done a great job with Gabby. He taught her that she is a human being and that humans should possess certain qualities that add to the world and make it better rather than worse. A striper hit Gabby's line, Dr. Westerfields and then mine. From the bend in the rods in appeared that Gabby had the biggest fish. I got up and told Gabby to go as close to the edge of the boat as possible on her side. I did the same. I didn't want the lines to get tangled. I reeled my fish up as fast as possible so that at least one line would be out of the water. I made Charles sit in my chair so that Gabby and her father would have some space. I didn't want to do this, but I lightened the drag on Gabby's reel so that she would have a little more fight. It would tire and kill the fish but I was taking that fish home for the clam-bake. Charles grabbed the Bud and took a big swig. I watched with the Captain and the mate as father and daughter fought their respective fish. It was beautiful. The Captain motioned for me to come over and whispered that I should come around more often. The boat hadn't been out for five years. I went back to the stern of the boat and helped both Gabby and Charles land their fish. I hadn't seen such a joyous celebration of fish catching since my father took me fishing when I was six. Gabby and Charles exchanged high fives and hugged each other. There was another round of Bud and another triple hit. Once again, I reeled my fish in as fast as possible and repositioned Gabby and Charles to the far chairs. Charles rod was severely bent and I knew he had a killer striper on the line. I was concerned that a man his age would tire and I watched Charles carefully. I was ready to take over at a moment's notice. I thought that he might take offense to this gesture so I told Gabby to help her father and I took over her line. I reeled her fish in quickly. I looked at the Captain and he nodded with approval. The most intriguing thing about fishing is that you never know what you have on the end of the line once a fish is hooked. Gabby and her father struggled together. They both worked the fish together huddled as close as two humans could get. As I watched them reel this lunker in, I would have bet that Dr. Westerfield would trade in any painting he owned for another ten fishing trips with his daughter. The Captain smiled. I motioned to the Captain to turn the boat around after the fish was landed. I grabbed the net but then let it go. The mate then grabbed the net with a smile and brought the striper on board. It was a 38-pound fish and that called for a picture. I had the mate take a picture of Dr. Westerfield alone, then Charles and Gabby and then all three of us. I wanted those pictures. No one inquired why the boat had turned around and was heading back to the harbor but I felt that Charles had had enough. I told the driver to go the BackSeat in Southampton. It was 1:00 o'clock in the afternoon. I ordered gin and tonic and a bowl of cold shrimp. For the next hour we talked art, politics and movies. My father had died right after my son was born. I would have loved to been able to have gone fishing and eat shrimp with my son and my father as I was doing with Gabby and Charles. When we got back to the house, Charles asked me what I was going to do with the fish that I caught. I told him that Gabby and I had been invited to a clambake down the beach at 7:00 p.m. "You mean with Murph the Surf," he said. "Yes, with Murph," I answered. "Well then, I expect you kids to wake me by five because I'm going." "Dr. Westerfield, it would be an honor to have you along," I informed him. Charles left to take a nap. Gabby and I sat on the back porch and had a gin and tonic. At 4:00 p.m., Gabby and I decided to take a nap. We both walked to our respective bedrooms. At the door Gabby turned and looked at me. I made a slight motion with my head for her to come over. She did. Gabby and I snuggled up closer to each other than we ever had. We went to sleep.

Dr. Westerfield woke Gabby and I up at 5:30 p.m. I was embarrassed. Gabby wasn't. We took showers and got dressed. All of us walked out towards the beach hand in hand. When we got to the beach, I walked over to the other side of Charles and put my hand on his bicep. I did it gently enough so as not to give Charles the impression that I was there to steady him. I meant it more as a sign of reassurance. We walked down to Murph's house and were greeted by Susan and Alan. They introduced me to all those present. I looked for a chair for Dr. Westerfield to sit in. I watched the smoke from the fire and positioned the chair upwind so Charles wouldn't be bothered. "Why are you so doting on my father?" Gabby asked. "I don't know. It's just who I am," I told her. "I think that people your fathers age should be looked after. Attended to. Made comfortable. They paid their dues and we owe them. It's as simple as that. I respect our elders. They have carried the great burdens in building this country. I feel like I owe them one," I said. "Nice, Stan. Very nice," Gabby said as she grabbed my arm and got up close to me. I handed the striper to Alan. Gabby and I took up positions on the sand right next to Charles. He put his hand on my shoulder. It was the first time in 20 years that I had the feeling of family. Good family. Periodically,

Gabby and I got up and helped Susan and Alan with the clambake. "We are a great couple," I thought. I checked on Dr. Westerfield and made sure he was comfortable and that his needs were met. The evening turned out to be wonderful. Charles wanted to go back to the house. I told Gabby that I was going to walk her father back to the house and that I would be back in fifteen minutes. I helped Charles up. He said his good-byes, patted Murph on the head, shook Alan's hand and kissed Susan on the cheek. Charles and I walked slowly back to the house. We didn't speak. When we got close to the estate Charles said, "this feels nice Stan, very nice. I'm glad you came and I'm sure you realize Gabby is happy as well." "Charles, it does feel nice." I walked Charles into the house and bid him good night. "See you in the morning. How about the Sunday Times and lox?" he said. "You could not have come up with a better idea, Dr. Westerfield," I told him. "Stan. Call me Charles," said Dr. Westerfield. I walked back to Murph's house and as I approached I overheard Susan telling Gabby that I was a sweetheart. Gabby told Susan that she thought we would be married soon. I intentionally slowed my approach until the ladies finished and then grabbed Gabby by the arm. "Did I miss anything, Gabby?" "No, we have been waiting for you," she said. I grabbed another chair and placed it next to the chair that Charles had been sitting in. Gabby and I sat down next to each other. Alan brought over two gin and tonics. We stared at the fire. Gabby put her head on my shoulder. "I think my father really likes you," she said. "Well, Gabby, I really like your father. He's an admirable man. Unfortunately, it's too late for me to ever be like your dad. Men like that are made over many years of hard work and devotion to principle. I have walked too many miles in the wrong direction and your dad has walked too many miles in the right direction. Spending time with your dad it both an honor and a pleasure," I told Gabby. "I think dad had a great time on the boat," she said. "I watched both of you today. I think that you and your dad had a great time." "We did, Stan, and we think that it had a lot to do with you. I bet that daddy puts that picture of all three of us on the wall in his study. Right up there with the Miro, Van Gogh and Rembrandt and I'll bet that he'll treasure that picture with as much delight that he gets from his paintings," Gabby said. "I hope so Gabby." Gabby and I stayed for another hour. We tried to get away sooner but Alan wouldn't have it. We each had another two tonics. We were tired, mellow and peaceful. Finally, we took our leave and walked slowly back to the house. I took a route through the dunes and looked for a spot that was dark and secluded. I found a place nestled among the high dunes that were hidden from the lights of the houses. I lay Gabby down on her back and sidled up next to her. I had one hand underneath her head to protect her hair from the sand. I didn't say anything. I just slowly unbuttoned her shirt and popped opened the snap on her wranglers. We made out for a long time. Gabby arched her back and pulled her jeans off. We made love.

The next morning I met Charles and Gabby in the kitchen and we all took a walk on the beach. I picked up a ball on the way that had been lying in the sand. I was hoping that Murph would be out. We just meandered on the beach picking up shells as we went along. Murph came running up behind me and grabbed the ball out of my hand. Murph put the ball on the sand and pushed it with his nose. I threw the ball down the beach and off went Murph. He came back, put the ball on the sand and pushed it again with his nose. Murph and I played ball for the entire length of the stroll. I threw the ball into the water but Murph didn't follow. I waited for the wave to bring the ball back to the shore when I saw Alan and Susan in the distance. I threw the ball to Alan and Murph followed. Gabby, Charles and I veered off towards the walkway and waved to Alan and Susan. We went into the kitchen and put on a pot of coffee. Charles went to the front door and picked up the Sunday New York Times and returned to the kitchen. I cut up some bagels and arranged the bagels, lox and cream cheese neatly on a large plate and we all went to the porch. Charles put on some classical music returned to the porch and we all sat down. No one spoke about anything of any great import. We were just chilling out. I wondered if anyone would get around to talking about the incident. I knew that it should be discussed but I thought that pushing the subject would not be to anyone's advantage.

The next twelve days was the longest stretch of happiness that I had in a long time. Gabby and I got to know one another again on a deeper level than we had before. My time with Charles was wonderful. We easily bonded. I lost my father to cancer a long time ago and Charles never had a son. I doted on him at every turn, which he easily accepted. There was never any hostility between us. Neither him nor I ever mentioned anything about Sam. It seemed to be some unwritten rule in the Westerfield household that when you're on vacation you leave the crap at the door. It was a no crap zone. You fight for your family and country on fight time during working hours and you leave it outside before you open the door, hug your wife and kiss your wife and children. A simple Charles Rule. He inspired me by example. "I should have this life," I thought. Not the trappings of wealth, but the ease of his convictions. If I had followed the rules, I wouldn't be so up and down. Having a set of rules of conduct evens out the peaks and valleys. Should you find yourself on a peak or in a valley you have the mechanisms to bring you to safety. I didn't have a good set of rules. On Sunday night, I told Gabby and Charles that I had to go back and get a change of clothing and check my mail and messages. Gabby offered to go with me. I asked Charles if he needed anything in the city. He did not. Gabby and I got up early and took a little walk on the beach. Murph appeared once again and we went through our usual routine. "You should consider getting a dog, Stan. You love them. You have the space and a backyard. Besides we can come out here anytime you want and let the dog roam. The estate is open year round and I'm sure daddy would love it," Gabby said. "As a matter of fact, Gabby, I have thought about that over the last two weeks. I spoke to my son recently and he said that the only time he ever heard me cry was when I had to put my dog down. His name was Taz. He died of cancer at the age of three. He was a yellow lab. My son picked him out and he picked Taz in the most interesting way. He picked up each pup in the litter and put the pup near his face. He picked the pup that kissed him the most and that was Taz. And that was exactly who Taz w̄as. He was the most lovable and caring dog a man could have," I told Gabby. "Well, you should consider getting another Taz. We'll call him TazToo or TazRedux," Gabby replied. "I'll think about it, Gabby." Everything that came out of Gabby's mouth was "we" and that all stemmed from Gabby's statement to Susan the night of the clambake about getting married. I felt comfortable with it and didn't stop her. Gabby and I headed back to the city around 10:00 a.m. I wanted the traffic to die down. We arrived at my apartment at 1:00 p.m. There was a ton of mail. Most of it was junk. There was only one message on my machine. It was my mother. I called my mom and told her where I was and true to form she requested the number at the Westerfield estate. "Just in case," as she always reminded me. I told Gabby that I wanted to buy a gift for her father, which she advised me, was unnecessary. I told her it was a done deal and that I was getting a gift. I asked Gabby if her dad smoked cigars, which he didn't. She thought for a minute and then stated that her dad loved kaleidoscopes. I went to the specialty antique shops on Madison Avenue. I found a little Russian made kaleidoscope for $800.00. I had the kaleidoscope gift-wrapped. I took Gabby for lunch at a Greek restaurant that had an outdoor café. Gabby and I were chatting about TazTwo when my cell phone rang. "Hello." "Is this Dr. Stanley Warlib?" "Yes. It is." "This is Dr. Abraham Mordowitz. I am with a private, let me say, somewhat discreet clinic and we have a person named Sam who will only talk to you. Is Sam your patient?" "Yes, Sam is my patient. When was Sam admitted to your clinic and what's going on?" I asked. "Sam was admitted late last night at about 2:00 a.m. Someone who claimed to be his relative brought him in. He was crying uncontrollably and kept on repeating, "I'm through, I'm through." He has spent the entire night and day huddled in the corner against the wall stating that he would only talk to the 'uber-shrink.' He states that you're the best and no one can help him except you," said Dr. Mordowitz. "Where are you located?" I asked Dr. Mordowitz and jotted down the address. It wasn't far from our restaurant. Gabby and I walked over. I told Gabby that neither of us should repeat the episode that had previously occurred between us. Sam was her Uncle and Sam was my patient. I advised Gabby to wait outside and met Dr. Mordowitz at the front door. He took me to Sam's room and I requested some privacy. "Sam, it's Stan. Get up and sit in the chair," I told him. Sam looked up and had an expression of relief. "What happened?" I asked. "I don't know. It felt like everything was beginning to shatter. I felt caught between two massive guys beating me up screaming at me that I was a fraud. Everything just closed in on me," he said. "Do you feel all right now?" I asked. "How can I not feel alright with the best doctor in the world at my side helping me," he said. "Thanks for the compliment, Sam. I want you to stay here for two days. I am going to prescribe a mild sedative to calm you down. I am continuing on my vacation for another two weeks and will see you the first Wednesday after Labor Day. That's September 3. Do you understand that Sam?" I asked. "When the best doctor in the world tells you to do something you take his advice," he answered. I struggled with my own abruptness and boundaries that I had just set with Sam. I left the room and told Dr. Mordowitz what I had told Sam. I told Dr. Mordowitz to call me if he had further problems or questions concerning Sam. I met Gabby outside the clinic and assured her that everything was all right. I thought about how Dr. Westerfield would play this out. Calm, honest and straight forward was what came to me. "Gabby, your Uncle showed up at this clinic at 2:00 a.m. He had some problems and everything appears to be o.k. I have advised the attending doctor to keep Sam there for two more days and prescribed some mild sedatives. Nothing has occurred with Sam that has anything to do with either you or I. It is his issue," I said. "I understand Stan. I'm sure he'll be fine," Gabby said. We walked hand in hand to the car and I opened the door for her to get in. "Gabby, before you get in the car, please give me a big hug," I requested. When I got in the car I immediately put on a cd that I had burned. The cd had the best of Motown. Al Green was the first cut on the cd. When the song came on, Gabby and I started singing together. "I'm so in love with you…times are good or bad or happy or sad." This little episode with Sam ended quickly and it was forgotten by the time we exited the Queens-Midtown tunnel. "If I got TazTwo, would you help me with him?" I asked. "As much as you would like, Stan," replied Gabby. I wanted to tell Gabby that I overheard her say to Susan that we might get married but I didn't. I couldn't see the point in bringing that up. It was private and I decided to let it stay private. It occurred to me that Gabby must have been miserable these last several months. I certainly didn't extend my hand to offer any truce. Instead, I was screwing Elicia, the human intel asset and getting the mother of all shaves. What seemed so natural at the time, in hindsight appeared so unnatural. I felt like a dog. "I can't wait to get back to Charles and give him the kaleidoscope that I bought him. I'm going to tell him that it's a gift from the both of us," I said. Gabby didn't say a word. She was just humming Poppa was a Rolling Stone, the Temptations great hit. She put her hand on mine, leaned over and kissed me on the cheek. When I looked her way she winked and said "Hi sweetie." I laughed.

Dr. Westerfield had dinner waiting for us. He opened one of his finest bottles of wine. "What's the occasion," I asked. "No, occasion, Stan. This is what people do when they're happy. They celebrate," he said. "I'll remember that Charles. You know, it took me awhile to notice this but every time my son was happy he sang. When you're happy you celebrate. Maybe later I'll sing and celebrate," I said. "Stan, I'll buy a karaoke machine if you sing," Charles said. It seemed everybody was happy and having a good time. I just saw Sam 3 hours ago and because I set boundaries I didn't get stuck on Sam's peaks or in Sam's valleys. Boundaries work. Charles was having a great time. He seemed younger around us. At the end of the evening while we were having dessert, I handed Charles our gift. "What's this, Stan?" "It's a little gift that Gabby and I bought you for permitting us to share with you a fabulous two weeks." "Well, well, well. Thank you both," he stated. Charles carefully opened the gift and knew immediately what it was when he saw it. He was truly taken aback. He got up and walked over to me. He gave me a big hug and then grabbed Gabby. He gave us both a big hug. He retired to his study and I could see Charles studying the kaleidoscope and then peering into it. He was lost in his new toy. Gabby walked over to Charles and kissed him goodnight. "Stan and I are going for a walk." She leaned over and whispered in his ear that I bought him the gift. He turned his head and looked at me peacefully. "Good night, Stan." "Good night, Charles." Gabby was doing her best to cast me in a good light with her father. She grabbed my hand and ran out to the beach. She told that she felt great and wanted to snuggle up to me in the dune. It was my signal for romance. "Slow and easy," I said to myself. I loved to create scenes from movies and this scene was the romance scene. We eventually made our way to the dune but not without lots of hugs, kisses and sexual banter. By the time we arrived at the dune we were both hot.

The last two weeks of August were better than the first two weeks. I left the Hamptons and went to my office to pick up my session notes, tapes and the DSM-IV manual. I was going to review my notes of each patient so that I would remember where I left off with my patients in July. If I had any concerns, I could always listen to my tapes of each session. It was homework, plain and simple. I decided to add meat to the skeleton of my patient Sam. I knew from my sessions with Sam that Sam was a real deal reborn Christian evangelical. However, I wondered how a not too bright reborn could become the leader of his family. Who was the group behind Sam that propelled him to national prominence? I remembered notes from earlier sessions with Sam wherein I scribbled "research, research, research." I explained to Charles and Gabby that I intended to spend the last fourteen days of August doing research and that I would be busy from 10:00 a.m. to 3:00 p.m. Charles provided a laptop computer for my use and had a desk put in his study that directly overlooked the dunes. On numerous occasions, I worked twelve-hour days. I got so involved in fleshing out Sam's skeleton that I couldn't stop doing research. On two occasions, I saw Charles and Gabby talking on the dunes. Charles made a gesture with his arm to Gabby and I knew he was telling her to leave me alone. Sometimes, Gabby pulled me off the computer claiming that I was "googling" myself to death. She had a point, but I just couldn't stop. I was uncovering dots of information and one dot led to another dot that led to another dot. Every dot of information showed an increasingly clearer picture of Uncle Sam. I had a more complete understanding of my patient and the "dots" only confirmed the diagnosis that I was leaning towards. My suspicions were that Sam had a narcissistic personality disorder that was propelled by a severe condition of anti social personality disorder. Sam was a psychopathic narcissist. It was an unusual combination and a frightening one at that. Sam was a psychopathic narcissistic who controlled the most dangerous weapons in the world. Sam was a psychopathic narcissistic that embraced a policy of military preemptive strikes based solely on Sam's own interpretation of reality. This was, on the Dan Abrams Chilling Index a 10. This was truly chilling. At the end of my research, I wasn't laughing because I knew the danger that Sam posed to himself, his family and the world.

In 1975, Gerald Ford, the head of the family, was pursuing a policy of containment and détente with Russia. Ford's Secretary of State was Henry Kissinger. The Chief of Staff to Gerald Ford was Donald Rumsfeld and his assistant was Dick Cheney. In order to appear more hawkish towards Russia, on November 1, 1975, Gerald Ford fired William Colby, then director of the Central Intelligence Agency and replaced him with George H.W. Bush and appointed Donald Rumsfeld as Secretary of Defense. Donald Rumsfeld, an unknown at the time, was advised to hook up with Albert Wohlstetter, at the Rand Corporation. Wohlstetter was the spiritual godfather to the Cold War's atomic hawks. Rumsfeld cemented his position as a hawk. Ford and Kissinger were attempting to conclude the SALT II treaty talks. The hawks were furious.

The Director of the C.I.A., George Bush came up with a novel idea. To assess the C.I.A.'s information concerning Russia, Bush set up a Team A/Team B approach. Team A was the C.I.A. and Team B was an outside agency. To my surprise, Team B had on its roster a young Dr. Paul Wolfowitz. Team B, the outside non governmental group assessed the Soviet threat to a much greater degree than the C.I.A and Team B's report was the basis for increasing the defense budget for the next fifteen years. I realized that defense needs a boogeyman to justify large military expenditures and ever increasing military budgets. It was easy to connect the dots twenty-two later. Once again, Donald Rumsfeld is Secretary of Defense. His assistant is Dr. Paul Wolfowitz. Sam is head of the family and Richard Cheney is Sam's assistant.

In 1992, Bill Clinton became head of the family and enjoyed a peace dividend from the breakup of the Soviet empire. Sam's Department of Defense had no boogeyman to fight. The Neoconservative hawks languished from 1992 to 2000 and retired to right wing conservative think tanks. The Neo-Cons tried to get Bill Clinton to pursue a more aggressive posture towards the world to no avail. In 2000, Sam, was elected the head of the family. Sam, prior to becoming the head of the family, was the leader of Texas. Whoever controlled Sam, surrounded him with the most politically astute aggressive infighters. Richard Cheney became Sam's assistant. Colin Powell became Secretary of State. Poor Sam was surrounded by aggressive, mean spirited ideologues whose pursuit of world domination through the use of their military was unparalleled in world history. I recalled The Art of War by Sun Tzu, who advised that every leader needed a spy. Dick Cheney appointed I. Scooter Libby as his personal assistant and as a liaison to Sam. My gut feeling was that Libby was a spy for Richard Cheney. Condoleeza Rice was appointed as head of the National Security Council. Most of the people surrounding Sam had connections to the oil industry. I asked myself over and over again, why would anyone want Sam, a "C" student at best and a reborn Evangelical Christian to be surrounded by this group of ideologues. It didn't take too long to realize that Sam was a dupe. What better person to pluck out of mediocrity than Sam and what better person to start wars in the name of God than a reborn Christian. This group surrounding Sam called themselves the Vulcans. The Vulcan was a Roman and Greek God who made Zeus's thunderbolts, Hercules weapons and the armour of Achilles. The Vulcans are a war machine and specifically choose Sam because he walked the walk and talked the talk of God. Good versus evil. Sam was perfect for the Vulcans. However, the world enjoyed eleven years of peaceful stability and the Vulcans needed a boogeyman. They wanted war.

Dick Cheney and Donald Rumsfeld took a page out of history, probably at the suggestion of George H.W. Bush. They took another try at the Team A/Team B approach. Once again, Team A was Sam's own C.I.A. Cheney and Rumsfeld set up the Office of Special Plans. The Office of Special Plans was all over the C.I.A. to influence and hype the threat of Saddam Hussein. Saddam became the Vulcans boogeyman and then 9/11 occurred. Not only did the Vulcans have a boogeyman in Saddam, they had a new war on terror. A war against an enemy you couldn't see, didn't know who they were or where they were located and more importantly, a war that had no end. It was to be a Godly war on terror. Indeed, the ultimate war of good versus evil in the name of God and Sam was the general. "Perfect," I thought, and dangerous. The whole world was against Sam and Sam was wrapped up in his psychopathic narcissistic grandiose fantasy of saving the world from evil. "How moronic," I mused. I felt sorry for Sam. He was a pathetic figure. I saw Sam through different eyes and was no longer as apprehensive as I had been. I could figure out his bullshit and his next move and if I could, so could the rest of the world.

Alan and Susan planned a Labor Day, end of season clambake, starting in the afternoon. Gabby, Charles and I attended. After we said hello to everybody, Gabby wanted to take a stroll to the sand dune where we had made love. "Come on, Stan, take a walk with me." "Gabby, it's the middle of the afternoon," I said. "Stan, just a quickie. I just want you in me a little bit. Now, come on." Gabby pulled me by the hand and we walked over to the dune. I checked out the backs of the houses to make sure that no one was standing on the decks or looking out the window. When we got to the dune, Gabby unbuttoned the top buttons of her shirt. She led me around the dune to a little hidden area. Tied to a stake was the cutest little yellow lab. A note read, "Hi, Stan, my name is TazTwo. Take me home." I was at a loss for words. I grabbed Gabby and kissed her. I picked up little TazTwo and we headed back to the clambake. "By the way, Stan, I choose TazTwo in exactly the same way that your son picked Taz out. I held up each puppy in the litter and asked for a kiss. TazTwo won," she said. I asked TazTwo for a kiss. It was Taz reborn. When we made our way back to the clambake everyone fawned over TazTwo. "Oh, Stan, there is one condition. Daddy requests that you and TazTwo visit him in the City or in the Hamptons once a month," she said. "Well, Gabby, that's an easy request to honor." I looked at Charles and gave him the thumbs up. My August vacation came to a conclusion and it was one of the most memorable in my life.

The first week of therapy sessions after August is get acquainted week. My main focus was to catch up on my patient's lives and make sure nothing terrible had happened during my absence. Everyone appeared well enough. Nothing of any great significance had occurred except one of my patients had broken up with her boyfriend during August, which had a major impact on her functioning. We discussed the situation and decided that she should double up on her weekly sessions at least for a month. She agreed. The most significant aspect of the week was what didn't happen. Sam didn't show up on Wednesday. I called his cell phone and left a message. I did not receive a return call. I was nearing the point of totally cutting Sam loose, however, I recalled our last conversation in Hung Fat wherein he told me that the worst thing that could happen was that I would go to jail and he would have a new therapist. I knew I wasn't going to jail. I decided to call Dr. Mordowitz who advised me that he followed my instructions and released Sam the next day, at Sam's insistence, without incident. Dr. Mordowitz stated that he would not have released Sam had Sam exhibited any behavior, which would warrant his retention. I left Friday for Dr. Westerfield's estate and brought TazTwo with me. Charles and I had a great time strolling the beach with TazTwo. It was difficult keeping him out of the ocean. I broached the subject of the "incident" with Gabby and we spoke at length, although not in depth. I didn't tell Gabby that I overheard her conversation with Susan about marriage. I thought about my issues with women and in particular Gabby. Maybe I did love her and everything was going to be fine. Being with Gabby felt so good and right. Sunday morning my cell phone rang. It was Dr. Mordowitz. Sam had been admitted again. I discussed at length Sam's condition and decided that a trip back to the city was not necessary. Sam assured Dr. Mordowitz that he would appear the following Wednesday at my office.

Sam appeared at my office looking quite well. He arrived on time and handed me an envelope containing $300.00 in cash and explained that it was for the missed appointment of last week. I advised Sam that such conduct was intolerable and would not be condoned for any reason. He assured me that it wouldn't happen again. I told Sam that to the best of my knowledge, he had three episodes of uncontrollable breakdowns, two of which required hospitalization. I further advised Sam that I was concerned that the frequency of such episodes appeared to be increasing. I asked Sam what was going on. He did not respond. He didn't have an answer, he told me. After some discussion, Sam admitted to me that he was under a lot of pressure and that on those occasions he just cracked. He assured me that it wasn't a big deal because he felt better soon thereafter. He told me that on those two occasions with Dr. Mordowitz, the one where I visited him and the other consulting on the phone with Dr. Mordowitz, he felt immediately better. After all, he told me, "if you have the best nothing can be a problem." I asked Sam why it was that he loathed me at times and at other times thought I was the best therapist in the world. Again, Sam didn't have an answer. I told Sam about group therapy and recommended that he attend. I assured Sam that he would be welcome. In addition, I told Sam that I wanted him to come three times a week, Monday, Wednesday and Friday. Sam willingly agreed to each request. He reminded me, again, that I was the best in the world and that when the best recommends something it had to be good advice. I was confident that increasing the sessions to three a week was a good idea because I was deeply concerned that Sam had three episodes, which at the present time I could not classify and that the time between episodes two and three was shorter than the time span between one and two. I was confident that some kind of breakdown was occurring. I was somewhat less confident about group therapy. I did not know how Sam would react within a group. There was only one person in the group that caused me concern and it was Rueben. Rueben was a no nonsense, fast-talking, knowledgeable street kid who traded commodities in the pits. Rueben had a severe cocaine problem, which only added to his fast talking speech. Rueben also had a habit of reducing every situation in life to money. Everything in life had at its source a money issue. His accuracy of analysis was sometimes uncanny. He always told me that in Sam's family "it's all about the Benjamins," and therefore the only way to analyze anything with Sam was to "follow the money."

GROUP THERAPY SESSION

The group had five patients, three women and two men. One woman was a local attorney in Westchester County handling small cases. She was wealthy. She played at law and played in therapy. She didn't want to get healthier. Another woman was also an attorney who worked at a major firm in New York. She was a constant victim notwithstanding her success. She loved to bait the other members of the group and suck them into an endless battle over anything. The third woman was a wealthy independent businesswoman who owned a large clothing manufacturing facility. She was bright, rich and extremely attractive. Unfortunately, like Rueben, she had an addiction to cocaine. She hid it well but it was beginning to impair her functioning. The remaining man in the group was a high-powered real estate developer who had major issues with his father. From his perspective, everything that went wrong in his life was a result of his father's meddling. Now there was Sam. The group assembled and I introduced Sam. I told Sam the group rules. I advised Sam that what is said in group is confidential and should not, under any circumstances, be discussed with anyone other then another member of the group. Sexual relations between members of the group were forbidden. In the past, that rule had always been broken. I explained to the group, that whatever concerns Sam might express in the group, must, under all circumstances be kept strictly confidential because of his position. As is often the case, when I introduce a new member the group goes silent. I never intervene to get the discussion going. Sometimes a group will remain silent for a considerable length of time. That's their business. However, I did watch their body language. Everyone knew who Sam was from the newspapers and television. The three women tried as best as they could to fix their hair. They were primping. If they could have taken out their make up they would have done so. The real estate developer fixed his tie and straightened his pants and sat up straight. Rueben was bored. He slouched in his chair and tapped repeatedly on the arm of the chair. It was a given, that when Rueben taps, he had snorted cocaine in my bathroom. The group was silent for fifteen minutes. "Rueben, will you please stop tapping," demanded one woman. "Did you do coke in the bathroom again, Rueben?" inquired another woman. "Dr. Warlib, I think you should refuse to allow Rueben in this group if he does cocaine." I looked around the room. "That's a good idea," said another. "I think Rueben is very destructive," the other cocaine addict said. "He reminds me of my problem every time I see him like this. I am trying very, very hard to control my problem. I think Rueben should leave," she suggested. It appeared that everyone was nervous about Sam. No one wanted to broach any subject with Sam. Generally, introducing a new member to a group drastically changes the dynamics and I fully expected the dynamics to change with Sam in the group. It is not unusual for the group to avoid discussing their feelings upon introduction of a new member. They re-direct their feelings to the person they perceive as the easiest one to pick on. In this group, it was always Rueben. However, Rueben was the strongest member of the group. The entire group was on medication except Rueben. The rest of the group felt above Rueben and so they attacked. Rueben kept on tapping and the group session was going nowhere. "How does everyone feel about Sam being in the group?" I asked. Everyone, except Rueben, agreed that Sam was a great addition to the group. It was clear that they were sucking up. "Sam, how do you feel about the group?" the businesswoman asked. Sam hesitated and remained silent. He clearly didn't know what to say. "Just tell us how you feel?" she asked again. Sam responded. "Well, I must admit I have been in other groups much more distinguished than this one. I am used to groups of heads of state and the chiefs of major corporations. I don't know what this group can contribute to me that might be of any benefit and I don't know if anyone here is capable of recognizing my unique talents and capabilities. My needs are somewhat different and might be beyond all of you. Dr. Warlib thought that I might gain some insight and help you people in resolving your issues and since Dr. Warlib is the best in the world, I decided to give it a try," said Sam. Rather than deal with what Sam had just said, the group once again re-directed their feelings and picked up on Sam's statement that I was the best therapist in the world. The group periodically goes through praising me as their therapist. I'm usually second in line after Rueben as a means of escape. Usually Rueben could only take 10 minutes of the adulation heaped upon me and then exploded in anger. He was bewildered that successful people would put me on a pedestal like a God. He always liked to point out matters about me that he thought clearly indicated my mortal ness. If nothing else, Rueben was always there to shake the group out of their usual lethargy. "Here we go again, Dr. Warlib is the best. Dr. Warlib is God. Dr. Warlib is right. You guys are jerks. What a bunch of smucks," Rueben said. "Well, why don't you just stop doing cocaine in the bathroom before you come in here. It's rude to the group," said the local woman attorney. "Fuck you too," Rueben responded. Sam spoke up and stated that, indeed, I was the best therapist in the world and the reason that he knew that to be true was because he only had dealings with the best. At that very moment, I was sure that Sam was having serious problems. His negative feelings about me over the last three months were too strong to be suppressed. His high opinion of me at this point of time only indicated that he needed me. "Who is this fucking moron, Doc? Is Sam another one of your fucking cheerleaders? I have never heard such bullshit in my life. You got all these yuppie assholes in this group and you don't think there going to suck up to this new guy. What a moronic bunch of wanna-be's. Sam is a moron," Rueben stated looking defiantly into the eyes of all the other group members. Having known Rueben for several years, he was about to launch into some financial analysis showing the group exactly why Sam is a moron. I looked at Sam to make sure that he was not distressed. He appeared fine. Rueben continued. "I'll tell you why this new guy is a smuck. He invades Iraq under some bogus theory of an imminent threat to our security. Big fucking mistake number one. The first thing he does is to run to the oilfields to protect his future investment. Fuck the water, food and safety of the Iraqi people. Sam secures the oil fields and starts rebuilding them to pump more oil. He wants to get the pumps pumping 2,000,000 barrels a day. At $30.00 a barrel it's sixty million dollars a day and times that by 30 days and you have $1.8 billion a month. But this little venture is costing $3.9 billion a month, leaving a shortfall under the best of circumstances of $2.1 billion. Now you can try to increase production to 3,000,000 barrels a day but that would only cause havoc in the oil pits and drop the price to $22.00. That's sixty six million dollars a day or close to $2 billion a month. You're still short $1.9 billion. Are you with me dummies? This is math 101. Now, you have totally fucked up the oil markets and every one of Sam's little oil buddies is taking a huge loss. But it's no big deal, right? We'll reduce our costs. Our biggest cost is labor. Our soldiers. So we'll remove our troops and replace them but the replacements don't have any money so they want us to put them on the payroll. Wow, no big costs saving there. So you need either the United Nations or some big guns like France, Germany, Russia or China. Well, now, we can't do that because we pissed them off so much they're laughing their asses off that big Sam is stuck in the fucking desert and paying $2.1 billion for the privilege of getting some young guy shot in the head in broad daylight standing on line waiting to get a coke from some fucking vending machine. But Sam can't leave because then he would have lost all credibility against some third rate sand jockeys and the whole world is laughing. Welcome to the Grand Plan of Sam and you guys are picking up the tab for his insanity. So that's my take." Rueben crossed his arms and stared at the wall. Sam leaned forward in his chair. "Not everything is done for money!" Sam barked. Sam took advantage of Rueben's crossed arms and pre-occupation with the wall that he was staring at and leaped across the room swinging his fist. He caught Rueben right on the chin and knocked him out. Rueben lay on his back. The entire group was stunned and sat riveted in their chairs. In a strange way I was glad Rueben was out cold. I didn't think I could have controlled an all out brawl between the two and I was sure that others would have been hurt in the melee. Calmly, I dismissed the group and advised Sam to leave. I checked his hand to make sure it wasn't broken. Within sixty seconds the room was clear. Everyone in the group marched silently out. I attended to Rueben who came around within a minute. Rueben could not sit up and so I advised him to lie on the floor until he felt better. I got a cold wet rag from the bathroom and applied it to Rueben's forehead. Rueben was up after fifteen minutes and I made him sit. It is extremely difficult to regain your bearings after you have been knocked out. It takes a long time and I felt that the prudent thing to do would be to take Rueben home in a cab. We didn't say a word to each other. Rueben said that he misjudged Sam. He didn't think that Sam would fly into a rage. Neither did I. Maybe group therapy wasn't a good idea after all. Sam was becoming clearer. I reviewed my notes and initial impressions of Sam. On Axis 1, I was convinced that Sam had a delusional disorder notwithstanding the fact that I had to take into account his religious beliefs. I was convinced that Sam had two personality disorders along Axis 2. Sam had a Narcissistic Personality Disorder and an Anti-Social Personality Disorder. I wasn't quite sure which personality disorder was prominent but I was convinced that both disorders existed.

When I got home I opened the DSM-IV manual and turned to the Diagnostic criteria for 301.81 Narcissistic Personality Disorder. I read the following:

> A pervasive pattern of grandiosity (in fantasy or behavior), need for admiration, and lack of empathy, beginning by early childhood and present in a variety of contexts, as indicated by five (or more) of the following:
>
> > (1) has a grandiose sense of self-importance (e.g., exaggerates achievements and talents, expects to be recognized as superior without commensurate achievements)
> >
> > (2) is preoccupied with fantasies of unlimited success, power, brilliance, beauty, or ideal love.
> >
> > (3) believes that he or she is "special" and unique and can only by understood by, or should associate with, other special or high status people (or institutions)
> >
> > (4) requires excessive admiration.
> >
> > (5) has a sense of entitlement, i.e., unreasonable expectations of especially favorable treatment or automatic compliance with his or her expectations.
> >
> > (6) is interpersonally exploitative, i.e., takes advantage of others to achieve his or her own ends.
> >
> > (7) lacks empathy: is unwilling to recognize or identify with the feelings and needs of others.
> >
> > (8) is often envious of others or believes that others are envious of him or her.
> >
> > (9) shows arrogant, haughty behaviors or attitudes.

The narrative provided is the manual was instructive and helped to further bolster my diagnosis. It stated:

> The essential feature of Narcissistic Personality Disorder is a pervasive pattern of grandiosity, need for admiration and lack of empathy….and is present in many contexts.
>
> Individuals with this disorder have a grandiose sense of self-importance. They routinely overestimate their abilities and inflate their accomplish-ments, often

appearing boastful and pretentious. They may blithely assume that others attribute the same value to their efforts and may be surprised when the praise they expect and feel is not forthcoming. Often implicit in the inflated judgments of their own accomplishments is an underestimation (devaluation) of the contributions of others. They are often preoccupied with fantasies of success, power, brilliance, beauty or ideal love. They may ruminate about long overdue admiration and privilege and compare themselves favorably with famous or privileged people.

Individuals with this disorder generally require excessive admiration. Their self-esteem is almost invariably very fragile. They may be preoccupied with how well they are doing and how favorably they are regarded by others. This often takes the form of a need for constant attention and admiration. They may expect their arrival to be greeted with great fanfare and are astonished if others do not covet their possessions. They may constantly fish for compliments, often with great charm. A sense of entitlement is evident in these individuals' unreasonable expectation of especially favorable treatment. They expect to be catered to and are puzzled or furious when this does not happen. For example, they may assume that they do not have to wait in line and that there priorities are so important that others should defer to them, and then get irritated when others fail to assist "in their very important work." This sense of entitlement combined with a lack of sensitivity to the wants and needs of others may result in the conscious or unwitting exploitation of others. They expect to be given whatever they want or feel they need, no matter what it might mean to others. For example, these individuals may expect great dedication from others and may overwork them without regard for the impact of their lives. They tend to form friendships or romantic relationships only if the other person seems likely to advance their purposes or otherwise enhance their self esteem. They often usurp special privileges and extra resources that they believe they deserve because they are special.

Individuals with Narcissistic Personality Disorder generally have a lack of empathy and difficulty recognizing the desires, subjective experiences and feelings of others. They may assume that others are totally concerned about their welfare. They tend to discuss their own concerns in inappropriate and lengthy detail, while failing to recognize that others also have feelings and needs. They are often contemptuous and impatient of others who talk about their own problems and concerns. These individuals may be oblivious to the hurt their remarks may inflict. When recognized, the needs, desires, or feelings of others are likely to be viewed disparagingly as signs of weakness or vulnerability..... These individuals are often envious of others or believe that others are envious of them. They may begrudge others their successes or possessions, feeling that they deserve those achievements, admirations, or privileges. They may harshly devalue the contribution of others, particularly when those individuals have received acknowledgement or praise for their accomplishments. Arrogant, haughty behaviors characterize these individuals. They often display snobbish, disdainful, or patronizing attitudes. For example, an individual with this disorder may complain about a clumsy waiter's "rudeness" or stupidity or conclude a medical evaluation with a condescending evaluation of the physician.

Associated Features and Disorders

Vulnerability in self-esteem makes individuals with Narcissistic Personality Disorder very sensitive to "injury" from criticism or defeat. Although they may not show it outwardly, criticism may haunt these individuals and may leave them feeling humiliated, degraded, hollow and empty. They may react with disdain, rage, or defiant counterattack. Such experiences often lead to social withdrawal or an appearance of humility that may mask and protect the grandiosity. Interpersonal relations are typically impaired due to problems derived from entitlement, the need for admiration and the relative disregard for the sensitivities of others. Though overweening ambition and confidence may lead to high achievement, performance may be disrupted due to intolerance of criticism or defeat.

The Diagnostic criteria for 301.7 Antisocial Personality Disorder were as follows:

A. There is a pervasive pattern of disregard for and violation of the rights of others occurring since age 15 years, as indicated by three (or more) of the following:

> (1) failure to conform to social norms with respect to lawful behaviors as indicated by repeatedly performing acts that are grounds for arrest.

> (2) deceitfulness, as indicated by repeated lying, uses of aliases, or conning others for personal profit or pleasure.

> (3) impulsivity or failure to plan ahead.

> (4) irritability and aggressiveness, as indicated by repeated physical fights or assaults.

> (5) reckless disregard for safety of self or others.

> (6) consistent irresponsibility, as indicated by the repeated failure to sustain consistent work behavior or honor financial obligations.

> (7) lack of remorse, as indicated by being indifferent to or rationalizing having hurt, mistreated, or stolen from another.

B. The individual is at least 18 years.

C. There is evidence of conduct disorder with onset before age 15 years.

D. The occurrence of antisocial behavior is not exclusively during the course of Schizophrenia or a Manic Episode.

Diagnostic Features

The essential features of antisocial personality disorder is a pervasive pattern of disregard for, and violation of, the rights of others that begins in childhood or early adolescence and continues into adulthood.

This pattern has also been referred to as psychopathy, sociopathy, or dissocial personality disorder. Because deceit and manipulation are central features of Antisocial Personality Disorder, it may be especially helpful to integrate information acquired from systemic clinical assessment with information collected from collateral sources.

For this diagnosis to be given, the individual must be at least age 18 years and must have had a history of some systems of conduct disorder before age 15 years. Conduct disorder involves a repetitive and persistent pattern of behavior in which the basic rights of others or major age-appropriate societal norms or rules are violated...The pattern of antisocial behavior continues into adulthood. Individuals with Antisocial Personality Disorder fail to conform to social norms with respect to lawful behavior. They may repeatedly perform acts that are grounds for arrest (whether they are arrested or not), such as destroying property, harassing others, stealing, or pursuing illegal occupations. Persons with this disorder disregard the wishes, rights or feelings of others. They are frequently deceitful and manipulative in order to gain personal profit or pleasure. (e.g., to obtain money, sex, or power) They may repeatedly lie, use an alias, con others, or malinger. A pattern of impulsivity may be manifested by a failure to plan ahead. Decisions are made on the spur of the moment, without forethought, and without consideration for the consequences to self or others; this may lead to sudden changes of jobs, residences, or relationships. Individuals with Antisocial Personality Disorder tend to be irritable and aggressive and may repeatedly get into of commit acts of physical assault...These individuals also display a reckless disregard for the safety of themselves or others. This may be evidenced by their driving behavior (recurrent speeding, driving while intoxicated, multiple accidents)..... They may be indifferent to, or provide a superficial rationalization for, having hurt, mistreated, or stolen from someone (e.g., "life's unfair," "losers deserve to lose," or "he had it coming anyway"). These individuals may blame the victims for being foolish, helpless, or deserving their fate; they may minimize the harmful consequences of their actions; or they may simply indicate complete indifference. They generally fail to compensate or make amends for their behavior. They may believe that everyone is out to "help number one" and that one should stop at nothing to avoid being pushed around. The antisocial behavior must not occur exclusively during the course of Schizophrenia or a Manic Episode.

Associated Features and Disorders

Individuals with Antisocial Personality Disorder frequently lack empathy and tend to be callous, cynical, and contemptuous of the feelings of the rights, and sufferings of others. They may have an inflated and arrogant self-appraisal (e.g., feel that ordinary work is beneath them or lack a realistic concern about their current problems or their future) and may be excessively opinionated, self-assured or cocky. They may display a glib, superficial charm and can be quite voluble and verbally facile (e.g., using technical terms or jargon that might impress someone who is unfamiliar with the topic)........ Individuals with Antisocial Personality Disorder also often have personality features that meet criteria for other personality disorders, particularly Borderline, Histrionic, and Narcissistic Personality Disorders..... Individuals with Antisocial Personality Disorder and **Narcissistic Personality Disorder** share a tendency to be tough minded, glib, superficial, exploitative, and unempathic. However, Narcissistic Personality does not include characteristics of impulsivity, aggression and deceit. In addition, individuals with Antisocial Personality Disorder may not be as needy of the admiration and envy of others, and persons with Narcissistic Personality Disorder usually lack the history of conduct disorder in childhood or criminal behavior in adulthood....

The next day I called Rueben to make sure that he was all right. He told me that he went to the hospital to get an x-ray. He wanted to make sure that his jaw wasn't broken. I told Rueben that I wanted to have dinner with him that night and pick his brains about finance. He told me that it was difficult to talk but that he would do it. We agreed to meet at Puglia's, an Italian restaurant with a lively outdoor café. It would not be unusual for all the diners to break out in song with the wait staff. It was a place full of energy. It was like Rueben. Rueben and I hooked up at 6:30 p.m. and ordered a carafe of the house red and a shot of Grappa. Rueben told the waiter to get the basement Grappa. That was the local brew that was distilled somewhere in the neighborhood. We picked up our glasses, said salute, and drank the Grappa. Nothing tastes more like jet fuel than Grappa. "Got to love that stuff, huh Doc," Rueben said. "Not for nothing, but that was a lot of fun last night. The best group session we've had in a long time. Man, that guy can punch. But he cold cocked me. I had my fucking arms folded and was staring at the wall. Hey, Doc, I promise I won't fuck him up, at least not in-group. So, what do you want to know about finances? I'm not a certified financial planner so I can't really help you out. I just understand money. Money is my game and Rueben is my name." "Rueben, I want to know about financial matters because it will help me understand Sam better. It seems that a large part of Sam's personality is influenced by religion and money. I have talked at length about religion with Sam but I can't get a handle on the money thing. He keeps on referring to his financial buddies," I said. "You mean you want my help, to help you, help Sam. That fucking guy just punched me out 24 hours ago. Hey, Doc, are you on drugs. I'm only kidding. I'm just fucking with you. I'll be glad to help. It's a big subject. I don't know where to start. Want to give me some help here?" asked Rueben. "I don't know, just start talking about money and Sam. Maybe something will develop," I said to Rueben. "All right, Doc. Kind of like free floating bullshit. O.K., first thing, when you say, 'financial buddies' you could just as easily say 'criminal buddies.' There isn't a clean corporation in America today. Let me start by just naming a few the biggest corporate names in America that have committed major wrongdoing and fraud: Worldcom, Qwest, Morgan Stanley, Imclone, MCI, Tyco, Impath, Charter Communications, AOL, Activision, Freddie Mac, HealthSouth, Merrill Lynch, AMR, Mattell, Xerox, J.P. Morgan, Adelphia, Arthur Anderson, Citigroup, Sunbeam, CSFB and the grand mofo of them all Enron. Oh, there you go Enron and Sam. Well, they got a long history together. How about that Doc? Those names big enough for you? There are hundreds more. Dirty to the bone. Restatement of earnings is nothing more than a euphemism for re-cooking the cooked books. In other words they cheated, lied, stole and manipulated the books and now they're coming clean before any prosecutions take place. They raped the companies and fucked over their employees. Hundreds of thousands have lost their jobs and pensions. It's the biggest fucking over in my lifetime. Does any body go out and hang these motherfuckers. Think of it this way. Suppose a lieutenant in the mob fucked with the books. What the hell do you think is going to happen? Bam. Right between the fucking eyes. But these corporate guys are so slick that they came up with all sorts of mechanisms to fuck with the books, like derivatives, that very few people really understand. I mean they aren't exchanging money they're exchanging paper. Are you with me, Doc?" "Yeah, I'm with you, Rueben," I assured him. "O.K., then let's move on. No one is moving on Enron mainly because they can't figure out the fuck they did. Even I couldn't explain what Enron did to a jury. Did you see those proceedings before Congress with Andy Fastow from Enron? I mean, they couldn't even ask the right questions because they couldn't understand what he did. That mofo Fastow stuck his chin out and almost said come on dummies, figure it out, and by the way, did you ever hear any of the names disclosed in the partnerships that Enron set up. There were hundreds of limited partnerships. I'll bet that reads like Hedi Fleiss's little black book of johns. I'll bet the names contained within those limited partnerships are the crème de la crème of American wealth. It also appears that the banks lent a hand in an advisory role besides supplying money. At the height of the scandals everyone is advising the poor little smuck in the street to beware of companies that beat Thompson First Call by a penny. That means they're managing earnings. It's a first sign of book cooking. So guess what. Most companies are still beating the street by a penny and the little guy is still buying stock. Now, those companies I named are big. What about the small cap corporations that are under the radar screen? What about the banks that are banging the little guy with $31.00 fees to honor checks? A huge percentage of their income is coming from fucking the little guy. What about the drug companies paying off the doctors to promote their drugs or rewarding the doctors for prescribing other uses of known drugs that are not permissible by the F.D.A. Sam doesn't have enough jails to house these mother fuckers. I mean, it's out in the open. Everyday. The whole place is corrupt. I wouldn't put a penny in the market. You have to be one dumb stupid ass hole to invest in any company. Take a look at Warren Buffett, the greatest investor of all time. He ain't investing in the market. He's sitting on the biggest cash hoard he ever had. He ain't stupid. Now, listen to this crap. In the height of the mania, you had Internet companies that had a market capitalization larger than the most established corporations combined. I mean these fucking companies didn't earn a dime. They lost millions and then they tell you that they have a negative cash burn rate and so they're poised to make billions. Think about that. Negative cash burn rate. What a fucking absurd idea. So I got out of the stock market and went into commodities. It's a cleaner game. I mean, you can't fudge a hurricane that wipes out the orange crop. You know the price is going up. It's supply and demand. Buy low and sell high, the two basic principles of money. Really, negative cash burn rate! Give me a break. Get into the corporate world and you're in a land of fantasy. It's all bullshit. Any questions, Doc?" "No, I'm taking it all in. I mean you're indicting all of corporate Sam," I said. "Now, we're talking out and out fraud. If you're not slick enough to cover your ass, you just make up numbers. You hear, Doc, there are companies that just make up numbers. They pick a revenue number and put it down, and why not? Look at the risk/reward ratio. You are a C.E.O. and you fuck over your own company and a year before you file bankruptcy you exercise your stock options at a high price and you're getting a high price based upon your own phony numbers and you walk out with millions. The risk is that you go to Fed-Med for two years and hang out with some of your old friends. Wouldn't you do it?" asked Rueben. "I don't think so. I don't think I could sleep at night worrying about 40,000 people who would lose their jobs and their pensions," I said. "Well, that's why you're a shrink and not a corporate CEO. You're not a cold-hearted nasty motherfucker. They don't care. They're running their own little fiefdoms. They are God in their companies. They don't run these companies for the shareholders. They run it for themselves. The shareholders are supposed to own the company. What bullshit. Who the fuck deserves the amount of money these guys get as compensation especially when their running the company, at best, marginally. Here, you want a simple solution. A corporation is a creature of the state. It can only live at the hands of the state that it is incorporated in. So, a corporation commits major fraud and fucks over a lot of people, revoke their corporate privilege. It's a good idea. Nobody is going to do it. Maybe Elliot Spitzer of New York would have enough balls to do it. Maybe he hasn't though of it yet. But Sam passed some legislation recently, which effectively took power out of the hands of all the attorney generals of Sam's family. So now I'll tell you what I think is going to happen. Corporations, Sam's financial buddies have no pricing power. That is, they can't raise the price of their product or service. Revenues will be flat or decline. Corporations got just about as much as they're going to get through efficiency and cost control. How do you increase profits? Simple. You go after the biggest cost factor you have. Labor. You hack away at raises, pensions, and increased employee health contributions and in the final analysis you fire the little bastards. You got that, Doc. You attack the very people that help run the company. Sam's workers are screwed. If they want to keep their jobs they're going to have to give back the benefits and money that they have received in the past. Management doesn't give a shit. If these guys can commit criminal acts you can believe that they're not going to lose sleep about fucking their workers. These guys can go anywhere in the world and get labor cheaper. Take a look at IBM transferring 5,000 jobs to India. Here's the deal. The workers in Sam's family are slowly going to become third world workers." I interrupted Rueben. "But doesn't that destroy the very thing they're trying to protect? It seems contrary to their own interests," I asked. "Doc, have you been listening. Their interests are themselves. It's all about them and they're willing to go so far as to commit criminal acts in the pursuit of their own well-being. Sounds crazy, but it's true. Money is green and green is an international language. You got green you got business. It doesn't have to be here. It can be in Russia, China, Iraq, anywhere. These guys don't care. They're Gods in their own right. I heard that you couldn't even look at that guy Ellison from Oracle. I mean literally. Subordinates are instructed to lower their eyes in his presence. Could be rumor or could be fact but that's what I heard. This criminality is systemic. You have to blow the whole fucking think up and start over again. That's what you're dealing with. What I don't get is that nobody out there seems to care. In my neighborhood where I grew up you would have the shit kicked out of you. Sam's family fell asleep. I mean they are getting raped everyday in everyway and they don't do a fucking thing. Not a fucking thing. That's why I jumped all over Sam last night. My kid brother is over there in Iraq and I don't have a fucking clue why he's there. Imminent threat! What a fucking joke. Any questions, Doc?" "I mentioned to Sam in one our sessions that he seems to be acting contrary to his own financial interests. That is, eventually, financial ruin. Sam stated that his financial buddies were actually prospering and then inadvertently, I think he mentioned a name of some group called the Carlisle Boys. Do you know anything about that?" I asked Rueben. "Oh, oh, oh. It's the Carlyle Group. It's either a private merchant bank or closed mutual fund. It is one of the largest of its kind. It has sixteen billion dollars under management and they buy and sell entire companies. It's called the ex-President's club. Not only that, they only have 500 members from 50 countries. Can you imagine? You have to be a really big heavyweight for the Carlyle Group to manage your money. I mean you just can't be rich. You have to be rich, powerful and influential. They specialize in aerospace, defense and security. Doc, I suggest that you do a google search on the group. Oh yeah, by the way, some guy just wrote a book, I think it's called "The Iron Triangle," and it's about The Carlyle Group. Research it. I'm sure you'll find out a lot about your new patient. He's not coming to group, is he?" "I don't know, Rueben. How do you feel about that?" "Oh, I don't care Doc. I'll get him back outside of the group, but I'm not going to be any different. You know me. I got a big mouth and I can't take too much of that yuppie bullshit from the rest of the group. I mean, if he pisses me off, I'm going to go after him. Except next time my arms won't be folded and I won't be staring at the wall. If he comes after me, I'm going to fight. I'm not kidding. So it's your call, Doc," Rueben said. "I'll think about the whole matter and make a decision. Sam might decide not to show up at all in which case the issue will resolve itself. Rueben, it's getting late. Let's call it a night and thank you for all your help. I'll check up on you in several days to make sure that your jaw isn't giving you any problems. Once again, thanks," I said. "It's been my pleasure, Doc and don't forget to check out that Carlyle Group. I know you're going to find that real interesting shit."

I called Gabby when I got home and told her that I wanted to go to her father's estate for the weekend. The Hamptons, after Labor Day, is the greatest place to be. The crowds leave and the place is mellow. Gabby agreed and told me that she would be at my place at 5:00 p.m. on Friday. I called Charles next and asked him if it would be all right if I came for the weekend. He reminded me that I had an open invitation and was always welcome. I didn't have to ask for permission. He reminded me to bring TazTwo. I picked up a copy of the Iron Triangle for weekend reading. Charles Westerfield reminded me of Anthony Hopkins in the movie "Meet Joe Black." Charles was a gracious, wise, kind elderly gentleman who lived life as it should be lived. He was a wonderful man. There was part of me that thought that the Westerfields were nothing more than Elicia's back up. More human intel. However, after meeting Charles, I was convinced that a man of this caliber would never stoop to such mindless games. As a matter of fact, I realized that it had been a long time since I ever met someone of Charles integrity. Men like Charles just didn't exist in this ego-centrist society. I think he wanted a son and was looking at me as a candidate. I realized that if I married Gabby, I could not and would not walk down dark alleys. I would feel horrible if I disappointed Charles. I thought that it might be a good idea to proceed with my own therapy if Gabby and I were going to be married. The Iron Triangle was a quick read and I finished it on the dunes in one day. Unfortunately, the book led to a Sunday of googling on the internet. The Carlyle Group was a private investment bank handling over sixteen billion dollars. Carlyle specialized in defense and security. The Chairman of the Board was Frank Carlucci, a former Secretary of Defense and Deputy Director of the C.I.A. It was said about Carlucci that wherever he went a coup or revolution followed shortly thereafter. Interestingly enough, Carlucci and Donald Rumsfeld were college roommates and teammates on the wrestling team. Current Secretary of State Colin Powell was offered a job at Carlyle. Colin Powell got swept up in the mud in the Iran-Contra affair. George H.W. Bush was head of Asian affairs but resigned when Sam was elected head of the family. There was John Major, the former Prime Minister of England and Fidel Ramos, the former President of the Philippines. The game plan was easy. Having heavyweights on their staff created the impression that whatever military or security company Carlyle bought, the companies would be in a better position to secure government contracts because of the contacts that Carlucci, Major, Ramos and Bush had. Carlyle had sixteen billion dollars under management from only five hundred investors. They only dealt with heavyweights and they only had heavyweights on their staff and the Senior Counselor to Carlyle was James Baker III. Sam pulled Baker to his side when the State of Florida was in flux and would have prevented Sam from being elected head of the family. Sam reenlisted Baker into service when he sent Baker around the world negotiating Iraq's debts with the central bankers of the world, the same James Baker III of Baker & Botts, one of the largest law firms in Houston, Texas. It was almost as if Sam was Baker and Baker was Sam. Carlyle returned 30% to their investors. I wouldn't have been surprised if Baker claimed that he controlled Sam. It seemed all the dots centered on oil and Texas. Sam was quite insignificant, notwithstanding his narcissistic grandiosity. I stared out the window of

Charles study looking at the nighttime sky. I was using the stars as my dots of information trying to make connections with Carlucci, Rumsfeld, Rice, Sam, Cheney, Powell, etc. On one Axis, the dots aligned themselves clearly. I was witnessing a huge struggle between groups of dots. Using bank robbers as an analogy, it was clear that the bank robbers were comprised of two groups. One group wanted to blow the bank up and steal the money and the other group wanted to quietly embezzle the money. I put Cheney, Rumsfeld, Wolfowitz, Frum, Perle and Feith in the "blow up the bank group." The embezzlement group was Rice, Powell and Carlucci. My gut told me that the rich from all over the world started complaining about the blow-em-up group and advised Carlucci to do something about it. They didn't like blowing up the bank. It is too messy and caused instability. I figured that Sam sent Baker around the world not to renegotiate Iraq debt but to calm down the rich boys and international bankers. "Business as usual," I'm sure he advised. "Don't worry," he must have said, "we'll be back in control." As a reminder to Rumsfeld and Cheney, Sam appointed Rice to head up the Iraq Stabilization Group effectively removing control of the war effort into the White House and away from Rumsfeld. I was sure that Rumsfeld believed that someone was going to get hanged and caused his Department of Defense to conduct investigations into Halliburton, Cheney's former company. Cheney and Halliburton were inextricably linked together and the investigations were hanging Cheney. Dick became the weakest link. My dots were starting to make sense.

SESSION NINE

Sam arrived on Wednesday at 2:00 p.m. There was much that we had to discuss. His rage at Rueben, the Carlyle Group, his admittance to Dr. Mordowitz's clinic and increasing his sessions to three times a week. . I was concerned that Sam was beginning to "crack." He had three episodes of crying within three months, two of which required brief hospitalizations. Sam's hand was visibly swollen. "I don't think I'm coming to your group sessions anymore. It's a waste of my time. What could I possibly get from these people? Nothing. They're going to suck me dry. They should pay me for my attendance. After all, I am Sam." "Why did you get so enraged?" I asked Sam. "Do you think I'm like you. A man who stands for nothing! I don't take that kind of crap from anyone. You heard what he said to me. I can't believe you would actually ask me a question like that. Someone like you would take that crap. Not me. No one talks to Sam that way." I recalled that several days ago Sam proclaimed that I was the best therapist in the world and that he would only talk to me. Now he was back to attacking me. Whatever was troubling Sam was now gone. Sam was not going to discuss his rage with Rueben. I realized that Sam was a rather simplistic person. He didn't see shades of gray. It was either black or white. Whatever answer he needed was in the Bible. All he had to do was ask "What would Jesus do?" and the answer would be provided. Rueben insulted him and so Sam was justified in slugging him. Sam continued. "Look here, Stanley, don't think you're going to get into the inner circle by back dooring me with Gabby. You don't belong in my circles. It's not going to happen. Never. It will never happen while I'm alive," Sam stated. "I don't think my personal life has anything to do with you," I told Sam. Whatever progress I made with Sam was gone. Sam was on the attack. I recalled that I heard on CNN in the afternoon that Sam's close advisor Colin was not returning should Sam be elected head of the family again. Colin appeared to be a voice of reason and moderation. I knew better. "I'm turning Colin into an international greeter. I only want him to say hello to people," Sam told me. It was clear that Sam did a lot of thinking during his vacation and that anyone who didn't agree with him was going to be squeezed out. Sam was doing a little belt tightening in his inner circle and encircling himself with only the most loyal and agreeable employees. He wasn't going to entertain any opinions other than the ones he wanted to hear. I think he made peace with his financial buddies. He must have given them his assurances that they could get their way as long as he got his. "Sam, I would like to discuss the three episodes that you have had over the last 90 days," I said. "There's nothing to discuss. They won't happen again. I have made sure of that." "I don't think you have any control over these episodes. You can't prevent them Sam no matter what you think," I told him. "Yes, I can. You don't know what you're talking about, Stanley. I don't think you're even an average therapist. You're somewhere at the bottom," Sam emphatically stated. This was going to be a very difficult session. "I think we should concentrate on these episodes, Sam. I don't think they're going away," I told him. "I'll tell you again. There is nothing to discuss. Nothing." Sam and I sat there for twenty minutes in silence. I decided to move on and asked Sam if he would consider coming to therapy three times a week. "Are you nuts?" Sam barked. "You're lucky I even come here at all. Three times a week! For the pleasure of being with me and bearing witness to someone who is and will become a great historical figure you should pay me. Three times a week! I can't believe it." I asked Sam why he had come today. I reminded him that in Hung Fat he told me that the only thing that could happen to him was that "they" would find him another therapist. I asked Sam if he had any discussions with his financial buddies during August. He told me that he had and they told him he didn't have to have sessions with me or anyone else. I told Sam that I didn't believe him. He assured me that it was true but that he was there for a different reason. I asked what the reason was and Sam refused to answer. Sam told me that he made a compromise with his buddies. They presented him with a "roadmap" much like the roadmap that was presented to the Israeli and Palestinians leaders to achieve peace. They decided that therapy was useless and wasn't proceeding as fast as they had hoped. Essentially, the roadmap required Sam to achieve specific goals within a specific time frame. The roadmap was drafted to their benefit. If Sam followed the roadmap, financing to help Sam get reelected as head of the family would be forthcoming. Sam told me that the first part of the roadmap was to marginalize Colin Powell and essentially make him a lame duck Secretary of State for the next one and a half years. I knew that was bullshit since Powell and the Carlyle Group were tight. Of course, Carlyle and Powell might have agreed that Powell was going to come on board after his term. Sam further advised me that his friend Newt Gingrich who sat on the Pentagon Advisory Board wanted a complete change in the Department of State. I asked Sam if he had any ideas for Powell's replacement. He told me his friend Paul Wolfowitz was being considered. I told Sam that it sounded like he was turning the Department of State into the Department of War. I told Sam that I thought Secretary Powell was doing a fine job and presented a voice of moderation and reason in his family. Sam told me that there was complete failure in that Department. Had the Department been doing their job they would have persuaded France, Germany, Russia, Turkey and China of the merits of Sam's plans. I asked Sam if it was conceivable that those other countries might be justified in disagreeing with Sam's plan, after all, I reminded Sam, he still didn't find any weapons of mass destruction. It appeared that those countries were correct in assessing the threat of Iraq. Sam reminded me, once again, of his ordained mission and that anyone who disagreed with him is by definition wrong. Sam was a true narcissist. He discounted and attacked every person who had a different view of matters and surrounded himself with those who only agreed with him. "So, Sam, getting back to my previous question, why are you here?" I asked. Sam hesitated for a moment and then told me that he wanted me to write a book. I told Sam that I never wrote a book and didn't feel qualified to do so. "You're educated. You can swing words into sentences and sentences into paragraphs. You'll do fine." I suggested Sam get a ghostwriter. "No, I want you, Stan. I want you for a very simple reason. You are one of the few who noticed that I used the word wonder in my speech. You didn't focus on those infamous sixteen words. You picked up on 'wonder.' I like that. Sometimes it's the little things that bring people together. Besides, a Jew writing a book on me has a lot of political pluses and I think you can be saved." "Sam, really, I'm not a writer," I advised Sam again. "Well, if you really want me to write a book, this is what I have in mind. Here's the title. "Sam, God's Man on Earth with a subtitle, The Man, The Mission and the Victory." We'll have a picture of you from mid torso up and a burning bush behind you." "I love it, Stan. I knew you were good. But two little changes in the sub-title. I want it to read, "The Man, His Calling and His Victories." "I could live with that, Sam," I told him. Sam and I discussed details and Sam was willing to come every morning, five days a week at 7:00 a.m. He told me that he wanted the book completed and on the bookshelves no later than January. He further told me that he had many contacts with "his" publishers and that a he needed a book as an aid in getting him reelected to the head of the family. He wanted me to bear witness to his greatness. I told Sam that I would sleep on it and call him in the morning. "So, our sessions are over." "Yes, our sessions are over. You are no longer my therapist, you are my witness. I want you to record for historical purposes the genesis of Gods return to earth and the reign of 1,000 years of peace and how I was God's General in the war," he said. I raised the issue of money and Sam advised me that I would receive a check for $2,000.00 a week and could keep all the royalties generated by the book. I told Sam that I needed a release from him, as the conversations between therapist and patient are privileged communications and could only be waived by him. I further advised him that I wanted to avoid all appearances of impropriety. Sam told me to draw up a release and he would review it. I asked Sam if I could ask him any questions that I wanted and he agreed. "How about the Carlyle Group?" I asked. "Unimportant," Sam responded. "What does the Carlyle group have to do with a book entitled Sam, God's Man on Earth," "How about questions about your family?" I asked. "Whatever you want to know, I'll answer. My family is important. If you're interested in a psychological profile, I have lots of them. I'll provide them to you. I don't want you wasting your time on my family. It's a book about me and to the extent that my family plays a part in explaining my greatness you can ask anything and have any information you want." I reminded Sam that I would think about the entire matter. I asked Sam why he appeared so joyful. "Sam, I am happy today because a Yale economist named Ray Fair, the absolute best, predicted that old Sammy boy here is going to win in 2004 even with this economy. He said in 2000 that Gore would get 50.8 per cent of the vote and he got 50.3. Now that is uncanny. He's the best, just the best and another great economist, internationally known, named Douglas Hibbs of Sweden's Goteborg University predicts the same thing. All that I have to do is follow the roadmap and keep the boys happy and by the way, I agree with the roadmap. So therapy is over and bearing witness has com-menced. I love it. 'Sam, God's Man on Earth. The Man, The Calling and His Victories.' I think we're talking bestseller. Call me, Stan." I assured Sam that I would. I wrote no session notes of any significance other than that attempting to treat a patient with severe Personality Disorders, such as Narcissistic Personality Disorder, is generally not successful. I toyed with the idea of continuing to treat Sam under the guise of writing a book. The question was whether I wanted to be a therapist or a scribe. I decided to dwell on that as well. I asked myself what would Charles Do? Sam was asking himself what would Jesus do? The answer was clear. The therapeutic relationship was over. There was no reason to think or act otherwise. The only question was whether I wanted to be a scribe. I had always wanted to write a book and after all I was going to get paid $2,000.00 a week which would put me back on sound financial footing at least for the next 4 months. I still had an interest in the psychological side of Sam and his family and decided to pursue that interest independently of writing "Sam, God's Man on Earth."

I called Rueben to see if his jaw was o.k. "Hey, Doc, how are you. What's up," said Rueben. "Just checking up on you, making sure you feel alright," I said. "Hey, Doc, check the news today. Let me read you this little blurb," he said. "I don't have time, Rueben," I told him. Rueben read on in spite of my admonition not to do so. They were articles about layoffs and outsourcing. After Reuben fin-ished reading the articles, I told him that I always thought he had an uncanny knowledge and grasp of money matters. However, I asked him about the day's headline that stated that, Rueben interrupted me. "You mean the Institute for Supply Management index that shot up to 65.1 from 60.6 the highest reading since 1997. Big fucking deal. Did you see what the markets thought of that? The DOW plummeted 108.00 points and the yields on treasuries went up. I know, Doc, you're bewildered. Why do the markets react negatively to good news? Well, the market thinks that the number is a fluke. Maybe it's even bogus. Now as far as the treasuries are concerned, here I'm a little confused. If the stock mar-ket believed the Institute's number were real than stocks would react favorably but since the market thinks it's a fluke the moneymen sell off the market. You with me, Doc?" Rueben asked. I assured Rueben that I was. "Why then doesn't the treasury market believe the number is a fluke and increase prices thereby reducing the interest rate? You'll hear a lot of explanations but nobody really has any answers. I think the buyers are losing confidence in Sam. Things are just too fucked up. Just a couple days ago, Sam and his boys were screaming that the economy is on the mend. Today, planned layoffs surged in July. The economy has already lost 700,000 jobs and it is only July. Now, listen doc, what are you going to believe, a psychopath screaming everything is o.k. or actual planned job layoffs. I'm telling you we're fucked. It's just going to get worse not better," Rueben said. I asked Rueben if he thought Sam's people would really make up numbers. Rueben laughed. "Are you fucking kidding, Doc. What planet are you from? You have systemic criminality running through corporate Sam and you ask me if someone would make up numbers. Oh no, heaven forbid, that's wrong, they might get in trouble. Hey, Doc, if you want to make money go to India. That's where all the jobs are going. I got to go, Doc. See ya." Rueben hung up. He probably needed to go to the bathroom to snort more cocaine. Rueben called back in two minutes. I knew he went to do some coke. "Hey, Doc, did you get a chance to check out the Carlyle Group," he asked. "No, not yet," I told him. I lied. "Well, when you get around to doing your research throw in Halliburton, Bechtel and Kellogg, Brown and Root. You'll find them interesting too. Got to go."

Gabby and I went to the Hamptons for the week-end. TazTwo was growing quickly. He had a nice square head and large puppy paws. I peeked into the study and without turning around, Charles said, "the laptop and desk are in your study. I created one for you." "Where is it?" I asked. "Through the door on the left. It's the study next to mine," he said. "Thanks, Charles." "No problem," he answered.

I bought a world map and tacked it up on the wall of my study. The dots of information that I was studying required a map. I could not visualize where the countries, that I was interested in, were situated. After I put the map up on the wall I stared at it for a long time. I had a peculiar thought. I wondered if Charles was staring at a map of the world through his window as I was staring at the map on my study wall. I walked into Charles study and stood next to him looking out the window. "What are you doing, Charles?" I asked. "Oh, nothing, Stan. Just gazing out the window." I peered out the window and looked for a formation of stars that could be aligned as France. They were there. Soon I found Germany, China, Russia and England. That old codger was reading the news and playing chess in the sky. He had been playing the game so long he didn't need a map. I went back to my study and stared at my map. It occurred to me that if you wanted to move soldiers and military equipment anywhere you wished, under the rational of defending your homeland, you couldn't get a better enemy than terrorists. They could be anywhere. Therefore, you could move your pawns anywhere. I thought about Afghanistan. Sam and the Pakistani's were launching a huge spring offensive in the mountains bordering both countries. The stated reason was to capture Osama Bin Laden. It was with some amusement that I recalled that the Bin Laden's and Sam's father George were dining together at the time of the 9/11 tragedy. It was a Carlyle Group function. I didn't believe that 50,000 troops were needed to capture Osama Bin Laden or roust al-Qaeda holdovers. During the course of my research I found articles about a pipeline that was to be built from the Caspian Sea in Turkmenistan through Afghanistan and into Pakistan. It was a two billion dollar oil pipeline project to promote oil and gas finds estimated to be worth close to six trillion dollars. Unocal, the lead oil company attempted to negotiate with the Taliban in Afghanistan to secure the area where the proposed pipeline was to run through Afghanistan. The Taliban visited the United States on several occasions and even offered to secure and turn over Osama Bin Laden that Sam never followed up on. Security was never established and Unocal broke off negotiations claiming that they wouldn't invest in the pipeline project if the area could not be made secure. I was not surprised to discover that Sam sent his soldiers into Afghanistan post 9/11 to rout the Taliban and capture al-Qaeda operatives. It was a ruse to secure the area for a pipeline. Unocal claimed that they would not negotiate unless Afghanistan had a recognized government. Sam immediately installed Hamid Karzai, a former consultant to Unocal as President of Afghanistan and within 10 days appointed Zalmay Khalilizad, a former aide to Unocal as Sam's special envoy to Afghanistan. It appeared that Karzai could not control the borders between Afghanistan and Pakistan and he became captive within Kabul, the capitol of Afghanistan. I drew the obvious conclusion that Sam was going to secure the area claiming he was fighting terror and going to capture Osama Bin Laden. The prize was the second largest known unexploited oil and gas reserves after Saudi Arabia. It has nothing to do with terror and everything to do with oil. Sam was using public assets for private purposes and putting his soldiers in harm's way. That was Sam's plan heading east from the Caspian Sea to service China, India and Japan. However, I learned that Sam was heading west from the Caspian Sea as well, presumably to service the European community. An oil and gas pipeline was being built called the Baku-Tblisi-Ceyhan pipeline. Baku was the capitol of Azerbaijan, a country bordering on the west side of the Caspian Sea and Tblisi was the capitol of Georgia. Ceyhan was a port in Turkey. I was not shocked to find that James Baker III established a law office in Baku. Nor was I surprised to learn that Georgia experienced a "Rose Revolution" late in 2003 replacing a pro-Russian President with a 36 year-old former American attorney. I recalled that I read that it was claimed that wherever Carlucci went a coup or revolution was sure to follow. Secretary of State Colin Powell made a point upon visiting Russia to advise Vladimir Putin to keep his hands off Georgia. I went into Charles study and asked Charles if he had any colored pins so that I could track of the players. "How's it going, Stan?" he asked. "Charles, simply fascinating," I told him. My understanding of the underlying reason for invading Iraq became clearer. Sam was establishing a beachhead in the Middle East. He had easy access to Syria, Saudi Arabia, Iran, Georgia, Azerbaijan, Turkmenistan, Afghanistan and Pakistan. Sam was protecting his current and future plans. Unfortunately, the blow-em up bank robber group was causing too much anguish among the world's wealthy. It's better to embezzle than implode the bank with bombs. Sam threatened world stability and instability is an anathema to wealth. It was the first time I felt that I knew the game that was being played. As Rueben once advised me, "it's all about the Benjamin's." Sam was out of control.

I decided that I wanted to finish my analysis of Sam's family notwithstanding the fact that Sam offered to provide several analyses. I couldn't recall exactly what I thought about Sam's family along an Axis 1 diagnosis. I did remember my block analogy and that the blocks hung in the air above my desk. I recalled that I wasn't thinking that Sam's family had a major manic or depressive attack or a combination thereof rising to an analysis of Bipolar 1 or 2 Disorder. I thumbed through the DSM-IV manual and focused on Cyclothymic Disorder. That was what I was looking for. I was firmly convinced that along Axis 1 the criteria existed for a diagnosis of Cyclothymic Disorder.

Diagnostic criteria for 301.13 Cyclothymic Disorder

A. For at least 2 years, the presence of numerous periods with hypomanic systems and numerous periods of depressive systems that do not meet criteria for a Major Depressive Episode.

B. During the two-year period, the person has not been without the systems in Criterion A for more than two months at a time.

C. No Major Depressive Episode, Manic Episode, or Mixed Episode has been present during the first 2 years of the disturbance.

D. The systems in criterion A are not better accounted for by Schizoaffective Disorder and are not superimposed on Schizophrenia, Schizophreniform Disorder, delusional Disorder, or Psychotic Disorder Not Otherwise Specified.

E. The systems are not due to the direct physiological effects of a substance (e.g., a drug of abuse, a medication) or a general medical condition (e.g., hyperthyroidism).

F. The symptoms cause clinically significant distress or impairment, in social, occupational, or other important areas of functioning.

Diagnostic Features

The essential feature of Cyclothymic Disorder is a chronic, fluctuating mood disturbance involving numerous periods of hypomanic systems and numerous periods of depressive systems. The hypomanic systems are of insufficient number, severity, pervasiveness, or duration to meet full criteria for a Manic Episode, and the depressive systems are of insufficient number, severity, pervasiveness, or duration to meet full criteria for a Major Depressive Episode.

What concerned me was the following:

Course

Cyclothymic Disorder usually has an insidious onset and a chronic course. There is a 15-50% risk that the person will subsequently develop Bipolar I or II Disorder.

I noted the following about the Criteria for Hypomanic Episode:

A. A distinct period of persistently elevated, expansive, or irritable mood, lasting throughout at least four days, that is clearly different from the usual no depressed mood.

B. During the period of mood disturbance, three (or more) of the following systems have persisted (four if the mood is only irritable) and have been present for a significant degree.

(1) inflated self-esteem or grandiosity

(2) decreased need for sleep (feels rested after only three 3 hours of sleep)

(3) more talkative than usual or pressure to keep talking

(4) flight of ideas or subjective experience that thoughts are racing

(5) distractibility (i.e., attention too easily drawn to unimportant or irrelevant external stimuli).

(6) increase in goal directed activity (either socially, at work or school, or sexually) or psychomotor agitation.

(7) excessive involvement in pleasurable activities that have a high potential for painful consequences (e.g., the person engages in unrestrained buying sprees, sexual indiscretions, or foolish business investments.

C. The episode is associated with an unequivocal change in functioning that is uncharacteristic of the person when not symptomatic.

D. The disturbance in mood and the change in functioning are observable by others.

E. The episode is not severe enough to cause marked impairment in social or occupational functioning, or to necessitate hospitalization, and there are no psychotic features.

F. The systems are not due to the direct physiological effects of a substance.

I ruled out true manic and depressive episodes. Sam's family couldn't function under such circumstances. For example, under a true depressive episode, Sam's family would find itself in an economic depression. I concentrated on Cyclothymic Disorder because it was in between, not full blown episodes but symptoms of hypomania and depressive symptoms. I recalled the impeachment of Sam's brother Bill. That was a mid level depressive episode. The mood of Sam's family was somber. The conduct of Bill's family largely controlled by Sam and his companions conveyed the gravity of the situation to the family. The family was going to fall apart. Bill lied about oral sex and disgraced his office. It was an international and domestic disgrace of such significant proportions that the republic was in danger of disintegration. I recalled how mothers were worried that they couldn't explain Bill's conduct to their children. The family was depressed but functioned. Then Sam's family went through a hypomanic episode with the stock market mania as it was called. I remembered that Alan Greenspan called the mania "irrational exuberance." I reviewed the stock market episode against the criteria for hypomanic episode and determined that the episode met the criteria. I realized we were going through another mood disturbance, this time it was the "war on terror." There was less travel and more talk of employment of the lack thereof. Personal bankruptcies were hitting monthly record highs. There was and still is a constant drumbeat of impending terror attacks. The mood of Sam's family was depressed and reinforced by daily news stories of terror, murder and rape. I became extremely concerned because Cyclothymic Disorder has an insidious onset and a chronic course. There was a 15%-50% risk that Sam's family could develop Bipolar I or II disorder. My main concern was a full-blown Depressive Episode and a resulting economic catastrophe. It would be a major depression, psychologically and economically. I was also deeply concerned that while Sam was off seeking self-glory in God's fight his family was going to suffer and was presently suffering distress. One thing that disturbed me was that the criteria called for "numerous" periods of hypomanic and depressive symptoms. I decided to look for more evidence of frequency. I was leaning towards stating that my diagnosis had "features" of Cyclothymic Disorder.

Sam called me the next day and demanded an answer. I didn't have one and this made him angry. I told him that I needed a little more time and that I would have an answer for him on Monday morning. I explained that I wanted to make the right decision and that would take time. Of course, Sam couldn't understand why I didn't jump at the opportunity to write a book about him. Sam reluctantly agreed but told me that Monday was the deadline. I agreed to have an answer. I had my appointment with Dr. P. on Thursday and explained what had happened. He was glad that therapy had ended between Sam and I. We fully discussed the issue of my writing Sam's book. The main issue was whether writing Sam's book was walking down a dark alley. After one full hour of discussion, neither Dr. P. nor I could see any damage that might occur to me. If I stuck to writing and clearly maintained boundaries between Sam and I, we could not see any downside risks. I asked Dr. P. what approach I should take if Sam had an "episode" either in my office or showed up at Dr. Mordowitz's clinic. We agreed that I must maintain my boundaries and not interfere. He was no longer my patient. I was relieved.

Gabby showed up at my place on Friday at 5:00 p.m. "Where's TT?" she asked. "Come on, Stan, you know, TazTwo." I told Gabby that TT was out on the back deck. She went out back and yelled, "he's going to be a horse." TT was getting big. We stopped in Southampton for dinner and then proceeded to the estate. Charles was waiting at the door and handed me a key and explained the security system. He advised me that I didn't need an invitation, ever, and that I should consider his house my home. I had TT in my arms and Charles grabbed him. "You guys settle down and unpack," he said. He took TT out to the dunes. I went into Charles study and watched him play with our dog. I didn't feel like unpacking and went out to the dunes and asked Charles to take a walk with me. We strolled down the beach like father and son. "Something on your mind, Stan?" "Several weeks ago at the Labor Day clambake at Alan and Susan's I came back to your house to get something. When I went back Gabby was talking to Susan. They didn't notice me approach but I did overhear Gabby tell Susan that she wanted to get married. I just want you to know that I haven't stopped thinking about that since I heard it. I didn't tell Gabby that I overheard her and she does not know that I know. It makes me nervous. I'm afraid I'm going to crash and burn. I'm afraid that somewhere along the way I'm going to screw up and cause both you and Gabby major disappointment," I said. "Stan, just the fact that you're thinking and talking about matters like this only inspires confidence. Settle down and let time pass. Enjoy Gabby, my home and TazTwo. I'm sure we'll talk again. It's the weekend. Work hard and then play hard. Never mix the two," Charles told me. Gabby came running up behind us and put her arms around both of us. "My two men," she exclaimed. "My two handsome men."

It was another wonderful weekend. I was sure that Charles was being nice to me as a prospective son-in-law. I was also sure that Charles would have thrown me out of his house if he did not like me. I expected that Charles had conducted a complete investigation on me and found some things that he didn't like and found some things that he did. I could only conclude that on balance, I passed inspection. The biggest plus in my corner was that Gabby loved me. I told Charles that I had to violate his work hard, play hard rule on Sunday and do a little research. He raised his eyebrow and looked disappointed. I told Charles that I didn't want to break the rules and that whatever research I had to do I would do late Sunday night or early Monday morning. He was pleased.

I dropped Gabby off at her apartment and went home. It was another great weekend. I poured a glass of white wine and settled on the back deck with TT at my feet and the manual in my lap. I was trying to get a handle on the personality of Sam's family. At first, I was sure that I was witnessing a mirror image of Sam. That Sam's family also had a Narcissistic Personality Disorder. I was bothered that I did not see in many of Sam's family the essential feature of a pervasive pattern of grandiosity. There were a lot of regular people in Sam's family that just didn't quite fit the criteria for Narcissistic Personality Disorder. In my manual were pieces of paper that I had scribbled notes on over the past 90 days. I love to think and scribble notes. Whenever I had, what I believed to be a moment of clarity, when a jumble of different ideas made sense, a breakthrough so to speak, I would write them down as notes. Unfortunately, my note taking was less than exemplary. Indeed, it was poor and almost useless. However, it appeared that I was working on some theory of a "sandwich" personality. An essential core personality, such as a Narcissistic Personality Disorder sandwiched between a Borderline and Paranoid Personality Disorder. To make matters worse, my notes further indicated that at some point of clarity, probably occurring on a toke of dope, I believed that the sandwich personality shifted in degrees of severity so that one might mistake the bread for the meat at any given time. As a result, I might determine that a person had at its core a Paranoid Personality Disorder when in fact it was only core at a given point in time and was actually subservient to the core in reality. I decided two things. First I was going to take better notes and second I was going to review my notes again until they made sense. I had an idea of where I was going but reading my notes just wasn't working for me. I was sure they would make sense after many reviews.

Sam arrived on Monday at 7:00 a.m. ready to go. I told him that I carefully reviewed the issue and decided to go forward. I further advised him that I did not have a release ready but that I would make sure to take of it. I told Sam I was taking hand written notes as well as taping the conversation. He understood and agreed. Sam asked me where we should start the book. I told him that the sub-title of the book was The Man, The Calling and The Victories and that the best place to start was with The Man. Asking a narcissist to talk about himself is absurd. A narcissist never has to be asked to talk about himself. Sam proceeded with his early childhood and continued with his monologue for 50 minutes. I only asked several questions that I thought would make the narrative clearer. Sam told me that he would pay me at the end of the week to which I agreed. "Is that going to be cash or check," I asked Sam. "A check," Sam responded. The overwhelming feeling that I had with Sam was one of boredom. There is never a conversation with a narcissist. They talk and you listen. They don't care about anything you have to say. I was going to let Sam talk for a week and then start to write.

After the day's sessions, I took TT to the back porch. I had a bottle of wine and I was going to drink the whole bottle. I spent a good 2 hours playing with TT and drinking the wine. Occasionally, I looked at my notes hoping that something would come together. I was having trouble because I had no interest in Sam anymore. Why should I? I reread an article about Fritz Holling who announced his retirement. There was one sentence in the Times article that I read over several times. It said:

The senator also saved a barb or two for apathetic voters in his home state, one that has grown increasingly inhospitable to Democrats.

"Riding up here," he said, "I saw this state could care less. I just saw Carolina license plates, tiger paw license plates. They just can't wait for the kickoffs here at the end of the month. They just don't worry about the 60,100 textile jobs alone we have lost since Nafta."

What struck me was Hollings statement that his constituents just don't worry about losing their jobs. For the longest time I had this deep rooted pain about Sam's family as well. They just didn't seem to worry or care. I was always fascinated at this apparent lack of concern. Where was the anger in Sam's family? It was like the entire land had been blanketed with some kind of "be nice" fairy dust. I was astounded. What was I looking at? What kind of personality did Sam's family have? Sam and his boys were gutting the country and everyone wanted to be nice. I looked at my notes and played with TT. I was starting to for-mulate an image. The notes were becoming clearer. The best way to explain what I had in my mind was to look at Sam's family as an image. Trying to explain what was in my head with words on paper wouldn't work. I saw one body with two heads. Imagine a blank face. At the top near the forehead area is number 1. The nose is number 2 and the chin is number 3. Now imagine the numbers changing places and that number 2, the nose, dropped down to the chin and the chin, number 3, moved up to the nose. Number 2 is the dominant personality disorder but fades in importance at some points in time so that the chin, number 3, appears to be dominant when in fact, it isn't. At that point in time, it is dominant but will eventually drop to its original subservient position. One face was clear to me. The dominant personality disorder in the number 2 position was a mirror image of Sam's Narcissistic Personality Disorder. In addition, this face had a Paranoid Personality Disorder and an Obsessive-Personality Disorder of equal strength. However, either the top or the bottom could shift position at any point in time depending on what was going on with Sam. It was clear that Sam had a profound effect upon his family shaping his families personality. The other face had at its center, the core, the number 2 position, a Histrionic Personality Disor-der sandwiched between a Dependent Personality Disorder and a Paranoid Per-sonality Disorder.

Diagnostic criteria for 301.50 Histrionic Personality Disorder

A pervasive pattern of excessive emotionality and attention seeking, beginning by early adulthood and a verity of contexts, as indicated by five (or more) of the following:

(1) is uncomfortable in situations in which he or she is not the center of attention.

(2) interaction with others is often characterized by inappropriate sexu-ally seductive or provocative behavior.

(3) displays rapidly shifting and shallow expression of emotions.

(4) consistently uses physical appearance to draw attention to self

(5) has a style of speech that is excessively impressionistic and lacking in detail

(6) shows, self-dramatization, theatricality, and exaggerated expression of emotion

(7) is suggestible, i.e., easily influenced by others or circumstances.

(8) considers relationships to be more intimate than they actually are.

Diagnostic Features

The essential feature of Histrionic Personality Disorder is pervasive and excessive emotionality and attention seeking behavior. This pattern begins by early adulthood and is present in a variety of contexts.

Individuals with Histrionic Personality Disorder are uncomfortable with or feel unappreciated when they are not the center of attention. Often lively and dramatic, they tend to draw attention to themselves and may initially charm new acquaintances by their enthusiasm, apparent openness, or flirtatiousness' qualities wear thin, however, as these individuals continually demand to be the center of attention. They commandeer the role of life of the party. If they are not the center of attention they may do something dramatic (e.g., make up stories, create a scene) to draw the focus of attention to themselves...

...Emotional expression may be shallow and rapidly shifting...They are overly concerned with impressing others by their appearance and expend an excessive amount of time, energy, and money on clothes and grooming. They may fish for compliments regarding appearance and be easily and excessively upset by a critical comment about how they look or by a photograph that they regard as unflattering.

These individuals have a style of speech that is excessively impressionistic and lacking in detail. Strong opinions are expressed with dramatic flair, but underlying reasons are usually vague and diffuse, without supporting facts and details. For example, an individual with Histrionic Personality Disorder may comment that a certain individual is a wonderful human being, but be unable to provide any specific examples of good qualities to support this position..... However, their emotions often seem to be turned on and off too quickly to be deeply felt, which may lead others to accuse the individual of faking these feelings.

Individuals with Histrionic Personality Disorder have a high degree of suggestibility. Their opinions and feelings are easily influenced by others and by current fads. They may be overly trusting, especially of strong authority figures whom they see as magically solving their problems. They have a tendency to play hunches and to adopt convictions quickly..... (Emphasis supplied)

I found in the section of associated features and disorders that people with Histrionic Personality Disorder also crave novelty, stimulation, and excitement and have a tendency to become bored with their usual routine. These individuals are often intolerant of, or frustrated by, situations that involve delayed gratification, and their actions are often directed at obtaining immediate satisfaction.

Although they often initiate a job or project with great enthusiasm, their interest may lag quickly. My original notes were starting to make some sense to me. There was one body and two heads with two different core personalities. However, both heads had the essential feature of being the center of attention. "Me" was at the core. I was also convinced that each had or exhibited to varying degrees, elements of a Paranoid Personality Disorder that their Uncle Sam fed into and nourished to his advantage for various reasons. I thought about the ubiquitous advertisements of Tom Ridge, the head of Homeland Security reminding me on a daily basis of the need to protect myself against acts of terrorism. It was not a question of whether or not we would experience acts of terrorism it was only a question of when, Tom Ridge reminded me. However, for the three years since 9/11 there was not one terrorist attack on Sam's homeland. I was bewildered by the fact that many people complained of the lack of adequate funding to protect against acts of terrorism. I was also bewildered by the fact that Sam always advised his family that the information supporting Sam's conclusions were sketchy and secret. Trust me Sam said. This would appeal to the Histrionic part of Sam's family, who are overly trusting especially of strong authority figures. I became convinced that Sam needed to develop and nurture a Paranoid Personality Disorder in his family and that development occurred among both across the Narcissistic and Histrionic heads of his family.

Diagnostic criteria for 301.1 Paranoid Personality Disorder

A. A pervasive distrust and suspiciousness of others such that their motives are interpreted as malevolent, beginning by early adulthood and present in a variety of contexts, as indicated by four or more of the following:

(1) suspects, without sufficient basis, that others are exploiting, harming or deceiving him or her.

(2) is preoccupied with unjustified doubts about the loyalty or trustworthiness of friends or associates.

(3) is reluctant to confide in others because of unwarranted fear that the information will be used maliciously against him or her.

(4) reads hidden demeaning or threatening meanings into benign remarks or events.

(5) persistently bears grudges, i.e., is unforgiving of insults, injuries, or slights.

(6) perceives attacks on his or her character or reputation that are not apparent to others and is quick to react angrily or to counterattack.

(7) has recurrent suspicions, without justification, regarding fidelity of spouse or sexual partner.

B. Does not occur exclusively during the course of Schizophrenia, a Mood Disorder with Psychotic Features, or another Psychotic Disorder and is not due to the direct physiological effects of a general medical condition.

In reviewing the diagnostic criteria, I was confident that none of the criteria applied to Sam. Sam was too strong financially and militarily to be afraid of anyone. He could destroy anyone at anytime. However, Sam truly needed his family across both heads to be paranoid. I recalled the propaganda war that Sam waged against the French and played upon each element of the criteria in turning his family against the French. I thought of the persistent grudge that Sam's family displayed against the French. French kisses and French toast were replaced with freedom toast and freedom fries. It was childish, but effective. Sam played upon his families' paranoia fears to great success. In order to invade Iraq for his own narcissistic grandiose plan he created fears in his family of imminent demise. Mushroom clouds of impending nuclear disaster and capabilities of a fourth rate nation, launching biological and chemical attacks in 45 minutes. I considered the entire basis of Sam's justification for invading a foreign nation and realized that the entire episode was made up and designed directly to feed into his families Paranoid Personality Disorder. Part of the diagnostic feature stated in the manual burned in my mind. It stated that individuals with this disorder assume that other people will exploit, harm, or deceive them, even if no evidence exists to support this expectation. They suspect that on the basis of little or no evidence that others are plotting against them and may attack them suddenly, at any time and without reason. I was convinced that if I read the material Sam brought me about his analysis of his family, it would contain the very same passage.

I petted TazTwo, took another sip of wine and went deeper into my head. I had constructed a one body image with two heads each head with a "me" core. I stared at the faces in my mind's eyes and tried to envision the forehead. There were names written across the top and they slowly came into view. On the head with the Histrionic core read Dependent Personality Disorder and on the head with the narcissistic core read Obsessive-Compulsive Personality Disorder.

Diagnostic criteria for 301.4 Obsessive-Compulsive Personality Disorder

A pervasive pattern of preoccupation with orderliness, perfectionism, and mental and interpersonal control, at the expense of flexibility, openness and efficiency, beginning by early adulthood and present in a variety of contexts, as indicated by four (or more) of the following:

(1) is preoccupied with details, rules, lists, order, organization, or schedules to the extent that the major point of activity is lost.

(2) shows perfectionism that interferes with task completion (e.g., is unable to complete a project because his or her own overly strict standards are not met.

(3) is excessively devoted to work and productivity to the exclusion of leisure activities and friendships (not accounted for by obvious economic necessity)

(4) is overconscientitious, scrupulous, and inflexible about matters of morality, ethics, or values (not accounted for by cultural or religious identification)

(5) is unable to discard worn-out or worthless objects even when they have no sentimental value.

(6) is reluctant to delegate tasks or to work with others unless they submit to exactly his or her way of doing things.

(7) adopts a miserly spending style toward both self and others; money is viewed as something to be hoarded for future catastrophes.

(8) shows rigidity and stubbornness.

I went on to complete my diagnosis and read the criteria for dependent personality disorder. The manual stated:

Diagnostic Criteria for 301.6 Dependent Personality Disorder

A pervasive and excessive need to be taken care of that leads to submissive and clinging behavior and fears of separation, beginning by early adulthood and present in a variety of context, as indicated by five (or more) of the following:

(1) has difficulty making everyday decisions without an excessive amount of advice and reassurance from others.

(2) needs others to assume responsibility for most major areas of his or her life

(3) had difficulty expressing disagreement with others because of fear of loss of support or approval.

(4) has difficulty initiating projects or doing things on his or her own (because of a lack of self-confidence in judgment or abilities rather than a lack of motivation or energy)

(5) goes to excessive lengths to obtain nurturance and support from others, to the point of volunteering to do things that are unpleasant

(6) feels uncomfortable or helpless when alone because of exaggerated fears of being unable to care for himself or herself

(7) urgently seeks another relationship as a source of care and support when a close relationship ends.

(8) is unrealistically preoccupied with fears of being left to take care of himself or herself.

There, before me, in my garden, with TT next to me and a glass of wine in my hand appeared Sam's family. One body, two heads, each with a "me only" core, supported by a paranoid chin and topped off with an Obsessive-Compulsive Personality Disorder on one head and a Dependent Personality Disorder on the other. I recalled reading a book by David Brooks entitled "Bobos in Paradise: The New Upper Class and How They Got There." These were the organization kids, the sleep deprived, goal oriented, resume builders types. Every minute is accounted for and directed towards some goal. This was my Narcissistic-Obsessive-Paranoid part of Sam's family. I saw them everyday with cell phones stuck to their ears at six o clock in the morning. They are the ones who talk overly loud in bookstores so that everyone can hear their conversations. They are very important people. In thinking about them, I realized that this part of Sam's family was the breeding grounds for entry into Sam's little club. There are those among this group that would step over the line into anti-social behavior and do anything to maintain their grandiose narcissistic dreams. The first anti social act is always the hardest and when you realize that God doesn't strike you dead, the second and continuing acts of anti-social behavior become second nature. It was clear to me that Sam hated that part of his family that was dependent. Sam could deal with Histrionic and Paranoid but the dependency of that part of his family irked Sam to no end. Sam didn't want anyone pulling on him in any way. Sam was making every attempt to cut the dependencies of that part of his family. Sam wanted to replace himself with voluntary faith based groups. I could almost hear him shout, "don't come to me, God helps those who help themselves." My diagnosis was as follows:

SAM

DSM-IV MULTIAXIAL EVALUATION

Axis 1   297.1 Delusional Disorder (Grandiose sub-type), severe and continuing

Axis 2	308.81 Narcissistic Personality Disorder-severe
	301.7 Antisocial Personality Disorder-severe
Axis 3	none
Axis 4	none
Axis 5	GAF-90 (current)*

* 90-Absent or minimal symptoms (e.g., mild anxiety before an exam) good functioning in all areas, interested and involved in a wide range of activities, socially effective, generally satisfied with life, no more than everyday problems or concerns (e.g., an occasional argument with family members)

FAMILY—NARCISSISTIC CORE
DSM-IV MULTIAXIAL EXAMINATION-

Axis 1	301.13 Cyclothymic Disorder, moderate
Axis 2*	301.81 Narcissistic Personality Disorder, severe
	301.4 Obsessive Compulsive Personality Disorder, severe
	301.0 Paranoid Personality Disorder. Moderate to severe

* Note: Narcissistic Personality Disorder is core personality. It is served by subservient and dedicated to by Obsessive-Compulsive Personality Disorder to achieve core's grandiose plans. Subservient paranoid personality is a creature of Sam's manipulation to serve his needs.

Axis 3	none
Axis 4	Generally no psychosocial and environmental problems, however fears of job loss are beginning to emerge.
Axis 5	GAF = 80 (current)*

* If symptoms are present, they are transient and expectable reactions to psychosocial stressors (e.g., difficulty concentrating after family argument) no more than slight impairment in social, occupational, or school functioning but generally functioning pretty well, has some meaningful interpersonal relationships.

FAMILY HISTRIONIC CORE
DSM-IV MULTIAXIAL EXAMINATION

Axis 1	301.13 Cyclothymic Disorder, moderate
Axis 2*	301.50 Histrionic Personality Disorder, moderate
	301.6 Dependent Personality Disorder, moderate
	301.0 Paranoid Personality Disorder. Moderate

* Note: Histrionic Personality Disorder is core personality. Subservient paranoid is a creature of Sam's manipulation to serve his needs.

Axis 3	Many medical conditions including but not limited infectious, obesity, neoplasms, circulatory, respiratory, digestive, musculoskeletal and symptoms, signs and Ill-defined conditions.
Axis 4	Has problems with primary support group, social environment, educational, occupational, housing, economic, access to health care and problems related to interaction with legal system.
Axis 5	GAF =60(current)*

* Moderate symptoms (e.g., flat affect and circumstantial speech, occasional panic attacks) or moderate difficulty in social, occupational, or school functioning (e.g., few friends, conflicts with peers or co-workers.

I was confident that my diagnosis about Sam and his BoBos in Paradise was correct. I was not that confident about my diagnosis of Sam's Histrionic family. The Histrionic part of Sam's family comprised the bulk of Sam's citizens. However, in view of the limited sessions, it was the best that I could do. I finished the book during the course of the next four months. I became engaged to Gabby with Dr. Westerfield's blessing. Two of my patients returned. Rueben constantly bothered me to check out the Carlyle Group. I should have told him that I had read the book but I didn't see the need to do so. I wanted to put as much distance between Sam and myself as possible. When I completed an initial draft of the book and gave it to Sam he freaked. He sued me seeking a preliminary injunction blocking the publication of the manuscript, which brings me back to the beginning of the story. I sat in the courtroom listening to all the arguments on both sides; first amendment rights, therapist-patient privilege and some collateral issues. I found that the legal mumbo-jumbo made me drift off and stare at the ceiling. At one point, I thought that if I won the case the real war would begin. If I really believed that Sam was a psychopathic narcissist why would I want to antagonize him? He would come after me with a vengeance. I knew that Sam's narcissism prevented him from ever imagining that I was writing something critical. I was being a wise-ass. I knew that writing a negative book about Sam was inconceivable to him. If hell had no fury like a woman scorned then it paled in comparison to the hell that a narcissist revealed would reap. This was a dark alley and I decided that I wasn't going to walk down it. I raised my hand and the judge acknowledged me. I explained to the Judge, much to the astonishment of my attorney, that I wasn't going to proceed to publication and that I was willing to hand over all notes, manuscripts and tapes and any other documents that related in any way to Sam, God's Man on Earth.... The Man, The Calling, The Victories upon the condition that Sam sign a stipulation waiving any monies that he had given me, a withdrawal of the lawsuit and the exchange of general releases. Sam's attorney triumphantly agreed to such conditions immediately. Another narcissist I thought. This smuck was claiming victory when I had conceded to abandon publication. What a joke. I didn't walk down this particular well-lit alley fraught with guaranteed danger. I was proud of myself. Walking through the Rotunda on the ground floor of the Court, I felt a sharp pain in the upper region of my back. I had been shot. As my lung collapsed, I slowly fainted. However, out of the corner of my eye, I believed I saw Elicia putting away a gun in her briefcase. She quickly walked past me.

Charles and I sat in Adirondack chairs on the dune watching the stars come out. Gabby decided that I should recuperate at the estate. It was getting cold and Gabby brought out two hooded sweatshirts. While Charles and I stared at the stars the doorbell rang. "I'll answer it," Gabby said. Gabby opened the door and saw Sam. She did not come back to the dune.

"So Stan, what do you think you know?" asked Charles. "About what?" I asked. "About what you have been researching in your study," he said. I knew that Charles was testing me. "You see that bright star up there. Use that as a starting point," I said. I then proceeded to outline with a degree of accurateness that impressed Charles, all the countries from western Spain to Russia. "You have been doing your homework," he said. "Yes, I have," I responded. "Well, ask me one question and I'll know exactly how much you know based upon that question," he said. "Charles, here's the question. If Carlucci and Rumsfeld were such good friends, college roommates, wrestling buddies, why did Rumsfeld cancel the Department of Defense "Crusader" contract that it had with Carlyle's company

United Defense?" I asked. "You really have done your homework, haven't you," Charles said. Based upon the question, Charles knew that that we could converse on a higher detailed plane. Charles asked me about my diagnosis of Sam and his family. I spent the next hour explaining to Charles the diagnosis and he agreed with my assessment. "Stan, this is what I want you to do for the next several weeks while you're resting. You're looking at life through a straw and giving Sam credence way beyond what he deserves. You're being myopic. Don't you think there are other powerful men out there? Sam is just one player. Now tell me who you don't see?" he asked. "That's diffifcult. Trying to prove a negative is always difficult," I told Charles. "Look at the stars, Charles, look *at* the stars," Charles said. I stared at the stars and reviewed the question. I saw France, Germany, China, North Korea and Iran. These were the countries that Sam and his media gave press time to. "I don't see Russia. I don't Vladimir Putin," I told Charles. "Oh, he's out there. He's a wrestler you know. Putin is a real fighter. He was champion of St. Petersburg for ten years. The point, Stan, is that he knows when to be aggressive, when to be defensive and when to be neutral. Sam's just a loud mouth bull in a china shop. You can see him coming. In two years, Russia will be the largest producer of oil. They are a stone's throw away from China. He's been consolidating his position with all the former Soviet states. Lukoil, Russia's state owned oil company signed an agreement with Saudi Arabia. Putin is building pipelines to supply oil to the east and west. He is revitalizing his military. The center of the world's business is going to be conducted within the boundaries of Spain, at the western tip, to Russia on the eastern tip with Russia sitting next to China, the world's largest consumer of industrial products. The world is changing, Stan. Sam is going in the wrong direction. Empires never last. Narcissistic Grandiosity has within itself the seeds of its own destruction. Watch Putin, Stan. In October of 2003, Putin said that he could accept Euros as currency for his oil. He was floating a trial balloon. If he accepts euros then the euro will become the world's reserve currency. The dollar will plummet and interest rates will sky-rocket. The housing and auto markets will collapse. In your studies, I want you to watch foreign central bank currency reserves. The trend of increasing euro reserves has already started. Don't worry, I have bought Gabby and you an estate in the South of France and placed a substantial amount of euros in an account for both of you. If Putin demands euros, many others will follow and he will have accomplished what ten thousand terrorists could not have. It's going to be a pay back for when his beloved mother Russia broke up without a shot being fired." Charles concluded his speech. Gabby appeared and stood behind us. It appeared that my discussion with Charles was over. I wasn't finished. "I'm not finished talking, Charles," I said. Charles understood that I was a little kid who discovered something he loved. I fell in love with psycho geo-politics. The subject was fascinating. "Charles, find Georgia in the sky," I asked him. He did. "You know the Baku-Tblisi-Ceyhan pipeline?" I asked. I knew Charles did. "Well, the newly installed, probably Carlucci installed, President Mikhail Saakashvilli of Georgia is having trouble with the renegade province of Adzharia run by Aslan Abashidze, who is pro-Russian. The province borders the Black Sea and will interfere with the pipeline," I said. "It will be the first of many confrontations between Sam and Russia. It will be a fight by proxy states. There are many smart people in Sam's family. The C.I.A. just released an initial assessment of Russia claiming that Russia will try to reassert itself. Putin won't try, Putin will. Stan, I know you're excited but I'm getting tired. Let's finish this off with two questions. I want simple answers. I'm tired," said Charles. "What are the two questions?" I asked. "What is your take on the November elections and did Sam have anything to do with 9/11?" he asked. I thought about the answers. I wanted to give a short answer. "Sam is appealing to the paranoid part of his family's disorder. Kerry is appealing to the 'me' core of his family. If job creation increases, Sam wins. If the economy weakens, Sam will put up a show trial of Saddam and Osama, if he is captured, as a diversion. If that still doesn't work, a psychopathic narcissistic would think nothing about creating another terror attack. Sam's family would not unseat him during an active terror attack. As far as 9/11, is there a difference between causing an attack to happen and letting it happen?" I asked. "Stan, welcome to world's greatest movie. You're a walk-on and you just earned yourself a bit part. Remember three things in this game. (1) Trust no one (2) always watch your back and (3) cover your ass."

An unlit pile of firewood was eight feet in front of us. "Stan, are you going to get off your ass and light that fire, or what? It's getting cold out here," Gabby said. "Yes, Stan, are you going to get off your ass and light that fire. I'm too old. You youngsters have to do that," he said.

0-595-32116-X

Printed in the United States
60563LVS00003B/335

9 780595 321162